C000165077

Gaby Hauptmann was born in Trossingen, Germany in 1957. She has worked as a TV producer, filmscript writer and has run her own press office. Her first novel, *In Search of an Impotent Man*, was published by Virago in 1998 and became an international bestseller.

Also by Gaby Hauptmann

In Search of an Impotent Man

a handful of manhood

GABY HAUPTMANN

Translated by Helen Atkins

A *Virago* Book

Published in Great Britain in 2000 by Virago Press
This edition published by Virago 2001

First published by Piper Verlag GmbH, Munchen 1998

Copyright © Piper Verlag GmbH, Munchen 1998
Translation copyright © Helen Atkins 2000

The moral right of the author has been asserted.

A CIP catalogue record for this book
is available from the British Library.

ISBN 0 1 86049 889 2

Typeset in Berkeley by M Rules
Printed and bound in Great Britain
by Clays Ltd, St Ives plc

Virago Books
A Division of
Little, Brown and Company (UK)
Brettenham House
Lancaster Place
London WC2E 7EN

To our victor
so that he has something to read
in heaven,
and to our Doris
so that her revue leg
will soon be better.

Thanks to the daring team at Piper Verlag,
who are prepared to take on
an author like me.

Sixty is no age at all, Günther reassures himself on his birth-day. Out of the corner of his eye he is watching his friend Klaus, who is almost the same age, dancing closely entwined with Regine. When he woke up this morning, at any rate, everything was the same as usual. He was only a year older, that was all. Well, more or less all, until he came down to the break-fast table. Disturbingly conspicuous, the number sixty was there, facing him for the first time, piped on the top of the birthday cake and looking almost maliciously vivid in pink icing against the dark chocolate cream. It was a blow, and his spirits sank a little, but that wasn't the crucial moment. It's only now, here at his own garden party, after he has had to listen sixty times over to 'Many happy returns' or 'Well, old man, you still okay?' or 'Welcome to the club, old chap' that it comes to him in a flash that he's not going to accept this. He's going to opt out of growing older like everybody else. And while he's thinking about ways and means – sport, a South Sea island, per-haps a new hobby – and watching Klaus, his financial adviser, with Regine, he suddenly knows the answer: what he needs is a new woman!

The idea hits him like a bolt of lightning. The excitement makes him close his eyes for a second. His thoughts are in a whirl, he can already feel his pulse racing, his senses coming alive.

Klaus laughs across to him, 'Hey, Günther, what's the matter? Are you auditioning for a waxworks? You look as if you're rooted to the spot!'

Günther rouses himself from his abstraction and waves to him. 'Something's just occurred to me. I must ask you about it straightaway!'

'That man never thinks about anything but business.' Klaus shakes his head in mocking disapproval, and Regine laughs.

'I must ask him how he started with Regine,' Günther thinks as he walks over to the buffet, oblivious of everything around him. He still remembers clearly what an outcry there was a year ago when, right out of the blue, Klaus left his wife and immediately afterwards married his secretary, twenty-six years younger than himself. Everyone was shocked. The small-town sisterhood resolved to punish him by giving him the cold shoulder – him and his new wife – ignoring him, no longer inviting him to their parties. They all went round to visit Monika, the shamefully abandoned wife, to comfort her and heap abuse on Klaus and Regine. But where was Monika now?

It would work out the same way for him.

With a sense of satisfaction, he takes a glass of champagne and drinks to himself, to his own secret birthday present.

Then he helps himself to a salmon canapé and looks around. His wife has organised everything perfectly: ordered a cold buffet, hired an excellent barman and found a musician with his own synthesiser. There are coloured lanterns and lights all around, and everyone who is anyone in this small town has turned up.

Günther yawns. How boring. Just like Marion, his wife. Perfect and boring. He helps himself to another salmon canapé and lets his eyes roam around again. That girl there, dancing with the mayor's son, near to Klaus and Regine – she would suit him. Slim, sexy, under thirty. She would bring a bit of fire into the bedroom! He studies her more closely. As she dances, the short skirt of her dress sometimes slides up a little over the black stockings. She laughs, throwing back her head. He imagines her facing him, in that same position, naked, her full breasts moving freely above him as she rides him with abandon.

A clap on the back almost makes him choke on his food. 'Well, old chap, how's it feel to be sixty?'

His old associate from the council, Manfred, is standing beside him. He's only showing off because he's two years younger. 'I feel just the same as usual. Maybe a bit poorer, because you're all drinking so much!'

Manfred gives a saccharine smile and to prove Günther's point drains his glass in one go. 'Yes, you're really hard up, aren't you?' He wipes his mouth with the back of his hand, casting a meaningful look at Günther's new house, which cost three and a half million marks to build.

It's late afternoon. Even though thunderstorms were forecast, the weather has been kind. Marion looks around with satisfaction. The landscape gardener was as good as his word: the garden is perfect for entertaining on a grand scale; it has plenty of variety but it's still spacious. If the young trees were already taller and could offer shade, then the garden – with its dance floor of light-coloured marble, the small level area for the buffet and bistro-style tables and the charming little goldfish pond with its wooden bridge – would really have a turn-of-the-century feel. Marion draws a deep breath. Everyone seems happy; they're all chatting, standing at the bistro tables or dancing. She smiles, with a sense of relief. Everything is going well, she has organised it perfectly, she can be proud of herself. And so can Günther! She looks around for her husband and sees him standing with Manfred. Marion looks at him affectionately. His sixtieth birthday.

They've been married for thirty-five years now and have been through quite a lot together, Günther out there engaged in the cut and thrust of business, she behind him, invisible but solid as a rock. She's always been there for him, shielding him from other worries, bolstering his will and his warrior spirit. Now the work is done and the seed is bearing fruit; soon they will reap the well-earned harvest. A feeling of happiness and security floods through her, leaving a pleasantly warm feeling in her stomach. She has chosen the right path in life. She has a wonderful husband, still an attractive man, who is respected by everyone and who loves and admires her – what more could a woman ask of life?

Linda is still dancing, though the music isn't exactly to her taste. But she'd rather dance one foxtrot after another than stand around on the lawn with a champagne glass in her hand. So although she never stops circling to the rhythm with Dirk, she observes the party guests and notices what goes on around her. Günther's appraising glances have not escaped her. She's not bothered by them. After all, what can he want, the old git? she thinks, wrapping her arms a little more tightly around Dirk's neck.

Dirk responds by searching for her mouth. He'll propose to her in thoroughly traditional style, he decides. Before the summer is out, somewhere down by the river, he will have a table set up under a weeping willow, a large table with a white damask tablecloth hanging down to the ground. On the table will be a huge champagne bucket with a magnum of champagne, two long-stemmed cut-glass champagne glasses, a silver candelabrum with lighted candles and a gigantic bunch of red roses. And, wearing his white suit, he will fall to his knees on the grass before her and, quoting some suitable line of poetry, ask her to be his wife, and then perhaps they'll make love on the spot – no, not perhaps, certainly, for he'll be a devoted husband to her, a husband who will always be there for her. Enraptured, he draws her close and kisses her passionately. In doing so he steps out of rhythm and treads on her foot. Linda laughs out loud. Her eyes meet Günther's. She starts to nibble at Dirk's ear-lobe. Let the old man have a good look if he wants to; she's young, she's desirable, her life is full of possibilities, and whatever happens things will turn out all right.

Marion has invited sixty guests to Günther's special birthday party, and exactly sixty guests have come. No one has turned down the invitation, and no one has brought an unexpected guest along. They all know that Marion plans her parties like a military operation and takes them extremely seriously. Sometimes she smiles about it herself, but she knows no other way. She comes from a Prussian family; her father and his father and grandfather before him all pursued military careers, winning decorations and honours by their single-minded zeal and always showing exemplary fighting spirit, discipline and integrity. It was a disappointment to the whole family when she was born a girl. Though this was hardly her fault, it was soon made clear to her that this regrettable caprice of nature excluded her from all the really important things in life. For a long time this made her unhappy, especially as, unfortunately, she also remained the only child. Then she found her own way to make up for her humiliation and lack of self-esteem: whatever she undertook was carried out with military precision!

Günther's new neighbours engage him in conversation, and Manfred strolls towards the house. It is too showy, too white – typically nouveau-riche. All the same, he has to admit to himself, however grudgingly, Günther has been many times more successful than he has. The thought produces a strangely gnawing

sensation in him. He's not sure, but he's afraid that it's envy.
Pure, naked envy. In fact he actually quite likes Günther. For
many years the two of them sat together on the local council,
until Günther could no longer spare the time and decided not to
stand for election again. During those years they have shared
many a useful piece of information with each other, and such
insider knowledge has often been beneficial for both of them.
They profited together. Even so, he would have been secretly
delighted if Günther's most recent speculations had not turned
out to be so astute. When, after the collapse of communism,
Günther expanded his civil engineering business into eastern
Germany and immediately invested recklessly, doubling the
amount of machinery he owned, everyone thought he was mad.
But he had clearly backed the right horse, especially in the area
of underground and surface engineering: a goodly portion of
the money that the state poured into road-building is now standing there for all to see, shining white, with its colonial-style
pillared porch, surrounded by green lawns. Oh well, Manfred
thinks, making a strenuous effort to suppress his negative feelings. It's Günther's monument to himself.

Günther Schmidt is not particularly well educated – he never
had either the persistence or the will to study, and failed to see
the point of it. For a long time 'learning by doing' was the only
English phrase he knew. But as a child of the war years he developed a kind of peasant cunning, and over time he acquired a
growing understanding of economics. Combined with the
opportunism and emotional coldness he had picked up from
his stepfather, this produced a mixture that gave him an advantage over many other people. It still does to this day. Feelings
mean almost nothing to him; his ideals are money and power.
Loyalty is directed only towards himself. Günther has no sense
of obligation towards either his country or his family. He's not

concerned with right and wrong, but only with what furthers his own ends.

Günther's real father never came back from Russia. Like thousands of others he had been sent to the front as a rifleman, and at some point he was reported missing. Günther was four at the time, and a mere six months later he could barely remember him. Not only had his own recollections faded, but Erich, the new man in his mother's life, did everything in his power to erase the memory of Günther's father.

Erich dealt in scrap metal, a good line to be in, especially after the war. Soon he was one of the first people in the town to own a car, and Günther's mother had a washing-machine. At that time it was thought that Günther should be taught good manners by a tutor, but he rebelled against this because Erich did not set him an example, and anyway he was much happier rummaging about in the scrapyard. There his stepfather taught him the basic principles of the free-market economy: always sniff what's in the wind, keep your ears pricked, fraternise with anybody who might be useful to you, build up connections that will be to your advantage, and stay one step ahead of the rest!

Günther observed closely the example provided by Erich, at first with unbounded admiration, later with an inner compulsion to outdo him. In 1973 his stepfather sold the scrapyard at a sky-high price to a firm that was planning to build a new sewage-treatment plant, but the project came to nothing because of a storm of public protest and an organised local campaign. That was of no concern to Erich: with his newly acquired capital he became a property developer and built shopping centres and DIY stores on the outskirts of nearby towns. When this market was exhausted, he changed tack once again, and on the strength of his experience in the field set himself up as a business consultant at

the age of fifty-five. In 1980 his antennae told him that it was
time for another change. At sixty-two, Erich set up a business
clearing old waste tips. Green had suddenly become not just a
colour but a political concept, and Erich recognised that Germany
was full of former waste tips, notably on the land around his
former scrapyard, where a school had since been built. The very
next year he was able ceremoniously to hand over to a Greenpeace
representative a cheque for a five-figure sum to be used for environmental conservation – a donation that he immediately put to
prominent use in his advertising, to the great benefit of himself
and his firm, and that he equally promptly set against his tax bill.

Günther exchanges a few polite phrases with his neighbours
and looks around impatiently for Linda. She's no longer on the
dance floor, and his guests are too densely packed together for
him to be able to pick her out among the crowd. He climbs
some of the steps up to the house to get a better view. Ah, there
she is, she and Dirk are making their way to the buffet. She
seems to glide along; her black dress fits her like a second skin,
revealing every detail of her body. Günther gulps. At her every
step he seems to hear the erotic sound of her stockings rubbing
against each other. He feels a surge of blood towards his nether
parts and simultaneously hears his stepfather saying, 'Whatever
the situation, keep a clear head.' But Erich is dead. And, annoy-
ingly, he went two years too soon, for now at last Günther could
prove to him that he's his equal – no, that he's surpassed him!
He's earning a lot of money, he's built a house costing millions,
and soon he'll possess a lovely young woman. What a triumph!

Linda walks over to the buffet with Dirk, smiling radiantly and
casting appraising glances to left and right. 'You're the most
beautiful woman here,' Dirk whispers to her suddenly. 'No one
can dispute that!'

'Are you proud of me?' she asks him softly. As they walk on he lightly places his hand just above her bottom.

'And how!'

Linda looks with amusement at his boyishly flushed face. 'And what does that do for you?'

'Everything.'

'And what do I get?'

'Whatever you want.'

Linda laughs, amused. 'You'd better be careful, making promises like that!'

Marion sees the two of them approaching. She and Günther were never a couple like that. Carefree, happy, relaxed. She tidies the napkins, straightens the cutlery, which is lying perfectly straight anyway, and says, 'I'm so glad that you've both come,' and then turning to Dirk, who is just about to take a plate, 'and your parents too.'

He looks up, smiling at her. 'No one would want to miss a party like this.'

'And you have such a beautiful setting for it,' Linda says, gesturing towards the house. 'A dream home! It's enough to make anyone really jealous!'

Under her pale-blue linen suit Marion gives a slight shrug. 'Oh yes, it is nice. But nothing is as nice as youth. And that's what you have.'

Linda nods slowly. 'That's true.' She adds, with a slight pout, 'Only – everybody has been young once, that's a gift everyone is given – unlike some other things . . .'

Laughing, Marion shakes her head and lays a hand on Dirk's arm. 'You'll be building a palace for her one of these days, won't you?'

The microphone crackles into life and everyone looks up expectantly. The mayor has climbed on to the small wooden stage and is standing there next to the synthesiser, clearly about to make a speech in honour of the birthday boy.

'Oh no, I can't bear it,' whispers Dirk. Linda watches as Günther steps forward to take up his position and Marion hurries to his side. All the guests fall silent and move closer. The mayor clears his throat twice into the microphone, but he can't start yet because the video camera has yet to be mounted on its tripod. When everything is ready and a new battery has been loaded, just to be on the safe side, Joachim Wetterstein lets his eyes wander over all those present before focusing on Günther. 'My dear old sporting comrade,' he begins, but then at once corrects himself, smiling, 'although on this special day perhaps I should say, "My dear still youthful sporting comrade"!' A few people laugh, and there is some restrained applause.

'Take me away from here!' whispers Dirk, groaning quietly.

'Why?' asks Linda. 'It's rather funny. And besides, you have to put up with it if you want to keep up with what's going on.'

'But I don't want to keep up with what's going on!'

She prods him gently in the side with her elbow. 'I do. So there!'

Günther is aware of the pack at his heels. He knows perfectly well that they begrudge him all this. The house, his success, and now, to crown it all, the mayor giving a speech for him. The one thing that they may not begrudge him is his stolid wife in her boring dress. And he can be quite sure that they don't envy him his acute hair loss, which has been causing him concern for weeks and is already making his forehead noticeably higher. Manfred has jokingly suggested that he should have his new property checked out for hazardous chemicals. And Klaus said with a wink that finally his potency was on the rise. It's easy for him to talk, with his sexy young wife! Involuntarily Günther's eyes seek out Linda. Ah, there she is, still by the buffet. With that good-for-nothing, the mayor's son, a student who shows no sign of completing his studies, always keen to criticise society's ills and full of ambitious plans for changing the world. Joachim really deserves better than that. And Linda? Günther grins at the mayor, without listening to what he is saying. She'll soon realise that she does too.

As she goes to bed that night, Marion is happy. What a pity her father didn't live to see this. It was a successful party: everything went as planned, no one stepped out of line, and it was a gathering of everybody who's anybody in Römersfeld. In the bathroom she has a new, almost transparent negligée laid out ready, for tonight she is going to seduce Günther – that's part of his birthday treat, a finishing touch for a perfect day. Marion carefully removes her makeup, has a shower and anoints herself from head to foot with a perfumed body lotion, while looking in the wall mirror at her problem zones. She notes objectively that her thighs and stomach would rule out a bikini nowadays, but as bikinis were always too daring for her and she has therefore never owned one this doesn't spoil things. Because of its roundness, her face has almost no wrinkles, and her hair isn't dyed yet. It still possesses the warm chestnut colour of her youth, although the short bob has long since given way to a perm. In three weeks you'll be fifty-five, she tells herself, dabbing some perfume behind her ear. I wonder what idea Günther will come up with to celebrate my special birthday. She slips into her negligée, performs a little twirl in front of the mirror, gives a satisfied nod, quickly runs a comb through her hair again and then softly and expectantly opens the door to their bedroom.

Loud snores greet her. She pauses indecisively, then gropes her way towards the bed in the dark. It's really true, Günther is already asleep! Disappointed, she switches on the bedside lamp and sits down on the bed. This has never happened before. It has been an unwritten but sacred law that on birthdays and special days they don't simply drop off to sleep. This rule has held for thirty-five years of marriage – until now. Uncertain what to do, Marion considers whether to wake Günther. It might be unlucky to end the tradition. But equally it might be a bad idea to wake her husband if he doesn't want to be woken up. She contemplates him for a while as he lies there in the foetal position with his back to her, and she's not sure whether that position makes him look child-like or rejecting. Finally she slips under the covers and snuggles up to him.

Günther has heard her come in. In his mind's eye he has followed her every movement in the bathroom, all her preparations for the ritual that have by now themselves become a ritual. When the door finally opens he pretends to be asleep and snoring. He doesn't want to touch her just now. He doesn't want to touch her at all ever again. He's sixty and has a right to a fresh, new life; he's earned it. Günther senses Marion looking at him, and feels her slipping into bed. Just keep away from me, he thinks, and he pictures Klaus with his young wife. Marion presses close against him, and he is repelled by the contact. That warm flesh that will one day be withered, the breasts that have grown increasingly soft; he doesn't want to see her one morning without any teeth or have to think about arranging care for her. He doesn't want to watch her grow old at all, he must get rid of her. As soon as possible. Günther thinks of Linda, of the provocative way she danced in her skin-tight dress; he remembers lunchtime's daydreams, immerses himself in them again, pursuing them further. He imagines Linda coming towards him. With a single movement he tears off her dress; she stands before him in nothing but her black stockings and high-heeled shoes; he sees himself throwing her on to the bed and hears her groaning and whimpering as he thrusts into her, thrusts and thrusts. He sees her open red mouth before him and feels himself growing hard. Just before he comes, he turns over and grabs hold of Marion.

It's Sunday. The birthday party at the Schmidts' went on into the early hours, and the church bells are calling in vain for the top people in the town. Even those who regard it as politically expedient to be seen in church on Sundays and holidays are thinking up some excuse for not going today.

But Klaus Raak is already up. Regine can hear the hum of the ergometer from his exercise room. She turns over in bed and looks at the clock. Eight o'clock! Far too early to get up after such a night. But she knows what he's up to. For an hour Klaus will secretly torture himself with all sorts of different machines and then, freshly showered, lie down quietly beside her and then wake up with her at about ten o'clock as though nothing had happened. She pulls the cover up over her head so as not to have to hear that monotonous drone. It irritates her, because it shows that Klaus isn't nearly as laid back about the age difference between them as he likes to pretend. Why can't he be open about the exercises he does to stay young? What's so awful? After all, other people also make an effort to stay fit. Since it seems to matter to him, though, she goes along with it and forces herself to say nothing. If that's all it is, he's welcome to his little secret. Regine closes her eyes tight and soon falls back into a dream-filled early-morning sleep.

Römersfeld, with is population of just about 50,000, was for a long time held up as the perfect small town. Firstly, because of its sunny position and the gently rolling hills that surrounded it, producing excellent grapes for the winegrowers who had been established here for centuries, and secondly – and this aroused much more envy among the neighbouring towns – because of two firms that were major suppliers to the motor industry and brought a great deal of money into the locality. As the icing on the cake for the town's finances, they were joined in the late 1980s by a large computer company, which brought not only new jobs but also a sense of progress. So Römersfeld, once wholly dependent on wine production, had for decades now been experiencing a boom. It had built a state-of-the-art high school equipped with everything that the younger generation could possibly require, and also an indoor swimming-pool and a heated outdoor pool. These were soon followed by a multi-purpose hall designed to be just slightly superior to that of the neighbouring town; in due course Römersfeld also boasted a concert hall, a modern equestrian centre and a high-class tennis club, and people were giving serious thought to a suitable location for a golf course. This was the period when shopping centres and DIY stores sprang up like mushrooms, and large car dealers and hire firms set up branches, so the small town, at least when viewed from the major road which by-passed it, lost its former idyllic appearance. And it was the heyday of the Schmidts of this world, who cared little for idylls but always knew well in advance when a particular site was about to become free for development, and always had enough useful contacts to enable them to use that knowledge to best advantage.

The phone rings and Regine wakes with a start. She's just about to reach for it when she hears her husband pick up the receiver in the next room. This suits Regine very well, as she was just having a lovely dream and would like to let it continue. So she rolls back into her sleeping position, but some scraps of conversation coming from the exercise room make her prick up her ears. 'Why do you suddenly want a divorce?' she hears her husband say loudly. And a little later, 'It'll finish you! You'd lose your house, at any rate.' Slowly Regine sits up. 'Don't do anything stupid. Just get yourself a girlfriend and have done with it!'

Who on earth is he talking to? Regine wonders. She also feels annoyed about that particular piece of advice. Wasn't she also just a girlfriend once? What does he mean, just get yourself a girlfriend and have done with it?

A little later she hears Klaus go into the bathroom. Apparently he's no longer in the mood for the exercise bike. Regine gets up and also goes into the bathroom. Klaus is in the shower, snorting as the water goes into his mouth. Regine slides the glass door open a little and touches his naked back. Klaus spins round. 'God, you made me jump out of my skin!'

'You're up early today. Good morning, darling!'

She blows him a kiss and starts to clean her teeth at the double washbasin, until Klaus reaches for a towel and comes over to her.

'The phone woke me up,' he says evasively.

Regine smiles at him through a lather of toothpaste. 'I heard it.' She reaches for the tooth mug and spits. 'Who is it then who wants to get divorced?'

Klaus hesitates briefly, then gives her a sideways look. 'I'm afraid I can't tell you that. Professional confidentiality.'

'The whole town will know soon enough.' Regine shrugs and slips out of her thin pyjamas. 'They did in our case.'

'But that was different.'

Regine puts on a shower cap. 'Divorce is divorce. And I think for you to advise a husband just to get himself a girlfriend and have done with it is in very bad taste. Demeaning to women. You make it sound like going to the butcher for a joint of meat!'

Klaus reaches for his bathrobe. 'Now you're exaggerating, darling. I only meant that he shouldn't do anything rash and wreck his career.'

'You're a fine one to talk!' Regine opens the shower cubicle but pauses for a moment longer to see Klaus's reaction.

'Honestly, Regine!'

So that's all he has to say, thinks Regine. She closes the cubicle and showers, with the water in turn hot and cold.

Deep in thought, Klaus searches for his slippers and goes into the kitchen. His house can't compare with Günther's, but it is also detached, a 1970s bungalow, which he has had extended since his divorce. This has made the garden much smaller, but that means less work as one grows older. He's also had to have the kitchen redone. Strangely enough, Regine didn't mind sleeping in Monika's bed, but she refused to cook in her kitchen.

Well, he says to himself, getting out the coffee and filter and grinning to himself, your divorce has cost you a pretty penny, though you've got a pretty young wife out of it! But Günther will have to pay much more, because Monika had money of her own, unlike Marion. More money than he has, in fact. She had, some years before, taken over her parents' car-spraying firm, so she wasn't financially dependent on him. Of course she made her divorce lawyer fight over every penny all the same, but that was for the sake of pride, not cash as such. That his children thought him an utter idiot was harder to bear. But his son, at thirty-five, is running the business in partnership with his mother, and his thirty-four-year-old daughter is trying, in her third stab at a career, to make her mark as a fashion designer. So they both have other things to occupy their minds, and they'll come to terms with the divorce eventually.

Regine's father is more of a problem. He's two years younger than Klaus, and maintains to this day that the relationship is practically incestuous, like father and daughter. Klaus can understand his attitude when he considers his own daughter, but with regard to himself he sees things quite differently. After all, as he protested during their last argument, he's an unusually lean, youthful and active type. But Karl-Heinz only laughed scornfully: he could say the same of himself. Whenever Regine goes to visit her parents, Klaus now finds some excuse not to go.

The coffee's almost ready. Klaus lays the table in the new conservatory, which Regine has equipped with bamboo furniture and palms and calls her 'island in the sun'. Madness, really, he thinks, returning to the kitchen and watching the coffee drip into the glass jug. A kitchen costing as much as a good mid-range car. And to do it just as Römersfeld's fortunes are in decline. The computer firm has already closed down, the auto-parts suppliers are laying off more and more people, and there are rumours that the firm producing electronic systems for vehicles and electric motors for luxury features in cars is thinking of relocating – moving closer to the car factory, which means no more storage, no transportation by lorry, direct transfer from the production line into the cars as they're built. The pubs and restaurants, the DIY stores and shopping centres are all feeling the pinch as purchasing power declines. And those people who still have enough money are stashing it safely away, because no one knows what lies ahead. The one thing they all share is the fear of Europe. Especially the thought that other countries might produce cheaper car seats and so bring Römersfeld's second-largest employer to its knees as well. Now it's not only people down the pub who grumble that you can't survive off the back of a concert hall. Or tennis courts and swimming-pools. Last winter saw the first demonstrations against the wasting of money and energy. If the unemployment level rises any higher, anger about the cost of maintaining the town's luxurious facilities will continue to grow.

And in such a financial climate Klaus has bought a kitchen costing 60,000 marks.

Klaus sighs. He knows no more than anyone else how his business will fare. He's lost some of his best customers as a result of their moving away. The computer firm was a good client, but when it went into receivership that was the end of that. Now he still has the men on the management floor of the two other firms, which also don't want to use their income to heat municipal swimming-pools but think more in terms of shipping loans or publicly subsidised housing. If he loses these clients too, he won't have much left to offer Regine. He wonders how seriously she took the words 'for better, for worse' at their wedding.

Klaus opens the fridge, puts butter, jam and the plastic dish with the sausage on to a tray, and carries it all into the conservatory. He pauses a moment in the doorway. As the morning light comes flooding in, it is broken up by the palms, which cast picturesque shadows across the table. This really has improved the house, he thinks. All the same, the extension wasn't necessary. He spent a lot of money at a time when everyone else was hanging on to theirs. With a sigh he puts the tray down. Everyone except Günther, that is – he has no problems at all. He's just swimming in money, like Donald Duck's Uncle Scrooge. Doing deals runs in his blood. And now something else runs in his blood too. But springtime fancies aren't conducive to keeping a clear head, everyone knows that. If your energy is concentrated below the belt, there's none left for your brain.

Klaus sits down and pours himself a cup of coffee. What should he do? He can try to dissuade him. Or he can help him.

If he tries to dissuade him, Günther will just go to a different financial adviser. So that would achieve nothing, except that he'd lose yet another good source of income.

If he helps him, then he stays in control. He can, for instance, arrange everything in such a complicated way that even Günther loses track of it. And then he would be indispensable. Klaus catches his breath. Such a thought has never crossed his mind before. For a moment he sits at the table completely motionless, pondering the enormity of his idea. Then his rigidity gives way to a shrug of the shoulders and a slight grin. One good turn deserves another, he thinks, and as you'll realise quite soon, Günther, old chap, young women don't come cheap.

'Welcome to the club,' Klaus says softly, raising his coffee cup.

Since early that morning Günther had been wandering around his house like a ghost, drinking one cup of black coffee after another and waiting restlessly for eight o'clock. He thought it was not unreasonable to make a phone call just after eight on a Sunday morning. It was vital that he should ring Klaus, because he wanted him to draw up a battle plan at once, a plan that would ensure him total victory in this divorce. All the money must be gone, or at any rate out of sight. He would need time to make it all disappear, but Marion mustn't notice that anything was going on. Since she knew nothing about his business affairs anyway, that would probably not be too difficult. The hard part would be to continue playing his role as a husband. What he would really like would be to go and ring Linda's doorbell right now and invite himself in for some steamy sex.

Thinking of Linda, it occurs to him that he knows neither her surname nor where she lives. But that just makes him keener still. It's a game! A game with one winner. And he, Günther Schmidt, will be that winner!

He had been waiting so impatiently for that phone conversation with Klaus, but now he feels annoyed. The fellow seemed so hesitant. All that stuff about getting a girlfriend! He, Günther Schmidt, doesn't want anything hole-and-corner. He wants to bask in his newfound happiness; he wants the whole word to see his latest acquisition and envy him for it!

He's just on his way to the kitchen to get himself another cup of coffee when he hears Marion coming down the stairs. He'll act the charming husband. He's already starting to enjoy this game.

Marion has also been awake for a long time. She's been lying in bed, her eyes wide open, listening as Günther wanders aimlessly around the house, and thinking. About the party and what happened afterwards in bed. She can't make sense of it. First it seemed like a sudden surge of passion, but then, because it was over and done with far too quickly and he immediately turned his back on her again, it felt like deliberate humiliation. Try as she may, she can't think of any reason for his behaviour. Everything had gone perfectly, there was not the tiniest hitch, the party had certainly enhanced his image. So what could possibly have made him angry with her?

Several times she was on the point of simply going downstairs and asking him. But a vague fear held her back. Then she heard the click of the telephone. He was ringing someone. Who could it be at eight o'clock in the morning? What could be so important on a Sunday?

As she goes downstairs, she resolves to act as though there's nothing at all the matter. She'll conjure up a delicious breakfast and talk casually about yesterday's party. Then she'll soon see what's what.

Monika Raak has also had a bad night. After getting up, she sat idly at the breakfast table for some time – alone, as she has done for a year now – then she picked some flowers and rearranged some of her books. She has now spent an hour cleaning out odd corners of her spacious three-roomed flat with its bright, modern décor. Just at the moment she would rather get annoyed with her cleaning lady, who steers well clear of the corners, than have to think about yesterday.

That Klaus was invited, together with Regine, makes her simply livid. She wishes she could have put some poison into their cocktails – what a scandal if they had just dropped dead at Günther's splendid birthday party! As for being alone, Monika has got used to that by now. In fact, she wouldn't have Klaus back now at any price. She only has to recall certain aspects of their life together to feel glad that they are divorced. But she has been robbed of her place in society, and for that she could kill him. She has lost their shared friends, their joint theatre subscription, and long-standing traditions like skiing at Zermatt over New Year. They had gone to the same hotel every single year for twenty years. Now Klaus's lifestyle continues as before, but she has had to pull her horns in. He sits in their old seats in the theatre with Regine as a matter of course; he's still invited to every party given by their friends; he has no hesitation in taking his new wife to Zermatt, where he is hailed as something of a lad and receives admiring comments. Whereas she has to find a different hotel for New Year's Eve so as to avoid the embarrassment of a meeting between the present and the former Frau Raak, and she can't be asked to certain parties for the same reason. It's as if she's got some leprous disease: she's the ex.

After their breakfast and the highly artificial conversation that accompanied it, Günther has retreated to his study. From there he watches Marion supervising the tidying up of the garden and wonders how he can get hold of Linda's surname and address. He thinks of Joachim, the mayor. He must know the name of his son's girlfriend.

Günther looks among his papers. Joachim has an ex-directory number that he made a note of only recently. But where? He goes through all the drawers of his massive writing-desk, takes out innumerable sheets and scraps of paper, reads what's on them, puts some back, screws up others and throws them away. Infuriatingly, he's written down some numbers without the people's names. So that doesn't get him any further. But he knows by heart the number of Joachim's direct line at the town hall, and before he's had time to think much about it his fingers are already dialling the number. To his surprise the phone is answered immediately.

'Wetterstein.'

'Oh, I wasn't expecting that – hi, it's me.'

'Günther!'

'Were you expecting a call from someone else?'

'Not exactly . . . but I'm glad you've phoned. I was going to ring to thank you for the wonderful party!'

'I'm the one who should be thanking you, for your speech. It was really good – everyone said so.'

'That's nice to hear. But Marion really excelled herself. She has set a standard that other ladies will find extremely hard to maintain.'

'Er, yes. I wanted to ask you, Joachim, that girl who was there yesterday with your son . . .'

'You mean Linda?'

'Yes, I think so. A little makeup bag was left behind, and Marion thought it might be hers. Have you by any chance got her phone number? Or better still her address, then we can got someone to take it round to her.' Günther is gripping the receiver between ear and shoulder and holding pencil and paper at the ready.

'Oh, she'll be very pleased.' Joachim's voice has lost its undertone of caution. He goes on, warmly, 'But there's no need to go to so much trouble. I'll mention it to my son this afternoon and he can drop by and get it from Marion. And many thanks once again, Günther, it was really first-rate!'

'You're welcome,' replies Günther, but Joachim has already hung up. Damn, thinks Günther, and breaks off the point of his pencil. Where is he to get a makeup bag from? And how is he to give it to Marion without arousing suspicion! 'Oh look, darling, the mayor's son's girlfriend left this behind yesterday in the men's toilet!' Or perhaps it was the mayor's son himself? How embarrassing – he must find some other way. But how?

Günther leafs through the telephone book. He'll ring Dirk Wetterstein. Perhaps he's a man who likes things to be done for him and won't want to drive right across town.

He's in luck. Dirk Wetterstein is listed in the book. Probably so that his fellow students can keep him informed of all the dates when demonstrations are going to be held, thinks Günther venomously as he dials, holding the pencil stub ready. It's some time before anyone answers.

'Hello, this is Dirk Wetterstein's residence.' A woman's voice. Is it Linda?

'Ah, hello, this is Günther Schmidt.'

'Hello. Do you want to speak to Dirk?'

'Well—,' Günther breaks off the end of the pencil stub as he hesitates. 'Were you at my birthday party yesterday with Dirk?'

'Yes, it was really nice. Thank you!'

Günther's mind works feverishly, but he can't think of anything better. 'Did you leave a makeup bag behind? We found one.'

'No, I'm sure I didn't. Shall I pass you on to Dirk now?'

'Many thanks, Fru . . . Fru . . .' But Linda doesn't oblige; she's already passed the receiver on to Dirk.

'Herr Schmidt? What a surprise!'

'I . . . really I was trying to get Joachim and I picked out the wrong number from the phone book . . .'

'He's ex-directory. After all, he's an important man! Are you ready to take it down? It's 60606. A real VIP number.'

'Thanks – I can even memorise that.'

'60606,' Günther scratches on his bit of paper with the broken pencil. That's made the situation even worse, he thinks. Joachim will tell Linda that tale about the makeup bag and she'll tell him that I've already asked her about it myself.

Annoyed with himself, he gets up to stretch his legs in the garden. Two men are clearing away the remaining rubbish; the stage and the long wooden structure that supported the buffet have already been removed. Marion is picking up cigarette ends and other small items of litter from among the bushes and stones. Günther watches her for a while, then suddenly thinks of the guest list. Of course, her name should be on that.

He'll get at that girl one way or another. No doubt about it!

Linda is lying in bed at Dirk's, dreaming of the future. Lost in thought, she gazes at all the books that are piled untidily on the simple wooden bookshelf or stacked on the floor and the political magazines lying in bundles against the wall. On the desk, which consists of a plain wooden table-top supported by two trestles, several books are lying open; a number of unwashed coffee mugs complete the tableau. On the floor, further thick tomes surround the folding chair where Dirk is sitting in a cloud of cigarette smoke, tapping away at his seminar paper. 'Bloody law,' he mutters now and then.

'Don't worry. Soon you'll be a famous lawyer and then you can laugh at all the Schmidts of this world!' Linda closes her eyes dreamily.

'I laugh at them already.'

'Maybe.' Linda says nothing for a while. 'Even so,' she continues, 'just think what that one garden party must have cost and what we could buy with that amount of money . . .'

Dirk stubs out his cigarette. 'Consumerism! For goodness' sake, Linda, there are other values – and besides, you earn good wages.'

'All things are relative.' Linda sits up and runs the fingers of both hands through her long black hair. 'Perhaps I should have accepted that makeup bag, since he bothered to ring up specially. It might have been worth having. Dior, Lancôme, Chanel, Joop, Jil Sander – who knows?'

'Give it a rest!' Dirk turns round to face her. 'What's got into you? And – in case you've forgotten – Günther didn't ring because of the bag, he just dialled the wrong number, that's all.'

'Yes, all right!' Linda throws back the cover and surveys her body. 'I could do with some sun. Do you want to come? A bike ride? Or down to the river? Or something else?'

He looks at her and his face brightens. 'Something else for sure, but I haven't got time for any of the other things.'

'Only if you bring me a nice breakfast in bed afterwards,' says Linda with a grin, patting her flat stomach.

'Whatever the fridge has to offer,' Dirk nods. He saves his work.

'That won't be much!'

Two hours later Linda is driving back to her flat in her red Polo. Dirk lives in an old building in the middle of the pedestrian zone, while she rents a flat on the outskirts of the town on the so-called 'new estate', six five-storeyed blocks, each containing a number of flats and designed in such a way as to form Italian-style inner courtyards, with grassed areas for playgrounds and barbecues. Linda likes it; it's anonymous yet homely, and it's also exceedingly practical. A lift takes her directly from the basement garage to her flat, and no bags of shopping have to be lugged across roads and up flights of stairs to the flat, as they do at Dirk's place. His flat doesn't even have its own parking space, and he sometimes has to circle around that old part of the town like mad, looking for somewhere to park. By the end of the month he's often spent more on parking tickets than Linda has paid to rent her garage.

As Linda turns into the road leading to her estate, a silver Mercedes is coming towards her. Whatever is a posh car like that doing around here? thinks Linda, and then she catches sight of the registration, GS 1. And as she slows down and drives close to the kerb in order to let the S-Class through, it dawns on her who the driver is: Günther Schmidt. He seems to have recognised her at the same instant, for he stops and lowers his tinted window.

'Fancy that,' he says from the dark interior. 'What a surprise. Do you live here too?'

Linda, driving with the windows open as it is a hot day, nods. 'Yes, why, who else does?'

'How do you mean, who else?'

'Well, I mean, you don't live here. So I suppose you must have been visiting someone who does live here.'

'Oh, I see, yes, of course. I was trying to call on a business associate, but he wasn't in.'

'On a Sunday?'

'Yes, it's something quite important.' He leans out of the side window a little. 'I was just wondering where I could wait until he comes back. Is there a café here?'

Linda thinks, but then shakes her head. 'Not on the estate. Only a pizzeria, but that's only open in the evening. Sorry!'

Günther pushes his sunglasses up a little. 'Could I invite you to join me for a coffee somewhere? Then I could come back here in an hour, and perhaps the man I need to see will be back by then.'

'Why don't you just go home for that hour?'

'Yes, why not . . .' mumbles Günther, and his sunglasses slip back on to his nose.

'Nice to have met you, ciao.' Linda waves to him, steps on the accelerator and drives off.

'Oh yes, very nice!' Günther first hits the horn and then his own head with the flat of his hand. 'Damn it all, man, you don't have a clue about picking up birds. Completely out of practice! I don't believe it! Thirty years of marriage and they won't even look at you! It's all Marion's fault!'

Furious, he slams his foot down on the accelerator, but by the time he's reached the turning for the centre of town he's already devised a new strategy. He's not going to give up just like that. Nor is he going to try for a different girl. He simply has to establish the truth now. Can it be that, at sixty, he's no longer attractive? Has his sexual magnetism diminished? Rubbish! He turns down the sun visor and uncovers the vanity mirror. He's looking good. Masculine. Austere. Mature – but not old!

Resolutely Günther heads for the nearest café.

An hour later he's on his way back to the new development with a colourful bunch of flowers in the car. He now knows where Linda lives. And also her surname, thanks to his wife's meticulously drawn-up guest list.

He parks the car in a conspicuous position in the inner courtyard, then slowly walks towards the big entrance door to her block. In his mind's eye he counts the doorbells. Her bell was at top right. He tries to look at the upper part of the building without being too obvious about it. The balcony just below the penthouse is most probably hers. Some yellow and white fabric is threaded between the iron bars of the railing, screening the balcony from view. What a pity. He can't see whether someone is out on the balcony. Perhaps even lying there.

Sunbathing.

Naked.

Stretched out sensuously on the sunbed.

Filled with desire.

For him.

He pictures Linda and at once feels something stirring. Sixty? Ha! he thinks. Ridiculous!

Now he is standing at the door. He still hasn't got any further. No arm has appeared, giving him an inviting wave from the balcony. On the contrary, he feels rather lost. Which bell should he ring next? Who should he leave the flowers with? Before it had all seemed so simple. Chance would come to his aid. Somehow Linda would appear at the crucial moment. Only now she's not here, although the crucial moment has arrived. Slowly Günther turns away. The courtyard is completely deserted. There's not even the sound of children's voices. Obviously everyone's gone out thanks to this glorious weather; they're swimming, having barbecues, cycling. It was idiotic to come here.

Günther turns on his heel, puts the flowers on the back seat and starts the car.

Slowly Linda emerges from the shadows of the basement garage. She pushes her bicycle out and follows the elegant silver saloon with her eyes until it is out of sight. Who was he planning to visit, bringing flowers? She at any rate has no wish to cross his path again. It might have looked as though she was trying to meet him on purpose.

Linda mounts her racing bike and pushes down on the pedals. Ah, that feels good. Exercise, sunshine, the warm air, a wonderful feeling. How can Dirk bear to stay in his stifling flat in weather like this? She decides to pay a visit to her friend Irena and persuade her to come cycling.

Irena has arrived at her mother's house, with Richi. It had occurred to both of them that Monika might be feeling a bit down after not being invited to the party, and each of them independently hit on the idea of going and cheering her up a bit.

'If you want all the details, I can always ask Dirk,' Richi is kindly saying to his mother. 'After all, he was there!'

Irena looks at him askance and taps her forehead.

Monika is in the kitchen, which opens on to the living room. Uncorking a bottle of Prosecco, she calls out, 'I couldn't hear you, Richi. What did you say?'

'That the firm is doing really well,' Irena answers for him.

'Thanks for telling me, but I know that already.' Monika comes back with the bottle and three glasses. 'It's nice of you to think of me, really touching.' She puts the glasses down on the small coffee table, carefully fills them and offers one to each of her children. 'Let's drink to us!' Then she sits down on the sofa next to Richi. 'So, how was it?'

'How was what?'

'Well, the party. I'm sure Dirk will have mentioned it to you . . .'

Richi casts a triumphant glance at Irena. 'Not yet. We haven't spoken today. But if you like I could ring him . . .?'

'Yes, go ahead, I'm sure you want to!'

Richi gets up, grinning, and goes over to the phone. Irena shakes her head. 'Oh, Mum! Must you torment yourself like this?'

'I've been angry about it all night and all morning. Before I decide to spring-clean my flat all over again I think I'd rather simply face the facts!'

'Mum, that Regine is nothing compared to you. She's just taking advantage of our poor idiot of a father – anyone can see that!'

'And she's making a good job of it, you've got to give her that!'

Monika picks up her glass and looks at her children. She's glad that she has them, and that they are so loyal to her. Richi, with his snub nose, so completely at odds with his masculine appearance, and his bright blue eyes, and Irena, whose brown hair is cut short with a severe parting, 1920s style, and who even as a child liked to appear daring and mysterious.

Richi comes back and plonks himself down on the sofa next to Monika.

'Well,' he begins, 'Dirk says it was a perfect party, as always, the whole clique was there, as always, his father made a stupid speech, as usual, and Günther, as usual, paid no attention to his wife.'

'Fantastic,' mocks Irena. 'Your friend ought to become a writer, not a lawyer. What Mum wants to know is: did Regine kick Dad in the balls, or not? Did she have a surreptitious snog with another man, some handsome young savage? Did Klaus cry his heart out on the bosom of some woman? Did the whole regiment of women stand there chanting, "We want Monika"?'

'Now, Irena, don't make me sound so silly. I just wanted to know if he's still alive.'

Richi bursts out laughing. 'Why, do you think Dirk should have bumped him off? Mum, he *is* our father!'

'All right, all right, of course he is! Let's change the subject. What was Regine wearing?'

Linda rings Irena's doorbell several times, but there's no reply. The neighbours, her landlords, nosily stick their heads out of a window. 'She's not in.'

'Thanks, I'd already gathered that.'

'She went off on her bike, so she can't have gone very far.'

'Ah.' Linda walks slowly back to the gate.

'She's probably gone to her mother's. But she didn't say anything specific to us.'

'No.' Linda opens the wooden gate and gets on her bike.

'You could try again in half an hour.'

'Thanks for the suggestion!'

'We'll tell her you came.'

'That's very kind of you!'

Of course she might have known. After that public snub yesterday Monika is probably in desperate need of moral support. Anyone who is dropped from Marion's guest list is well and truly left out in the cold as far as Römersfeld is concerned. That's a bitter pill for a businesswoman like Monika to swallow, especially when she could show most of them a thing or two in business matters. But a woman without a man is powerless against Marion's social pecking order.

For the next party we ought to find a Latin lover for Marion, thinks Linda as she starts to pedal. Then she'd have a man at her

side and everyone's eyes would be popping out of their heads!
She must say this to Monika and Irena straightaway. Full of
anticipation, she races through the town. Ten minutes later she's
ringing the bell at the entrance to the elegant apartment building. Richi's convertible is in the car park, with Irena's orange
bicycle leaning against it. Just as she thought. Even the son has
hastened to his mother's side to console her. Let's see if she can
make a contribution too.

In Günther's fairytale villa everything is back to normal, almost
as if there had never been a birthday. The presents had been
displayed on a large table, but now Marion has made a list of
them and tidied them away. She'll compose a personal thank-you
note for each one and get Günther to sign them. Some of the
gifts are just right for the tombolas that are constantly being
held to raise money for all sorts of good causes, and the rest will
help to restock the wine-cellar. One of the presents, a newspaper
from the day of his birth in 1938, Marion immediately dropped
into the paper recycling bin. Günther didn't need that visible
reminder of his age: he seemed to be finding it quite hard
enough to cope with being sixty as it was.

Marion hears the electric garage-door mechanism. He's been
out a long time. She takes a quick look round: the house is
immaculate. She walks through the kitchen to the garage – she
had really wanted this American-style feature – and opens the
connecting door. Günther is just getting out of the car, with a
bunch of flowers in his hand.

'Oh, Günther, how sweet of you!'

Actually he had intended to stuff them into the biological
waste bin, but this works just as well. At least this way he doesn't
have to worry about it any more.

'Because you organised everything so splendidly. You really
are a superb organiser!' Marion puts her arms around him and

kisses him on the mouth, which he submits to passively. Then she takes the brightly coloured bunch of flowers, cuts off the ends of the stalks, fills a vase with tepid water, adds flower preservative and puts the vase on the dining table. In the meantime Günther has sat down in an armchair and is turning the pages of the telephone book.

'Are you looking for somebody's number? Can I help you?'

Günther snaps the book shut. 'No, it was nothing in particular.' Linda isn't ex-directory. Great, he'll simply ring her up.

'Are you hungry?' Marion walks round the table towards Günther and stops right in front of him.

He looks up at her. 'What's on offer?'

Marion is tempted to say, coquettishly, 'Me,' but she holds back, seeing the mood he's in. 'Whatever you like,' she says instead, smiling encouragingly and lightly stroking her blue pleated skirt.

'What I really fancy is pig's tail with sauerkraut. Have you got some?'

'I haven't . . .'

'I thought not. I'll go down the pub.'

In his study Klaus is brooding over Günther's papers. He went to fetch them from his office just after breakfast and has been immersed in them ever since. Regine is annoyed because she would much rather have spent such a lovely sunny day out somewhere rather than sitting alone in the garden at home, but Klaus has explained that it's urgent and that he's not likely to have any time during the week. So now she's lying on a sun-lounger among the rose bushes, leafing through some women's magazines. But this makes her no happier. Quite the reverse. She has just come to a fashion feature on the latest swimwear, photographed on the beach at St Tropez: pictures of slim, tanned models in tiny bikinis at a beach bar, playing volleyball or in the water, attended by gorgeous men with Roman profiles and sexy figures, with cool cocktails in their hands and hot rhythms in their blood. And here *she* is, Regine Raak, née Meermann, lying behind a rose bush in Römersfeld. The other magazine is even worse. It shows sun-drenched islands and holiday paradises across the globe, one brightly coloured picture after another, each more tantalising than the last. Especially for Regine, who will be spending the summer here at home. Only yesterday, at Günther's birthday party, Klaus explained to her that he had neither the time nor the money to go away anywhere with her. The divorce and the alterations to the house had simply cost too much to allow for anything like that. He must get his bank account topped up again before they could think of going on holiday. When Regine argued that she still had some money of her own and that if need be she could go by herself, his reaction was almost aggressive. That was absolutely out of the question – after all, he hadn't got married in order to be left alone in Römersfeld while his wife went gallivanting off somewhere, having fun with God knows who.

Regine closes the magazine and picks up the next one. The cover story is about 'Tensions in a Marriage'. Well, I haven't got any of those, thinks Regine, furiously hurling the magazine into a rose bush.

For hours Klaus has been looking through Günther's papers, copying out figures from them. His company, East and West; his real-estate property; his shares in various banks; his fixed-term investments: Klaus has methodically listed everything and it adds up to a total fortune of 21 million marks. It could be difficult to make all of that simply disappear. Klaus fills a pipe, lights it and starts pacing up and down the room. As he does so he sees Regine lying on her lounger among the rose bushes, turning the pages of a magazine. Quite picturesque, he thinks; his face relaxes into a smile. She restores his youth, and he's going to make sure that she can enjoy life. As she is doing now, lying there on the lounger, carefree and beautiful, and on their own property too. A woman really couldn't ask for more! For some seconds he loses himself in contemplation of her, then all at once a solution to Günther's problem occurs to him. Years ago he set up a limited company in Liechtenstein for another client. The company has never been wound up, and the shares are now in his own name. This could provide a suitable basis for a complicated financial model. Klaus immediately sits down at his computer and starts to draft a plan.

Monika and her daughter are just in the process of creating a spaghetti sauce. They have spent hours pulling Regine to pieces and discussing Linda's suggestion, which made Monika laugh heartily. She thought that a fiery Latin lover was well worth thinking about. Towards evening their stomachs began to rumble, and Monika put a pan of water on to boil. Linda is in charge of making sure the pasta is properly *al dente*, while Richi takes responsibility for the salad. As Monika finds various ingredients for them, she suddenly declares that the separation wasn't Regine's fault at all.

'If Klaus hadn't been ready for an affair it wouldn't have happened. It always takes two. Perhaps, objectively speaking, Regine is quite a nice girl. Perhaps she didn't deserve to get saddled with a man like Klaus!'

Irena is frying the mince, mushrooms and tomatoes. She turns, spoon in hand, towards Monika. 'How do you mean, Mum?'

'In the case of the party, it's Marion's fault really. She acts as if Regine were everything and I didn't exist any more. Though perhaps it was Günther who wouldn't let Marion invite me.'

'Never mind, Mum. It was a stupid party anyway!' Richi, who is chopping onions, wipes his nose with the back of his hand.

With a disapproving look Monika tosses the roll of kitchen paper over to him.

'I don't think Günther cares about anything like that.' Linda adds the pasta to the boiling water, sets the timer and reaches for two peppers and a knife. 'He probably wouldn't even notice. Do you think he knows exactly who was there yesterday? I very much doubt it!'

'Damn!' Richi tears some sheets off the kitchen roll and wipes his eyes. 'Why don't you get your own back by giving a party and not inviting those two? Or better still, invite Günther with somebody else. With,' he looks round, 'Irena, for instance!'

Irena gives a yell and threatens him with the wooden spoon. 'You can keep that old baldie, you idiot! I might as well go with my own father!'

Monika laughs and waves the bottle of wine at them. 'I'm going to lay the table. Keep an eye on that sauce!'

It's already dark when Linda arrives home. Richi has driven her back because her racing bike has no lights. Cheerfully she goes into the bathroom and takes a shower. While she's drying herself, singing loudly, she hears the phone ringing. Oh dear, that'll be Dirk. He's probably been trying to get hold of her all evening. Bother. She could have called him from Monika's.

Linda wraps the towel around her and walks into the living room.

'Hello, darling,' she coos into the receiver, settling down on the sofa.

'Darling? I like the sound of that!' The voice is deep, and it's quite certainly not Dirk's. Linda gives a start and sits bolt upright. 'Who . . . I mean, I thought it was my boyfriend.'

'Well, you never know what may happen.' A throaty laugh. 'No, I'm sorry, that was a joke. I've just been with my business associates in the next building to yours, and I thought the perfect way to end the evening would be to have a glass of wine with you.'

Linda catches her breath. 'Herr Schmidt?' she asks hesitantly.

'Oh please, not so formal! Do call me Günther.'

'Where . . . where are you?'

'In my car, in front of your flat. If you step out on to your balcony I'll flash my lights. There, you see? As I said, I was just about to drive home when I suddenly had this brainwave.' Yes, his car is there.

'I just don't understand . . . I mean, do you know what time it is?'

'Ought I to know? On nights like these, warm summer nights, I don't think about the time.' How unspeakably stupid, thinks Linda. She decides to nip this conversation in the bud as quickly as possible.

'I have to go to work tomorrow morning.'

'Take the morning off, then you can have a lie-in. I'll make up your loss of earnings. What's your job? What do you earn? I should think 500 marks would be adequate compensation, okay?'

Rigid with astonishment, Linda stands on the balcony, staring at the two halogen lights of the car, which is impudently placed in the middle of the inner courtyard. But 500 marks? For a glass of wine? He must be completely off his head!

'Am I wrong? Do you earn more than that in a morning? Perhaps 600 marks? For a nice little chat with you, my budget can extend to that. Think about it. I'll walk round my car ten times; and if you agree, switch your light off quickly twice in succession. I'll only ring your doorbell after you've done that. Is that a fair offer?'

Linda hears the blood rushing in her ears. Automatically she cuts off the call, but she still holds the receiver in her hand, watching, fascinated, as down below the man gets out of his car and slowly starts to walk round it. He must be crazy. He thinks she's a tart! What a nerve! she ought to ring Dirk straightaway. Or, better still, Marion! Yes, Marion, guardian of all virtues; she ought to let her know what a fine specimen her husband is! Linda thinks of that afternoon's conversation, and of how effortlessly Marion had swept Monika off the social scene. Now here's an opportunity for revenge: she could invite Günther up and secretly record the whole meeting on tape. Who knows what Günther may have to say, over a glass of wine – and for 600 marks, out of the household budget! That alone would destroy Marion at a stroke. At least emotionally. Linda is sure of that.

She turns the light on and off twice, then she runs into the bathroom, quickly pulls on jeans and a T-shirt, puts on a bit of lipstick and, with the doorbell already ringing, runs a brush through her black hair.

'Yes, fourth floor, on the right,' she says through the intercom. After pressing the buzzer, she takes her dictaphone out of the drawer, checks the cassette, presses 'Record' and places it under the armchair. Her heart is pounding when soon afterwards there is a knock at the door. Barefoot, she opens it.

Taller and more heavily built than she remembered, Günther is standing before her, wearing a white, short-sleeved linen shirt with his blue trousers. In the dim light of the landing he actually looks quite good, and his broad smile is attractive.

'I hope I haven't made you feel at all alarmed,' he says as she asks him in. 'It's only just struck me that all this must seem very odd to you. But don't worry, I was really only thinking of a quiet drink in pleasant company to round off the evening. I wanted to think on my visit to your neighbourhood . . .' He laughs heartily, showing his white teeth.

'Oh, yes.' Linda thinks for a moment. 'Who were you visiting?'

'Oh, just a business acquaintance. Important to me, but irrelevant to the two of us.' He stands in the middle of the room and looks around.

Linda indicates the armchair. 'Won't you sit down? That chair's very comfortable.'

'Oh, I'd rather sit at the table there with you. That's less formal. Also it's easier to put your glass down.'

Damn, thinks Linda, now the tape recorder's in the wrong place!

'Do you have any wine? And glasses?'

He goes past her into the kitchen. 'Oh, the way you've done your kitchen is interesting. You have very good taste – it's most original!' He looks around the kitchen with its free-standing pieces of furniture. Linda follows the direction of his eyes, which have come to rest on a wine crate serving as a storage unit. 'Yes, I saw that the last time I was in Rome. I thought it was rather a good idea, for bottles of oil and vinegar . . . and that sort of thing.'

'Oh, what did you see in Rome? I love Rome!'

'Oh, all the usual places you visit when you're in Rome.' Let's hope he doesn't insist on pursuing this topic. Linda has never been to Rome, but that's none of his business. Günther goes over to the crate and with his finger slowly traces the letters branded into it. 'It had good wine in it too, Barolo.' He nods at her, acknowledging her taste. 'It's natural to want to keep something like that as a souvenir.'

'And it's practical too!'

'Yes, that too!' He looks at her, and Linda starts to feel embarrassed. Why did he have to come into her kitchen? She's twenty-seven years old: where would she find the money for a fitted kitchen? The old refrigerator is one she talked her parents into parting with, the dresser comes from the flea market, and she bought the cooker last year when the electrical shop round the corner from Dirk's was having a clearance sale. When she has any money to spare she prefers to spend it on travel rather than furniture.

'Do you think you've got a bottle of wine?' He smiles encouragingly.

'Oh, yes, of course I have.' She opens the fridge. 'Red, white, and a bottle of champagne. Whichever you like!'

'May I?' he reaches for the bottle of red wine. 'A fine Italian one. But it's better for it not to be chilled. Keep it outside the fridge.'

A Chianti Classico, which her parents brought the last time they visited. She didn't think it was especially good. After all, everyone drinks Chianti. 'Who drinks warm wine in the summer? It's much too hot for that!'

'I would have said the same a few years ago. But, take my word for it, you drink white wine chilled but you always keep red wine at room temperature.'

Did Marion tell you that? The question almost slips out, but instead she reaches for the bottle of white wine in the fridge. 'Well then, this one should be all right!'

He glances quickly at the label and chuckles. 'With a home-grown wine one can hardly go wrong. Do you have a corkscrew and glasses?'

At the table he opens the bottle and then looks around as if searching for something.

'Is there still something missing?' asks Linda, who is starting to get irritated. 'A thermometer, perhaps? Or ice cubes for the champagne bucket?'

'Not a bad idea for next time. I was really just thinking of a candle to put on the table.'

There won't be a next time, Linda vows to herself. Letting myself in for this stupid business tonight was quite idiotic enough.

She goes into her bedroom to fetch some candles.

I'll soon be in there too, thinks Günther, following her with his eyes. She has a stunning figure, he observes with satisfaction, even in those casual clothes. That firm round bottom in those jeans. If she puts on a suspender belt I'll be twenty again! Take it easy, he tells himself as she returns with the candles. Mustn't scare the child. We'll just take things as they come. And above all as *I* come. He grins at this thought.

'Is something amusing you?' asks Linda.

'No, I'm just pleased that you're willing to spend a little time with me. And I'm wondering if we shouldn't sit down.'

'Yes, please do.' Linda points to a chair and sits down opposite him. It's a small table, intended as a breakfast table for two. Linda lights the candles. Now she doesn't know what to talk to him about. Why on earth has she got herself into such a ridiculous situation? She hopes Dirk will ring soon.

'What job do you do, if you don't mind my asking?'

Aha, now he's going to haggle over the money. 'Because of the so-called compensation?'

'Heaven forbid! No, no, we've already agreed on that. No, purely out of interest. With your looks, I would guess that you do something connected with beauty. Are you a model?'

Linda is tempted to embroider the facts a bit. She does do something connected with beauty: she's a sales assistant in a shop that sells beauty products. And she does a bit of modelling too, selling lingerie on the side. But need she go out of her way to tell him this, when he is making much more flattering assumptions?

'A bit, as a sideline.'

That's even true.

'Anyone can see that straightaway. You ought to place yourself in the hands of professionals. Get an introduction to a proper agency. You're as beautiful as any of the girls in the magazines.'

He's trying to flatter her, it's pathetic! Still, it's all the same to her.

'I'm twenty-seven. That's too old to start a proper career. And

I'm less than five feet seven tall, which isn't enough. And of course that's always been the case, so I never had a real chance. But that doesn't worry me – I'm happy as I am.'

'That really does you credit! And Römersfeld would have one star less without you.'

He does talk a lot of rubbish!

'You've got a star on the bonnet of your car. I should think that's enough.' She reaches for her glass and raises it to him.

'Ha, ha, ha,' Günther laughs, 'that was really witty. You're an interesting woman, Linda,' and he raises his glass, 'quite uncommonly so.'

Then he takes out his wallet and counts out six 100-mark notes on to the table. 'May I come again? It's been nice being with you.'

'I . . . I thought you wanted to stay for an hour? It's not been that long yet.'

'I'd rather leave earlier today, but then come a bit earlier next time, ha ha.' Linda tries not to stare in fascination at the money. He has actually put 600 marks on the table. For half an hour's chat. She barely earns that much in a week! Good heavens, the man must be incredibly rich. Stinking rich.

She slowly gets up. Günther is already standing, holding out his hand. 'I'll say goodnight then. And I wish you a pleasant morning for tomorrow. Thank you for the wine.' Like someone in a hypnotic trance Linda accompanies him to the door. He's hardly touched the wine, so how can he thank her for it?

'What do you like to drink?' As he goes, he turns back to her again.

She can't immediately think of anything. Tomato juice, but that sounds too childish. 'Champagne,' she says at random.

'You have good taste.' He nods and goes to the lift.

Linda slowly closes the door, then puts out all the lights and, in the dark, goes to stand at the living-room window. She watches him walk to his car, get in, flash his lights on and off twice and slowly drive off. Did he guess that she was at the window?

Hesitantly she relights the candles. Beneath the flickering flames she looks at the banknotes that are lying, fanned out, on the table. Then the phone rings. Dirk! What on earth is she to say to him? Hey, listen, Günther Schmidt visited me and put 600 marks down on the table – for absolutely nothing. No one could possibly believe that! Before saying anything she'd better play back the tape and see if it's recorded anything at all.

'Hello?' she says.

'I enjoyed my visit. I just wanted to say goodnight!'

Günther Schmidt! From his car!

'Oh, thank you. Thank you very much,' she replies quietly, then hangs up.

Günther is sitting in his car, feeling triumphant. Now she'll be sitting there like a tame mouse looking at the money and wondering what to do. First she'll think that she must give it back, then she'll drink another glass and by the time she goes to bed she'll be convinced that she's earned it! As he drives along he turns down the sun visor and opens up the illuminated vanity mirror. 'Sixty, huh,' he grins at his reflection. 'New blood, twenty-seven years old – it's like cell-replacement therapy. And fun as well!' He puts on a cassette and loudly sings along, 'Pretty maid, oh so sweet, tell me, when can we meet . . .' He makes a slight detour in order to drive past his financial adviser's bungalow. Aha, there's still a light on in the study. Klaus seems to have got the message. Günther nods, satisfied: things are going along nicely.

Next morning Linda wakes up at six o'clock. An hour early. She has a strange sense of unease. What's the matter? she thinks, and looks at her alarm clock. Did she forget to set the alarm? Then suddenly she sits bolt upright. Oh God, the money! Schmidt! Was it a dream? She leaps out of bed and runs into the living room. No, the two half-empty glasses and the candles are still on the table, and lying in between them are the banknotes. She left everything untouched last night, wanting to sleep on it. But no inspiration has come to her.

Slowly she climbs back into bed, moodily plumps up her pillow and rolls herself up in the duvet. She's not going to get up an hour early just because Günther Schmidt chose to put 600 marks down on her table. She has never yet got up unnecessarily early, not for anything or anybody. Not in her whole life. So she won't do it today either. She'll have this last hour of sleep. Just as usual. Like any other day.

Regine has just got up to make breakfast for Klaus and herself. She'll go back to bed again afterwards, but they have made it a rule to spend this quiet quality time together each morning. As she puts the coffee on she hears Klaus going into the bathroom. Regine fetches the newspaper from their mailbox and skims the pages. It's July, everyone is looking ahead to the summer holidays, and there's very little real news. She turns to the back page, which is a mass of travel offers. With a sigh she closes the paper and lays it next to Klaus's plate. Perhaps she ought to talk to him about it again. After all, she could go on holiday with one of her women friends. Then he need have no anxiety about her and could work to pay off the cost of the extension and the kitchen without any worries. But when Klaus finally appears he looks really old, for the first time since they have been together. Regine doesn't dare to broach the topic of holidays.

'Did you sleep badly?' she asks, alarmed.

'I worked half the night. It was three o'clock when I headed into the bathroom!' He gives her a kiss and moves his chair up to the table. 'I suppose my age is starting to catch up with me. Short nights never used to bother me in the past. I hope you won't come to regret your decision!'

'Oh, darling, how can you say such a thing!' She pours him some coffee and passes the plate of cold meats to him. 'I can get a job again if you're having to work so hard. We can do it together!' Then I would also have some rights again and could go on holiday when I choose, she thinks, as she cuts two slices of bread.

'As long as you're with me you don't need to work. I've had one wife who was a career woman and that was enough for me! She was never there, never free; I even had to get my own breakfast. There were always strangers in the house: the cleaning woman, the ironing woman, the laundry woman, the tutor giving the children extra lessons, the music teacher, the au pair, and God knows who else.'

'Well, surely that's not so bad,' says Regine. 'I bet everything functioned perfectly.'

'Functioned! You've said it. They all fulfilled their functions. Even I, the head of the family, fulfilled my function. It was horrible. I never want to function again. I want to live. In the way that I choose!'

So where does that leave me? thinks Regine, furiously slapping fresh cream on to her bread. Now I'm lumbered with an egotist, just because Monika never paid proper attention to him! She's messed him up for me, the cow!

In Römersfeld it's the start of another glorious summer's day. Everything is following its usual course: Günther is driving to one of his construction sites to see how the work is progressing, Marion is preparing for her afternoon bridge party, at around eleven o'clock Dirk is searching for his car because as usual he's forgotten where he last left it, and Monika is discussing with her son Richi a letter from the tax office announcing that they want to check up on her details.

Only Linda still feels as if she has suffered an electric shock. She has got up and tried listening to the tape, but the only record of last night's events is a hissing sound and the faintest trace of voices – nothing she could use to annoy Marion, still less to explain things to Dirk. And it doesn't alter the fact that the bank-notes are still lying there on the table.

At last, acting on a sudden impulse, she puts the money into her purse, drives to work and then in her lunch break goes to the Animal Welfare League. There she hands over the whole sum as a donation in the name of Günther Schmidt, and asks for a receipt to be sent to his address as soon as possible. Then she drives back to work, but finds she can't concentrate either on her customers or on the products. She's constantly picturing Marion's face when she receives the letter from the Animal Welfare League, and also she's burning with impatience to tell the whole tale to Irena.

Around six o'clock Günther is on his way home after doing the round of his building sites. He is in buoyant mood; his projects are going well, all his plant is being used to full capacity and there's no sign of a fall-off in business.

Now, on his homeward journey, he's been on the phone con-tinuously. He's rung his major clients to tell them how the work is going, arranged a meeting with Klaus for tomorrow after-noon, told Marion that it's time for the bridge ladies to leave because he's on his way and wants his evening meal served at seven on the dot, and then, finally, as a sort of little dessert for himself, he's phoned his wine merchant and ordered a case of champagne to be sent to Linda's address. To be delivered this evening, at about eight o'clock if possible. Then at nine he'll be able to enquire innocently whether he's hit on the brand she prefers. He rubs his hands at the thought of this coup then moves out into the overtaking lane.

In order to make the most of the warm summer evening Marion has laid supper on the terrace. To please Günther she's cooked his favourite meal, a roast with sauerkraut and bread dumplings. Günther first demands a cold beer and then leans back in his chair.

'Do you think this is a suitable meal for a man who's been on the go non-stop on a hot day?'

Marion, who is just piling food on to his plate, stops nonplussed. 'What do you mean?'

'I think you might give a little more thought to what you cook. A summer salad would have been the right thing for a day like this!'

'What? But you don't like . . .'

'You might consider my figure!'

Marion lowers the serving spoon and stares at him. 'But you've got a good . . .'

'Ever heard of cholesterol?' he interrupts her brusquely, pushing his plate away. 'You might as well put a gun on the table in front of me with detailed instructions for committing suicide!'

'What on earth's got into you?' Marion sits down, shaking her head in disbelief.

'I've just reached sixty, Marion, in case that fact has escaped your notice, and I want to go on living for a few more years. Living, do you understand?'

'All right.' Marion stands up to remove the platter with the roast and the dishes with the sauerkraut and dumplings. 'Just as you like. But I did it with the best of intentions and . . .' The sound of the doorbell forces her to break off. 'Whoever can that be at this hour?' She turns to Günther. 'Are you expecting anyone?'

'Possibly.' For a moment the thought flashes through Günther's brain that it might be Linda, and his pulse starts to race. Nonsense, he tells himself, there's no reason why she should come here.

Marion is already at the door, opening it. A woman in her mid-thirties is standing there, beaming. 'I simply had to drop by personally, to thank your husband!'

'Oh,' says Marion, trying desperately to think whether the woman's face is familiar. 'What for?'

'Oh, for his generous donation. It's not every day that someone shows such kindheartedness. Is he at home? May I come in?'

Marion leads the way, still unable to make head or tail of this. Normally gifts to charity are her domain. Or has Günther been making a donation to a political party again, which will only lead to trouble in the long run?

She can see from the look on Günther's face that he's no wiser than she is. The woman holds out her hand to him, and he rises hesitantly to his feet to shake hands.

'On behalf of the Animal Welfare League I want to express our most heartfelt thanks. Your money will help towards enlarging our premises, and I'd like to extend a warm invitation to you right now, both of you of course,' she nods, smiling, towards Marion, 'to come along, when we've eventually managed to make up the full amount that we need, and attend the opening. And of course there'll be a plaque on the extension listing the names of donors.'

Günther doesn't know how to react. Is this some kind of a joke? The woman seems too genuinely euphoric for that. Perhaps there's been a mix-up?

'Oh, thank you,' he says cautiously, trying to free his hand, which she is still gripping with fervour.

'Oh, yes, and here's the receipt for your donation, just so that we've observed all the proprieties!' She laughs coquettishly, lets go of his hand, takes an envelope from her shoulder bag and places it on the table. 'And if you have any questions, just ask for me, Annemarie Roser, I'm the honorary chairwoman of the League. Or you can contact me at work at the job centre.

'Ah, yes. Yes, thank you!' He examines the envelope out of the corner of his eye. A letter bomb? But that would probably look different, and it would hardly be delivered in person. Is Klaus at the bottom of this? Perhaps he's used Günther's money to buy up the animal sanctuary. Has he made the millions a hundred per cent safe from discovery by hiding them under the dog mess?

Annemarie Roser puts her card down next to the envelope. 'Well, I won't keep you any longer. It's been nice to meet you, and once again many thanks. Every good deed brings its reward some day!'

Marion escorts her to the door as fast as she can. She doesn't want to let Günther deal with this ominous envelope on his own. She wants to know what sum of money the woman has been talking about. When she gets back Günther has already torn it open. A single glance tells him what transaction lies behind this.

Aha, he thinks, the little beast.

'Good heavens,' he laughs, as Marion comes back out on the terrace. 'I'd completely forgotten about this. Fancy them making such a fuss about it!'

Marion takes the receipt from his hand. '600 marks,' she reads, incredulously. '600 marks to the Animal Welfare League? Why? Was there some special reason?'

Günther tops up his beer and drinks off the head before answering. 'A bet. I lost a bet I had with Klaus. It's as simple as that. But I'd forgotten all about it!'

Marion holds the receipt right under his nose. 'But this shows that the donation was made today! How can one forget something like that?'

'What does it matter, Marion? Klaus dealt with it for me. Do you think I have time to mess about like that? Why don't you pass me the dumplings!'

Linda hasn't found anyone to tell her news to. Irena has gone to Munich for a training course, and Dirk isn't the right audience for a story like that. He would spoil the fun by taking it all much too seriously. Monika might be a possibility, but somehow she feels awkward about appearing in that kind of light to a woman of an older generation. After all, she did let Günther into her flat late at night, and he left a lot of money on the table in return. No, stories like that should only be heard by bosom pals.

So after work she drives round to Dirk's. Looking over his shoulder as he sits there studying, she suggests they go to the pictures.

'The pictures,' he groans. 'As if I didn't have enough drama in my life as it is! In the written paper today I had one mental block after another. If I don't pass the exams my old man will kill me!'

'Your old man?' Linda sits down on his lap, putting her arms around his neck. 'I'm the one you ought to be afraid of! After all, you can't use someone as a meal ticket forever!'

'As a what?' Dirk pushes back his longish, light-brown hair; his grey eyes look tired.

'A meal ticket,' repeats Linda, standing up and pulling down the hem of her short skirt. 'Why don't we at least have a glass of red wine together? Then I'll leave you to work in peace!'

Dirk stretches in his chair and yawns. 'If you like,' he says, turning round to her. 'Have a look in the fridge and see if there's still a bottle in there.'

Linda walks round the big oil heater and into the small side room that serves as a makeshift kitchen. 'You're not supposed to put red wine in the fridge,' she calls to him.

'Where did you get that idiotic idea from?' answers Dirk, putting his legs up on the desk. 'You're really starting to sound like my parents! Who would want to drink piss-warm wine in summer?'

Linda comes back with a bottle and two glasses. 'Well, connoisseurs,' she says, vaguely, pushing the ice-cold bottle between his naked thighs.

'Ow, bloody hell!' He jerks his legs off the desk and jumps up. 'Are you in a sadistic mood today?'

'Well, if it turns you on . . .' she grins, tugging at the curly hairs on his legs.

'Well, that gives you some indication.' Dirk points to his shorts.

'The things chilled red wine can do.' Linda playfully pushes her index finger into his belly button.

'You'd better stop doing that if you are serious about wanting me to become a lawyer!'

'Oh well, I do earn quite good money myself.' Delicately, with her fingernail, Linda scratches a line from his navel to the waistband of his shorts.

'If that's the way you feel.' Dirk buries his hands in her thick hair and bends his face down towards her earlobe.

At exactly half past ten that night Linda is driving into the basement garage. She and Dirk have been to Römersfeld's one and only beer garden, and she's a bit tipsy and shouldn't really be driving. But since Dirk had also had a few drinks he reckoned that it amounted to the same thing. He was also at an advantage because he could easily walk home through the town centre.

In the lift Linda giggles to herself.

It's really funny, the way all the establishments in Römersfeld make a special effort for the son of the mayor. As though he could do anyone any favours. And the way he gets so annoyed about it every time, because he doesn't want to be identified with his father.

When the lift comes to a halt she sees something in front of her door that doesn't belong there. Has she ordered anything by mail order? She can't remember. Coming closer, she finds that it's not a parcel but a small case of drinks. Linda bends down and reads what it says on it: six bottles of champagne. She straightens up, stands stock still and rubs her arms because they've come out in goosepimples. Now there's no doubt about it. Günther Schmidt wasn't just visiting a business associate yesterday. Günther Schmidt has definite intentions. She, Linda Hagen, is his business associate.

At the other end of town, Günther Schmidt has just made his tenth attempt to phone Linda at her flat. Damn it all, she must come home some time! He's tempted to drive over there, but he's afraid of arousing Marion's suspicions. He did just about manage to wriggle out of that business with the Animal Welfare League, but Marion knows perfectly well that he would rather pay to have a home for war veterans covered in gold than build a dog kennel. So he joins Marion in the living room to watch a news programme and grumbles about politics. He always does this, so there's nothing suspicious about it. Damn it all, he sends the girl champagne and then she's not even at home! He wonders what she's doing right now.

Wild fantasies chase through his mind while he stares unseeingly at the television.

'Poor woman,' he hears Marion saying.

'What?' He tries to focus his attention on the screen.

'Aren't you even listening?' Marion, lying on the couch with her mohair blanket around her, looks across at Günther, who is sitting in her last Christmas present to him, a leather TV chair.

Between them is the coffee table laden with nibbles, a bottle of white wine in the cooler and two clean glasses.

'What did you say?' Günther meets her eyes and calmly looks back at her. 'I didn't catch you.'

'That woman who is going to have quintuplets. It's awful.'

'How would you know?' Günther pulls a lever and the footrest comes up with a jolt. 'You didn't even manage one!'

Linda, meanwhile, has put the champagne down in the middle of her kitchen and is standing looking at it indecisively.

What exactly does he think he's doing? He knows perfectly well that she's with Dirk.

On the other hand no man has ever given her champagne before. Still less a six-pack of it.

The best thing to do would be to put the whole case into her car straightaway and leave it on Schmidt's doorstep. From Marilyn Monroe, with best wishes from the Beyond. Or, better still, she could go there each night and leave one bottle in the middle of the splendid columned porch with a condom over the top. Ringing the changes between a black one, a red one, a banana-flavoured one and, to finish with, a ribbed one. Guaranteed ultra-sensitive and suitable for the eyes of the newspaper boy.

Grinning, she looks in her cupboard for condoms. There was a packet left, she's quite sure. But when she finds it she's disappointed. They are simple, everyday ones, to fit all sizes but not all occasions. And they're past their sell-by date. She flings the packet into the bin and goes on thinking, but finally decides to leave it till tomorrow. She goes into the bathroom and then straight to bed. When, soon after midnight, the phone rings again, persistently, she doesn't even hear it.

Just over a mile away as the crow flies, Klaus is lying awake beside Regine, going over everything in his mind again. Since yesterday he's been unable to sleep; his plan is good, no doubt about it, but it also troubles his conscience. He has never yet cheated a friend. Not even in his thoughts. Klaus sighs and turns over. In the half-light he can see his wife, buried up to the chin beneath her duvet. Her face is relaxed and her features appear childishly soft, almost doll-like. He thinks way back to the days when, at weekends, he used to put his own children to bed and would stay sitting beside them for a long time even after they had fallen asleep. He could simply never get enough of looking at their peaceful faces. They were like little angels, cherubs with full, soft lips. He was almost overcome with emotion when he watched them like that, but before long an oppressive sense of impermanence would creep up on him. Some day, he thought back then, all this would be no more than a memory.

Günther starts the new day with tremendous expectations. This afternoon, with Klaus, he'll lay the foundations for the new phase of his life, and in the evening he'll drink to it with champagne. With Linda, his new partner in life, though without telling her the real reason for this small celebration. He drives through the town in high spirits. It's just after nine, and he decides to pay a quick visit to the barber. He could do with a fresh haircut, in a shorter, more dynamic style. After all, Heiner Lauterbach also has a high forehead and he still looks quite good. He grins to himself while trying to park. A car is just leaving a space in front of that shop selling perfumes and cosmetics. He takes that as a sign: a new after-shave wouldn't go amiss either. He can imagine that scents have changed over the last few years and he probably smells of something hopelessly old-fashioned.

Günther parks, thinks about buying a ticket but decides to take the risk, and walks in through the open door.

Linda is advising a customer in the far corner of the shop. She stiffens as, in the mirror surface of a display cabinet, she sees

Günther Schmidt briskly approaching the nearest assistant. How embarrassing if he should discover her here in her white coat! She feels like a fraudster who's about to be found out, and looks for a place to hide. 'Could you please excuse me for a moment, I don't feel at all well,' she whispers to her customer and vanishes through the nearest door. She stands behind it, trying to clarify her thoughts. She could just tell him straight out, here and now, to take his stupid champagne away again and leave her alone. This would be the perfect opportunity. She opens the door just a crack and peers out. By now Günther Schmidt has two assistants fully occupied with him. One is searching the shelves of perfumes for suitable men's fragrances and setting them out side by side on the counter, the other is adding all the appropriate scented products to go with them. They are all very busy. Linda's own customer remains standing in the corner, with no one ministering to her, watching. In the end she leaves without a word. No one really notices, for Günther Schmidt keeps the shop busy for a full quarter of an hour. When he leaves he's carrying a bag full of purchases.

'We could do with more customers like that,' says Renate, tapping the cash register. 'We've just sold more to him than we sold all day yesterday!'

Linda looks at the copy of the receipt. Two lady's perfumes costing ninety marks each, body lotion and shower gel for a further hundred and a set of men's products for 250 marks.

'But yesterday was a very poor day,' she comments.

'Well, yes.' Renate is putting the bottles away. 'But he paid cash too. So there aren't even any bank charges to deduct. I mean, that really is pretty good!'

'He must have a girlfriend.' The second assistant examines her long, black-varnished fingernails. 'Cash payment! Typical! No credit card, no receipt, no evidence!'

'I'm sure you know all about it!' Renate pulls a face. 'Why

don't you two busy yourselves with marking up the new stock? He may not be the only customer we get today.'

Marion is also making her way through town. She has a vague feeling that there is something in the air. It was rather like this in 1989, soon after the fall of the Iron Curtain. Günther was distant and often bad-tempered, and Marion wondered whether perhaps there was another woman. In the end she had to find out through Klaus, or rather through Monika, that he was speculating recklessly in eastern Germany, to such an extent that he was risking everything they possessed. Without telling her a word about it! Monika, who was then still married to Klaus, rang her up one evening and asked, without beating about the bush, whether she was financially secure, independent of Günther and his businesses. Marion thought it was an impertinence on Monika's part to pry into her private life, but at least she was warned, although she never forgave Monika for that intrusion and above all for having information that she herself did not.

She can't stop thinking about that donation to the Animal Welfare League. Günther would never do a thing like that unless there was something more to it. But what? Certainly not a bet, she's quite sure of that. It would never occur to either Klaus or Günther in that situation to give the money to an animal charity. The only possible explanation is that the ground adjoining the centre could be useful to them and that they're cooking up some sort of business deal. Marion decides to look into this more closely.

Regine is angry. Since Sunday, Klaus has been hiding himself away in his study every night, appearing at breakfast looking like death warmed up and unapproachable for the rest of the day too. And if she does speak to him, the word 'holiday' immediately provokes a very hostile response, even in conjunction with the suggestion that she might go away, at her own expense, with a girlfriend.

What did I really get married for? she thinks this morning, once the house is tidy and there's nothing more to do. She looks out at the garden for a while, and then phones Klaus at his office.

'Klaus, would you like a child?'

'What?'

'Shall we have a baby? I could come off the pill immediately!'

'Regine, I'm sorry, but I'm in the middle of a meeting!'

'Shall we?'

'Regine, please!'

'Shall we?'

'No!'

'Then at least a dog!' 'What?'

'I'm so lonely! You're never home!'

'I . . .'

'Otherwise it'll be a baby!'

'Regine!'

'Then a dog!'

'If you like . . .'

It was just like this with her parents! Regine shakes her head as she thinks about her own predicament. When you come to think of it, it's humiliating always having to ask for things, no longer being able to make any decision for yourself.

Still, she's got what she wanted. By the time Klaus comes home this evening there'll be a dog here. With no option of returning him. She grabs the keys to her little car and drives to the animal sanctuary.

She and Marion arrive at the same moment at the junction where a gravel track leads off to the Römersfeld animal sanctuary.

What on earth is *she* doing here? thinks Marion. Her mind starts working overtime. It looks as if Regine's been let in on her husband's latest plans, just as Monika was that other time. As before, she's the one who's left in the dark, made to look stupid. But she must act as if nothing were the matter.

Regine waves and smiles, and lets Marion go ahead. She knows that Marion would otherwise die of anxiety about the paintwork of her beautiful car. Then she follows in her wake. Bits of gravel fly up, hitting her radiator, and she's enveloped in a cloud of dust. This doesn't bother Regine. Soon her childhood dream is going to be fulfilled – a dog of her own! First her parents wouldn't have one, then she had to start work and had no time for a pet – but now at last it lies within reach.

All the same, she wonders what Marion can be doing here. She can't imagine that the Schmidts are interested in an animal in any shape or form, except roasted or grilled on their dinner table.

In front of the big iron gate they park side by side and say hello. 'Our husbands are honorary members now,' says Marion, shaking Regine's hand.

'Are they?' answers Regine, surprised. 'I thought the connection was only a business one.'

So I was right, thinks Marion, and resolves for the time being just to wait and see. Honorary members. Regine sighs inwardly. She's always coming out with that old military stuff. Honorary member, guard of honour, battalion of honour, I wonder whether Günther has to hoist the flag at home every time he gets an erection? She rings the bell.

At once there's a cacophony of barking, yapping and howling. At the second ring a young girl opens the gate and motions to them to come in but then pays them no further attention. 'Feel free to look round, we need to get on,' she yells above the din and immediately disappears into one of the huts.

So we chuck 600 marks at people like that, thinks Marion. She's glad that Günther appears to have plans other than building another animal enclosure. She looks at the surrounding land. Fields and meadows, but at the back there's a large empty building. It looks like an old aircraft hangar and doesn't seem to be in very good repair. Marion nods inwardly. Yes, obviously Günther and Klaus are on to something and they're making themselves popular with the Animal Welfare League so that they can more easily sound out the situation, wait for the planning permission and then bulldoze the lot. She can go home reassured. This time there really doesn't seem to be a threat to their whole way of life. It's just some little secret.

'If no one here has time to speak to us, I'm going,' she calls out to Regine. She brushes down her light-coloured linen dress as though mere proximity to the animal pens might have soiled it, then heads for the gate.

At this moment Annemarie Roser emerges from the office. 'Oh, Frau Schmidt, wait a moment, please stop!' But Marion has already slammed the gate behind her.

'What a pity, I would have loved to show our benefactress round the sanctuary and tell her how we plan to use that splendid donation,' she says to Regine, looking upset.

'Benefactress?' asks Regine, baffled, looking towards the closed gate; she hears a car engine being started up beyond it. She's sure she must have misheard. 'That was Marion Schmidt.'

'Yes, exactly. How annoying that Sonja didn't tell me she was here. What must she think of us?'

'Well, the same as I do. Except that I'd like to buy a dog. Small to medium-sized, cuddly, but a good watchdog too. Have you got one like that?'

Two hours later Regine is driving away with a fully grown sheepdog. His name's Bobby and he's three years old, has a long, light-coloured coat, and was found over the Easter weekend tethered to the bicycle rack outside a supermarket. Regine has also learned that the Schmidts donated 600 marks and that the League would like to buy the old building, with a suitable amount of land, to provide a retirement home for larger animals that are too old to work. Regine has promised to help with fundraising. After all, she has enough time to spare. It's better than counting the buds on her rose bushes.

In his office in the centre of Römersfeld, Klaus has everything ready. But when Günther arrives at precisely four o'clock Klaus has difficulty in concealing his agitation.

'Well, let's see then.' Günther heads straight for the desk on which Klaus has spread out his papers. 'All this will vanish again afterwards, won't it?' he says, indicating everything on the desk.

'That goes without saying.' Klaus comes and stands beside him. 'I'll explain it all in a minute. I can certainly guarantee that with my assistance you'll soon be a poor man,' he chuckles.

'I hope you know what you're doing. Then I'll be laughing along with you!'

'Absolutely. You'll see!'

Klaus and Günther sit down at the desk. 'Now then, you've got that half-finished office building in Berlin, haven't you? If you sell your shares now, you can pay off the mortgage on that project. The point is that I have a limited company in Liechtenstein that could buy your office building.'

'And what do we gain by that?'

'Well, the building isn't quite finished yet. So no one can check whether your asking price is appropriate. Therefore you can sell it to the Liechtenstein company at a knock-down price. In that way your firm makes an enormous loss because it can't show any return on the building.'

'Sounds good to me. And this . . . company belongs to you?' asks Günther, and has to take a sip of water.

'Oh, it's just a residential address, and the shares are in my name,' Klaus reassures him.

'Aha!' Günther is still not quite happy. 'And how would I retrieve my cash again? And what happens to my building firm?'

'The Liechtenstein company buys your building firm, which has been weakened by all this, and the eastern German subsidiary too while it's at it. And how much is a loss-making company going to be worth?' laughs Klaus, demonstratively shrugging his shoulders.

Günther nods. 'Okay, that's clear enough,' he agrees. 'But the money?'

Klaus lowers his voice. 'You get a contract, drawn up by a lawyer, entitling you to purchase all the shares of the Liechtenstein company. Of course this is agreed in a separate legal document.'

'Then at a later date the shares are transferred to me?'

'Exactly!' Klaus nods. 'And at a price that we might as well agree on here and now. What do you say?'

Günther gets to his feet and walks up and down the room several times, thinking. With this arrangement he can regain his whole fortune at a nominal price. Klaus is right, it sounds really good. Also, the land transfer tax in connection with the office building will be lower, and there will be no taxable profits – two further bonuses on his road to freedom. He stops in front of Klaus. 'Okay, let's go for it.'

'I think so too.' Klaus gets up and goes over to the computer.

'And the rest?' asks Günther. 'What do we do with the money I have deposited?'

'The million? You withdraw it. Vaduz is a beautiful city – why shouldn't one pay it a visit?'

'You're right there. Hope you enjoy it!' Günther gives him a wink, grinning, and runs through the whole thing again in his mind. The way they envisage it, everything he owns will gradually find its way abroad. And at some point he and his bird will go out and join it, and then they'll fly off on a jet-propelled case full of money. To the French Riviera, to Marbella, to Malibu and all the other places where he can admire her scantily clad body and enjoy life to the full.

Klaus is watching him. 'You seem to like my plan.'

'Is it so obvious?'

'It is to me.'

'Well, then, my friend, open the cognac and let's drink to it – to all the Regines and . . .' – he almost lets Linda's name slip out – 'and all the young women in this world!'

'And to ourselves,' adds Klaus, approaching the built-in cupboard. As he pulls down the front of the small bar unit, his face in the illuminated mirror confronts him like that of a stranger. His eyes are shining; they reflect his relief and joy, but also a feeling of power and victory. Klaus examines his image in the mirror. It's true, the first battle is won! What was it that Günther said so aptly a moment ago? To all the Regines of this world – *et voilà*!

Klaus has switched on his laptop computer, and the two of them are working on the finer points of their plan. Suddenly there's a knock at the door. Klaus looks up in surprise. 'Where's Frau Zeller got to this time?'

Günther looks at his watch. 'She's probably already gone home.'

'Oh?' The knock comes again. 'Come in!' Klaus calls.

The door is slowly pushed open. A large dog's muzzle appears and then immediately withdraws again.

'What on earth is that?' Klaus stares at the door.

'Come on, Bobby, be brave.' It's a light female voice.

'Regine?'

'No, Bobby!' The door flies open, and there's Regine standing in the doorway with a huge dog, laughing. 'May I introduce the new member of our household, Bobby, the flying shag-pile rug?'

'Ah!' Klaus can't think of anything to say.

'He's a bit big, isn't he?' asks Günther, standing up to greet Regine. 'Is it safe to shake hands with you?'

Regine comes in, with Bobby on a lead. 'Well, we'll just have to try it and see!'

Klaus also stands up. 'Günther's right. I was thinking more of a, well, a smaller kind of dog. Er, a Miniature Pinscher for instance!'

'But I took a shine to Bobby!' Regine fondles his neck; she doesn't even have to bend down to do so.

Klaus tries again. 'A big dog like that is a lot of work.'

'Are you the lady of the house, or am I?' Regine shakes her head uncomprehendingly. 'What is this? Aren't you pleased? Don't you want to welcome Bobby into our family?'

Klaus looks at Günther helplessly. 'Well, yes.'

Günther laughs heartily.

'Just wait and see what *your* wife brings home,' interjects Regine.

'Why?' His laughter stops abruptly. 'What do you mean?'

'Well, she was at the animal sanctuary too. So she must have something in mind as well.'

'Marion? At the animal sanctuary?' Günther looks at her incredulously.

'Don't you believe me?' Bobby cranes his neck forward to sniff at him.

Günther looks at the dog, then at Regine. 'Oh yes. I'm just surprised, that's all.'

'By the way, have you bought up a whole perfume shop?'

'Me?' Günther folds his arms defensively. 'Whatever makes you say that?' The dog sneezes and turns away.

'You smell like one. Quite a mixture. Bobby doesn't like it either!' The two men exchange glances.

'Anyway, come on, Bobby, let's go! You can take your time, Klaus, we'll take a walk round the park.' She gives her husband a kiss.

'But – I'll be finished in a minute!'

'No hurry . . .' With that she's gone.

'That's a turn-up for the book! Up to now she's always resented every minute that I was late.' Shaking his head, Klaus goes back to the computer.

'Well, now you've got a stand-in. Very useful. And without any risks attached!'

'So *you* say.'

'Better than a rival, at any rate, don't you think?'

'As long as he lets me into the house at night.'

Half an hour later Günther is sitting in the car, thinking about Marion. She's obviously spying on him. And if she's spoken to the Roser woman she also knows what the girl who handed over the cheque looked like. Not like Klaus, anyway.

The traffic light ahead of him changes to red. Günther stops, and pursues his thoughts. It could have been one of Klaus's staff. However you look at it, at this moment a marital crisis would be very inconvenient indeed. Much too soon. He must make sure that things don't start running away out of control. Behind him someone sounds their horn twice. Idiot! He looks up. The light's green, and he pulls away. Then he glances in his rear-view mirror. It's Regine, who's now waving to him from behind. She needs watching too, he thinks. She has enough time on her hands to notice everything, and plenty of experience of her own to enable her to smell a rat. He must be really careful. Günther raises his hand to wave to her and turns off.

At her flat Linda is laying the table. She wants to talk to Dirk about Günther Schmidt, so she phoned him late this afternoon and invited him to supper. Dirk asked twice if they couldn't have it at his place, saying that with his next exam coming up he simply couldn't take the whole evening off. But Linda knew that he would only sit over his books and not listen to her properly at his own place. 'I'll cook you a real risotto, with mushrooms and cheese and all the trimmings,' she said, to tempt him.

'What sort of trimmings?' he asked, sitting up and taking notice.

'You'll see . . .'

'Have you got some new lingerie?'

'I haven't even sold the last lot yet!'

It's quite true. Linda hasn't been particularly busy with her second job recently. She has an arrangement with the biggest lingerie boutique in Römersfeld, and she goes to people's houses showing the new collections, modelling them if she's asked to. It snowballs from there. Usually the women who come to the party as guests then hold their own lingerie parties and invite their own friends. Most of them find it great fun, and for Linda it's quite lucrative. At the last party she sold seven items, although only five women were there. That wasn't at all bad. Perhaps it's time she got things moving again.

She goes into the kitchen to make the risotto, and has to make a detour round the case with the six bottles of champagne, which is still standing in the middle of the floor. She takes two sachets of ready-made risotto out of the cupboard and tears them open. Dirk won't notice the difference. Then, to give it an extra something, she opens a tin of mushrooms and takes a bag of grated Parmesan from the fridge.

Günther is on his way home for supper. Marion is in an excellent mood, as she now feels that she has gained an insight into Günther's plans and is thus armed against his attacks. She admires his haircut and tells him the latest gossip. She doesn't mention her visit to the animal sanctuary, and Günther too decides to leave that topic alone for the time being. Marion has made a mixed salad and to go with it she's put together a platter with various kinds of liver sausage, bacon, Parma ham, radishes and chillies. Günther has already eaten three slices of bread and sausage, but hasn't so far touched the salad.

'Would you like some salad?' asks Marion, filling her own plate. 'I thought . . .'

'Later,' interrupts Günther. He knows what she's referring to – his outburst yesterday.

As from tomorrow he'll keep a strict watch on his figure.

Klaus still hasn't left his office. After seeing Günther out he found that the whole place really was empty; everyone had gone home. He was alone with himself and his thoughts. He poured himself another generous measure of cognac, sank with relief into his ample leather armchair and put his feet up on the desk.

He is there still, lost in thought. 'To the future,' he says aloud, taking a goodly sip, leaning back and closing his eyes. For him the agreement with Günther represents hard cash. If he goes about it the right way, he can make a lot of money. Klaus isn't thinking only of his high consultancy fees but also of the additional salary that he will be entitled to receive as manager of the company. For years.

He drinks his own health again. The tension in his stomach, there ever since his divorce from Monika, gradually subsides, and he breathes in and out deeply. Since this afternoon his financial worries are over. He has nothing to fear now. Even if the remaining auto-parts supplier should close down or relocate, it won't affect him much.

Klaus lets this welcome feeling of relief course through his body, and then he permits himself just the tiniest thought of what would happen if by any chance Günther were unable to exercise his right of first refusal on the shares. Klaus empties his glass in one go. That would be the peak of his financial success. But it could only come about if something were to happen to Günther.

For a whole hour Linda has been pacing up and down in her flat. Then she goes and sits on the balcony again and looks out for any cars driving this way. At eight o'clock she opens the case of champagne and puts a bottle into the chill compartment of the fridge. She could do with some now, for she can feel the anger rising in her. Dirk should have been here ages ago. Is he standing her up? It's just as well that she didn't make the risotto straightaway. It would be a soggy mess by now. At half past eight the phone rings. Linda snatches up the receiver. 'Hello?'

'Darling, I'm sorry, I've looked for my car everywhere but I think it must have been towed away!'

Linda takes a deep breath. 'Where did you leave it?'

He hesitates. 'That's just it, I can't remember . . .'

Linda twists the telephone flex between her fingers. 'That could only happen to you. Well, come on your bike then.'

'Linda! All that way on my bike? You can't be serious!'

'Then take a taxi.'

'Are you mad? The cost!'

'But it's important!'

'But darling, surely you can tell me whatever it is when you come tomorrow.'

'Oh, go to hell!' Furiously Linda bangs down the receiver and runs to the fridge. She's close to tears. What a pathetic specimen. Where is he when she needs him? Thinks his car's been towed away? What a feeble excuse. Bet *she* would find the car in no time. She uncorks the bottle of champagne with a loud pop. Okay then, *she'll* drink it. All by herself. And curse all men, the lot of them!

The phone rings.

Let it ring, she's not going to answer it. If he cares about her at all he'll find a way to get to her. Where there's a will there's a way!

She turns on the television and flicks through the channels. But nothing manages to capture her attention; her mind is elsewhere. Perhaps she should tidy up her wardrobe. She feels angry enough to hurl everything on to the floor, and energetic enough to tidy everything back again. But she doesn't do it, because she's afraid that as soon as everything's lying on the floor she'll have lost the urge.

The phone rings again, for a long time, making a nerve-shattering noise. Linda drinks up, listening to it, and finally with a jerk pulls the plug out of the wall. If he can't think of anything better than to keep trying to ring her, then he should just forget it. She pours herself another glass and sits down in front of the television. The champagne sparkles, tasting cool and luxurious, and surfing through the channels again she settles for some rubbishy love story. As long as there isn't a happy ending – she couldn't bear that just now.

During a commercial break she goes into the kitchen to pour herself another glass. She hasn't eaten anything, and the alcohol is going to her head. She looks at the clock. Ten o'clock, just the right time for a plate of risotto. She puts the right amount of water into a saucepan, stirs in a sachet of risotto, adds butter and switches on the heat. There! She'll have a nice evening in on her own.

At this moment the doorbell rings.

He's come after all! Joyfully she picks up her champagne glass and runs to the door. She presses the intercom for the entrance downstairs, but already there's a knock at her own front door.

Linda flings open the door and holds out the glass with a loud 'Cheers!'

'What a nice welcome!' Günther takes the glass from her.

'You!' Linda stares at him. Then it occurs to her that she could just shut the door on him. She considers whether that's what she wants.

'Do you like it?'

Linda still doesn't know what to do. The light on the landing goes out.

'That switch is set to go off very quickly.' Günther shakes his head. 'Typically thrifty!' His white shirt gleams in the darkness. Linda stands there uncertainly and says not a word.

'Were you expecting someone else?' Günther playfully raises the glass and grins. His arrogance annoys Linda.

'Yes, my boyfriend!'

'Aha! And where is he?'

A good question! 'And why are you here?' Linda asks, remaining firmly planted in the doorway.

'I wanted to ask how you liked the champagne. You haven't answered that question yet.'

'Couldn't you have phoned?'

'I tried several times, but there was no answer.'

So it was Günther. Dirk hasn't even thought it necessary to ring her again.

'Come in.' She steps aside. He walks past her, smiling.

'Thank you.' He stops and sniffs. 'Mmm, that smells good.'

'Oh, yes.' Linda relaxes. 'I'm just making a risotto. Do you like risotto? Will you have some?'

'If I may.'

Serves you right, you stupid son of a mayor. Now someone else is eating from your plate. 'Well, come through then.'

'Can I give you a hand?'

'You could pour me a glass of champagne.' She points to her glass, which he's still holding.

'With pleasure!' In no time at all Günther has filled her glass, moved the champagne case to one side and put another bottle on ice. Linda likes the way he takes charge of things. Dirk would have left it all to her. She clinks glasses with him, and then asks, 'Why are you doing this?'

'What do you mean?' He puts his glass down.

'You know exactly what I mean. Money, champagne . . .'

'You didn't benefit from the money much.' He grins. So he

already knows. She says nothing and carries on stirring her risotto. 'Frau Roser was delighted with the donation and brought the receipt round in person straightaway,' he continues.

'She's a very capable woman!'

'Are you such a great animal lover, or were there other reasons?' Günther studies her as she stands before him in her short summer dress, which is made of a very bright green stretchy material. It clings to her body like a second skin, and the vivid colour contrasts with her brown skin and black hair. She has long, slim legs and beautiful feet, with red-painted toenails.

'What are *your* reasons?' Linda turns sharply round to him. They look at each other. 'The answer's written all over your face,' she says slowly, putting down her wooden spoon. Günther feels she's caught him out, and scratches his head. 'But you know I'm with Dirk Wetterstein. I love him and I'm going to marry him.' Am I? she wonders as she says it.

'I don't want to offend you in any way.' Günther raises his hands apologetically. 'I find you attractive. I would just like to talk to you a little!' Among other things, he thinks, but his face betrays nothing.

'Well,' Linda frowns and turns to her saucepan, 'we can do that now – the meal's ready!' Günther looks for a suitable bottle of red wine but can't find anything that appeals. 'Pity the Chianti Classico has gone,' he says, shrugging his shoulders regretfully as he comes to the table with a cheap bottle of Kalterer See and two glasses. 'May I arrange for some red wine to be delivered to you? I have a very good wine merchant!'

Linda is just lighting the candles, which are the ones from the day before yesterday. She says nothing because she doesn't know what to reply. If she says yes, that's like giving him an entry ticket into her life; if she says no, that's not quite what she wants either. To be spoilt like this is a new experience, and rather a pleasant one.

She fills their two plates, and Günther pours the wine. As they
raise their glasses, Günther, with his other hand, pushes a small
gift-wrapped package across the table towards her. Linda recognises the paper; it's from the cosmetics shop.

'Isn't this a bit extravagant just for a little chat?' With her
index finger she touches the elaborate bow.

'I don't like to come empty-handed,' Günther says, making
light of it. 'It's just a small token. Instead of flowers.'

Linda knows what this small token consists of: two perfumes,
ninety marks each. After all, she did see the till printout. She's
tempted to tell him that another time he should make his purchases through her, since she gets a staff discount. But she keeps
quiet, and unwraps the package. 'My birthday isn't actually until
April. That's still quite far off.'

'It can just as well be a belated present for your last birthday . . .'

Linda thanks him and sprays a little on to her wrist. Her colleagues advised him well; this is one of the new, light fragrances.
Should she thank them tomorrow? That would be fun, but
unfortunately she can't – how could she possibly explain it?

This time, too, Günther stays for barely an hour. Linda watches
him go to his car. Once again he simply left his car in the middle
of the courtyard. One of these days someone's going to notice,
because there aren't all that many silver Mercedes saloons in
Römersfeld. Particularly not with the simple registration GS 1.
But apparently this doesn't bother him at all.

She goes out on to the balcony and waves to him as he starts
the car. He signals to her briefly with his lights and drives off.

He certainly makes an effort, she'll give him that.

With mixed feelings she gazes after the departing car.

The mystery of the animal sanctuary is preying on Marion's
mind. For half the night, while Günther was snoring beside her,

she was thinking who might be able to clear things up for her. Just as the distant church clock was striking four, the solution came to her. Manfred Büschelmeyer must know; he's on the council, he's sure to be able to give her some information. But the prospect that this time she won't be left in ignorance on the sidelines is so exciting that she's now wide awake.

No sooner has Günther left the house, at about eight o'clock, than Marion sits down by the telephone and rings the DIY store where Manfred is manager. She's in luck; he's already there.

'Marion?' She can hear the surprise in his voice.

'Yes. This may sound strange to you, Manfred, but I've got a question which probably only you can answer.'

'Really?' Manfred thinks about it. 'Well, fire away then!'

'Do you know that piece of land next to the animal sanctuary?'

'Yes, of course. Quite a way out, a lot of meadows and fields and a dilapidated old barn. Why?'

Marion clears her throat. Let's hope she's not going to wake any sleeping dogs. Günther would murder her. 'Do you know if there are any new plans for that piece of land? I mean, for housing, or perhaps commercial development?'

Manfred frowns. 'Commercial development? Now, just as everything's going down the pan? I shouldn't think so.' As he says this he wonders whether in fact it *is* a possibility. Could Günther be on the track of something that he himself hasn't heard about? Is it possible that by failing to attend the last council meeting he missed something important?

'You don't think it's possible?' Marion persists.

'Possible . . . anything's possible. I just haven't heard anything.'

'Can you find out?' Marion sounds agitated. It sounds as if a lot of money is involved . . . so that Günther can build himself a palace next time? He must lose no time in finding out what secret plots are being hatched.

'You can depend on me, Marion. But . . . why don't you just ask Günther directly?'

She clears her throat again and lowers her voice. 'You know what Günther's like, Manfred. I don't want to be left in the dark again, do you know what I mean?'

'Of course,' says Manfred, thinking hard. If she's afraid of the sort of thing he did after the fall of the Iron Curtain, when he gambled *everything* on a single horse, then this must be a huge project. Thanks for the tip-off, Marion! 'You can depend on me, Marion. I'll give you a call.'

'Yes, please do, Manfred. The best time is in the morning, after eight o'clock – you know?'

'I understand!'

Annemarie Roser has set off. Spurred on by Regine's promise of help in raising funds to buy the building, she has made some fresh calculations to assess the financial position of the League and has come to the conclusion that it should be possible. A street collection, perhaps some sponsorships for the retired horses, and if the owner is willing to agree a reasonable price the project should be quite feasible. Above all she could use the social prestige of the Schmidts as an inducement: 'Look, Herr and Frau Schmidt have donated 600 marks for these poor animals – what is the fate of these horses worth to *you*?'

That money was a real stroke of luck!

She's made an appointment to visit the farmer who owns the land and the old barn. In order to make a good impression on his wife, she stopped at the bakery and bought a plaited loaf. In her childhood memories, farms and plaited loaves always somehow went together. Like the hot milk with the thick skin on it, and in winter the roaring of the wood-burning stove in the kitchen while frost-flowers covered the windows of all the other rooms. But it's summer now, and the ghosts of her past are far away. She'll drink a cup of coffee and talk business.

Max Dreher is astonished. He's never actually thought about selling that piece of land with the old barn on it. Years ago, when he was farming more intensively and his young sons were still helping him, he used the barn to house his machinery and sometimes to store a surplus of hay or straw. But those times are long gone. His sons have moved to the city, he's getting on for seventy, and for some time he's been thinking of giving up the farm, but his wife, Bertha, won't hear of it. This is where she has lived ever since her wedding day, where she gave birth to her children, and where she wants to stay till she dies, even if she gets buried under all the work and everything collapses around her.

So Annemarie Roser changes tack and tries to make selling the land seem an attractive proposition to the wife. 'With the money you could visit a spa for a cure. Have a real rest and let yourself be pampered.'

The farmer's wife, who Annemarie thinks looks utterly worn out, shakes her head decisively. 'I don't need a cure. All this new-fangled stuff. There weren't any cures in the old days and people were perfectly healthy. And besides, if I go and take a cure who will look after the animals?'

A good question. Annemarie Roser doesn't know the answer to that one.

'Don't you have any children?'

'In town,' Max Dreher says dismissively, as Bertha pours him a cup of coffee. The plaited loaf is well received – that was a good idea. The farmer's wife immediately put it on the well-scrubbed wooden table, together with some butter and home-made raspberry jam. In honour of the visitor they were eating in the parlour for once.

'What do you want the barn for, anyway? It's no good for anything any more!' Dipping her piece of bread into her coffee, Bertha fixes her small, dark eyes on Annemarie, who explains her plan, but it produces only a baffled shake of the head from Bertha. 'What a fuss over a few old nags. They all have to go to the knacker's yard in the end.'

'Well, yes, but these are horses that aren't ready to be slaughtered, and yet they would otherwise be sent to the knacker's simply for profit.'

'Well, if you don't make money out of animals, why have them? What would be the point?'

Annemarie stirs her coffee. She mustn't lose her nerve. 'We just want to help the animals or, when necessary, protect them. That's what the Animal Welfare League is all about.'

Bertha breaks of another piece of the loaf and dunks it in her coffee.

'Help them! Nobody helps us,' she barks. 'Every animal has its purpose. The dog barks, the cat catches mice, and the others give eggs and meat. It's the law of nature! It's what God intended, or else it would be different!'

Annemarie can think of nothing more to say.

The farmer asks his wife for another cup of coffee, then sits with his head propped on his hand. 'Let's just think about this, Bertha. We don't need that land. But we do need to repair the silo before this winter. This could be a golden opportunity – it might save us having to ask the bank for money.'

The small brown eyes peer up at the chairwoman of the Animal Welfare League.

'How much land do you want, and what are you prepared to pay? After all, there is a building on it. That's worth something.'

'It's in a very bad state, Bertha,' the farmer puts in, slurping his coffee.

'But it hasn't fallen down yet!'

'Perhaps we could all go over there together now?' Annemarie wants to strike a deal as quickly as possible. 'Then I'll show you how much land I have in mind – I would estimate that it's about a hectare – and you can tell me what your price is. If it's within our means I'll have an agreement drawn up right away.'

'Honest people settle that sort of thing with a handshake,' Bertha interposes, wiping the breadcrumbs from the table.

'That too, of course,' agrees Annemarie Roser. 'But all the same I will bring a lawyer along as well, so that everything's done properly.'

'But we won't sell any more than that one hectare!' Bertha says, her eyes flashing. 'We're not parting with everything!'

'It's all right, Bertha, don't worry. We'll go with the lady.' Giving a slight sigh, and with one hand in the small of his back, Max Dreher gets to his feet.

Dirk looks at his watch. It's already after three, and there's been neither sight nor sound of Linda. Is she really angry about last night? Okay, so he lied to her. He simply didn't feel like going to so much trouble just for a meal. Also he was getting on well with his revision, so he couldn't break off just like that. She ought to understand that; after all, it affects her future too.

He lights a cigarette, leans back in his chair and looks out of the window. She's not normally so touchy. He takes a few deep pulls on the cigarette. He feels a bit uneasy all the same. It's unlike her not to contact him during her lunch break. Perhaps she's doing it as a challenge to him – it's probably something to do with the female psyche. Dirk stands up and walks across to his overfilled bookcase. He soon finds what he's looking for, his guide to women. He looks up 'Aloofness'. What's the cause of it? What is the woman trying to convey by it? And how should the man react to it? Dirk stubs out his cigarette and immerses himself in the chapter.

Annemarie Roser has returned to her office in a state of high excitement. The sum is affordable; the price of one mark per square metre has exceeded her wildest hopes. It's such a low price that she simply must act as quickly as possible. There must be some way to get together the 10,000 marks for the hectare of land including the building. The League could provide about half the sum from its own funds. As for the rest, the Schmidts have already made a first contribution. That leaves 4,400 marks. On the spur of the moment she rings Regine Raak.

'How are things with Bobby? Is everything going well?' she begins. Before she can say any more Regine has impulsively invited her to come round.

'Come over and see for yourself. We'd love to see you, Bobby and I!'

Without further deliberation Annemarie jumps into her car and sets off. When she arrives at Regine's bungalow she parks the car in the shade, smooths her cropped, light-brown hair and gets out. Her back is damp, because it was stiflingly hot in the car, but she ignores it; the blouse will dry out.

She rings the bell. Regine opens the door, wearing a T-shirt and shorts. From somewhere inside the house Bobby comes trotting up to greet Annemarie, wagging his tail. She had a particularly soft spot for this big fellow. If she could have, she would have liked to keep him herself. But a small flat isn't the same as a bungalow.

'Do come through.' Regine leads the way into the garden, where she has laid a small table underneath a sunshade. 'My goodness, it's so idyllic here! Really enviable!' Annemarie sits down on the chair Regine offers her and looks round. 'A house with a garden – it's what everybody dreams of!'

Regine nods. 'Yes, and it's especially great for Bobby! Can I offer you a Campari and orange? It's really refreshing in this heat.'

Annemarie agrees, and she tells Regine about her successful meeting with the Drehers.

'My God,' says Regine, 'that's amazing. They're always regarded as being so dour and stubborn. How did you manage it?'

Annemarie describes the meeting, then looks at Regine. 'The real reason I've come is that you kindly promised to do something for the League. Have you any useful links with sponsors, or an idea for a campaign?'

'How about a stall on the plaza? And I could also try to get my friends involved. What do you think?'

Annemarie takes out her notepad and they write down all their ideas. Finally Regine goes into the house and comes back with her cheque book. 'You know what? I was hoping to fly off somewhere on holiday, but nothing's come of it, and' – looking fondly at Bobby – 'I can't now, anyway. I'm so happy to have Bobby that I propose to launch our campaign here and now by donating my flight!'

'What do you mean?'

'This!' With a flourish Regine writes a number on the cheque and passes it over to Annemarie. 'I'd like to make a contribution – after all, not all animals are as fortunate as Bobby.'

Annemarie looks at the cheque and her face becomes flushed with excitement. 'A thousand marks? That's madness!'

'It's a week's holiday somewhere. I think it's a better use of the money to give it to you rather than some travel agent.'

'You're right.' Annemarie carefully puts the cheque away in her bag. 'I haven't got that much money, but I'll also give up my holiday in the Bavarian Forest. I can go hiking around here just as well. So I'll add 500 marks, and then we only need another 2,900. Aren't we doing well?'

'Absolutely!' Regine laughs and hugs Bobby. 'When women want something, they find a way to get it!'

*

Several days pass, and Dirk hears nothing from Linda. For his part, he's been following the advice given in his book. Women need space, it says, and women cling to what they are used to. Even when circumstances are unfavourable, the female psyche will keep on trying to make the best of things, mainly out of a need for security. So there's nothing to fear, Dirk thinks. He need only wait; whatever the circumstances may be, Linda will try to make the best of him.

In the meantime Regine has been busy fundraising and has managed to collect another 500 marks from former colleagues. Marion is waiting impatiently for the promised phone call from Manfred, but Manfred is now making enquiries on his own behalf, not hers. That piece of land is classified as agricultural land, and the building was also formerly used for agricultural purposes, that's definite. So the price per square metre is between one and three marks, depending. A real bargain for Günther, for if the land is to be designated as commercial or industrial land – and Günther seems somehow already to have found out that it is – then he could sell that piece on, undeveloped, to the town at a price of thirty-five to forty marks per square metre. With two hectares of land, a purchase price of two marks and a sale price of say, thirty-seven marks that would represent a profit of 700,000 marks. And of course a great deal more if he were to develop it himself. Günther, you're a sly fox, Manfred thinks, but not quite sly enough. I'll get you this time!

Over the past few days Linda has deliberately been keeping a low profile. She hasn't wanted to see Günther, and certainly not Dirk. He evidently sees no need to ring her up or to drop in at the shop. It's incredible! And she knows for a fact that he lied to her. On her way to work the following morning she made a small detour and, lo and behold, there was his car neatly parked in front of his own building. It hadn't even got a parking ticket, let alone been towed away. She'd have loved to write 'I am a pig' with her finger on the dusty bonnet, but she didn't want to risk the humiliation of being seen.

Günther, too, is considering his next moves. He's already withdrawn the million marks from his account and handed them over to Klaus in a small lockable case. It's now up to Klaus somehow to get the money to Liechtenstein and make it work for him. Everything has gone well so far and there are no obstacles in sight – except for one. Linda's iron resistance. He must break that down. When he phones her she doesn't answer. Twice he's rung her bell at the entry door, but she hasn't responded, although a light was on up in her flat. He's even begun to wonder whether she's the right girl for him at all. But he dismisses that thought. It's become a matter of honour now. He's a real man, and he wants to go on seeing himself as such when he looks into the mirror. Fortress Linda has got to be stormed, whatever the cost.

On Monday, acting on a sudden impulse, Regine goes to the bank and withdraws 3,000 marks from the joint account. It's all taking too long and if the Drehers don't see their money soon they might change their minds. She takes it straight to Annemarie, who is at work at the job centre and goes almost wild with delight.

'God, you make me feel so much better! Have you seen that queue? Just frustration, nothing but frustration all day long!'

'You're not married?' asks Regine, looking at the desk as though expecting to see the obligatory photo of the husband and two children standing in front of a detached house.

'Not likely,' Annemarie says brusquely, but then she does give a smile. 'I've never quite been able to see the advantages of marriage . . .'

'Well,' Regine gives a cheeky grin, 'for instance, I've just withdrawn 3,000 marks from the bank. There isn't that much in my own account. There never has been, actually, now I come to think of it.'

'Well, okay,' Annemarie weighs the envelope in her hands, 'but is that sufficient reason for getting married? I've always hoped that I might achieve that sort of financial security on my own some day . . .'

'Does the job centre offer good promotion prospects for a woman? I mean, could you in theory become president of the National Institute of Employment?'

Annemarie laughs heartily. 'That's a political post – I could never get there via this job.'

'Then you should hand in your notice and try some other route.'

'You may be right. But I'm afraid that I'd get stuck somewhere along the way. That wouldn't help anybody. Least of all me!'

'Okay.' Regine turns to go. 'It's easy for me to talk. I can simply spend the money and don't need to earn any. Talking of which, as soon as we've raised the 3,000 marks through our campaign I'll pay it back into the account. I've only borrowed it because I want to see this deal completed.'

In the farmhouse on the outskirts of the town – a once imposing building now in decay, a relic of better times – Bertha Dreher is laying the table. She's content, although she secretly wonders whether they couldn't have squeezed more money out of the deal. But it was her husband who fixed the price.

'Leave it be, Bertha,' he said, 'after all, they're not rich either. And 10,000 marks is a lot of money for a useless bit of land!'

She left it at that, although she's quite certain that they would have been prepared to pay 12,000. But when half an hour later

Annemarie Roser and Regine Raak count 10,000 marks out on to the table, she's quite satisfied.

Max Dreher has put out some of his own cider and some big-bellied glasses. Now, taking his time, he reads through the contract prepared by the solicitor, Peter Lang, an ex-boyfriend of Annemarie's who has been able to do this job at short notice for his old flame. Max Dreher carefully signs his name. 'There you are, ladies,' he says, nodding, 'and you too, Herr Lang. Now let's drink on it. Bertha, fill the glasses up!'

Peter Lang, the lawyer, leaves straight after that, as he has to hurry on to his next appointment.

Twenty minutes later Regine and Annemarie are driving happily back into town. 'Now *we* must have a drink to celebrate!' Annemarie is as elated as if she had just bought her own dream house.

'Yes, to mark the deal but also the fact that we've become good friends,' suggests Regine, who's driving.

'Great idea! Both things! But where?' Annemarie looks at her enquiringly.

Regine glances quickly at her watch and winks. 'Just gone six, that's perfect. Klaus won't be home before eight today. We can get a cold bottle of champagne out of our cellar, and a couple of glasses, and go and christen our new building and our friendship! That's the obvious place!'

Linda is just popping out of the cosmetics shop to go to the post office. She's made up two parcels for customers and would like to mail them before the end of the day. On the way back she sees Günther coming towards her. Lots of people are about, and she considers a quick dash to the opposite pavement. Perhaps he hasn't spotted her yet. But no, he's already waving to her. He comes up to her and stops.

'What a very pleasant surprise!'

Linda can't avoid stopping too, if she doesn't want to seem rude. She hesitates, wishing she could just disappear into thin air.

'I think it's a great pity we haven't seen each other for so long,' he says, frowning.

'It's only been a few days!' Linda folds her arms, irritated.

'You look stunning!'

Linda doesn't feel stunning. The situation is making her feel out of sorts; she finds it hard to stomach the fact that she's heard nothing at all from Dirk. But her face is tanned, a few freckles give her small nose a jaunty appearance, her light eyes form an interesting contrast with her black hair. Her bad mood doesn't show itself.

She's the one, thinks Günther, she really is the one! I must think of something!

'May I invite you out to dinner this evening? In a top-class restaurant of your choice?'

Linda thinks about it. Why not, when all's said and done? A bit of distraction can do no harm; she'd only spend yet another evening brooding on the reason why Dirk is behaving like this. And nothing much can happen to her in a restaurant.

'I don't know one!'

'I'll choose. Let's say I pick you up at half past seven?'

'That's too early for me. Can you make it eight, please?'

'I'm looking forward to it very much, Linda.' He is, too. Now he just needs to find some way of telling Marion – she's bought theatre tickets for this evening, a show based on texts by Karl Valentin. The title is *A Midnight Serenade*, if he remembers rightly. He'll have that this evening without the help of Karl Valentin. Perhaps even a midnight getting laid! He smiles at her.

Linda nods and walks on, but then she turns back towards him again. 'And, Herr Schmidt, just to avoid any misunderstanding, I'm not included in the price, okay? I don't see myself either as zabaglione or as a cream gateau. I'm not interested in an affair!'

Günther stiffens. He hopes to goodness no one overheard that. He moves closer to her. 'I'm not after an affair, I can assure you. Don't worry! I'll just pick you up, and bring you back afterwards. I won't lay a finger on you. Agreed?'

She nods and goes on her way without another word. Günther had actually intended to mount a new attack by turning up again at her door with a bouquet of Baccara roses, but now that fate has so miraculously come to his aid he can adjust his plans accordingly. He buys a mixed bunch of roses for Marion. 'Dragon food,' he murmurs mockingly as he puts them on the passenger seat beside him.

Regine and Annemarie have left the car in the animal sanctuary car park and made their way to the old barn, carrying the bottle of champagne in a chill-bag. Bobby leaps around them excitedly. He runs ahead into the cooling building and noses about. There is any amount of rubbish lying around, rusty bits of machinery, old tyres, mouldy hay.

'Oh, no,' groans Regine, 'it's all stuff that's awkward to dispose of. That'll be a real problem! We should have bought it only on the condition that the Drehers clear it out first.'

'You'd have had to wait a long time – they just aren't up to it. They can barely cope with their own farm!' Annemarie stretches out her arms and spins around several times. 'What does it matter? We've got it, and everything else will follow in due course, I've no worries on that score!'

'You're right!' Regine swings the bag. 'Come on, let's drink to it!'

They sit down in the shady doorway, right on the dusty concrete floor, with Regine leaning against one doorpost and Annemarie the other. Bobby stretches out on the ground between them.

'Okay then, let's get the bottle opened!' says Annemarie, laughing happily.

They drink one glass to the building and christen it 'Anngine'. Regine refills their glasses. 'Just don't tell anybody, else they'll think we're a pair of stupid kids!'

Annemarie giggles; in her jeans and short-sleeved checked blouse she's lost all resemblance to the official role that she was performing this morning.

Suddenly Bobby growls and jumps up. Regine immediately grabs hold of his collar. 'What is it, Bobby?'

Curiously, Annemarie looks round the corner outside, but at once she draws her head back in. 'There's a man coming towards us!'

Regine can't see. 'Who is it?'

'No idea. I don't know him. I wonder what he's after.'

Regine slowly peers round the corner. 'It's Manfred Büschelmeyer,' she says softly. 'One of Günther Schmidt's friends – he's the manager of the DIY store, a town councillor, and so on. A very careful sort of man . . .'

'Maybe he wants to make a donation?'

'A donation? Him? No more likely than the Schmidts, if you ask me. I still can't get over those 600 marks!'

'Perhaps their social conscience was giving them a hard time.'

'Or even a *beastly* time!' Regine looks round the corner again. 'He's coming closer!'

'What shall we do?'

'See what he's up to!' Regine is already retreating, with Bobby, into the darkness of the building. 'Shh, Bobby, nice and quiet now, no barking!'

Annemarie follows her, carrying the bag and the bottle and glasses. 'This is awfully exciting,' she whispers as she joins Regine and Bobby behind an old trailer.

Manfred is having a good look at the piece of ground. He's not interested in the barn – except perhaps in what it would cost to demolish it. But that would be nothing in relation to the huge profit that could be made. Really, it's all perfectly straightforward. The turning off the main road is already there, and would only need to be widened and properly surfaced. The land is located comfortably within reach of the neighbouring communities, and it's right at the other end of town from the industrial zone on its east side, which can't be extended because it borders on a conservation area. Here there's no danger of restrictions and conditions. These are just ordinary meadows and fields. It wouldn't occur to anyone from an environmental group to try to get this project blocked. Actually, it's surprising that the town developed eastwards first.

Manfred is busily making notes and pacing out the piece of land in every direction, pushing a meter-wheel ahead of him.

Regine and Annemarie, together with Bobby, have crept along the side of the building, and are watching him. 'Is he off his head?' asks Annemarie, tapping her forehead. 'What on earth is he doing with that funny wheel? He looks like a polar bear rehearsing his act.'

'I don't know, I don't know!' Regine is frowning. 'There's something fishy about this. He's measuring the land – but why?'

When Klaus arrives home at eight o'clock, Regine confesses her impulsive raid on their joint account, but Klaus's mind is currently occupied with such large sums of money that he can only laugh. 'I'm all in favour of your helping with a cause like that,' he says, lifting her off her feet.

'Hey, what's all this about?' Regine laughs.

'Just that I love you.' He swings her through the air, kisses her and energetically sets her down on her feet again. Bobby dances around the two of them, barking.

'Then you're not horrified? I thought you'd throw a fit!'

'Do you really think I'm such an old misery?'

Regine trips ahead of him into the garden, where she has laid their evening meal on a table with a blue and white cloth. 'No,' she laughs, 'but I saw the balance and, to be honest, it gave me a bit of a shock!'

Klaus sits down and with pleasurable anticipation opens a chilled bottle of beer, looking at her with just a hint of a smile. 'Don't worry about it. Sometimes things can change in no time. I have a fantastic new client. If we're very lucky we'll even be able to fly away on holiday, to the Caribbean, Sri Lanka, the Maldives, anywhere! Only of course,' he adds, pointing to Bobby, who has stretched himself out on the ground next to the table, 'with him we can't go any further than the Bregenz Forest.'

'I've always liked the Bregenz Forest!'

At about the same time Günther is on his way to pick up Linda. The garage door is just closing behind him, and before him lie all the possibilities of the night. He told Marion that he had a vital business meeting that would bring in a great deal of money in the foreseeable future, and he piled on the lies until Marion seemed to have grasped its importance. Marion let him go, at half past seven; what she had in fact grasped was that an important deal was about to be concluded this evening while Manfred had made no progress with his enquiries on her behalf.

Furious, she phones him at work the moment Günther has left, but nobody answers. Then, contrary to what they agreed, she tries ringing him at home. All she gets is an answering-machine, which annoys her even more. No wonder no woman has married him and he's still an employee at that stupid DIY store – he's obviously quite useless! He's had plenty of time to look into the matter.

While she's still striding about the room in a rage she has

another, devastating thought. Perhaps Manfred knew about the whole thing all along and is at this very moment taking part in the negotiations about the piece of land – it's quite obvious that the mysterious meeting this evening must be connected with that project. Everything Günther said to her pointed that way. Is this the reason Manfred hasn't phoned her, because he's right in the thick of it all too and is secretly laughing his head off about her?

She must go after Günther; she must find out where this conspiratorial meeting is being held and who's involved. Her honour demands it! She grabs her car keys and goes into the garage. With a bit of luck she can still catch up with her husband.

The road from their wealthy suburb into the town is long and absolutely straight. Marion goes roaring off, and sees some brake lights far ahead. She wonders if that could be Günther's Mercedes, but it's too far away for her to be sure. She's driving faster than usual; the speedometer's showing fifty miles an hour. The car in front turns off. Marion accelerates. She's never raced through Römersfeld at well over sixty before. But then she's never had such good reason. A blinding flash dazzles her; startled, she slams on the brake. Her pulse fluttering, she draws up at the kerb. A speed trap on her road! There's never been one there before!

She turns to look back at the speed camera. It's like a nesting-box, fixed permanently in place and camouflaged among some trees rather than one of those small mobile cameras. When the police run through the film she can say goodbye to her driving licence. She can't afford to do that – and besides, the press would have a field day. Marion Schmidt guilty of reckless speeding! Doing over sixty in a built-up area! She of all people! What will she say to Günther?

Marion looks up and down the road; it's pretty quiet at the moment, but in any case it's too early and still much too light to start interfering with official property. Also the thing looks much too strongly made to be destroyed with one's bare hands. Marion thinks hard. This is a new situation for her to be in, and it's vital she keeps a cool head. Slowly she drives towards the town centre. She's lost sight of Günther now, but that's the lesser evil. She looks at her watch. Nearly eight o'clock. She needs a hacksaw, one that's small and manageable, battery-powered and suitable for cutting through a thick iron pole. The nearest place where she can be sure of getting one is Manfred's stupid DIY store. Stepping on the gas, she makes it just before closing time and goes up to the first assistant she sees. 'Is Herr Büschelmeyer still here?'

She gets a surly look in return. 'The boss has already gone.' Then, after a pause, and no doubt a deep inward sigh, he says without much enthusiasm, 'Is there anything I can do?'

That's all she really wanted, and in addition she now knows for certain that Manfred is making a fool of her. Just wait, she'll get to the bottom of this. 'I'm looking for a hacksaw for my husband, small, handy, lightweight – a cordless one. And also a small aluminium stepladder. Sturdy, but portable.'

He looks at her as though she'd just suggested they should spend the night together. 'It's a bit late for me to start showing you all our products; we have a large selection, you know.' He takes a deep breath. 'Couldn't you come back tomorrow?'

'No, I couldn't,' says Marion. 'Just bring me the best you have. I'll go straight to the checkout.'

At a quarter past eight she drives off with a hacksaw and a stepladder in her boot. It's just as well Manfred wasn't there. Otherwise you could be quite sure that this bit of news would have reached Günther's ears in no time. Real old gossips, those men.

Marion is satisfied: so far, so good. Now she'll find out where that veterans' club is holding its meeting, and then she'll confront Günther with the facts. Perhaps then he'll finally realise that it's a mistake to treat her like some silly young bimbo, shutting her out of all his business affairs.

Günther has booked a table for two at the Lake Restaurant. The 'lake' is a small flooded gravel pit, and the fish is flown in, but even so this is the best restaurant in Römersfeld, and Günther is well known here because he comes quite frequently with business associates and once a year with his wife. There's an arrangement of red roses on the beautifully laid table, and the owner, Katrin Christiansen, comes up in person to greet Günther and his guest and to light the two candles on the silver candelabrum.

Though she doesn't show it, Linda is impressed. Among her friends the Lake Restaurant is regarded as a flashy venue and up to now none of them has so much as seen its menu. And now here she is, right inside – and she can't tell anybody about it.

Günther acts the part of a man of the world. He senses that this is a good opportunity to impress Linda, and so he begins by ordering two glasses of champagne and then asks the chef to tell them what specialities are being offered today. Eventually he chooses jellied rabbit with a tomato sauce and green salad as an hors d'œuvre, followed by iced melon soup with tarragon as an *entremets*, then as the main course fillet of *loup de mer* in a thyme crust with parsley potatoes, and for dessert a Grand Marnier flan with lime butter.

When he has put together the four courses and chosen suitable wines to accompany them, he beams across at Linda.

'How do you come to be so knowledgeable?' she asks, as the waiter serves her her aperitif.

'It's simply a matter of social know-how,' says Günther, flattered, raising his glass to hers. 'Some people have it, others haven't!' He can hardly tell her that Marion insisted that he attend a whole succession of courses in order to acquire these social skills. And that he only went along with it under pressure from that old militarist, his father-in-law.

But now, lo and behold – he smiles winningly at Linda across the table – it's paying dividends. Like the piano lessons you have as a child. You only remember them when you've almost forgotten them.

Linda has decided simply to let events take their course. What's the point of suffering heartache for Dirk when he can't even be bothered to phone her? And why should she tell Günther to get lost when at the moment he's the only person taking any interest in her? She's wearing a close-fitting summer dress of dark-red raw silk and black strappy shoes with stiletto heels, bargains that she snapped up in last year's summer sales and then stowed away in the back corner of her wardrobe waiting for some special occasion.

And lo and behold, her foresight has paid off. Like the rules of etiquette, almost forgotten, that her mother taught her: remember that at smart dinners the cutlery for each successive course goes from the outside inwards. For the first course you take the cutlery from the outside, and don't forget, child, to dab your mouth with your napkin before you drink! At the time she thought her mother was hopelessly old-fashioned. If only she could see her now . . .

'This is pleasant, isn't it?' says Günther at last, when nibbles are served. 'Fresh goat's cheese garnished with radish shoots,' announces the waiter, 'with the compliments of the kitchen.'

Did we actually order this? thinks Linda, and then shakes her head about herself. What does she mean, 'we'? *He* orders, and *he* pays. There's no 'we' about it!

But she has to admit that he's right. It *is* pleasant. It's like having a birthday.

Yet again!

Marion is driving all over town. First to the animal sanctuary, because it seems most likely that they'll meet actually at the piece of land in question. But she can't see any car that she recognises, so she drives on. Her next port of call is the clubhouse at the football ground, where the men regularly continue their council meetings into the small hours. The car park is packed, with innumerable cars and even camper vans crammed in side by side. There must be some event going on, thinks Marion, and mutters crossly: Römersfeld Losers versus Nonentities United. Of course, it's possible that Günther lied to her simply because he was intent on going to this proletarian entertainment. Marion has never had any time for football, and she and Günther always used to quarrel about it. Only now does it strike her that this hasn't happened for some years. That doesn't mean he hasn't been going any more, it means that he's stopped telling her. Angrily she drives up and down the rows of parked cars. This is going to be an evening of revelations. She'll run him to earth somewhere!

Günther and Linda have reached the iced melon soup. They're in high spirits, laughing about all sorts of things, whether or not they're funny. Katrin Christiansen is already opening the second bottle of wine and asking if everything is to their satisfaction. This sets Linda laughing again, because it seems mad to her even to ask such a question. Giovanni ought to ask that when he serves one of his stodgy pizzas. Next time she'll throw that circle of stodge back at him. The idea makes her laugh even more. As she tosses back her black hair, her cheeks are glowing and her eyes shining, and Günther feels that he's almost attained his goal. He raises his glass: 'You're so beautiful, Linda. I'd love to spoil you, please give me the chance.'

Linda freezes for a moment. He has used 'du', the familiar form of address, just like that, without warning or invitation. Günther senses the slight change of mood. Take care, you old stallion, he says to himself. Mustn't frighten the young mares.

'May I suggest we say "du" with each other?' He is still holding up his glass. 'It's for me to propose it, since I think that I'm

the older of us two . . .' He laughs at his own joke, but Linda still
hesitates. Although she also raises her glass, she finds it difficult
to use the familiar form just like that. After all, he's thirty-three
years older than she is. Apart from her own father and a few
other relatives, she's never used it with a man of his age.

'Spoil me in what way?' she asks, clinking glasses with him.

'Well,' Günther gives her what's meant to be a mysterious
smile but it turns into more of a leer. 'Help you to enjoy life.
Have fun. Really live!'

'I enjoy life as it is.' She puts her glass down next to her empty
soup plate, which is immediately taken away. 'Every day I feel
glad to be alive. I'm young and healthy, I have a good job, a
loving boyfriend, everything's fine – what more could I want?'
What a load of nonsense, she thinks; I have a second job in
order to scrape together a bit more money, I have an idiotic
boyfriend who couldn't care less about me – and I might really
have a chance here, I could use my youth to good advantage,
have my own business, buy a flat of my own, drive an Alfa
Spider.

And end up dead in a bathtub . . .

'Linda?'

'What?'

'Are you dreaming?'

She comes to with a start. Günther is fondling her hand. She
automatically withdraws it and reaches for her glass again.

'Let's drink to life!'

'Yes, I'm in favour of that!' Günther clinks glasses with her.
'Have you ever been to Paris?'

'Paris?'

'Yes, it's great. Shopping in Paris – summer fashions, or winter
fashions, as the case may be. Going up the Eiffel Tower, visiting
the Pompidou Centre, Sacré Cœur – have you ever done that?'

Günther Schmidt and shopping – she can't believe it.

'No, I haven't, actually.'

He laughs, feeling victory within his grasp. Just then he happens to look out through the window towards the car park, and despite the growing darkness he can see a BMW approaching, a convertible that he recognises. It's his wife!

The shock makes him choke on his food, then he thinks feverishly. What's she doing here? Has she got another man? Or is she spying on him?

He can't afford to have a confrontation.

He leans forward across the table. 'Don't be alarmed,' he says to Linda in a low voice. 'My wife has just driven up; she doesn't know that the two of us are here. It's probably best if we quickly nip out to the toilet.'

The toilet? This is just how she imagined an affair would be. One minute it's Paris and the next minute the toilet.

'But nothing at all's been going on,' she says, trying to reassure him, but she knows that's silly. Of course something's been going on. They're sitting here in the best restaurant in town, eating and drinking by candlelight – what is a wife to think?

Marion would never have expected to find him at the Lake Restaurant. And she'd really intended to go back to the speed camera now, because it was getting dark at last. But the silver saloon was visible from the road. As ever, Günther had parked his car right in front of the entrance as though there were no parking bays.

The man's a fool, thinks Marion, as she drives into the car park. Or else he has nothing to hide. She looks around. There's no other car that she recognises. Who is he with?

She parks in a proper space, quickly smoothes her hair, applies some bright red lipstick, picks up her handbag and walks up to the entrance.

Katrin Christiansen is already coming towards her. 'I'm afraid you've just missed your husband,' she says in a low voice, raising both hands apologetically.

'What do you mean?' asks Marion, looking around. The restaurant is fairly empty; five tables are occupied and there's a small table that has obviously just been vacated.

'Where's he gone?' she asks, studying the small table from a distance.

'He called a taxi, and left ten minutes ago with the other gentlemen.' Katrin Christiansen points to a table which has been cleared.

Günther has come home way over the limit before now, but never by taxi. 'Are you sure that was my husband?' Marion asks.

'May I offer you something? Some refreshment perhaps?' Katrin Christiansen makes a gesture of invitation.

Marion doesn't take up the offer. 'And whose is that small table that's unoccupied?'

'That one? Oh, a young couple, they were suddenly in a hurry, you know what I mean?'

'No, I don't.' Marion gives the table another searching look. But there's nothing to suggest that Günther had been sitting there. And anyway, why should there be? She's puzzled by her own suspicion. 'I'm sorry to have bothered you,' she says to Katrin Christiansen. 'Goodnight!'

Two minutes later her BMW is leaving the car park, and three minutes later Günther is in the kitchen. Katrin Christiansen has just helped herself to a brandy. She goes up to him with the empty glass in her hand. 'You know, Herr Schmidt, you're a very good customer. But I'm not up to this sort of thing. I don't want any scandal.'

'I seem to remember a little difficulty about parking spaces.'

Katrin Christiansen sets her glass down with a bang. 'We have parking spaces.'

'Yes, but not enough for the number of seats in the restaurant. There are planning regulations with guidelines for . . .'

'We know that, Herr Schmidt, and we do appreciate the help you gave us at the time. And I think that whenever you've dined here, in all the years since then, we've shown our gratitude for your support. But I wouldn't like to have to become a liar on that account.'

Günther turns towards the door, shrugging his shoulders. 'I think, Frau Christiansen, that we'd like our main course now!'

Marion is driving slowly back through the town on her way home. Once she's back there, in the garage, she'll read the instructions for the power saw and then try it out. On Günther if necessary. Because if he is cheating on her he won't live to tell the tale. She owes that not only to the honour of her family but above all to herself.

The house is dark. Just as she expected. Günther didn't take a taxi home. Frau Christiansen was lying. But why? Or did he go by taxi to some place where he didn't want his car to be seen? Where could that be? A nightclub? The brothel?

This almost makes her laugh. All the time that he was on the council, Günther waged a passionate campaign against that non-descript little house on the edge of the town. The morals of the townspeople were at risk, he thundered, youngsters were led astray and respectable family men endangered by that den of vice. Could it be that he himself is endangered now?

Marion opens the garage door using the remote control, drives in and unwraps her booty. An excellent little machine. She brandishes it in the air several times and climbs up the stepladder holding it. No problem, she's strong enough. Marion looks at her watch. Half past ten, still too early to launch her attack. But perhaps she could find some more practical clothes. She decides on a black trouser suit, canvas shoes with rubber soles and a black woolly hat. Then she sets off. By now it's eleven o'clock, and peace has descended upon Römersfeld. Most people are in bed.

She drives along a road parallel to the main road and into a small car park beside the patch of ground where the trees are. If she's judged it correctly, she can walk straight across it and come out right by the speed camera. The nearest houses in any direction are a good hundred yards away. If she's quick she'll have sawn off the box before anyone has been woken by the noise.

She finds that it's not so easy to walk through the little copse at night carrying a stepladder and a hacksaw. She's constantly bumping into the trees and undergrowth, and she soon starts to perspire. When she at last reaches the camera, she wonders how she'll ever be able to get the box, hacksaw and stepladder back to the car. She can't possibly carry them all at once.

But the thing has got to go.

She puts the ladder in place, climbs up and lifts the hacksaw into position. Just as she's about to switch it on, car lights approach. Quickly she climbs down and hides in the bushes, together with the ladder and saw. This happens three times, and she's just wondering, crouched in her hiding place, whether she shouldn't postpone the deed for another couple of hours when a car comes racing by. Marion sees it, a silver Mercedes driving well above the speed limit. Obviously Günther's been home in the meantime and is now out looking for her. Marion closes her eyes as the flash goes off. Just as she did a few hours earlier, Günther jams on his brakes and then comes roaring back in reverse. Not ten feet away from her he gets out and has a good look at the camera. Marion watches him. What will he do now, mystery man that he is? For the moment he seems to be quite at a loss. Eventually he gets into his car, slams the door shut and drives on.

As a good wife she should now be all the more intent on sawing off the camera and discreetly disposing of it. But does she want to do him that favour? He was driving at least as fast as she was. Günther without a driving licence would be like a hawk with a broken wing. She'd have him completely under her surveillance. And he's changed the inevitable newspaper headlines – now they won't be about her but about him. He'd have done better not to set her against him!

She drags the saw and the ladder back through the trees to her car and drives home. An hour and a half later, when she's already in bed, she hears the automatic garage door opening. Will he ask her where she was? But then in return she'll want to know how his car got home from the Lake Restaurant when he was supposed to have left by taxi.

Marion's arrival had put an end to Linda's good mood. How humiliating to be sitting in the toilet while the jealous wife was having a good snoop round outside. And yet she could have shaken her hand without embarrassment, for after all, apart from the decision to call each other 'du', nothing had happened between her and Günther. After Marion left, Günther acted as though he had everything under control, but it didn't escape her that he was keeping a watchful eye on the car park.

'Are you afraid of your wife?' she asked as they were eating their dessert.

Günther nearly split his sides laughing. 'For heaven's sake! That really is too funny for words! What man is afraid of a woman!'

'He might be afraid of his own wife.'

'You really shouldn't worry your pretty little head about that.'

'You can be rather nice, Günther Schmidt, but sometimes you're just a bit big-headed, don't you think?'

Günther could think of no answer to that. He asked for the liqueur list and ordered an apricot brandy for each of them. No one had ever said that to him before. He wasn't big-headed, simply a big man. Not at all the same. She'd come to realise that soon enough.

When, at her front door, he put his arm round her to kiss her, she quickly turned her head a little so that he only kissed her on the cheek. 'That was a wonderful supper, Günther, thank you ever so much – and we did agree that I'm not included in the price!'

'Now you're in danger of hurting my feelings,' he said, taking a step backwards. 'Am I so repulsive that I don't even get a good-night kiss?'

'Oh no, you can have one.' She kissed him lightly on the mouth and slipped quickly indoors.

Just you wait, thought Günther. You can be as coy as you like, but I'll get you in the end!

Shortly after he had driven out of the inner courtyard, another car's lights went on. Dirk had seen enough. It had been worth the wait. No wonder she hadn't contacted him – that fat slob Günther Schmidt had got his paws on her now. They'll both pay for this, he vowed as he drove back to the town centre in a frenzy of pain, helplessness and thirst for revenge.

The next morning brings the first rain for weeks. It'll be good for the garden, Marion thinks as she cleans her teeth in the bathroom. She's still tired and would have liked to sleep on a bit, but she never likes to show any sign of weakness. Günther will also be getting up any time now. Will he ask her anything about last night? When he came to bed he didn't even turn the light on. She co-operated by pretending to be asleep. But surely now he'll want to know what was going on. And so will she. No more guessing about the land by the animal sanctuary, no more strange meetings, she's his wife and she has a right to expect him to be open with her.

Marion is laying the table for breakfast in the living room when she hears him coming down the stairs. 'Nothing for me,' he calls to her, already reaching for his coat, 'I have an urgent appointment.'

If she were in the kitchen now she'd be able to confront him. 'Günther!' she calls, trying to stop him, but she can already hear the sound of the garage door. 'Don't just go like that!' Angrily she pursues him into the garage, but he's already in the car and driving away as though he hadn't seen her. The door slowly closes again. She stands there in the dark, seething with fury. He saw her perfectly well. He just chose not to. Why on earth not? What scheme is he hatching?

She's just turning towards the kitchen door when she stops in surprise. Out of the corner of her eye she notices a strange box that wasn't there yesterday. Marion reaches for the light switch. She almost laughs, it's just too ridiculous. There is the speed camera, sawn off, leaning in the corner, fixing her malevolently with its single eye.

All right, so he's done her a favour without realising it. But of course he's done himself a bigger one. This is why he got home so late. He still had to get hold of the things that she already had in her boot. And he's sawn it off much too low down. Half of the pole is still attached to it. A thoroughly unprofessional job!

All the same, stolen public property doesn't look too good in the house of a respectable building contractor. She goes into the living room and calls his secretary. 'When my husband gets in, please tell him that he's put the nesting box up too late and in the wrong place. The breeding season is already over!'

Manfred Büschelmeyer is sitting by the phone, his face flushed with rage. He's just learned that the Animal Welfare League has beaten him to it. That stupid female has nothing in her head but Friskas and Tasty-Treats – and she has got in first! Max Dreher has calmly told him that as far as he's concerned the deal is done. He's got his money, and that's all there is to it. And there's no more land on offer at present.

He refused even to tell him what price per square metre was paid.

It's enough to drive him mad. The one remaining hope is that the Roser woman doesn't realise what a prize she's got. In which case he must take steps immediately, because once Günther works out what's going on it'll be too late for him and his money.

The phone rings, and he sees from the display that it's an internal number. It's the young assistant wanting to tell him that a Frau Schmidt was asking for him in the store yesterday, just before closing time.

Manfred breaks out in a sweat. No doubt she wanted to tell him about the deal in person yesterday evening. But perhaps she herself is behind the Roser woman and did it in order to push the price up higher? That would be just like her. Once a Schmidt, always a Schmidt – male *or* female.

'I've got to dash out,' he says to his secretary. 'I'll be back in a couple of hours. I'm not available to anybody, not even on my mobile!'

And with that he's gone.

He wants to find out from the bank how much credit he could get, but although he drives around for some time he can't find a parking space, so he carries on to the animal sanctuary without having got approval for a loan. But a young girl who looks after the animals tells him that Annemarie Roser won't be there until 4.30, and that even then she has several appointments straightaway. So he can't see her before 5.30 at the earliest.

Ah, that tells him all he needs to know. He must beat the others to it.

'Frau Roser works at the petrol station, doesn't she?'

'At the petrol station? No, at the job centre!'

Twenty minutes later he's in his car outside the job centre. While he's about it he can tell her that she never sends him anything but time-wasters. He needs people who are prepared to work for their money, not the sort who skulk around in corners just filling in time till it's their break. But perhaps it would be better to say nothing . . .

Approaching the door to Room No. 25, he ignores the long queue, knocks loudly and goes in without waiting for an answer.

He's met with a disapproving look.

'Please can you wait outside like everybody else!'

'But I haven't got time for that. I'm an employer, and there's something I need to discuss with you.'

'I'm busy, as you can see. Come in when I call you.'

How he detests these close-cropped domineering bitches, these women's libbers who've been spreading across the country like a plague. He goes and stands in the corridor outside the door and tries to ignore the mocking glances of the other people there. Okay, so he's been thrown out, so what. He'll have the last laugh.

Manfred waits for twenty minutes. He'd have left by now if there weren't so much money at stake. She's called in two men before him, and now a woman. This is getting beyond a joke!

The next 'Will you come in, please?' is clearly meant for him.

He goes in and makes an effort to adopt a friendly manner. She hold all the trumps, so he must keep his true feelings hidden. He forces a smile as he shakes hands with her.

'So you're an *employer*,' she says. She makes it sound as though this were some peculiar form of human life.

'Yes, but that's not why I'm here,' he says, trying to move the conversation on.

'Oh, isn't it? Are you looking for a job, then?'

'There's no need to be funny.'

'I'm sorry, but what is it about, then?'

She points to the old brown chair facing her desk. He's damned if he's going to sit down on such a penitent's seat.

He declines the offer and remains standing. 'It's about the piece of land that you've bought from Max Dreher. I'd like to make you an offer for it.'

'An offer?' Her face is a picture of astonishment. 'Why ever should you do that?'

Damned silly question, thinks Manfred. 'Because I'd like to have it,' he says pleasantly.

'What for?'

What for indeed? What should he say? Because he just would? 'To fulfil my mother's one remaining wish, to build her a house.'

'Next to the animal sanctuary? Have you any idea what that means? The dogs? The noise? You can't inflict that on an elderly woman!'

Damn it, he's taken a wrong tack here. He should have thought it out more carefully beforehand.

'She wants it all the same!'

Annemarie Roser takes her time before replying. She sits at her desk, twiddling her pencil in her hands.

'That's interesting,' she says at last, for by now she's recognised him. He's the man who was measuring the plot of land when she and Regine Raak were sitting in the old barn. What can he want? This stuff about his mother is a lie, she can tell.

'I'm afraid the plot of land isn't for sale,' she says, smiling at him.

'Even if I make you a good offer?' Manfred takes a deep breath. This is his only chance. He must grab it somehow.

'How good?'

This sounds more promising.

'Ten marks a square metre?'

Annemarie Roser has to exert great self-control so as not to show her astonishment. Is there oil under the ground there? Or some mineral deposit? Or something else she's completely unaware of? Have they unwittingly bought a treasure? She must ring Regine as soon as possible.

'Ten marks?' she repeats slowly.

'Fifteen,' says Manfred. Now the blood is rushing to his face. 'But then you'd have to come to a lawyer with me straightaway.'

'Why, do you have one lined up already?'

Manfred grips the back of the chair. He can feel his heart pounding. If she says yes he'll be paying more than he'd intended, but he'll still make a killing. And if the Roser woman agrees to sell at this price it shows that none of the pros are behind her. That's the best thing of all: he'll have put one over on the Schmidts.

'No, but I can arrange it, don't worry.'

'There are still people waiting outside, they have a right . . .'

'It'll take no time at all!' He's already looking around for a phone.

'Are you afraid I might die between now and tomorrow?' Annemarie does the sum in her head. Fifteen marks a square metre; for a hectare that makes 150,000 marks. In a single day they'd make a profit of 140,000 marks. But why? What's behind it all?

Annemarie stands up. 'I'll think it over.'

Nervously Manfred wipes his right hand on his trousers and holds it out to her. 'When can I ring you?'

'Tomorrow morning.'

'It's my mother's birthday tomorrow, her seventieth. I'd like to surprise her with it first thing in the morning. You know old people are early risers. Couldn't it be later today?'

Annemarie gives him a good long handshake. 'I'm an early riser too. You can ring me tomorrow morning at six. I'm in the book!'

Back in his car, Manfred is so excited that he goes into reverse instead of forward gear. He's never done that before in his whole life, but then he's never before been so close to pulling a fast one on the great Günther Schmidt. Will Marion ever invite him to a garden party again? Grinning broadly, he drives through Römersfeld, back to his store.

Monika Raak just happens to be looking out of the window of her office when a small, battered-looking car drives on to the large forecourt of her car-spraying firm. Absent-mindedly, she looks at it. That little car could do with a respray, but on the other hand its owner presumably can't afford to have it smartened up or it wouldn't be in such a pitiful state to start with. All the same, the driver has a healthy sense of his own importance. He parks right in the boss's space and gets out. Now she recognises him – it's Richi's friend, Dirk Wetterstein. As far as she can remember he's never been here before. The two of them usually meet elsewhere, away from work, and since Dirk has been struggling with his revision they've hardly been meeting up at all.

She's only just moved away from the window when there's a knock. Dirk is standing at the door, pale, wet and looking as if he's had no sleep at all.

'Dirk, this *is* a surprise,' she says, shaking his hand firmly.

'Yes.' He looks around. 'Is Richi not here?'

'Richi has his own office, across the corridor. But he's out at the moment – he should be back in half an hour. Can I do anything for you?'

'I don't think so.' The way he looks at her reminds her of Snow White in the forest.

'Well, come and sit down, anyway.' She leads him to the sofa in the corner. 'Coffee? Something to eat? A croissant perhaps? They're fresh from the baker's.'

'No thanks, I feel sick already!'

Whatever is all this about? The telephone rings. 'Would you

excuse me?' Monika lifts the receiver. It's Irena, eager to tell her the latest bit of amusing gossip from the fashion world.

'Irena, I'm sorry, but I've got a visitor. Dirk's here.'

'Dirk? Then you can ask him where Linda's got to. I've been calling her and she's never there. Has he locked her away somewhere?'

'Ask him yourself!'

Monika passes the receiver to Dirk.

'A fine friend you've got,' Dirk says by way of a greeting.

Ah, so that's the way the wind's blowing, thinks Monika using the internal phone to ask for some coffee and croissants.

'I'm not interested in any of that,' she hears Dirk say. 'For me it's all in the past, over and done with, okay? Ancient history, of no interest. As far as I'm concerned she doesn't exist any more, she's finished with, dead and buried, d'you understand? I've never seen a woman so dead, do I make myself clear? No? Well, too bad!' He passes the receiver back to Monika. 'I can't be bothered with slow-witted women just now. If Richi isn't around I'll go again.'

'But they're just making you some fresh coffee. It'll do you good!'

'What do you mean, do me good? Is there anything wrong with me? Do I look as if there is? I'm fine, great, never better. If Richi doesn't come soon, I'm off.'

Monika considers what to do. It's impossible to get any sense out of him in the state he's in. The one thing that seems clear is that Linda's finished with him. That's a pity, but Monika isn't surprised. It was only a matter of time before the right type of man happened to find his way into the cosmetics shop. Dirk simply isn't mature enough for a woman like Linda.

The door opens and a young man serves coffee and croissants on a tray. 'Don't you have a proper secretary?' asks Dirk with an utter lack of political correctness.

'Why, don't you fancy me?' the young fellow retorts.

'Marc is our token man in the office,' laughs Monika. 'I wouldn't have thought you'd be so old-fashioned, Dirk.'

'I . . .' Dirk sits down rigidly but then slumps down into the sofa. 'Oh, forget it. What difference does it make? We're ruled by women in every area of life anyway. At work, in love, and now they even provide themselves with token men. Take yourself, Monika – are you a woman, or aren't you?'

'I should say so,' Monika says, pouring his coffee.

'And does this whole set-up belong to you or not?'

'Yes, you could say it does.'

'Well, there you are. I'm off!'

When Richi arrives ten minutes later, Dirk has gone. While he's still on the forecourt, Monika runs out to tell him about his friend's brief visit. Walking back to his car, she holds the car door open. 'Go on, you must go and look for him. I thought he seemed drunk, quite beside himself. He was talking really wildly, as if he'd been taking drugs!'

Meanwhile Günther is sitting in his office. He's in a foul mood and is finding it hard to concentrate on the work that has piled up on his desk. Damn it all, yesterday evening started off so well, and then his own wife mucked it all up. Robbed him of the night of love that he'd been working up to so successfully. And then that silly business with the speed camera. Having to go and cut the wretched thing off its post that same night. At least he was lucky enough to have the workshop keys with him. And all that bother just because his old woman was still flitting around town late at night and he was afraid that she might go to Linda's door and lean on her doorbell. After all, she might have been crouching behind a bush in the car park there, watching them. An army officer's daughter like her would be capable of anything. Just as well that the money will be gone by the time the fighting gets really dirty. She'll soon run out of ammunition. Wars are an expensive business.

He stares out at the rain. He'd been so close. It's maddening! And then that message from Marion about the nesting box. He'd meant to dispose of it this afternoon, but he can hardly drive through town with a sawn-off iron pole sticking out of his boot. Especially as the story will no doubt be all over tomorrow's paper. But trust Marion to go poking her nose in! A person like her, always trundling through the town at twenty-five miles an hour, wouldn't have an understanding of irrepressible male energies.

Günther is sorting through all the enquiries, notes and letters. All this interests him very little at the moment. He feels a pressure in his head that won't be released until he's been to bed with Linda. He picks up the phone, rings the best florist in Römersfeld and orders thirty red roses to be sent to Linda. Long-stemmed, he adds, thinking: *like me*.

Regine has just brought the garden furniture in out of the rain when the phone rings. She hurries from the garden into the house, with Bobby bounding happily after her. 'Oh no!' she says, as she lifts the receiver.

'Oh no?' asks Annemarie Roser at the other end. 'Does that mean me?'

'No, Bobby! He's bringing a whole lot of dirt in from the garden. Bobby, sit! And I'd only just washed the floor. I don't think I shall ever be able to manage this stupid house!'

'Are you sitting down?'

'I am now.'

'What would you say to making 140,000 marks' profit in a single day?'

'Has the Russian Mafia been advertising down at the job centre?'

'It's no joke, Regine!' And Annemarie gives her a detailed account of Manfred's visit that morning.

'Manfred Büschelmeyer. Well I never. That's amazing!'

Regine thinks about it. 'Shall I ask my husband what he makes of it? After all, he's a financial consultant – he'll probably have some idea of what might be behind it.'

'Annemarie hesitates. She knows the networks that operate in the town – too many cosy arrangements of the 'you scratch my back and I'll scratch yours' type – and she's wary of the sleaze factory in these hearty male bonds. And she's not sure whether Klaus Raak isn't part of all that. On balance she would guess that he is.

Without Annemarie having to spell it out, Regine understands. The two of them started this ball rolling and they're not going to let anyone else muscle in.

'Shall we meet? Here?' she asks.

'Fine,' Annemarie agrees. 'I'll be glad to come over.'

'Now, Bobby,' Regine puts the phone down and addresses the sheepdog, who is lying on the floor with his coat all wet, vigorously drumming the tiles with his tail, 'how about fetching the bucket and scrubbing brush? In the meantime I'll put a bottle of champagne in the fridge, because I'm just beginning to see why Marion was at the animal sanctuary. It looks rather as if there's something quite important hidden there. And Annemarie and I are sitting right on top of it without having a clue what it is. Now we just need to find out how high we can push up the bidding. And then we can turn Römersfeld upside down!'

Richi drives straight to Dirk's flat. As usual, he can't find a parking space. Losing patience after going around the whole district three times, he leaves the car in a no-parking zone. It'll be okay just for five minutes. Anyway, he doesn't think Dirk's at home. He hasn't seen his car, at any rate. He rings the bell loudly and insistently and, as he expected, there's no response.

A traffic warden is taking down his registration number just as Richi returns a moment later. 'I notice this car quite often,' she says, giving him a reproachful look from under her wet cap.

'There are lots of convertibles in Römersfeld.'

'But not with this registration number!'

'Let me explain . . .'

Undeterred, she goes on writing, carefully puts the ticket into a waterproof plastic sleeve and tucks it behind the windscreen wiper. 'If you really want to explain, you can do it just as well in writing.' With a perfunctory smile she moves on to the next car.

Grinding his teeth, Richi takes the ticket and gets in. That's thirty marks down the drain for a start. A fine rescue operation this is turning out to be!

For another twenty minutes Richi drives all over the town, but he can't see Dirk's car anywhere. In front of the cosmetics shop he wonders for a moment whether he should ask Linda, but on reflection it doesn't seem appropriate. What business of his is Linda's love life? Also it's bucketing down now. In the end he drives back to work.

Meanwhile Annemarie Roser has arrived at Regine's house. She leaves her wet umbrella in the porch and takes her shoes off.

'No, really,' protests Regine, but Annemarie only laughs.

'One Bobby in the house is quite enough!'

The two women sit down in the conservatory and try to guess what could be so special about that piece of land.

'Well, the Animal Welfare League can't afford to turn down 140,000 marks, land or no land. We can find another field for our animals somewhere else. And with that amount of money we can build some first-class stables. And other things too. We'll become a showpiece sanctuary!' Annemarie shakes her head. She still can't take it in.

'The only catch is that Manfred Büschelmeyer wouldn't be investing 140,000 marks unless there was a great deal more to be made. He's on the council and he keeps his ear very close to the ground!'

Briskly Regine uncorks the bottle and pours the champagne with a flourish. 'I've got it!' she says, not noticing that the glass she's filling is overflowing. 'Of course! The area's going to be developed! That's what the buried treasure is!' She bangs the bottle down on the table. 'And Marion knows it too. That's why she turned up at your sanctuary. Schmidt and Büschelmeyer are both after it!' She sits down slowly. 'Isn't that incredible!'

They look at each other.

'And here we are right in the middle of it all!'

Annemarie gives a peal of laughter. 'We've snatched it from under their noses! What's the betting that they've also rung the Drehers? But we got there first!'

'Without having the faintest idea!'

'It's unbelievable! Let's drink to it!'

They raise their glasses. 'And to us!'

Each of them takes a long sip.

'Ooh, that does you good,' sighs Annemarie.

'It certainly does,' agrees Regine. 'But what now?'

'Good question!'

The rain beats down on the conservatory roof as they sit in silence, racking their brains.

Regine watches the rivers of raindrops pouring down the panes of glass. 'We must apply some leverage somewhere,' she says finally.

'But where?'

'How much money could a person make out of a piece of land like that?' Regine reaches for the bottle and, deep in thought, tops up the glasses, which are still only half empty.

Annemarie shrugs her shoulders, takes a sip and thinks about it. 'No idea,' she says finally, 'but it must be a lot, otherwise they wouldn't be trying so hard for it.'

'What if we play them off against each other?'

'To do that we need at least some basic information.'

For a time neither of them says anything.

'A present for his mother on her seventieth birthday!' says Annemarie, shaking her head. 'Who does he think he's kidding?'

Regine looks up. 'You've just given me an idea. I'll ring my mother. She used to work for the council. She must know a bit about these things.'

Dirk goes to Stuttgart. He's decided to work off his anger on a prostitute. That'll show Linda exactly what he thinks of her. Even if she doesn't get to hear about it. When he reaches the city centre it's early afternoon, and he's not sure where the notorious red-light district is. Also he wonders whether he'll find any member of that profession working at this time of day. For a while Dirk drives round the city centre, then he parks his car in a multi-storey car park close to Königstrasse, deciding to try his luck on foot. But the mere price of parking there takes the edge off his vengeful pleasure. This is going to cost him a packet. His head down, he trudges through the rain. To be ready for all eventualities, he withdraws 400 marks from a cash machine on Königstrasse. That's probably cleaned out his account. Dirk looks around and goes down some steps into another street. He'll find some girl who's willing. He'll show Linda that she can't treat him like that. Schmidt – who is Schmidt, after all! Apart from his money, there's nothing to him!

Meanwhile Regine has got hold of her mother and now knows the going prices for land. She rings off, grinning, and then frowns. 'Really, we need only wait for the town to approach us. If they're interested in our plot, the price for undeveloped land is about thirty-five marks per square metre. That would be 350,000 marks . . .'

'But what if they don't approach us?' Annemarie's hand goes to her heart. 'This is all horribly nerve-racking. If they don't, we'll have nothing. We'll have played for high stakes and lost everything. On the other hand, if we sell it tomorrow we'll have the money safely in the bag and we needn't care what happens after that!'

'And what if your sanctuary has to move as a result?'

Annemarie leans back in her chair. 'Then we get compensation and build somewhere else!'

She draws a deep breath, rummages in her bag for Manfred Büschelmeyer's card and asks Regine for the phone. Regine passes it to her with an enquiring look.

'I'm going to go ahead now, because a bird in the hand . . . you know.' She's already dialling.

'Ah, Herr Büschelmeyer, I'm really glad to have got hold of you so quickly. It's Annemarie Roser here. I've got a bit of a problem. The thing is, there's a lady who's also suddenly shown an interest in that piece of land. She'd like to build a stable there, which of course appeals to us more than you building a house for your mother. So I'm sure you'll understand if we have to decline your offer!'

Regine claps her hand to her mouth, suppressing her laughter.

'Well, I don't know whether the lady would wish to match that,' Annemarie is saying, earnestly. 'But of course I'll ask her and then tell you the outcome right away.' She winks at Regine. 'No, I can't tell you that. A lady who moves in all the best circles, but I won't mention names. After all, I'm not revealing your name either, Herr Büschelmeyer. I'll ring you later. Bye for now!'

And she hangs up.

'He's offered seventeen marks. I think I'll accept that!'

'He thinks Marion's bidding too.' Regine raises her glass. 'But my guess is that he's even greedy enough to pay twenty marks!'

Dirk has eventually found a pub that looks disreputable. Hesitantly he goes in. Grotty dives aren't usually his thing, but this time he has no choice. He walks slowly over to the bar. He can't see much of his surroundings because his eyes have to grow used to the semi-darkness. There are two men behind the bar. They don't look very trustworthy types, but they're sure to have the sort of information he wants.

He sits down on one of the bar stools and waits. Eventually one of the men turns to him. 'What's it to be, mate?'

'A beer and a girl,' answers Dirk boldly.

He is answered by a neighing laugh. 'A girl! Bloody hell, d'you think this is a knocking shop?'

Dirk can't answer that, and takes a while to reply.

'What d'you want, then?'

'A beer!'

He wouldn't have touched a girl in this place anyway. You can catch all sorts of things. He'll drink up his beer and then look around for something better. 'Have you got a phone book here?' he asks the other barman, a fellow with a boxer's face and skin-head haircut who's pulling his Pils.

'D'you want to order a girl from Telekom? I can give you an address, mate, if you're that desperate!'

Dirk wouldn't have known what to look under anyway. 'Bars'? 'Establishments'?

'Okay then,' he says, stretching out his hand.

'What? For nothing?' He guffaws across to the other guy at the bar. 'It'll cost you fifty, mate. This bird's top quality. That's absolute peanuts for pussy like that!' He reinforces his words with gestures. 'She'll give you a really good time.'

Dirk has already stopped having a good time. Fifty marks for a scrap of information?

'How much does the . . . er . . . bird charge?'

'Depends what you want.'

That leaves him none the wiser. All this is starting to make him feel very uncomfortable. What's he doing going after this woman when he doesn't even know what she looks like or what she charges? Dirk takes a good look at his informant. He doesn't look as if he won all his bouts in the ring. On the other hand his broken nose shows that he's actually been in some fights, not just read about them and then analysed them as sociological phenomena. So much the worse for Dirk. He wonders how he's going to get out of this situation in one piece.

'What's the problem, mate?' The fellow is facing him, big and brawny. His friend is staring across.

'I . . . I'll think it over.'

The other's expression changes to an ugly scowl. 'Don't give me that crap.'

Dirk is glad that Linda can't see him. Perhaps this expedition wasn't such a good idea.

Tensely he holds his breath. Then he feels a blow across the shoulders, which he takes as a signal for him to retaliate. But firstly he's no fighter, and secondly he's a pacifist.

'Don't bother,' says Stuttgart's answer to Mike Tyson in a patronising tone, grinning at him.

Dirk breathes again. This sounds quite promising.

'Another beer?'

He hasn't even half finished the first one yet. 'No, I'll pay now.'

'Fifteen marks.'

Dirk is staggered and feels he's being taken for a ride. On the other hand it'll be worth fifteen marks to get out of here. He'll put down twenty and then be off. He reaches into his back pocket, but his hand finds nothing. His wallet's not there. He gropes along the dark bar counter. Had he already put his wallet down? A dark foreboding brings out the sweat on the back of his neck. He feels around his left-hand back pocket. Nothing.

The two men watch him suspiciously.

'What are you up to now?' the boxer finally says, baring his teeth in the semi-darkness.

'I can't pay.' Sheepishly Dirk holds up his two empty palms. 'Somebody's obviously nicked my wallet!'

Günther can't bear to stay in the office any longer. Somehow or other he must dispose of that speed camera. He takes one of the company vans and drives towards home. He'll take out the film, wrap up the camera and later on throw it into the river. In this weather no one will be out walking there, and it won't be possible to trace him afterwards because he was wearing gloves and the Römersfeld police won't examine the evidence all that carefully when it's just a matter of a sawn-off camera. If it should come to the worst, he knows a few people of influence, or at least he knows certain things *about* them. Up to now he's always been quite able to look after himself.

And this evening he'll find out how his long-stemmed roses have gone down with Linda. And he'll enthuse a bit about Paris, about the boutiques with the sort of clothes that leave little to the imagination, about the cabarets like the Moulin Rouge or the Lido, and about the first-class hotels with the king-size beds, not forgetting lots of champagne and Alain Delon in the room next door.

Revelling in these thoughts, he feels better again, especially as he sees that Marion is obviously not at home. He reverses towards the garage, uses the automatic mechanism to open the door and parks the van right in front of it. This escapade is starting to be fun. If there's a piece in the paper tomorrow about the sawn-off speed camera, he'll be able to show Linda what a lad he is. There's no adventure for which he's too old – or too tired either.

'Look, son, just hand over the cash. First you're all mouth and now you give us this crap. I wouldn't try it if I was you.' The boxer thrusts his fist under Dirk's nose. Dirk swallows. He's thinking of his teeth. They're his best feature – straight, regular and pearly white. Images from films crowd in on him, and in his mind's eye he sees a face smashed to a pulp.

'My wallet's been stolen, that's not my fault,' he says in an attempt to appease the man. 'I want to pay, but I don't see how I can at the moment!'

He feels a firm grip on his wrist. 'Now what?' Before he knows it his watch is lying on the bar.

'Right, that stays here until you come across with the dosh. Or I can punch you one if that's what you want. Fifteen marks' worth. Just enough to flatten a little turd like you.'

Dirk goes red. 'That watch is worth 500 marks! We're talking about fifteen! That's called extortion, or using undue force!' He sees the other's face and adds automatically, but more quietly, 'Paragraphs 253 and 255 of the criminal code.'

'Oh, we've got a bloody lawyer here! And a little shit like you thinks he can screw us?' Dick can already smell his breath, for the flattened nose is moving dangerously close to his own.

'All right, all right. You can keep the watch until tomorrow and then I'll come back with the money and get it back. But in that case could you lend me another fifty marks? The thing is, I've got no petrol left to get me home.'

First he feels a fist on his collar, then the pavement under him as he is thrown outside. The door bangs shut behind him. Two passers-by give him a wide berth as though he were a drunk. Dazed, he scrambles to his feet. 'And you have to sign for it too,' he mutters, as he tries to brush the wet dirt of the street off his clothes. That watch was a present from Linda. A gift to show her love, as she said at the time. 'At the time,' – it was less than two months ago! The tears start to come. He feels like sitting down in the gutter and bawling his eyes out.

Richi is just about to finish for the day and leave the office when the call comes from Dirk. Dirk has gone to seek help from the police, but they have no time for sentiment, only for facts. The wallet's gone, sure. Thefts like that happen dozens of times every day. The officer opens a book so that Dirk can see for himself how many cases have already been reported today. The wallet business must be booming. His mistake was to use a cash machine in public view. Someone must have been watching and then . . . However hard he thinks back, he can't recall having noticed anything. But the outcome's clear, at any rate. His account's overdrawn, the cash has gone, he's probably lost his watch, and Linda as well. All he needs now is to fail his exam, be evicted from his flat and have his car stolen. No, at least that won't happen. No one would intentionally steal his car. That car is his fortress against the world. And if a lack of money prevents him from driving it, at the very worst he can always sleep in it.

But first he needs to get home, and the only way he can think of is by contacting Richi. The policeman writes down the number, gets the switchboard to put him through to Richi and, when Richi answers, announces, 'Buchholz, Stuttgart Central Police Station.'

Richi is so startled that he almost drops the receiver. Why are the Stuttgart police phoning him? His mind races through all the possible offences he might have committed, but he has an even greater fright when the policeman says that it's about Dirk Wetterstein.

He's killed himself, is his first thought.

But then he hears Dirk on the other end of the line, his voice sounding strangely thin.

Attempted suicide, is Richi's next thought.

'Richi, I'm sorry, but could you possibly come and pick me up? I've been robbed!'

A mugging! Richi leaps from his chair, imagining the most horrible scenes of violence.

'That's terrible!' he exclaims. 'Of course I'll pick you up. Are you okay? Can you walk? Are you still in one piece?'

'It's not that bad, Richi. It's just that my money's gone, and I've run out of petrol and can't buy any more.'

'Oh, I see.' Richi subsides on to the edge of the desk. 'You gave me a real fright. No problem, I'll come straightaway if you can tell me exactly where to find you.'

Dirk tells him, and then says in a low voice, 'And bring a bit more money. I've got to get my watch out of hock.'

'From a pawnshop?'

'No, of course not. It's at a pub, a thug has got it, an ex-boxer or something!'

'Or something,' mutters Richi, putting the phone down with a sense of unease.

Günther has dropped the speed camera into the river and then exchanged the van for his car again. Now he's driving, in the best of spirits, to Linda's neighbourhood. It's almost eight, the rain has stopped, and the bright, hard light coming through the cloud gives the estate a newly washed look. Günther is feeling on top of the world. He's turned the radio on loud and is singing along to a pop song and looking forward to seeing Linda.

Linda is sitting on her balcony, varnishing her toenails, when she sees the car coming round the corner. Her first impulse is to make herself as small as possible and simply not to react. He can't see her from down there. Then she thinks of the huge bouquet of roses, now standing on the small breakfast table, which absolutely took her breath away. A bouquet of thirty Baccara roses is something she's only ever seen in a flower shop, never in someone's home. And it's not even a special occasion.

She hesitates and peers cautiously over the edge of the balcony. She could at least say thank you and offer him a glass of champagne in return. Well, it's hardly giving him something in return, she thinks immediately – the champagne came from him anyway.

The phone rings. It's obviously him, at his usual game: I'm down here in the car. Please, Rapunzel, let down your hair.

And what if I don't happen to feel like it? she asks herself, but she finds that she's already on her feet. She waves briefly over the side of the balcony and is answered by a signal from the lights of the Mercedes. Then the car disappears into the basement garage, and the ringing stops before Linda has reached the phone. Well, well, this is the first time he's put his car away out of sight. Walking on her heels so as not to mess up the fresh varnish on her toenails, Linda takes a quick look round the flat, tidies up using the open-the-cupboard-and-shove-everything-in method, and then presses the buzzer as the doorbell's already ringing.

In a few moments Günther is leaping out of the lift with youthful vigour, running up to her, kissing her hand and laughing as he asks, 'Isn't it a glorious day?'

'A glorious day?' she repeats, closing the door behind him. 'It's been raining nearly all day!'

'I didn't notice, I was so much looking forward to the evening!'

'How did you know' – she suddenly realises that she's reverted to the polite form of address and changes back to the familiar 'du' again – 'how did you know I'd be here?'

He stops in front of the voluminous bunch of roses. 'An inner voice whispered it to me.'

'Thank you for the wonderful roses.' Linda kisses him lightly on the cheek. 'I've never seen such a bouquet in my whole life. It's fantastic!'

'It was my pleasure, and I'm glad you like it – but possibly that bucket isn't quite appropriate,' he grins.

Linda looks at the blue plastic bucket that she's put the roses in.

'It was all I could manage, I haven't . . .'

'Tomorrow I'll bring you a champagne bucket,' Günther interrupts. 'That'll do for everything. From champagne cooler to flower vase to chamberpot.' He roars with laughter at his joke.

Linda clears her throat. 'Would you like a drink?'

'Red wine out of the fridge?'

'Or champagne . . .'

'Is there something to celebrate?' asks Günther, giving her the look that, years ago, his wife had said could melt icebergs.

Linda hesitates. She knows where it will lead if she says yes now. She studies him. He's not exactly Leonardo DiCaprio. On the other hand, he's past the age of youthful egotism. She's getting proof of that delivered to her door every day.

'Maybe,' she says, with a slight smile. 'Who knows what life may bring?'

What rubbish, she thinks, it's perfectly obvious what it'll bring.

It'll bring what I want it to, thinks Günther, nodding towards her. 'Why don't we just wait and see?'

He opens a bottle and fills two glasses, while Linda puts a second chair out on the balcony. He won't start trying to tear my clothes off out here, more or less in public view, she tells herself. She smiles at Günther, who is following behind her with the two glasses. 'Very romantic,' he says teasingly.

'It was romantic yesterday too – until there was that minor interruption,' she returns, taking a glass from him.

'Wives generally have little sense of the romantic,' he says, raising his glass.

'When it comes to romance with other women, you mean.' Linda takes a sip of her drink and sits down.

'So censorious today?' Günther sits down opposite her. His face is tanned, his blue polo shirt, with white stripes on the open collar, gives him a look of freshness; he makes you think of leisure and sunshine and radiates the relaxed aura of the good life.

Linda thinks of Dirk, of her desire for him, that constant ache in her stomach – but what was there apart from that? She was expected to organise everything, and as far as possible finance everything, and be available when the lord and master had time – but did he ever have time for her? The things she cared about didn't interest him, while she was automatically expected to share *his* interests.

Really she was just stupid.

Physically satisfied, but stupid.

'I'm thinking,' she says, looking into Günther's face. 'I'm thinking about where this will lead.'

Günther holds his breath. This is going faster than he'd expected. He leans a little towards her across the table and places his hand on hers. 'That's up to you,' he says softly. 'From the moment I first saw you at my birthday party I fell in love with you. I can't sleep or eat or think any more because of you. But it's your decision.'

Linda doesn't know what to say, and picks up her glass. She's not the slightest bit in love with him. But can she tell him that? Wouldn't that be unkind, especially just now, when he's being so open about his feelings?

'I . . .' she says, and then breaks off and takes another sip. She looks at him over the rim of the glass, feeling like a mouse being watched by a snake. 'I just don't know!' She puts her glass down. 'It's all going too fast for me. You're married, I'm in a relationship, I like everything to be clear and straight-forward.'

'What's clear to me is that you are the woman I've always dreamed of.'

'Yes, but what does that mean? For me?' Linda puts her legs up on the seat and clasps her arms around them. She's agitated and she feels shivery. What is she doing? Haggling over her own life?

'It means that I'll treat you like a princess if you'll let me!'

If you'll let me? Yes, of course, only then.

'I need to think about it. Honestly, Günther, I can't decide just like that. I mean, it's a matter of feelings . . .'

'I have those,' he interrupts, 'deep, sincere feelings.'

Linda withdraws her hand.

'What I'm trying to say is that *my* feelings come into it too!'

Günther clasps his hands together. 'Take your time. I've told you that the decision is yours.'

They study each other in silence for a while, then Linda gazes out over the balcony rail, letting her eyes wander. She looks towards town. There, beneath one of those roofs, lives Dirk. What's he doing? Why hasn't he been in touch?

'Do you still love him?' Günther asks suddenly. Involuntarily he holds his breath. If she says 'yes' now, he may as well give up. His heaviest guns would be powerless against that.

But Linda hesitates.

Love, she thinks. I've no idea. I really don't know any more what I feel towards him. Anger? No, really she only feels hurt. Longing? Above all she'd like to know what's going on in his mind, how he could part from her like that, from one day to the next, without a word. As though there had never been anything between them.

No, it's not love. At least, not any more.

But that doesn't mean that she can simply switch over from Dirk to Günther.

She leaves his question unanswered; Günther doesn't pursue it. 'Are you free tomorrow evening?' he asks instead. Tomorrow

Klaus will be driving to Liechtenstein with Günther's million marks, laying the foundations for his future life. 'There'll be something to celebrate, and I'd like to take you out somewhere special.' He smiles, and a look of pleasure comes into his eyes. 'As a sort of taster of Paris.'

Linda doesn't answer. She takes a sip from her glass, then nods thoughtfully. 'That would be nice.'

'Perhaps it would be even nicer if you bought yourself a really super dress for tomorrow evening.' He ceremoniously pulls a 500-mark note out of his breast pocket and places it next to her champagne glass.

'That's . . .' protests Linda, but Günther is already rising to his feet.

'I've got an appointment, so I'm afraid I haven't got time to discuss it. Just take it, and think of it as being for both of us.' He walks round the table to her, and bends to kiss her on the forehead.

Linda stands up slowly. Günther puts his arms around her. She leans her head against his, smells him, breathes in his slightly tangy dry-grass fragrance; it wouldn't be so difficult to succumb.

She releases herself and kisses him on both cheeks.

'Thank you. See you tomorrow!'

A few minutes later she is watching from the balcony as he drives out of the basement garage.

Next morning Marion is already sitting at the breakfast table when Günther comes down at seven o'clock. Silently she places the local news section of the paper in front of him. 'Speed camera sawn off' is the main headline plastered across it. 'Obviously the work of hooligans,' Marion reads out gleefully, smiling at him. 'Günther Schmidt, a hooligan. I like that!' With a single slice she decapitates her egg.

'What are you trying to say?' Günther pulls his chair up to the table. Marion is wearing an ice-blue trouser suit, and even at this hour she's already perfectly groomed and made up. Just as Günther has asked her to be all these years.

'Nothing,' she says, offering him a basket of freshly baked rolls. 'I just find it funny. There are things about you that I would never have thought possible. And yet we've been married long enough!'

'You said it,' he mutters, choosing a roll. Then he looks up quickly. 'What things do you mean?' he demands. Has she been following me again? he wonders, trying to think of anything he may have overlooked.

'Well, that you go around sawing off speed cameras, for instance!'

'Oh, that!' Relieved, he cuts his roll in half.

'Why, what did you think I meant?' Marion looks at him thoughtfully and feels something building up inside her. She already knows this feeling: suspicion.

'I thought you meant my latest deal,' Günther says, trying to lead the conversation off on to something innocuous. He reflects on what sort of deal he can fob her off with if she should pursue the matter.

But Marion has understood. He means that piece of land. Obviously once again there's been more going on than Manfred has got wind of. Or more than he's prepared to tell her. She'll go to the land registry today, find out who owns that plot of land and do something about it herself. After all, some of the money in their account is hers. She brought it into the marriage, so he can never tell her that she's wholly without means. There is some money that she can do exactly what she likes with. Even use it to get the better of her husband!

At this early hour Klaus is already on the road because he wants to arrive in Liechtenstein in good time. The lockable executive

case that Günther grandly handed over to him in his office is in
the boot. Together they counted the notes, sorted them into
bundles, stacked them in the case and set the combination.
Somehow they felt as if they'd just pulled off some particularly
successful coup. Like the Great Train Robbers in England in
1963, or like Huckleberry Finn and Tom Sawyer after their
escape from Indian Joe. It makes them feel strong, having a
secret like that. True comrades, men standing shoulder to
shoulder.

That heroic mood lasted for some time, but now Klaus puts
on a classical music CD and simply enjoys the feeling of having
a million marks in cash behind him. The things he could do
now! Get on the next plane, disappear to South America, enjoy
the rest of his days with a coffee-coloured beauty. But would the
money last for the rest of his days? And wouldn't Günther eventually come and spoil the rest of his days for him?

He drives to Ulm and from there takes the motorway towards
Bregenz. It's a long time since he's been to Lake Constance, and
he decides that on the way back he'll drive into Lindau and find
a good restaurant there. By then he'll have earned a treat. In the
Pfänder Tunnel in Austria the traffic comes to a complete stand-
still. Klaus is wedged in between other cars and imagines what
it would be like if this traffic jam had been created deliberately.
What would he do if he found himself surrounded by armed
men? Flight would be impossible, and so would attack; he's no
Pierce Brosnan. Klaus loosens his tie, turns the air-conditioning
to a cooler setting and looks anxiously around. In front there's a
green Opel Kadett of indeterminate age, and behind him a family
camper van. Nothing too intimidating. Or is there? Wouldn't the
camper have room for at least six people? He tries, by looking in
his mirror, to see the driver's face through the windscreen. A
woman, that's good. Klaus relaxes. But wait a minute, when it
comes to terrorism aren't women the most brutal and cruel and

sometimes actually the leaders? Then he sees the passenger door open and a man get out. His heart starts to pound; the guy comes past the boot and walks with obvious determination towards Klaus. Klaus takes the precaution of pressing the central locking button. The gentle pop all round reassures him, but then it occurs to him that the windows aren't made of bullet-proof glass. Any idiot can shoot right through them. Is the guy carrying anything? Now Klaus is looking straight into the bearded face pressed against his side window.

'Go away!' he yells, flapping his hands at him. Any moment now there'll be a bang. Sawn-off shotguns are supposed to make terrible holes in you. Wipe out your whole face, just like that! And he wasn't planning to pinch the money. He had no evil intentions. Just to live, to have a few more happy years with Regine – oh my God, the fellow's shouting something. This is it!

'Turn the engine off, stinker!'

Klaus sits there, rigid with terror.

The man beats against the window with his fist.

'Engine off, this is a traffic jam, you fool!'

Turn the engine off? Gradually it dawns on Klaus that he's not the victim of a robbery. On the contrary, those people in the camper see themselves as the victims of his exhaust fumes.

'Oh yes, absolutely, of course, right away. I'm terribly sorry!' His heartbeat hasn't calmed down yet. The guy has made a gesture with his middle finger and gone back to the camper, but it takes a bit longer for the sweating to stop. 'It wasn't intentional,' says Klaus, more to himself this time, 'honestly!' Then he sees the car in front of him starting to move. Trembling, he turns the key. As he starts the engine he avoids looking in the rear-view mirror.

Manfred Büschelmeyer is sitting in his office, sharpening pencils. That cow at the job centre still hasn't phoned. Is she trying to wear him down, or what? He can't go any higher than seventeen marks. He'd be cutting his own throat. Anything above seventeen marks would be risky.

The phone rings. Ah! At last! He quickly lifts the receiver.

'Hello, Manfred, Marion Schmidt here!'

Oh God, if he'd known he'd have got the receptionist to say he wasn't there.

'What's the latest from the front?'

She talks as if she'd served in the forces, that officer's daughter who'd never be declared fit for anything. And as if she didn't know the answer perfectly well herself. Competing with him and feigning ignorance so as to get information out of him.

He tries to sound as indifferent as possible. 'It doesn't seem to be such a hot property after all. At any rate, no one on the council is interested in it!'

Aha, thinks Marion, now he's trying to pull the wool over my eyes. She looks out into the garden: the day promises to be fine, and she can see the gardener coming in through the gate.

The gardener is always the murderer, it occurs to her. 'So, it was just hot air?' she asks.

'Nothing but hot air,' answers Manfred, breaking off the pencil points that he's just sharpened. 'You really can forget about it, Marion, sorry!' Does she already have a contract signed? Did she offer more than seventeen marks? Does she know that he's the other bidder? Is she just revelling in his defeat, playing with him, enjoying his attempts at evasion?

'Pity,' says Marion slowly. 'Perhaps next time, Manfred. It's a case of losing the battle but not the war, if you know what I mean.'

I don't know anything at all, he thinks, furiously slamming down the phone, I only know that that bitch from the job centre hasn't rung. And she won't ring, because she's already done the deal. Game, set and match to Marion! So much money, and it's slipped through his fingers! It could so easily have been his.

For once, at last, he had thought he held the winning card. Those Schmidts ought to be wiped off the face of the earth!

Annemarie Roser is lying back in her chair at the job centre, daydreaming. So this is how you make money. 160,000 marks in an afternoon, just like that. 160,000 marks. For that money, on her salary, she'd have to work for three years and eight months without ever spending anything. 160,000 marks could mean new furniture for her living room, a new kitchen and a new car. Or she could simply move to a new flat. Perhaps even a little house out in the country. Or alternatively a world tour every year, and skiing in the winter. Actually that's the version that appeals to her most. She closes her eyes, puts her feet up on the desk and loses herself in her fantasies until she's jolted out of them by loud knocking. Oh heavens, yes, there are all those people sitting outside because they're looking for jobs. If only she could just offer them her own job and float off into a new life.

Klaus is approaching the border In Feldkirch, still in Austria, once again his heart's in his mouth. He doesn't quite know why, because nothing can actually happen to him once he crosses into Liechtenstein. There's no requirement to declare cash. Only when it's invested abroad does it have to be declared for the sake of the balance of payments statistics, together with any interest it earns. Klaus also knows that this declaration applies only to foreign trade and investment activity and the exchange of goods and services between countries. And he knows that the statistics are subject to data-protection regulations. Information cannot be released for any other purpose, either to the tax office or to any other body.

Although he tries to use his knowledge to calm himself down, his nerves are on edge because the unknown quantity in his calculations is the customs official. He doesn't know how a customs man will react if he finds bundles of notes amounting to one million marks in Klaus's executive case. Nothing can happen to him personally, because he has the documentation from the bank to prove his legal ownership of the notes. But it could still be awkward because the man would be bound to investigate whether or not there is some link with blackmail, kidnapping, robbery or drug-dealing. And even if the outcome is negative, notes on the investigation might find their way to who knows where. And although the million in his boot has already been taxed, the one thing Klaus doesn't want is to leave any kind of a trail in the official records.

At this thought Klaus begins to perspire again. He resolves to calm himself down a bit before approaching the border. He feels sure that dollar signs are flashing in his eyes. Any border guard worth his salt will see straightaway that he's taking a million marks for a drive in his boot. He parks in a car park and walks up and down a bit to try and get a grip on himself. He daren't go far, otherwise someone might pinch his car. BMWs are popular – even without a million marks thrown in as a bonus.

I must try to think about something trivial, he tells himself, applying some autogenic training techniques. But all he can think of is his divorce from his first wife, and Regine saying she'd like to fly away on holiday, and his ailing bank balance, and there he is back at the million again. After circling the car park for a third time he feels that this isn't doing any good. His shirt is sticking to his back; it's simply too hot to keep on walking round and round the car.

He gets back in, listens to Brahms's Variations on a Theme by Haydn and feels himself gradually relaxing. After eighteen minutes the piece is at an end, and Klaus hears it through again. As he plays it for the third time he starts the car and drives to the border. With Brahms giving him moral support, he passes calmly through Austrian customs and greets the Swiss customs officials as blithely as Alice in Wonderland. 'Nothing to declare,' he says, and they wave him through. As he rolls along the road to Vaduz a broad grin spreads over his face. He's done it. The money is about to disappear.

When Linda is called to the phone at work she's afraid it may be Günther. For him to find out where and how she earns her money is the last thing she wants.

But it's Greta Kremer, confirming the details of the lingerie party at her house in Kirchweiler.

'I wouldn't have forgotten you,' Linda laughs, relieved.

'I just wanted to make sure, because we've got a good number of people together. I'm sure it'll be terrific fun, and I think you'll be able to sell quite a lot.'

'Thanks, I could do with that!'

'Yes, I bet you could!'

Linda slowly hangs up. She has to work herself silly for a whole long evening, talk till she's blue in the face, laugh at stupid jokes and let people stare at her, and all for an amount of money that Günther can simply put down on the table for her.

Now you're thinking like a tart, she immediately reproves herself. Take care, Linda, that on your way up you don't slip and fall!

Dirk has had a sleepless night. Richi proved himself a true friend yesterday: he collected him from the police station and they marched together to the pub in a sort of closed formation of youthful male force. Dirk found the pub again at once and went boldly in. As before, he could see nothing at first, but when his eyes had got used to the twilight he whispered over his shoulder to Richi, who was standing right behind him, ready for anything, 'This is the place!'

'Good, let's get on with it then!'

'Here are your fifteen marks,' said Dirk to the barman, who was standing behind the counter with his back to him. He turned round, looked at him briefly with his deep-set eyes and held out his hand. 'Thanks.'

Dirk hesitated. The barman snapped his fingers, then quickly opened and closed his hand encouragingly. 'Come on then, let's have it. I don't know what for, but if you want to get rid of some money, son, that's fine by me!'

Was this some sort of a bad joke?

'I left an expensive watch with your colleague earlier on as security because my wallet had just been stolen and I couldn't pay for my drink.' Dirk was making an effort to speak very clearly in order to hide his agitation. 'The drink cost fifteen marks. Here they are. And now I'd like my watch back!'

'My colleague? What is all this crap? I haven't got a colleague, as you call it. This is a one-man show!'

'That's not true!' said Dirk indignantly. 'An hour ago, maybe a bit more, a bloke with a broken nose served me. And pocketed my watch. And now I want it back!'

The fellow facing him eyed him coldly, then his eyes narrowed to slits and he roared with laughter. 'If I tell him that, you'll soon have a broken nose too, you tosser! That was Eddy, pal, and if you've got a score to settle, you'd better go and sort it out with him. He's a customer, like you!'

'Eddy who?' puts in Richi.

'Eddy's just called Eddy. Sometimes he's around, sometimes not. If he's got a valuable watch on his hands he probably won't be around for a while. But you can wait if you like. It's all the same to me who buys drinks here.'

'I'm going to the police.' Dirk turns on his heel.

'Well then, leave the cash here. Or do you want me to have the law on *you* for not paying?'

*

Dirk didn't go to the police because he would have felt too much of a fool, and now he's still lying in bed, but feeling terrible, a total wreck. A prospective lawyer hoping one day to handle difficult cases, and he can't cope with a simple case of a stolen wallet! Law books versus life: how ironic. He can't get yesterday's experience out of his head – that fellow with the shifty eyes, and the distinct feeling that during their conversation Eddy was sitting in the next room and that afterwards the two of them probably rolled about laughing at him. Dirk, the laughing stock. He really has had better days. But it's all Linda's fault.

She hasn't contacted him.

She's acting as though he doesn't exist!

For a while he tosses and turns, pulls the cover up over himself, pushes it down again, lies on his front, then turns on to his back; he feels edgy and restless.

And then suddenly he sits bolt upright.

He shouldn't have ignored her invitation to supper. Perhaps that really hurt her feelings. More than he suspected.

He runs the fingers of both hands through his hair.

Should he phone her?

A glance at the clock tells him that it's almost time for her lunch break. Perhaps . . . With one bound he's out of bed, then under the shower, drying himself with lightning speed and slipping, still damp and unshaven, into his jeans and T-shirt. A moment later he's pulling his clothes off again: she likes him better in the black jeans and black polo shirt.

And she doesn't care for stubble, either.

In his agitation he cuts himself twice, then he runs down the stairs of the old building, taking three steps at a time. Who knows why Schmidt was with her? There was probably some perfectly innocent reason. He's going to throw that crappy female psychology book away. How can a book know what's going on inside the head of his Linda? As he turns into the street where Linda's shop is located he sees her on the opposite pavement. For a moment he catches his breath. She really is stunningly beautiful. The way she moves, her confident manner, her wonderful black hair: everything about her follows a mysterious rhythm, it curves and flows. And this total work of art is mine, thinks Dirk proudly. Joyfully he waves to her, but Linda disappears into a shop. She hasn't seen him. And it looks as if she didn't even feel that he was close by. Aren't lovers supposed to have a sixth sense for that sort of thing?

Dirk walks on further and then stops, still on the opposite side of the road. He looks incredulously at the name of the shop. 'Indra's' – of all places, she's gone into the most expensive, most fashionable boutique in Römersfeld. What's she doing there? Is she looking for a new job? Has she perhaps lost her old job, and he didn't even know about it?

From the other side of the road Dirk can't see what she's doing in there. So he saunters inconspicuously on, then crosses the road, walks quickly back and approaches the large windows of the boutique.

He takes the last few steps slowly and cautiously. Just when he's reached the front of the shop and is able to look in, Linda spins in front of a big mirror, holding in front of her a dream of a dress in black lace. As she does so, their eyes meet for a fraction of a second, Linda inside, Dirk outside. Linda stops for a moment with her back to him, then turns first her head and then her whole body towards the window and towards Dirk, holding the dress in front of her like a protective shield. Dirk stands rooted to the spot, staring fixedly at her. Linda waits for him to show some reaction. But she can't detect any trace of emotion in his face. So she slowly turns round again, goes over to the dresses hanging on a long rail and looks at one dress after another.

Dirk is completely paralysed. He feels like a dog that's been beaten, but he doesn't know why. Why didn't Linda come rushing out, thrilled to see him? What has come between them, apart from that thick pane of glass? Of course I could go in and ask her, he thinks, but would that be right? She's obviously more interested in new clothes.

Out of the corner of her eye Linda sees him walk away. So that's how a great love dies. He can't even be bothered to come in and talk to her. He doesn't give a damn how she is. Or what she's thinking or feeling. He simply stares at her and then runs away. Just like that.

She's lost all desire to buy a dress. She goes outside, but Dirk's already out of sight. The pain is intense, she can feel it between her heart and her stomach. He was never really committed to her, and this realisation hurts. He's probably already got some other girl installed in his grotty place, and now *she* thinks she's really lucky to have got him. The idiot!

Linda goes back to work. Work is the best remedy for heartache, even if it's only unpacking goods and arranging them on the shelves.

Klaus, meanwhile, has opened an account at a bank in Vaduz and paid in the million marks. This was the easy part: the Liechtenstein banker didn't bat an eyelid at the size of the sum. The meeting with a counterpart of Klaus's, a Liechtenstein financial consultant, will be more tricky. He's to become the chief executive of the company in order to preserve anonymity. Otherwise the trail would be too easy to follow. And this is precisely what Klaus wants to prevent. However matters develop, the shares will be in his name, but the superstructure will screen him.

On the stroke of four Annemarie Roser reaches for the phone. Time to knock off at last! She doesn't even need to look at her watch – after all these years she knows instinctively. Slowly she dials Manfred Büschelmeyer's number. It takes only one ring before the receiver is picked up. Annemarie smiles to herself. He's obviously been waiting for her call.

'Herr Büschelmeyer? Yes, in principle nothing stands in the way of our deal.'

She hears him hesitate.

'But?' he asks at last.

'Well, as I said, there is a lady bidding against you.' Tensely, Annemarie stares at a point on the white wall opposite.

There's a moment's silence, then he asks breathlessly, 'And what does that mean?'

'I could decide in your favour in return for a small premium.'

'How small?'

Annemarie's demand seems huge to her, but she must go through with it now. You have to play for high stakes to win.

'10,000 marks.'

'Aren't you making enough on the deal as it is?'

'I'm only the intermediary between you and the Animal Welfare League. Or, of course, between . . .'

Manfred Büschelmeyer knows what she means. Between Marion Schmidt and the Animal Welfare League. But would Marion Schmidt pay such a high commission? He can't ask her that. And he daren't assume that she wouldn't.

'Just a moment, please,' he says, getting out his calculator. Assuming a middling selling price of thirty-seven marks a square metre for the undeveloped land, a hectare bought at seventeen marks a square metre plus a commission of 10,000 marks would still leave a profit of a cool 190,000 marks.

All the same, he says, 'Rather high, your commission.'

'Agents take more than that.'

That's true enough.

'Well,' he says, grinning, 'one's bound to ask oneself whether it's worth it – but you know, my mother . . . and sons will go a long way to please their mothers!'

'Yes, sometimes even too far!'

'Pardon?'

'I hope she'll be happy in her little house next to the animal sanctuary.'

'It's my dearest wish.' He clears his throat. 'When and where shall we draw up the contract?'

'Peter Lang, my lawyer, will draw it up. If it's acceptable to you, everything will be finalised, once we've been over it with Herr Lang, by tomorrow evening. Oh, and before I forget, in cash, of course, Herr Büschelmeyer!'

'The commission in cash – or what?'

'The commission in cash, and if you want to give me a cheque for the rest I'll obviously have to clear it through the bank before I sign the contract. Then it may take a day longer. I'm sure you'll understand.'

Cash? How can I get my hands on so much cash right away? Manfred Büschelmeyer writes one figure after another on a piece of paper: 180,000.

'Of course,' he says. After the numbers he draws three big exclamation marks.

Dr Jürgen Berger is an absolute pro, Klaus can see that at a glance. They've arranged to meet at his office in Vaduz. Klaus nearly arrives late, not having managed to find the place right away. It's in a modern building, and among the many name-plates is one indicating Berger's office. When at last, on a spacious landing, Klaus is standing outside the right door, his Liechtenstein associate answers the bell in person, then leads him down a narrow corridor and in through the first door on the right. Klaus cannot see into the adjoining rooms, but as he can hear phones ringing non-stop he assumes that it's a pretty busy place. Dr Berger – the complete businessman in his grey suit and discreetly striped tie – looks thoroughly sound to Klaus, apart from the signet ring on the little finger of his left hand. Klaus is always suspicious of men who wear jewellery, but as this ring bears a family crest, Klaus can just about tolerate it. In all other respects Berger seems irreproachable. A full head of hair with a rigorously straight parting, a high forehead, a forceful chin and not too feminine a mouth. Full lips are another thing that Klaus doesn't like to see on men. He classes such men as half-baked youths, sentimental and unreliable types, wimps. Berger seems to him, at first sight anyway, to be just the right man for the job.

Berger gets straight down to business. He offers Klaus a leather chair as he himself sits down at his desk, then he asks Klaus to run briefly through what he's already told him over the phone, and he makes a few notes. Finally he looks up. 'I see no difficulty in reactivating your company,' he says. 'You are the sole proprietor, Herr Raak, and you and two businessmen from Liechtenstein, whose names I'll give you later today, will constitute the board of directors. I shall be the chief executive and hence the company's authorised representative. I shall effect purchases and sales.'

Berger leafs through his notepad for a moment. 'The share capital at present amounts to 100,000 Swiss francs – is that correct?'

'Exactly.'

'Right.' Jürgen Berger picks up his ball-point pen. 'The next step will be for the company to take out a loan with a Liechtenstein bank in order to finance the purchase of the firms and property from Günther Schmidt.'

Klaus nods.

'What sum are we talking about?' asks Jürgen Berger, looking up.

'About 500,000 francs.'

He makes a note for his own reference, snaps his pad shut and gives Klaus a quick glance. 'My salary as chief executive will be 1,000 francs a month, and the two members of the board will receive 3,000 francs each for their expenses. Paid annually.'

'While we're on that point,' adds Klaus, 'you'll need to know that I shall be getting 10,000 francs a year as chairman of the board.'

Berger acknowledges this information with a nod. 'Right. Since we appear to be agreed on all points, I'll have my name entered on the legal register as chief executive.'

'How long will that take?' Klaus glances at his watch, though even as he does so it strikes him as absurd.

Berger impatiently dismisses the question. 'That's not a lengthy process here in Liechtenstein. For the German end, set up a meeting for Günther Schmidt and myself with a solicitor in' – he looks quickly at his notepad – 'Römersfeld. But first Herr Schmidt must make sure that there are no obstacles to the sale; in other words, he needs to check whether the banks are willing for a sale to go ahead. Obviously I don't know to what extent his building and his land may be mortgaged. As soon as that's clarified, the company will buy the firms and property from Herr Schmidt at the agreed price. If everything goes through reasonably quickly, the company will be awash with funds inside a week!' He laughs, revealing large, uneven teeth.

Klaus joins in the laughter. This is a pleasant prospect; what appeals to him still more is the idea of what might follow. If Günther were to overdo it with Linda and have a heart attack or depart this life in some other way, he'd be able to dismiss his chief executive, Dr Jürgen Berger, with no trouble at all.

Towards five o'clock Günther starts to feel vaguely unsettled. He's looking forward to this evening immensely. He's reserved a table at the Palace, a first-class hotel with a three-star restaurant, far enough from Römersfeld for them not to meet anyone they know, but close enough for them to stay in the mood on the journey back. Or would he do better to book a room for the night there? Yesterday Linda seemed pretty receptive to his advances, not to say really up for it. He tries to play through the situation in his mind, but there's always a catch: Marion. If he stays out overnight, she'll pursue him like a fury for days. He needs an alibi. Where could he plausibly have to go off to for the night at such short notice? Whom could he get to back up his story convincingly? And what reason could he give to explain why Marion wouldn't be able to contact him at the place where he claimed to be staying?

Thinking about it in his car on the way from one of his building sites to his office, he can't find a solution. Which of his friends could he confide in? Manfred Büschelmeyer comes to mind, his old comrade in arms. But is he really a friend? Wasn't it just the council, and the game to see which of them could use information to better advantage, that had forged the link between them?

A game that he had always won, incidentally.

Just before Römersfeld the traffic slows to a crawl. At the head of the queue Günther can make out a tractor. The drivers directly behind it obviously aren't willing to risk trying to overtake, and for him, twenty cars back, there's no chance. Günther inches along, swearing out loud, and finally, as a distraction, turns the radio on. News, followed by the traffic report with details of the usual hold-ups. He listens with only half an ear, but suddenly he starts to feel overheated.

'A81 Stuttgart to Singen, congestion causing interruption to traffic flow north of Sindelfingen, delays expected.'

Interruption, delays . . . what a humiliation if that were to happen to him this evening!

He tries desperately to remind himself how it was last time

with Marion. On his birthday it was still okay – but does that signify anything with an organ which has a mind of its own?

What if *it* doesn't want to?

He'd never get over the humiliation, it would be just too embarrassing.

But is there a danger of that happening?

He tries to imagine Linda naked. Or wearing a suspender belt, with her rounded bottom, and topless. God, not so long ago it worked like clockwork. The very thought of her moist anticipation on the balcony had a phenomenal effect. Even though at that time he wasn't anticipating anything. Moist or otherwise.

And what about now?

Günther looks down at his lap doubtfully.

There's nothing doing, except that the tractor is turning off down a farm track. Here we go, things are moving again, he says out loud, addressing his flies.

Then he consoles himself. I guess I'm not in the mood yet. Out on the building site all day, sweaty and weary, how is one to get a hard on? It'll be different tonight!

He passes the sign for Römersfeld.

And what if it isn't? a voice inside him asks. Can he risk it?

Günther grabs his phone and calls his usual chemist. Frau Mattuscheck answers. He can't tell *her* what he wants.

'Could I possibly speak to your husband, Frau Mattuscheck?'

'What's it about?'

Damn!

'Oh, sorry, we're about to get cut off – I'll call again later!' He rubs the receiver to and fro a bit on his trousers and then switches off. He can be pretty sure Frau Mattuscheck is no expert on mobile phones, not enough to know she's not genuinely been cut off. Even assuming she knows what he meant at all.

*

After putting the phone down Manfred did a little dance of joy round his desk. That was settled; now he could get on with the day's business with his mind at rest. First he did the rounds of the DIY store, hoping that moving around would calm him down, then in the general office he asked for a coffee and had himself filled in on the latest store gossip – his personal 'Big Brother is watching you' routine – and now, an hour later, he's back in his office. He casts an eye over the desk. Next to the signature folder, still waiting to be dealt with, there are piles of letters, faxes and figures, and he comes to a halt before it. Only one question still remains: his credit-worthiness with his bank. The deal has to be done quickly; he'll have to make that clear to them. Only he doesn't know how banks feel about quickly done deals just at present. Unfortunately Annemarie Roser's phone call came too late for him to go to the bank and find out. The only thing he can do after four o'clock on a Wednesday is have a statement printed out, and that's no use.

With a sigh he sits down, picks up the faxes and skims through the first one. A job application. By fax. Amazing! But he's got one thing right, this young fellow, and that's the respectful way he has addressed the fax to him as 'The Manager'. And damn it all, quite right too. He's the manager of the biggest DIY store in Römersfeld. So why should any bank deny him a small loan?

Günther is now driving round the edge of the old town centre for the fifth time. He needs a parking space near the chemist's – and soon, because time's moving on. And somehow he has to have a word with Herr Mattuscheck at a moment when his wife isn't standing next to him or pricking up her ears two shelves away. A phone call will be safest. If need be, he can always say it wasn't him. A practical joke, somebody imitating his voice. Probably a Red. Or better still, a Green, who wants to turn the chemist's into a muesli shop. Third World and all that kind of thing. Your typical red-socks-with-green-stripes. The application's already with the committee.

The phone's already redialling. Günther's in luck – Arno Mattuscheck himself answers. While the chemist is still doing his phone-answering spiel, Günther suddenly thinks of a way he can keep himself out of the firing line.

'Herr Mattuscheck, you know that it's our mayor's birthday soon.'

'Oh, is it?'

'Yes, it is. We've thought of a special kind of . . . well, let's say something to fortify him!'

'Really? Well, I dare say I've got something suitable, just a minute – along the lines of vitamins perhaps . . .'

'Sex, Herr Mattuscheck, along the lines of sex!'

Silence at the other end. Surely they haven't really been cut off? Günther looks frantically at the display. No, full output. 'Herr Mattuscheck, did you get that?'

'Isn't that . . .' Herr Mattuscheck obviously can't think what to say, and perhaps his wife's standing next to him too. Günther drives to the edge of the road and switches on his warning lights, because now he's afraid that his reception really might get worse.

'You know that you need a prescription for that!'

'But not when it's to be a surprise for the mayor, Herr Mattuscheck, surely! We're all prepared to make a decent contribution, we'll pool our money for it. How much would it cost?'

'1,100 marks for thirty!'

'Well, there you are.' In his rear-view mirror Günther can see a police car moving over to his lane. 'Our mayor's worth that much to us! Can I pick it up straightaway?' He drives off before the police car can pull in behind him and signs to its occupants apologetically as they catch up and draw alongside him. They're obviously discussing what they should do. Günther looks across at them again. He knows one of them. Don't make a fuss; us guys have to look out for each other.

'This really puts me in a difficult position,' he hears Mattuscheck saying.

'Me too, in fact doubly so!' Surely that policeman's not going to pull him over now? That's all he needs.

'How do you mean?'

'Well, the mayor fancies Viagra for his birthday, and we're stuck for a prescription. His wife will be livid. Which is not very pleasant for you . . .'

'Oh, his wife . . .?'

'Even so, you're taking professional confidentiality seriously, aren't you, Herr Mattuscheck?' The police car is gradually over-taking him and driving on. Günther breathes again.

Mattuscheck's voice sounds muted and husky: 'Birthday night and all that?'

'And all that! Precisely!'

'I wouldn't have thought it of her!'

Günther grins and pictures Ilse Wetterstein's next visit to the chemist's. 'Nor would we, but we're glad to grant her that bit of pleasure.'

'But you'll have to come to the back door in ten minutes' time if you can manage it. And cash, if you don't mind!'

Manfred has looked through his mail and made a list of what he needs to do tomorrow. Today he just can't concentrate, he keeps having distracting thoughts. He'll sign a few more papers and then go. Of the documents that his secretary has left for him to read through and sign, one batch consists of letters, another of suppliers' offers, and finally there are a few cheques. He won't do anything with the offers today; tomorrow he'll have a clearer head for them. The letters are fine – he scribbles his initials on them – and then he looks at the cheques. They're mainly payments for the alterations for the extended gardening section, which is expected to produce an enormous volume of sales. People in Römersfeld like gardening; they all compare their own front gardens with those of their neighbours, and now that economic downturn has left some of them with more time on their hands, where better to work off their frustration, fury or surplus energy than in the garden? That's Manfred's calculation, and he's confident of being proved right. With a flourish he signs the first few cheques, and then pauses.

He sits motionless for a few seconds, then riffles through the cheques and does a rough calculation in his head. Something like 240,000 marks.

He puts the cheques aside and gazes into space for some time before allowing himself to admit what's taking shape in the deep recesses of his mind.

He looks at the dates of the invoices. The accounts department has responded quickly in order to make sure of getting all the discounts. Quite right, given the size of the sums involved. Even so – what firm pays quite so promptly? Six weeks is the norm, so for these payments there would still be a good three or four weeks to play with.

And in three or four weeks he'd certainly have his deal with the municipal authorities done and dusted.

Tense with excitement, Manfred reaches for his calculator.

Interest at the going rate of six per cent on a loan of 180,000 marks will be about 900 marks a month. That's not a vast sum, but it could be avoided if he were to divert cheques amounting to 180,000 marks to his own account. As the authorised signatory that would be no problem. Then, as soon as the town has paid up, he just pays the appropriate sums into the suppliers' accounts.

He scribbles hypothetical figures all over his pad.

He must take his time and think this through carefully. A

manoeuvre like that would certainly be feasible, but it had better not involve his own account. It needs to be subtler than the scheme he has just conjured up.

He puts the cheques back in the folder and closes it, then leans back in his swivel chair.

But would it be worth the risk? he wonders. Only if the bank were to refuse him a loan.

As soon as Günther sees Linda crossing the courtyard towards his car, in her black off-the-shoulder dress, he can't help laughing at himself and his earlier fears. She looks so sexy – the way she walks, the way her long dress clings to her legs with every step she takes, the way her breasts are defined beneath the silky material – that he wonders how he could ever have doubted his virility. After all, ever since he saw her at his garden party he's been thinking of nothing else. He gets out of the car and goes to meet her.

'You look stunning,' he says by way of a greeting, and kisses her hand.

'Thank you,' she smiles. 'You look good too!'

That's not exactly a fervent declaration of love, he thinks as he leads her round the car to the passenger door, but it's a start.

'I'm sorry I'm a little late,' he says, opening the car door for her to get in. 'I just couldn't get away from the office today.'

For 'office' read 'Marion', thinks Linda, but she makes no comment. She is letting things take their course. She can always say no.

Günther settles himself behind the wheel and looks Linda up and down with hasty appreciation before turning on the ignition. 'You have real taste,' he says approvingly. 'Where does one find such an exciting dress in Römersfeld?'

'At Indra's!' She doesn't mention that it took her two attempts to get it. Why should she? Dirk could have seized his opportunity. Well, it was his last.

They drive slowly away. Linda notices that he immediately turns off to the left, so as to get out of town and out of danger as quickly as possible, but she doesn't mind. She enjoys driving through the countryside in such comfort, the world outside floating by, all sounds muted, the engine barely audible, everything around her acquiring a new dimension.

How nice it is to have money, she thinks, leaning back contentedly.

The little wild cat's getting tame – Günther watches her out of the corner of his eye – but not too tame, he hopes. Just a hint of the wild animal would be good.

Klaus has left the motorway. Now, feeling rather weary, he's taking the shortest route to Römersfeld via the main road. In his mind he's running through the day's events. He doesn't notice the approaching silver Mercedes until it's almost gone past him. In the rear-view mirror he gets a quick look at the registration number, GS 1. It's Schmidt. Where can he be off to at this time of day? And who with? Has he already made that much progress with the girl? Klaus wouldn't put it past him. He concentrates on the road again and gets a shock: a small red car comes shooting out of the blind corner right ahead of him just as Klaus is turning into it, and it is heading straight down the middle of the road towards him. In the nick of time Klaus wrenches at the wheel and swerves to the right, almost ending up in the ditch. He pulls back on the steering and skids, only just managing to regain control.

With his engine stalled and his nerves fluttering, he comes to a halt facing the wrong way. It's lucky there was no other traffic on the road after that maniac. There's no sign of him any more. He must have raced on at full speed. Klaus would have liked to go after him and give him a piece of his mind, but his adrenalin level is so high that he can barely manage to get his car started.

Marion is sitting crossly at home in front of the television. She went to the council offices today to enquire at the land registry about the plot of land next to the animal sanctuary, but she was told that the man she needed wouldn't be there until tomorrow. Nobody else could give her any information, they said, which reinforced her suspicion that the whole affair was a set-up. First thing tomorrow, at eight o'clock, she'll collar this man and refuse to leave until she knows what's going on. Otherwise she'll have to instruct her lawyer to place her own money somewhere safe, because if Günther is hatching another diabolical plan like the one a few years ago and plunders their joint account, she doesn't want to end up penniless if he pours all the money down the drain in some senseless scheme.

Added to which, his constant meetings are getting on her nerves. All right, so today one of the veterans of the bowling club is being ceremoniously awarded the much coveted title of Senior Honorary Bowler, but why it has to be Günther giving the speech of congratulation and staying on for the stupid celebration dinner is beyond her comprehension. That's just the way men are, Günther told her before he left; they need that sort of thing from time to time.

Why he always refers to other people when he evidently needs it himself is even more incomprehensible. After all, if he didn't need it, he wouldn't go.

And why does a man need to indulge in such childish activities? she asked as he was knotting the turquoise tie he was wearing with his dark blue suit. 'Because we like to play,' he answered with a shrug. That's another thing she'll never understand. Girls put aside their urge to play games by the time they're eighteen or even sooner. Men, on the other hand, only seem to develop it properly after the age of eighteen and pursue it more and more into their old age. It probably won't stop until they're asking St Peter at the Pearly Gates how much he's betting.

Marion puts on the television to take her mind off things. It's twenty past eight, and she flicks through the channels and ends up watching a film. Günter Strack's in it, so that'll be watchable. She presses the teletext button on the remote control to find out what she's watching and reads the title *A Man Deceived*. I'll certainly make sure that it doesn't turn into *A Woman Deceived*, thinks Marion, fetching herself a glass of wine and settling down to a solitary evening.

Günther parked his car among all the other flashy models in front of the Palace Hotel, which had a splendidly festive appearance and really did look like a palace. Then, with Linda, he expectantly mounted the flight of steps up to the double-doored entrance and waited in the spacious, red-carpeted foyer until the *maître d'hôtel* came to show them to their seats. Now, as Günther slowly follows Linda to their table, passing through the two classically decorated dining rooms, both full of guests, he takes pleasure in the attention she attracts. He wouldn't care to know how many of the men here wish they could change places with him. Or rather, he *would* like to know; it would be worth the price of standing everybody a drink. All these men, their eyes popping out, must be wondering how *he* comes to be with such a tasty bird. Because he's a super-stud! That's just the way it is!

Dirk forced his wretched little car to its limit, keeping the silver Mercedes with that swine Schmidt and the treacherous Linda just in sight. But in this stupid town, where he doesn't know his way around, he suddenly lost them. At a junction several cars got between him and the Merc, and they were gone. He's been driving round at random for half an hour now. What if they went off somewhere completely different a long time ago?

After another five minutes he stops. Dirk, he tells himself, you need to approach this logically. They must have been going somewhere specific. It's too late for the theatre, so it must be the cinema or a restaurant. The cinema is too unexceptional, so it's got to be a restaurant. If so, it must be a special one, and the people here will be able to tell you the most likely candidate.

If it turns out to be a hotel, I'll kill the pair of them.

Günther has ordered two glasses of champagne as an aperitif. He now raises his glass to Linda, his cheeks flushed with delight. Linda notices and smilingly touches her glass to his. Günther has not only booked a window table but has arranged for twenty long-stemmed roses to be waiting on the table. To make space, the waiter now moves these from the centre of their table to a little extra one placed beside it.

'This is a fabulous place, Günther. Thank you!'

Then Linda looks out of the window and Günther follows the direction of her eyes. A few more guests are sitting at white-clothed tables on the terrace, with its sandstone balustrade, but when making his booking Günther had opted for indoors; he was determined to prevent Linda from concealing her figure under a jacket.

'Isn't the park superb?' Linda would love to run out into it barefoot. The lush green of the close-trimmed lawn tempts her almost irresistibly. 'The mixture of elegance and wildness is brilliant.' She eyes the gardens with their old, gnarled trees, hedges cut in steps and rampantly proliferating shrubs and flowers.

'I have to agree with you there. It is a brilliant combination!' Günther picks up his glass. Perhaps I should try popping one of those pills this evening, he thinks, who knows whether I'm up to anything wild, especially with alcohol inside me . . .

'The rooms must be fiendishly expensive.'

What, already? Is she a mind-reader?

Linda picks up her glass too.

There's so much promise in the air that he feels almost giddy.

She laughs happily. 'But the prices needn't concern us. Luckily we each have a roof of our own!'

Luckily isn't the word Günther would have used. And he's taken quite an interest in room prices already; in fact, he has a reservation for one.

The waiter interrupts his thoughts, proffering the menus and wine list and enumerating today's special recommendations.

'Don't you have a surprise menu for people in love?' asks Günther after the waiter has finished, secretly delighted at remembering this. Marion had asked that at one of their wedding anniversary meals and he had been enormously impressed, even though he hadn't let her know it.

'Chef will be delighted to put together a suitable menu, I'm sure,' nods the waiter, taking back the menu cards.

'Is that all right with you?' Günther asks.

The soft evening light entering through the big window panes gives Linda's complexion a bronze sheen. She smoothes back her black hair and looks obliquely at him. 'That sounds wonderful!'

She would have preferred to ask him what sort of things to expect, but she's reluctant to reveal her lack of knowledge, while Günther doesn't seem to be the ignorant peasant that she's always taken him for after all. Even so, she knows what he wants, but she doesn't know yet what *she* wants. Maybe this evening will help her make up her mind.

*

Dirk has found the Palace Hotel. As darkness falls, he creeps into the car park and starts by peeing up against the registration plate of the silver Mercedes, GS 1. I could tell him where to stuff his GS 1, he thinks furiously as he leaps over the waist-high hedge into the hotel gardens. In the process he is scratched on his bare forearms, but the pain doesn't bother him – if anything it intensifies his self-tormenting sense of profound emotional distress.

One step at a time he creeps towards the main part of the hotel. The terraces of the magnificent building are now deserted, the windows brilliantly illuminated, the guests clearly visible from outside, and through the open door to the terrace comes the reek of wealth and greed, vanity and lust for power. Dirk stands motionless. Then with a shudder he sees, not twenty yards away, Günther Schmidt and Linda sitting at a table, laughing, talking and raising their glasses to each other.

So it's true.

Dirk sinks down on to the grass just as, on the other side of the window, the main course is being served.

The waiter serves Günther and Linda duck with ginger, and Günther has accepted his recommendation of a suitable red wine to accompany it. Now they are enjoying the food and chatting about unimportant things, in order to avoid having to discuss serious subjects such as Marion and Dirk or their jobs. Whatever Linda talks about, Günther hangs on her every word, asks questions, acts the part of the sympathetic listener and keeps trying unobtrusively to test the water. Is he there yet? Will she go upstairs with him? If so, the dessert had better not be too long in coming, or it might get too late. Marion might think of looking for him at his bowling club.

'How do you feel?' he asks Linda after she's put down her knife and fork, and he reaches across the table for her hand.

'It's just like being in a fairytale,' she answers impulsively, and she really means it. The food is fantastic, surpassing in concept and quality anything she could have imagined before today, the wine puts her in a relaxed, contented mood, and she's quite carried away by the ambience created by the sumptuous period furniture, lavish flower arrangements and silver chandeliers. It all feels a little unreal, like Cinderella putting on her glass slippers for one night knowing that she'll be sweeping floors again next morning.

'Might this lead to something even better, do you think?' Günther squeezes her hand.

Linda looks up in surprise. 'I should think Paris would be terrific too!'

'Yes, of course, we'll do Paris together, absolutely – but I mean *now*. Today. Here!' He gazes imploringly at her. Linda averts her eyes and looks outside. What's that lying in the grass? Difficult to make it out, the glass reflects everything; she can see herself, Günther's double chin and the whole dining room, which is gradually emptying. Even so, that dark patch wasn't there before. A dog?

'Linda!' says Günther, not giving up. 'You're so lovely. It's almost more than I can bear!'

I can bear it, thinks Linda, gradually coming down to earth. Now the gentleman wants his contribution from me.

She squeezes his hand, which is still lying on her own, and then withdraws her own. Günther is at a loss. Has she just signified her willingness or not? This calls for a different approach.

He opens a frontal attack. 'Don't you feel like it as well?'

Linda casts her gaze around the room, with its palatial furnishings, and suppresses a sigh. She's losing her glass slipper sooner than she expected. 'Look,' she says, gently fending him off, 'you're a really fascinating man and in incredibly good shape for your age' – Günther feels the collapse inside his trousers – 'but it's all happening much too fast for me!'

Don't give up now, thinks Günther, you're too close for that.

'Just a little cuddle to round off a lovely evening, a little ten-derness, nothing too much, just being affectionate, lying in each other's arms . . .' He gazes at her expectantly.

'Perhaps,' she smiles at him. 'The dessert to follow the dessert – I understand. We'll see. But first I just need to . . .' she leaves the sentence unfinished and stands up. Following her with his eyes as she moves through the room on her high heels, the black backless dress clinging to her figure and her bottom lifting provocatively with every step, he reaches into his breast pocket and takes out a blue pill. It'll take effect in an hour; with any luck he has the timing just right, and Linda will have a tiger, a ravening wolf in bed. And then, if not before, she can give her knight of the sad countenance, that Don Quixote of legal sophistry, the *coup de grâce*.

Dirk waits for Linda to return. Then, just as she's about to sit down, he jumps up and hurls the stone with all his might. It crashes against the window; the glass becomes a mosaic of cracks but doesn't shatter. Linda has leaped up in terror, and Günther has also taken cover. Totally taken aback, they gaze at the window. Fragments would have slashed them to pieces if it hadn't been shatterproof.

Other guests are also on their feet, and the staff have rushed over. 'It came from outside!' the *maître d'hôtel* exclaims agitat-edly. 'Somebody go and see what it was!'

But nobody dares to go. 'All the senior management have already left,' says a young woman in a business suit. She approaches Linda and Günther, who are standing close together. 'We do apologise most sincerely, nothing like this has ever hap-pened here before. But I'll telephone our manager immediately, and he'll do everything necessary. Naturally we'll give you another table, and your whole evening will be with the compliments of the hotel!' With a slight nod she departs.

Linda is shaking all over. If that huge pane of glass had shattered she would now be lying here with splinters of glass in her face and across the parts of her body revealed by her low-cut dress. She'd be disfigured for life. She no longer has any appetite for dessert, and orders a brandy. So does Günther. He's wondering whether this was a random attack or whether he, Günther Schmidt, was the target. If so, it would mean that Marion was behind it.

Involuntarily he looks towards the window, but apart from the damaged glass there's nothing to be seen, no face grimacing at him, no gun barrel pointed at him.

The brandies are served, and Linda and Günther drink them standing up.

'I don't know,' Linda says, looking regretfully at Günther. 'I'm not really in the mood any more. I think I'd like to go home.'

Günther thinks about the mood *he'll* be in. In an hour it'll start – no, less than an hour, in forty-five minutes he can expect to have a hard-on – and what is he to do with it?

Dirk is already driving homewards. Half triumphant and half miserable, because he's not sure how he feels about what he's just done. He gave them a real shock, they jumped up like startled rabbits, sure enough. But what if they'd ended up lying on the ground covered in blood? As a committed pacifist he'd rather not think about that. At the time of his military call-up, when he applied to be treated as a conscientious objector, wasn't one of the questions something like: 'What would you do if your girlfriend was being attacked in the woods and was about to be raped – would you just look on, or talk, or take action?'

Well, no harm's been done, he tries to reassure himself. But I meant harm, he thinks a moment later, I just don't want to admit it to myself. And this thought is anything but reassuring.

Twenty minutes later Günther and Linda are also on their way home. Linda is silent. The incident has not only wrecked the happy mood she'd been in but has set her thinking. What is she doing here really? Is this what she wants? A relationship with a married man whom she doesn't love but who can offer her things that she hasn't experienced before?

Günther can see all his hopes coming to nothing. He does his utmost to cheer Linda up.

'That was the postman, I swear it – I sent you a telegram declaring my love this morning, and he was trying to deliver it by the most direct route possible . . .'

He glances towards her, but her eyes are fixed ahead, as though the solution lies before her, on the road, in the beam of the car's headlights.

'That was pure chance, Linda. Why are you letting it bother you? It's in the hands of the police – what happens now doesn't concern us.'

'But it could have marked us both for life. And it would even have been obvious that it had happened to us both at the same time!' Her tone is aggressive, more so than she intends.

Günther lays a hand soothingly on her thigh. 'I intend to make our relationship official, anyway.'

'What relationship!?' She fires off the words like a gunshot.

Ah, his thoughts had moved a step ahead of reality. That was a bit of a mistake. He drives past the sign marking the end of town and on to the country road. 'If it were to come to a relationship,' he finally clarifies, 'that would be a reason for me to make a complete change in my life.'

'That can mean all sorts of things,' Linda replies dully. She stares blankly forwards, feeling somehow paralysed, switched off, totally lacking in energy.

She's certainly right there, thinks Günther, speeding up. The road is empty and he switches on the full beam of the headlights, lighting up the carriageway far ahead and picking out the trees to right and left.

'It's only supposed to mean that I wouldn't go in for any compromises,' he says at last.

Linda looks out of her window at the dark landscape rushing by. 'You'd get a divorce?' She says this challengingly, only meaning to draw him out.

'If you'll give me your love, yes!'

Linda wasn't prepared for this answer. She looks at him in amazement.

Günther smiles at her in confirmation, as though this spontaneous declaration was a decision that he'll now stand by, as a man of his word. But he's also smiling over something else, because the double meaning of what he said has just struck him, and while he's thinking about this he remembers his pill, which ought to start working any moment now.

Half an hour later, outside her flat, Linda has mixed feelings as she climbs out of the car.

'Can I come in with you? Just for a coffee?' Günther has walked round to her side of the car and rests both arms on her shoulders.

Linda looks at him. 'I don't understand. You'd really get a divorce? But why – surely not just because of me?'

'Nothing else in my life would make me do it.' He gazes straight into her eyes.

'I'm sorry, but it's all too much for me to cope with right now.' Linda gives him a kiss on each cheek. 'Thank you for everything, and for this evening, and for this,' she vaguely indicates her dress, 'but now I just need some air!'

'Air?' Günther looks questioningly at her.

'To breathe, I mean, space. Time to think, call it what you like.'

'Pity. I'd have liked to talk it over with you.'

'Another time. Don't be cross, but right now there's so much going on all at once that I can't handle it.'

Günther puts an arm round her shoulders and walks her to the entrance of her block. 'You can think it over when you're up in your flat. You have my mobile number – I'll be straight back if you want me, I guarantee!'

Linda isn't at all sure that she wants this guarantee. She unlocks the door and goes inside.

Marion is already asleep when she subconsciously hears the garage door, and she weaves it into her dream before actually waking up. She looks at her clock. Gone midnight, but not all that late. That's in his favour and suggests that he wasn't just spinning her a tale about the bowls evening. That's reassuring, anyway. She decides to pretend to be asleep, so that he doesn't think she's been waiting jealously ready to pounce on him.

Günther is glad to get his car safely back into the garage. His eyesight seems to be playing tricks on him: there's a blue veil over everything, and his heart is pounding like mad. *Mors in coitu* is the phrase that crosses his mind as he gets out of the driver's seat. He doesn't know any Latin, but this term has stuck in his mind because it refers to sudden death during intercourse. Something that he's always found amusing until now – anyone who dies while on the job was asking for it. But now he has this blue pill in his system . . . Might he even die beforehand? Hasn't Viagra already caused a number of deaths? If he were next in line, without even having enjoyed Linda's young body . . .

Günther tries to shake off this idea as he passes through the house on his way upstairs.

And what if the pill doesn't even work? Up to now he's felt nothing, apart from having cloudy vision. If he'd been with Linda it would have been a real fiasco. But then perhaps looking at her would have made the difference. Isn't it said that the erectile tissue reacts only when you are sexually stimulated? In the bathroom he sees what tricks his imagination can perform, strokes himself a little, although he doesn't really like doing it, and then he proudly observes how his noblest part rears up and stretches out and hardens to a quite undreamed-of degree. Oh, Linda, he thinks, there would be something here for you now. He stands sideways before the mirror, turning his body to the left then a little to the right, looking at the frontal view and lavishing copious admiration on himself. But Linda isn't there – how frustrating! He simply can't let his super-erection subside unseen and unused, and he can hardly leave a photographic record of it for posterity. Would Marion . . .?

Scarcely has Günther disappeared round the corner when Linda gets her car out of the basement garage and drives into town. A vague yearning impels her to be near to Dirk, or merely near to his home. At first she looks for his car, cruising along one street after another without finding his battered old crate. Finally she stops in the no-parking zone outside his door, takes out his key, which she still has, and unlocks the main entrance door. Her heart pounds as she goes up, stair by stair, getting closer to him with each floor. What if he just laughs at her, doesn't want to know, or has another woman in his bed? Perhaps she should have changed her clothes first, because her dress will certainly startle him. But even as she's thinking about it, she's already unlocking his door and stepping quietly inside. He'll think I'm a burglar!

'Dirk!' she calls softly, feeling for the light switch, 'Dirk, don't worry, it's me, Linda, I've got to talk to you!'

She moves towards Dirk's unmade bed and feels her way along the covers. Is he lying somewhere under there? Disappointed, she eventually sits down on it and gazes into space. Wherever could he be at this time of night? After a while she gets to her feet, goes over to the fridge and looks inside. A saucer with some slices of cooked meat, already starting to curl at the edges, half a packet of butter, a few pots of yoghurt, a bottle of white wine and another of red. She considers pouring herself a glass of the white, but doesn't bother and instead goes into the bathroom. There it comes fully home to her how out of place her expensive dress looks in these surroundings. Dirk would just look at her, quite disconcerted, and that would make any conversation impossible from the start. But she still can't make up her mind whether to go or stay. Finally she lies down fully dressed on the bed and thinks. About herself, life, Dirk, the future, her original hopes. Mulling it all over, she falls asleep.

Marion is totally confused. For days Günther has been treating her as though she had a nasty rash – and now this! Is she to understand it as an expression of love? Is he trying to make up? Asking her to forgive him? Or simply getting something out of his system? Since the moment he crept into bed he's been trying to persuade her. First he caressed her breasts sensitively, then his hand slid lower down and became insistent. Finally he grunted, 'Come on, Marion, come on – you *are* my wife!' Marion doesn't know how to react. Actually she wouldn't mind just shoving him out of the bed. But what would that lead to? The thought of the days that would follow holds her back. While he tries to stimulate her, more painfully than pleasurably, she suddenly thinks that perhaps her distrust is unfounded after all and that she's being unfair in rejecting him. And a few moments later she tells herself, as she turns over to face him, that she hasn't had it for a long time – and, what's more, she has a right to it.

Dirk was in far too much of a state to drive straight home. He stopped off at his regular pub and was in luck, as a few late drinkers were buying freely and keeping the landlord in a good mood despite the hour. He was able to order a Pils, and then a second, and by the third he was managing to erase what had happened from his mind. At first he was standing at the bar by himself, but gradually a few people joined him, having had enough of sitting down, and he started a conversation with a dark-haired girl who somehow reminded him of Linda, though she was nowhere near as pretty. She introduced herself as Petra, and as she was a student too they were soon swapping anecdotes about fellow students, lecturers and overcrowded lecture theatres.

Now, at four in the morning, the landlord finally turns them out. 'Would you like a coffee?' Dirk asks the girl when they are outside in the street. It's a perfectly innocent invitation, because he means no more than he says. 'I live quite near here.'

Petra turns to her friends and says goodbye to them. The boys grin, and Dirk suddenly realises what they're all thinking. Never mind, he tells himself; if they see me as a bit of a lad, that's fine by me.

As she wakes up, Linda at first has difficulty in working out where she is. In Dirk's flat? Then she gradually remembers how she made her way there without his knowledge. It must have been all the alcohol she'd had, or something – with one quick movement she's out of bed. She smoothes her dress and looks for her shoes. She must get out of here. How could she have thought that coming here might change the situation? Or put it right, or – she herself doesn't know what. Was she hoping for some kind of forgiveness? – forgiveness for what? – and looking for a fresh start? Did the initiative for that have to come from her?

She crosses to the door and as she steps out she's about to press the landing light switch when the light comes on of its own accord. Linda starts back. Then she hears voices from below. One deep and one high-pitched, extremely animated, both laughing and joking. Linda stays rooted to the spot and listens. She's not sure who it is, and tries to peer down the stairwell, but the shaft is too narrow. Damn! She leans far out over the banister, but it's no good. The pair remain out of sight, only their voices come nearer. But a few moments before they turn the last bend in the stairs there's finally no doubt: it's Dirk. With a woman. Linda takes a deep breath and considers what to do. Should she go straight up to them and belt him one? Should she coolly pass between them as though there were absolutely nothing amiss? Such scenes aren't her style, and anyway she wants to know what's going on. Quietly she climbs a floor higher. There she crouches down and peeps through the banisters. And while she waits and tries to make sense of the scraps of conversation that reach her, she goes hot and cold at the thought that she might still have been sleeping peacefully in Dirk's bed. In her naivety she'd supposed that talking would sort everything out; in truth she would just have made herself look ridiculous.

Dirk has a sense of well-being that he hasn't experienced for a long time. He's able to laugh heartily, and even if it's all down to the alcohol, it's still doing him good. And he's got a girl at his side, who isn't Linda, admittedly, but who's good fun and seems uncomplicated. While he's taking her up the flights of stairs towards his flat and the jokes are coming thick and fast, he's thinking, supposing those lads were right? What if Petra fancies him? Does he still have a few condoms in his flat? Then right in front of his door, just as he's about to fish the key out of his jeans, it happens: he notices Linda's scent. Confused, he stands motionless for a moment, not trusting his own senses. Just for an instant there had been a really strong scent of Linda. He looks around, and Petra prods him in the chest with her index finger. 'Something the matter, Robin Hood? Caught sight of a sheriff?' She laughs resoundingly at her own witticism. Linda ducks down even lower, and Dirk opens the door. 'No, all clear, the night is ours,' he says, more to himself, giving his words the intonation of a magic spell designed to banish the evil influence.

For a few minutes more Linda sits on the landing, without moving, until the automatic light switches itself off. She can't believe what she's just seen: the fact that Dirk has got another woman is obvious now, once and for all, and that this other woman isn't remotely in Linda's class is equally clear. What can he possibly see in her? she asks herself as she begins to feel her way down the stairs. With a shudder she imagines what is unfolding behind the door that she's just passing. Is he wearing his boring old grey underpants? Or has he invested in a new pair for this super-erotic occasion? Will he offer her some red wine from the fridge, or let her start straight in on him? Full of angry thoughts and inwardly cursing him, Linda goes down another flight before switching on the light. Then she feels another surge of panic. What on earth did she do with her key? What if she's left it in Dirk's flat and the main door down below is locked? Then she'll be trapped here until six in the morning. But she finds it in her pocket – anyway, she could safely have relied on Dirk's sloppiness, on his 'anti-bourgeois behaviour', which he always calls his ABB for short: the door's open, there's nothing to impede her flight out of Dirk's life.

A clap of thunder wakes Marion with a start on Thursday morning. What was that? Burglars? Then she hears the deep rumble of a storm and a few moments later another deafening crash. The storm must be directly above Römersfeld. She gets out of bed and opens one of the thick curtains just a fraction. Heavy black clouds are lowering and now it's starting to hail. How annoying, thinks Marion as she watches the hailstones rattling down; they'll flatten my flower beds. With a sigh she lets the curtain fall back into place and looks at the clock. The alarm will go off in twenty minutes. She glances from the bedside table towards Günther, but his side of the bed is already empty. How unusual, he's up first. Marion reaches for her dressing-gown and goes into the bathroom. He's just shaving and gives her a look in the mirror that is anything but friendly.

'Good morning.' Marion forces herself to sound cheerful and goes to the wash-basin alongside him.

His reply is barely intelligible.

'You're rumbling away like the storm outside. Is something wrong?'

He's standing in his vest and underpants in front of the mirror, his legs apart, contorting his face in every direction. 'You can see I'm shaving,' he says finally.

'Is there some special reason why you're up so early?' asks Marion, reaching for her toothbrush.

He pats after-shave on to his face, and Marion takes the bottle from his hand. 'Aha, Cool Water, the shaving lotion for the man with a body of steel!' She throws him a mocking look, because in his underwear he can't conceal his tummy by drawing it in. There's a noticeable bulge above the broad waistband of his briefs.

'I keep telling you not to cook such fattening things. This is what comes of it!' he snorts, picking up his comb. He dampens it to comb his not exactly abundant hair towards the back of his head.

Marion scrutinises him closely.

'What now?' he barks at her, growing increasingly irritated.

'Surely I can take a look at my husband once in a while. I did marry you, after all,' says Marion, amazed to find herself answering him back like that. Günther can't think of a suitable reply, and goes past her into the bedroom to get dressed. Marion follows. 'It's my birthday in five days' time, Günther. What shall we do? A long weekend for two? Or invite some people round? Or just go out for a meal in the evening?'

Günther turns to face her. She's leaning against the doorpost with her arms folded. What's got into her? thinks Günther, and while, still at a loss for words, he goes over to the wardrobe and takes out a white shirt, he hits on a possible reason for her sudden assertiveness. It *was* she who threw the stone, just as he suspected. She saw him with Linda, and now she thinks she knows everything and has got him where she wants him. But if she thinks that, she's making a big mistake.

'Are you thinking of the Palace Hotel, by any chance?' he asks sweetly but with a bitter undertone, unfolding the shirt.

'What a wonderful idea,' Marion says with a spontaneous smile. 'We haven't been there for ages. I'll make a reservation for next Tuesday straightaway.'

Günther doesn't say another word, because he no longer knows what to think. Is she putting on an act? Or does he only think she is?

At eight o'clock Manfred is standing outside his bank. He is the first customer of the day, entering as soon as the steel barriers have been raised. He finds it unpleasant having to ask for money, but since he can't produce 180,000 marks out of thin air there's no option but to go cap in hand to the bank. He's more punctual than the man he has to see, who keeps him waiting for ten minutes, even though the bank's already open for business. Herr

Biber, in dark-grey suit and yellow tie and with cropped hair
stiffened with gel, apologises for his late appearance, which he
attributes to an unexpected meeting. Manfred interprets this as
meaning a quick read of a motor-racing magazine in the loo.
Then they get down to business. Herr Biber turns to his computer screen and calls up everything that the system has on
Manfred Büschelmeyer.

'What security could you offer for 180,000 marks?' he asks at
last. From the way he says it, Manfred knows exactly what will
follow.

So he says slowly, 'Nothing that's worth 180,000 marks, otherwise I wouldn't need to come to you. But I only need the
money for a short period, eight weeks at most. I'm using it for a
business investment that is absolutely secure!'

The other's look says it all. 'Don't take this personally, Herr
Büschelmeyer, but nowadays absolutely secure business investments are, let's say, rare to non-existent.'

For a moment there's silence. Manfred moves forward on his
rather small chair and scrutinises the calendar behind Herr
Biber's back.

'But I could make you a proposal based on your income.'

'How does that work?' asks Manfred dubiously.

'You tell me what you earn and what regular monthly outgo-
ings you have, including your car, housing and insurance, and
we can calculate your borrowing capacity and make you an
appropriate offer of a loan.'

'That sounds just great,' says Manfred sarcastically.

'Well now, in your case I would guess that we'd come to a
figure of, well, let's say 25,000 to 30,000 marks.'

Manfred stands up. 'Most generous. Let me think about it!'

As Manfred leaves the bank he knows that he'll do things his
own way.

*

Günther left the house in a very unsettled state of mind. He feels somehow as though he's floating in the air, and on top of that he has a terrible headache. He didn't sleep for half the night, and then came Marion's peculiar hints, and now to cap it all this splitting head. He'll press charges against that idiot of a chemist. In America he'd have a good chance of getting millions in compensation for having had to use the pill on the wrong woman.

He arrives at work earlier than usual. It's still pleasantly peaceful, not a trace of frantic activity anywhere, and he asks himself why he doesn't come in early more often. The carpet on the way to his office muffles his footsteps, and the connecting door from the secretarial office into his room is open. He enters and is about to say a loud 'Good morning' but the words die on his lips. Sitting on his desk, with her back to him – pretty to look at, but quite out of place – is his secretary, speaking English. She's quite obviously making a call to America on his phone. What a nuisance that he doesn't understand the language, because it would certainly have interested him to know what she's saying. Apparently something very entertaining, as she's gesturing and laughing and chatting and laughing and gesturing, but after two minutes she puts the receiver down, horrified, when Günther taps her lightly on the shoulder.

'Do you do that every day?' he asks her as she slides off the desk-top, blushing furiously and hastily smoothing her red suit.

'It . . .' she stammers, 'it was a call for you, and we just got talking!'

'I can have the call checked – where to, how long, how much it cost. But do we need to go into such detail?'

Her blush has given way to pallor, and she's looking down at the floor in embarrassment.

'I've . . .' She looks up. 'I'm sorry. I'll pay you for it.'

'Who were you phoning?'

'My boyfriend . . . he's in the US army.'

'Known him long?'

'We met in New York three years ago.'

Günther snorts through his nose as he walks round the desk. 'And since then you've been phoning him on my line every day? Do you imagine your salary would be enough to repay all that?'

His secretary runs her fingers through her short ash-blonde hair.

Günther drops into his chair. 'I'll have to think about this. Bring me a coffee.'

Marion is also just making herself some coffee, her 'good morning' coffee with frothy milk with which she always starts the day as soon as Günther's left the house. She leafs through the pages of the local news section of the daily paper: nothing more on that stupid speed trap, and it evidently didn't think the presentation to the bowls club member was worth a mention either. Marion turns over the pages as far as the business section, and decides to let the day start gently, particularly as it's still raining slightly.

Shortly after eight she remembers the man at the land registry office, who ought to be back at work today. She picks up the phone and rings the council offices. She's in luck; she's put through to him.

The official at the other end of the line tells her, without wasting any words, that to get information about the ownership of a piece of land it is necessary to have a legitimate interest in it.

'My interest is perfectly legitimate,' Marion informs him, 'I should like to buy the land.' Though he objects that such matters are not normally dealt with by phone, she chooses to ignore this.

Finally the official declares that he'll have to consult the land register. Marion rates this as a success. 'I can wait,' she says, stirring her coffee.

After a while the receiver at the other end is picked up again. 'Frau Schmidt?'

'Yes, I'm still here.'

'Frau Marion Schmidt?'

'The same.'

'Right. According to my records this plot of land, registration number 4377/3, is the property of Max and Bertha Dreher. I must just add, though, by way of caution, that that hasn't been checked right up to today's date. I wasn't in the office yesterday.'

What difference can that make? thinks Marion. In high spirits she thanks him, and puts the phone down. Max Dreher, she murmurs, poring over the telephone directory. Aha, the farm adjoining the land. She might have thought of that herself really. Should she phone them? No, with that sort it's sure to be better to turn up in person. Quickly she stands up and goes to get herself ready.

Günther has never before caught anyone out doing that kind of thing, or not so blatantly anyway. Who knows who else may be on the fiddle in his firm? Who knows what sums of money are being siphoned off if there's some individual like his secretary in the accounts department? He toys with the idea of firing her, but he isn't sure that what she's done would count as sufficient grounds. And besides, by the time a replacement has learned the ropes it will have cost him more effort, nervous energy and cash than whatever her little phone calls are likely to amount to. Even so, it irks him to have been deceived. A Günther Schmidt is not to be deceived, that's something they should all know by now.

His telephone rings. Günther is unwilling to be disturbed in his train of thought and lifts the receiver reluctantly.

'A call for you. Shall I put it through?'

'Who is it?' Now she'd better not say that she didn't catch the name properly. She's blotted her copybook enough for one day.

'A Frau . . .' She hesitates. Come on, come on, thinks Günther. 'Hagen.' She sounds relieved.

'Hagen?'

'Yes, she gave her name as Frau Hagen.'

Günther's heart misses a beat, his hand goes automatically to his shirt collar. 'Put the call through!'

'Morning, Günther!'

'Good morning, Linda. I'm really pleased to get a call from you . . .' Günther sits tensely. After last night's fiasco, is this going to be his marching orders?

'I just wanted to ask you when we're flying to Paris.'

The tension in his spine increases. 'To Paris?'

'Yes, Paris . . .'

Her tone is different from usual, gentler, more relaxed.

More promising!

'Yes, of course, whenever you like!' He feels himself growing hot. Has he managed to pull it off? 'Where are you?'

'At home.'

His eyes go to the clock. 'At this time? How's that? Are you not well?'

'I thought you might like to come over for a late breakfast . . .'

Late breakfast? Günther is still sitting bolt upright and tense on the edge of his leather chair. Can it be . . .? Can it mean . . .? Why so suddenly?

He clears his throat. 'What shall I bring?'

'Nothing. Everything is here. Ev-ery-thing!'

She has emphasised the 'everything' so strongly that Günther gets up out of his uncomfortable position and stands motionless. He clears his throat, because this is so completely unexpected. 'I'll be with you right away!'

Manfred has arrived at his DIY store and is arranging an interest-free loan for himself. For the time being he'll hold back three of the cheques he's signed, to the value of 182,350 marks in all, and then alter them to be payable to himself. As soon as the money from the town council comes in, he'll settle the bills by making cash payments. It won't be noticed unless somebody delves deeply into the books. And there will be no reason why they should. In cheerful mood, he phones Annemarie Roser to tell her that she can have the money to complete the deal that evening.

'But you haven't read the draft contract yet,' she protests.

'I'll look over it this evening, that'll be soon enough.' Manfred rubs his hands with satisfaction. At last this DIY store is being of some use to him. A manager who's only an employee – in the eyes of people who own their own businesses that's like being a dog on a leash. With the leash held by somebody smarter than you are. But now he'll show them all that he's the master, not the dog.

All that remains now is for him to open an account at a bank where he's not known and pay in the three cheques and a bit of his own capital, and then he can take the money out again and be Mr Big in Römersfeld.

Linda has decided to throw overboard everything she's ever believed in.

When her alarm went off she brought the flat of her hand down on it and decided to sleep on for another hour. Then she phoned the cosmetics shop to say she was ill. Pretty bad stomach cramps – flu or something, not her appendix, she hoped. Given that she was normally quite a robust type, no one was suspicious: on the contrary, the other assistants were full of sympathy and suggested all sorts of strange remedies.

Next Linda put a bottle of champagne into the chill compartment, showered and washed her hair, and phoned Günther. She knew he would come over at once. And what he could expect to get. She's in the mood to drive him to a heart attack, to give him what Dirk is never going to get any more – and not just that, but much more than Dirk ever got from her. She'll wear him out until he's on his knees whimpering, coughing up banknotes, because all men are pigs.

The night with Petra was just what Dirk needed. She had coffee and then she had him, and it was like healing balm to his spirit. At last he had someone again who was obviously satisfied with him. But then, in the cold light of day, Petra simply wasn't Linda, and when she had left for the university he began to suffer again. He settled down at his desk to work, but his thoughts kept wandering until finally he realised that he was making notes about something quite different. 'Plan for revenge,' he had written right across a sheet of paper, and beneath this he was listing effective ways of getting back at Günther, starting with 'Tell Marion' and ending with 'Shoot him'.

But now it's becoming clear to Dirk that he's just going round in circles. He thinks over what he did yesterday and what the results might have been, and he resolves to draw a line under the subject once and for all. He crumples up the piece of paper and hurls it with all his might in the direction of the waste-paper basket. It's really quite pointless to let Günther blight his life! He reaches for his keys and gets up. A short walk will do him good, he needs some fresh air. And he also needs to think what to say if Petra phones. Sorry, it was nice, but that's it? Or should he stall her in case he fancies another session? He opens the door and steps out on to the landing. That wouldn't be fair on her, he thinks, and that's not my style. Or is it? The door slams to behind him and he runs lightly down the stairs.

Marion is sitting in her car mulling things over. Bertha Dreher, in filthy rubber boots, greasy skirt and stained jumper and with her hair tied into a straggly bun, turned her away immediately and in no uncertain terms from the yard of the house. The plot of land was sold and she'd have nothing to do with thieves from town. She couldn't be induced to say any more than that. Marion wondered whether the farmer's wife might already be drunk even at this time of the morning. She remained standing by her car for a while, hoping to see someone who could enlighten her, but there was no sign of Max Dreher, and Bertha gave her an angry look before disappearing into the cowshed. So she stood there alone, surrounded by the dilapidated barns and cattlesheds and the weather-beaten farmhouse, as out of place with her smart BMW convertible and her pink dress with the gilt buttons as if she'd dropped down from some distant star on to this concreted yard with all its cracks and potholes.

Now she's sitting in her car, trying to collect her thoughts. It can't be true. Hasn't that idiot at the land registry office only just told her that the plot belongs to this old couple? Is the woman too stupid to know what's hers, or has somebody really beaten her to it by a few rotten hours?

At last she starts up her car, because now she's determined to get at the facts. She'll go straight to that land registry fool and demand to know what's what.

After looking at his list of appointments for the day, Günther goes through to his secretary whose expression shows that she's prepared for the worst. 'For the next two, or let's say three hours, I shan't be available,' he says curtly, 'so postpone my meetings.' With these words he crosses to the door, turns and adds magnanimously, 'Look, we can forget that business with your boyfriend.' Opening the door, he takes a step outside, but then he turns back once more: 'But you owe me a favour! In one way or another.' He can see from her face what she's thinking, but he doesn't care. He had never had sex in mind, only repayment.

Günther races straight to the nearest florist's and buys a whole vase full of flowers. 'Don't bother to tie them fancily, just put some paper round them as they are.' Then, burning with impatience and only with difficulty keeping his speed below forty, he drives straight on to Linda's.

Klaus can't believe it. Yesterday he pushed through the transaction of his life, and now Günther has cancelled their meeting just like that. He tries Günther's mobile, but all he gets is his voicemail. He only says, 'Call me back urgently,' because he makes it a rule not to entrust confidential information to the German telephone network.

'What's the matter? Why the black looks?'

Regine has come up behind him. She takes the phone out of his hand and massages his neck. 'I expect it was tough, your business trip yesterday.'

'Tough, but successful!' Klaus takes and kisses her hand.

They're still having breakfast in the conservatory, later than usual, which is why Regine has laid the table more elaborately than usual: crockery with a daintily coloured flower pattern and a matching tablecloth, a basket filled with fresh croissants and assorted rolls, home-made jam, a dish of sliced meats and cheeses, freshly squeezed carrot juice and, to celebrate their having a quiet, leisurely breakfast together, omelettes with bacon and mushrooms. And now the first rays of sunshine are shining through the glass roof, bathing everything in a warm and cheerful light. The thunderstorm has finally passed over, the alarming hailstorm has finished, and even the rain has stopped. Klaus draws Regine on to his lap. 'I'll make a suggestion: I'll fetch us a bottle of champagne from the fridge, and you can decide in the meantime where you'd like to fly with me. I'm thinking of a nice little city break: Milan, Paris, Rome, Venice, Amsterdam – the choice is yours.'

'Are you serious?' She throws her arms around his neck. Bobby, stretched out on the floor, eyes her attentively and growls.

'Yes, you jealous old thing! Just watch this!' Klaus kisses Regine vigorously on the lips, to which Bobby responds with a burst of barks. 'I'll have to watch out that he doesn't pinch my wedding ring one of these days,' laughs Klaus, detaching himself from Regine and giving the dog's head a quick pat before going into the kitchen.

'Wow, Bobby, did you hear that? A city break. He's really pulling out all the stops!'

The dog listens, his ears pricked, as she enthuses about Italy, the canals of Venice, Milan fashions and Roman monuments and museums, but then she suddenly remembers that Bobby can't go on a plane. 'We could go to Paris,' she consoles him, 'we could drive there in the car. Plenty of room for all of us!'

'I was thinking you could entrust this feather-duster here to your friend Annemarie Roser – that shouldn't be a problem.' Klaus has followed her into the conservatory and is putting the bottle and a pair of glasses on the table.

'At the sanctuary?' asks Regine in consternation.

'It's called going back to one's roots,' jokes Klaus, but he sees from Regine's expression that this hasn't gone down well. 'We'll get him an au pair,' he says soothingly, and to Bobby, who has lifted up his head, 'a pretty one . . .'

Manfred has stowed the three cheques plus a few blank ones in his briefcase, and he has given the signature folder with the remaining cheques to the secretaries with instructions that they must be taken to the bank today. He's also told them that he won't be available until this afternoon, because he absolutely has to go and see a rival DIY store in Stuttgart that everybody's talking about. Much too much for his liking, he says chattily, so now he positively must go and see what all the fuss is about.

They all readily accept the need for this important trip, or at least they pretend to, and Manfred sets off in high spirits. On the drive to Stuttgart he goes over his plan again, step by step. Cash for the cheques will be safer, because a credit transfer to his own account would be too risky. Then he has to hope that the firm's accounts office will only pay attention to the amounts and compare them with the debit payments. By the same token, it will be best to let the three cheques pass through the accounts as three separate cheques and not appear as a debit for the total amount. Manfred fumbles a piece of chewing gum out of its wrapper. Any other way would be impossible in any case, he tells himself as he unwraps it, because the woman wants to get her hands on the dough today, and a transfer would take far too long.

Günther's white shirt is sticking to his back, even though he has turned down the air-conditioning in the Mercedes to the coldest setting. As he runs the car down into the basement garage, just to be on the safe side, a myriad thoughts are tumbling through his mind. What if he's completely misunderstood Linda's meaning? Up to now it hadn't looked as if she was just waiting for the chance to leap into bed with him. Or is it to do with the storm this morning – has she been struck by lightning, is it a reaction to electrical energy or magnetic fields, is she weather-sensitive and therefore changeable, unpredictable?

Now you're being silly, old man, Günther says to himself as he carries the huge bouquet of flowers towards the lift. Basically you don't care what she's like: you want to screw her and you want to show her off. Still enough of a stud to please a young filly! Anyone can see that, and you want them to see it. Even if that's not the decisive factor any more in this age of Viagra. Damn, he's forgotten the Viagra tablets. Wherever did he leave them? But does he want to inflict that on himself again? And what if he swallows another of the pills now and she has quite different ideas? Should he take his stiffie to the office and demand his favour?

He grins, because the idea of an omnipotent boss amuses him, and it really seems a shame to him that women have a will of their own. The world has gone to pot since the demise of proper leaders. Actually he would be exactly the type of man that the Germans need: authoritarian, a man of iron will, unshakeable, clean-living.

But the lift is arriving and Günther steps in. He pats his flies with his free left hand: we're nearly there, my dear friend, my nose tells me that our waiting is finally over.

It's driving Marion mad. That wretched man, that dreary official, isn't there again. A woman who shares the same office points to his overloaded desk and says apologetically that something among the new documents might be relevant to Marion's query, but unfortunately she doesn't deal with that kind of thing. Her colleague is in an important meeting and won't be available until after lunch. And with a little swipe at Marion she adds that members of the public would normally have to phone and make an appointment.

'I can't make an appointment with somebody who isn't there,' snorts Marion before pulling the door to behind her. She wishes she could just go through the idler's mail herself; she's sure she'd find what she needed to know in five minutes. Hesitating, she stops halfway down the long corridor. What if she waits until the woman has to leave the room, for the toilet or something, and then darts in? If she had a mobile on her she could phone her and ask her to go down to the entrance. That would give her enough time. But what would happen if she were caught poking around? What would that count as? Unauthorised sorting through official correspondence? Prohibited examination of confidential documents? Trespass? Burglary? Espionage? She puts these thoughts out of her mind and walks slowly towards the broad stone stairs and the exit. She doesn't know who has bought the plot of land, or for how much, it's true, but if it had been Günther he would have let out a whoop of triumph this morning, if not before. So perhaps she's still in the game. Maybe somebody has an ace in their hand without realising it. But certainly she needs to prepare for this eventuality, because before she joins in she'd better at least know how much she can stake. She glances at her watch: still ample time to pay a visit to her bank.

Through the spyhole in her door Linda sees Günther approaching. You can still change your mind, she tells herself. You don't have to open the door if you don't feel like it! But she does in fact feel drawn to a man who woos her so persistently and is eager to place the world at her feet. It's her game, and she has the first move. Decisively she opens the door before he has a chance to ring. 'Welcome, Günther, I'm glad you could come so quickly,' she says, taking a step out on to the landing to meet him.

'Good Lord!' Günther's jaw drops. He looks so surprised that Linda can scarcely help laughing. But then his expression changes to one of sheer admiration, and he clicks his tongue. 'You look like the goddess Venus, with an exquisite touch of the goddess Diana!' He puts his enormous bouquet into her arms. 'A small token from the house of Schmidt!'

'Not from your wife's vase, I hope?' she can't resist saying.

He merely laughs and kisses her on both cheeks. '*You'll* soon be my wife,' he whispers, so softly that she isn't sure that she's heard correctly. Linda turns and goes ahead of him into the flat. Her short black skirt swishes about her long legs, and above it she's wearing a loose-fitting, close-meshed black net top that only reaches down to her navel. She knows perfectly well that this outfit is utterly provocative, but that's her intention. She decided during the night that she'd do it, and now she wants to see the effect.

Günther grins in satisfaction as he follows her. What a start, absolutely out of this world, he thinks. He can't take his eyes off her skirt, which as she walks swings up almost to her knickers. Is she even wearing any?

Linda goes into the kitchen, gets a bucket, rinses it out and puts the flowers into it. Günther relieves her of them and crinkles his forehead. 'That's something I've forgotten, you know, I intended to bring a champagne bucket – well, two really, because we'll need another one for the champagne.'

'How about a champagne bucket and a flower vase?' asks Linda, already kneeling in front of the fridge and fishing for the bottle.

Aha, thinks Günther, that's the first thing she's asked for in the time we've known each other. Up to now she's just accepted gratefully – and with reservations that she hasn't tried to hide. Now she's expressed her first wish, which means that the game has started.

'Crystal? Murano? Blue smoked glass? Or orange? What's Madam's preference?'

'As big as possible!'

Günther can feel something stirring in his trousers. As big as possible? By all means!

'I'm quite demanding in that respect,' she adds, handing him the bottle. Slight doubts creep into Günther's mind. What if that scruffy student Dirk is better equipped than he is? Longer, thicker, harder? He should have taken that pill after all, damned fool that he is. Yesterday his size was colossal. But what good is yesterday? Marion probably didn't even notice!

'Come on,' says Linda, picking up the glasses. 'Let's go into the living room. The sofa's getting on a bit but it's quite comfortable.'

Aha, the sofa, thinks Günther, following her. The next subject to come up will be the car, and then the terms of the deal will be clear.

Linda sits down and looks up at him. It's amazing how clearly his thoughts are written all over his face, she thinks, smiling at him. 'Come on, sit here,' she says, patting the sofa next to her. 'Will you open the bottle? Let's drink to our short break in Paris. I'm already looking forward to it tremendously.'

Perhaps she isn't after a sofa at all but is genuinely keen on me, thinks Günther, sitting down close beside her. He could very well understand that.

Marion is frozen to the spot, speechless. She's sure her heart's about to stop beating; blood surges up to the roots of her hair, and finally she starts to shiver. With her current bank statement in her hand she stands at the cashier's window, steadying herself against the counter. Pull yourself together, she tells herself, it must be a mistake. The computer's gone crazy, or at a pinch the whole bank. But a million doesn't vanish just like that. A million just evaporating into thin air – it's impossible. She turns round, intending to ask the bank clerk some questions immediately or, better still, go straight to the manager.

Behind her stands an old man who has evidently been watching her closely. 'Do you need any help?' he asks. 'Do you know, that's just how I feel every time I come here. The pension is just too . . .'

'Mind your own business,' Marion snaps. She strides rapidly towards the big glass door of the manager's office. A million! gone! She can prosecute the bank for a mistake like that. The value of the lost interest alone! When she tells Günther he'll hit the roof!

Günther has already poured himself a second glass and is drinking as Linda's still sipping her first. He's telling her about this morning, but Linda can't see anything wrong. 'Other firms have to pay for expensive courses for their secretaries to improve their English – yours is providing her own training. She'll soon be asking for a rise in recognition of her language skills!' She looks at him and bursts out laughing. 'You should see your face,' she says at last.

'Well, I mean!' He shakes his head. 'Those are pretty revolutionary ideas! Just what I need in my office!' Linda laughs again. Günther lays his hand, as if accidentally, on her left thigh.

'I could give you some lessons.' Linda's tone has changed. Günther pricks up his ears.

'What in?' he asks, increasing the pressure of his hand.

'In this!' Linda puts her hand on his and pushes it a little further up.

Günther's heart rate immediately doubles. He felt the twitch in her leg; the invitation is clear enough. Slowly, tentatively he advances. He feels himself growing hot. If only he doesn't start sweating. Beads of perspiration on one's forehead are no turn-on. He can still feel Linda's hand lying firmly on his own; now she moves it away and places her bare leg across his lap. Günther swallows with a dry throat; he can hear the surging of his blood. She's wearing almost non-existent panties, and that arouses him more than if she were wearing none at all. With fevered fingers he explores the narrow strip of material. Beneath it lies his target; at last he's got to where he wanted to be from the start. He pushes the material aside and with his fingertips feels his way through the soft warm skin. A gentle sigh tells him that he has reached the right spot; he slides down from the sofa and stimulates Linda with his tongue. He feels her long fingernails on his head, behind his ears, on his neck, her pelvis moves faster and faster, he must get up before the train leaves without him. Hoarsely, he says, 'Take your knickers off,' and he fumbles with his own trousers, pushes his shoes off his feet, tosses trousers and underpants together on to the floor (which is quite unlike him), throws himself down on her and plunges his honourable member (firm enough, thank God) into bliss while his mouth searches for hers. He's detached from his rational mind; he can feel only how everything in him is pulsating, tensing, he hears the crash of the glass that he must have swept off the table in his excitement, then he explodes – and a second later he thinks: Shit, too soon!

He feels himself lying drained and heavy on top of Linda, and raises himself up apologetically. With a slight smile on his lips he asks, 'How was it for you?' – the question all men have had to ask since 1968.

'Oh, it was wonderful,' Linda lies, as generations of women have lied before her.

Günther gets up, goes into the kitchen and comes back with a kitchen roll. 'You're a fabulous woman,' he says, holding out the paper to her. 'But next time we'll do it differently – I'd like to be able to see you naked as we do it, and have more time.' He pulls gently at her top. 'Would you like the bathroom first?' Linda nods and gets up. He follows her with his eyes as she goes towards the bathroom door, naked except for her top. Her bottom has just the right curves – not too boyish, but not too ample either, firm and youthful like a racehorse in training. Günther allows himself a proud grin as he bends to pick up the broken pieces of the glass. Carefully he gathers them up. Symbolic of shattered virginity, he thinks complacently, and briefly strokes his wilted penis. 'Well done,' he praises it. He feels at least twenty years younger. Today marks the beginning of his second life. And nobody had better stand in his way!

The manager confirms to Marion what she simply isn't willing to believe. Günther himself, in person, withdrew the money. She can see the date and signature, and there's no doubt about it: he's cleared out the account! Including her money. 'And what about my shares?' she asks, trembling. The shares have been sold, the notice account emptied. More than that, not even the hastily summoned customer adviser can say.

The manager himself seems surprised. 'Is it possible that your husband has changed his bank? Was there any cause of dissatisfaction?' This sounds more like a threat addressed to his subordinate than a question.

'I don't know,' Marion replies, feeling close to a heart attack. Her head is buzzing, and the wood-panelled customer consultation room is dancing around the circular table. She struggles to regain her composure, and at length says, with a degree of self-control that she would not have thought herself capable of, 'I'll have to ask my husband about it.' Her voice has an icy ring, and both men stand up simultaneously as she prepares to go. As though on automatic pilot Marion leaves the room and passes through the bank hall to the exit. So she was right. Günther is staking everything on some venture or other. Without asking her, he's made a clean sweep of everything. He's gone too far: even if the profit could justify the risk, he can't take such liberties with her. Or her money! It's so monstrous that even in the car she can't think straight. Her pulse is racing, but apart from that she is incapable of any emotional reaction. She feels neither sorrow nor anger. What if Günther is backing the wrong horse and loses it all? Could a whole world collapse, virtually from one moment to the next? It could, she tells herself, clenching her teeth. If her father knew, he'd be turning in his grave.

Linda stands under the shower, thinking things over. Do you really want to let yourself in for this, she asks herself as she showers. He's so many years older than you – he could easily be your father! The thought makes her shudder. She avoided taking hold of him under his shirt because she finds flabby flesh a turn-off. What's all this in aid of? She still hasn't fathomed her own motivation. Why is she doing this? Taking revenge on Dirk? Or is it the prospect of easy living? She can't find an answer; the way into her soul seems blocked and her subconscious is denying her access to any information.

Linda dries herself and is about to come out with her towel round her hips. Günther comes over to meet her with a freshly filled champagne glass.

'To a wonderful future, my lovely,' he says as he hands her the glass. 'From tomorrow, everything will be different!'

She stops and takes a mouthful. 'What will be different?' she asks suspiciously.

Günther makes an all-embracing gesture. 'You'll see!'

Linda's eyes follow the movement of his hand. Does he mean her living room? Is he planning to refurnish it? 'Is there something you don't like?' she asks, on her guard.

'I like everything tremendously, but it'll get much, much better!' He lowers his voice. 'And *we*'ll get much, much better too, when we have a whole night to ourselves!'

What's all this 'we'? thinks Linda, but she makes no comment.

Marion has composed herself sufficiently to be able to start the car. She won't phone Günther beforehand; she'll drive straight to his office. Then he can explain himself on the spot. She hasn't been there for a long time because she has no business there, as Günther has reminded her on occasion. She was too trustful, and now she's annoyed that she didn't at least sort out her own finances. He could always be certain that she'd never help herself to money from their joint account, but he obviously didn't have the same scruples. As soon as the money is back again she'll make some fundamental changes!

She drives faster than usual through Römersfeld. As she does so, she remembers the sawn-off radar camera. Since Günther's birthday her life has somehow gone off the rails. And then the way he pounced on her last night. Without tenderness, almost impersonally, selfishly. Nothing is the way it was any more. It's almost like the pieces of a jigsaw puzzle without a pattern to refer to. However she tries to put them together they still don't make a picture.

Marion drives into the big yard in front of her husband's company. The building was put up without any unnecessary expense, and it's completely plain and functional. The external walls are made of exposed aggregate concrete, the frames of the curtainless windows are of dark brown plastic, and the whole area at the front – the car park, the drive and the space near the entrance – is asphalt. No flowers, no trees, no grass, nothing. It dawns on Marion that this building is an apt reflection of her husband. Lacking soul, aesthetics or taste. If Günther shows any warmth, it's calculated. If he adopts a sophisticated manner, it's superficial. His craving for status is the product of a limited intelligence with no depth to it. The whole man is governed by base instincts – the desire for possessions, power and gratification. It's never been so obvious to her before.

Marion is shaken by her new insights. It takes her a moment to notice that Günther's parking space is empty. He's not here! Then why did he get up so early this morning? Is the fateful meeting taking place today? Is he passing her money across the table at this very moment?

Marion quickly gets out of the car and approaches the entrance. In the glass door she can see her own reflection, and it strikes her as ridiculous. A pink dress with gold buttons – quite the kept wife, with time for expensive shopping trips and beauty care. She should have put on a simple black trousersuit; that would have suited her mood better. She storms down the long corridor and without knocking wrenches open the door to her husband's secretary's office. The desk chair is empty and the door to the boss's room is closed. Surely he and that blonde slut . . . she thinks, but then remembers that he isn't even here. To make quite sure, she pulls Günther's door violently open. That room is empty too. That's something.

For a moment she stands there, irresolute, then she decides to ask other people working there where he is. Even at the risk of making herself look foolish. She simply must find him. She shuts the door to his office behind her and is just going to open the door to the corridor when it is suddenly flung wide.

Günther's secretary is standing facing her, holding a large mug from which an arc of spilled hot coffee is splashing down on to the grey industrial carpeting. 'God, you made me jump,' she says, checking her short red suit for stains and giving Marion a reproachful look.

Marion ignores it. 'Is my husband not here? Where is he?'

Just like a puppy shaking its paw, the young woman waggles her hand, which obviously got in the way of some of the hot coffee, and then shrugs her shoulders in a way that seems to Marion to be deliberately provoking. 'There was a phone call, and he suddenly went off in a terrific hurry.'

Indignantly Marion snaps at her, 'You're his secretary – you must know where he is! Look in his appointment diary. It's urgent!'

'This appointment isn't in there, I can tell you that straight-away.'

Her defiant look makes Marion suspicious. 'What's that sup-posed to mean?'

'That he didn't say anything. After the phone call, he went off. That's all.'

She doesn't know why, but for the second time today Marion hears warning sirens in her head. 'Who called?'

'A woman!' With her fingertip she catches the drop of coffee that's hanging from the bottom of the mug.

Marion is almost bursting with impatience. She'd like to pour the whole mugful over the girl's head. 'For God's sake, just tell me! What was this woman's name?'

'I didn't make a note of it. Sorry!'

Marion thinks it over. Could it have been the secretary of the sinister person he's doing his deal with? Or – she catches her breath – does he have a girlfriend? But then what would he need so much money for? Her theory that the big deal's being done right now, at this very second, is much more likely. Naturally he wouldn't tell this silly little cow about it.

Marion takes her leave curtly, maintaining her dignity, and decides to call on Manfred. And if that's no good, she'll go and ask Wetterstein in person. He must know what people are up to.

And maybe, she thinks as she gets into her car, that's where she'll find that whole treacherous bunch of crooks.

Manfred is amazed at how easy it is. At one of the big banks in the centre of Stuttgart he's opened an account with 500 marks of his own money and paid in the three cheques adding up to 182,350 marks, then from the total amount he's had exactly 180 1,000-mark notes counted out into his briefcase. Now he's strolling along Königstrasse, feeling that his triumph must be written all over his face. How maddening that he can't celebrate it! He's desperate to tell somebody of his heroism. After all, he's just managed, thanks to his cunning, to lay the foundations of a fortune and get one over on all the Römersfeld wannabes. And now he's having to keep it all to himself! What a waste. But he controls himself. As soon as the municipality has bought the plot from him and he's used the proceeds to pay the diverted money into the three firms' accounts, there will be opportunities enough for people to slap him on the back. And many will. All those people who can't stand Günther Schmidt's inflated sense of his own importance. Grinning maliciously, he starts daydreaming, savouring the pleasures of anticipation in every possible variation, then he buys himself a bottle of champagne; at least he'll be able to celebrate the day's work by sinking a few glasses at home.

In the car, having put the bottle and his briefcase on the passenger seat, he notices the display on his mobile telling him that his office has been trying to contact him. Before switching on the ignition he returns the call. Marion Schmidt has been round wanting to talk to him urgently, he's told, and she has asked him to call her back. Instinctively Manfred puts his hand on the briefcase. What's she up to? Has she got in first, despite everything? He can feel his pulse racing. Frantically he gets connected to the job centre. Only when Annemarie Roser confirms that their arrangement still stands does his pulse settle down, and he sinks back into the car seat in relief. 'Can you hurry the paperwork along a bit?' he asks. 'I'd like to get it all tied up as soon as possible!' He can feel Marion breathing down his neck, and he doesn't trust her.

'I've already got the contract on my desk. If you give me a call just before we arrive, the solicitor can be here in no time – his office is only round the corner from here.'

'And he won't make any difficulties with this?' A solicitor available at such short notice is something he's never encountered before.

'He's an old schoolfriend of mine, and that's what we've arranged. So come over whenever you can make it.' As soon as possible, thinks Manfred, taking a deep breath and starting the car.

Linda has sat back down on the sofa with Günther, who is telling her how he built up his business. 'From nought to sixty in three seconds, real Formula One stuff,' he grins, then he asks what Linda does for a job.

Linda considers what to say. Since he took her for a model to begin with, her actual job seems rather paltry by comparison. 'Not quite up to sixty yet,' she temporises, 'but I'll get there.' She takes a mouthful from her glass, so as not to have to say any more.

'So why haven't you been at work today?' He glances meaningfully at his gold Rolex.

'I wanted to make you happy,' she declares, amazed to find that she can say it without a blush.

'You've certainly done that.' Günther grins and pats her knee. 'That's what I call having a good time!'

Something in his look tells her that he wants more. Quickly she stands up. 'But there are things I must do, you're quite right, otherwise I shan't have seen today!'

Günther runs both hands across the closely cropped top of his head. 'I have a few little jobs to attend to as well,' he says, getting heavily to his feet. 'And now I feel more motivated to do them.' He stretches, and flexes his back. 'I've left you a little something in the bathroom. For afters, as it were. Or as an aperitif for next time. Whatever you prefer!' He kisses her on the forehead. 'I hope it won't be long till the next time. Think about whether you're doing anything tomorrow . . .' He nods at her. 'And check whether you still have enough champagne. If not, I'll bring some. And maybe something else too.'

'Something else?' Linda puts her head on one side.

'It's a secret. But I know you'll like it.' He pats her skirt.

After being told at the DIY store that Manfred won't be back from his business trip before this afternoon at the earliest, Marion is seething with fury. He's conned her; he's in cahoots with the others. She's angry with herself. What else did she expect? 'Networking' is the trendy new name they give to what her father used to call corruption. All the people they need for this deal have probably been put in the picture and had their palms well greased. She roars out of the car park, taking a protruding kerbstone with her, but she doesn't care, even though she may have buckled the wheel rim. She's in the process of discarding all her principles. And she has no intention now of knocking politely or letting some secretary hold her back. She'll break up this lousy meeting, even if Günther tries to stop her. For years she's spared herself annoyance by turning a blind eye to things, but self-deception is one thing and breach of trust quite another. Theft within a marriage – that really is too much!

Absolutely livid, she tears through Römersfeld like one possessed, straight through a red traffic light. The road's empty, she sees no point in stopping. If she has no money left, she can't afford a car. So if she loses her licence, what's the difference?

Linda waits on her balcony to see Günther's car come out of the garage, then goes straight into the bathroom. She's curious to see what his little 'aperitif' is, but in truth she already knows: it'll be money. She glances round, but can't see anything, so she takes a more careful look around. This is just like hunting for Easter eggs, she thinks, then suddenly she spots a tiny corner of paper peeping out from under her tooth-mug. That'll be it. She stops in front of it with her arms folded. What's she worth to him as a main course? 200? 500? She lifts the mug and pulls a carefully folded note from under it. Slowly she smoothes it out. He's left 1,000 marks for her. Linda collapses on to the toilet seat. That's absolutely crazy, she thinks; nobody would pay 1,000 marks for a quickie like that. Whatever does he want from her? Is he kinky, is he trying to soften her up for it? What did he mean when he said he'd bring 'something else' next time? Those were the words he used. She stands up. There won't be a next time. He can stick his 1,000 marks.

Marion has parked in the no-parking zone and is hurrying across the plaza towards the town hall, which was built ten years ago, in a blaze of publicity and civic pride, in neo-Renaissance style. Nowadays no one would countenance squandering money like that, she thinks, using all her strength to push open the massive wooden door. The glass kiosk prominently marked 'Reception' is empty. That's fine, then she won't need to tell anyone that she's thinking of murdering three men. His Worship the Mayor, no less Manfred the traitor and her husband the swindler. As fast as the hem of her dress allows, she runs up the stairs. She needs no signs, she knows exactly where to find that gang of three. The clatter of her heels echoes down the long corridor, and her fury grows with every step. On either side are departmental offices, and at the end of the corridor the mayor's office is on the left and the council chamber on the right. She doesn't meet a soul, the whole place is deserted. This infuriates her even more, because it's nowhere near the end of the working day. And this is what I pay my taxes for, she thinks angrily, as she tries to fling open the chamber door. But it won't give. She presses the gilt handle further down and puts her shoulder to the door, but the outcome's the same. Nothing doing. But hang on – she can hear voices inside. The sound is muffled, but there's definitely something happening in there. Something so secret that they've locked themselves in! 'Open up!' she shouts, banging on the door with her knuckles, then with the flat of her hand, and finally her fist. Before she can start making a real racket, she hears the key slowly being turned in the lock on the inside. She pushes the door open. Joachim Wetterstein is facing her, looking startled. So she was right! 'Where's my husband?' she demands, not bothering with the normal courtesies.

'Your husband?' asks Wetterstein in confusion, trying to keep the door partially closed. 'I don't know anything about your husband!'

'Tell me where he is at once!' Marion pushes against the door but meets resistance. The mayor has evidently put his food behind it. It's obvious that they're in there, why else should he be so keen to keep her out?

'Believe me . . .' begins Wetterstein in a soothing tone, but before he can get any further Marion has hurled herself at the door and swept his foot aside, the door crashing heavily inwards. Wetterstein steps sideways, startled, but then immediately blocks the doorway again when Marion tries to get past him and enter the room.

'Why are you being so obstructive if he's not here?' she yells.

'Shh, there's no need to shout.' He puts a finger to his lips, trying to calm her down. 'There's absolutely no problem. I can assure you that your husband isn't here!'

'Why are you behaving so strangely, then?' asks Marion, trying to look past him into the chamber.

'I'm . . . in a meeting. But not with your . . .' He gets no further before Marion thrusts him aside and enters the room.

Monika Raak is leaning against a table, smiling at her with her arms crossed. 'Satisfied?' she asks sardonically.

'What . . .?' Now it's Marion's turn to be utterly flabbergasted.

'He thought you were his wife!' Monika points to Joachim, who is now quietly pushing the door closed.

'Are you reassured now?' he asks Marion. 'Would you mind leaving?'

Marion has recovered from her surprise. 'No, I'm sorry, I didn't intend to disturb you, of course, but I've no intention of leaving. There's something I want to know!'

'Do you need me for this?' Monika has detached herself from the table. 'If not, I'd like to leave!'

Marion considers. It's a fair bet that Monika Raak was never stupid enough to trust her husband with her money. On the other hand, she can't forgive her for that phone call. One humiliation is enough.

She nods. Without offering to shake hands, Monika walks out past her. Joachim Wetterstein sees her out, but comes straight back.

'It's not what you think!' be begins, closing the door behind him.

'I hadn't thought anything at all until now, but I'm beginning to,' she replies, a hint of disgust in her voice.

He looks at her thoughtfully for a moment and then gives what's obviously a forced smile. 'Now, what can I do for you? You said you were looking for your husband?'

Marion is no longer sure that she's asking the right person. Perhaps she'll wreck Günther's plans if she tells Wetterstein anything. But since Günther hasn't considered it necessary to keep her informed about important matters affecting them both, she can't be certain. So any risk is of Günther's own making.

'You can give me some information that I need about a particular plot of land,' she begins, but promptly interrupts herself. 'Should we perhaps discuss this in your office?'

For a talk of any length, their present position – the mayor standing by the door and she in the middle of the chamber – seems too rigid.

'After you.' He opens the door. 'Is Günther going after another lucrative bit of business?' he asks, his curiosity aroused, as Marion passes him on her way out of the room.

'That's exactly what I want you to tell me!'

Günther is astonished to hear that his wife has been round to his office. 'What did you tell her?' he asks his secretary.

'Only that you had to go out again in a hurry.'

He stands in front of her desk, glaring down at her. 'And did you also tell her where I was going?'

She doesn't bat an eyelid. 'How could I? I didn't know myself!'

'Get me my home number. Immediately!'

He slams the door behind him and comes to a halt by his desk. That's the absolute limit! His wife's spying on him again! He hurries back to the door. 'Hold it!' he barks at the secretary. 'First I must speak to Klaus Raak! And make it snappy!' Then he withdraws into his own office again, and it's not long before his phone rings.

'At last,' says Klaus before Günther can get a word in. 'Didn't you get my message? I tried to get hold of you this morning.'

Günther comes straight to the point. 'Is the cash safely stowed away? Is everything going according to plan? What about the sales? Tell me!'

Klaus is silent for a moment, then asks, 'Where's the fire?'

'Marion's been here, and I wouldn't mind betting she's been to the bank. I've got to know whether I can give her the push today or whether it's still too soon.'

'By the time she's even begun to grasp what's going on, she won't be able to get her hands on anything. Things are under way and there's no stopping them now.'

'Thank goodness. That's really good to hear. Thanks, Klaus.' Günther sighs with relief and sits down on the edge of his desk. 'What happens now? Are we going to get together? I'd like to know the details!'

'Sure. Whenever you like.'

'I'll be right with you!'

Manfred is almost back in Römersfeld now. He's been really stepping on it. For the first time in his car-driving career he's noticed how many people crawl along the motorway in the fast lane, holding him up. Actually he is normally one of those who take it fairly gently, but today, when he's in a real hurry, he sees everything differently. By the time he's reached the exit for Römersfeld he's identified three categories of annoying driver: the pedants who like to point out to everybody that seventy miles an hour is quite fast enough and who therefore drive in the fast lane even when the inside lane is empty for miles ahead; a second group, mainly elderly people or sometimes women, who cling nervously to the outside crash barrier because they're afraid that if they move over to the inside lane they'll never ever get back out into the fast lane; and lastly the fat cat executive types who are simply convinced that their car is better, faster and more expensive than anyone else's and that when they bought the vehicle they naturally bought the fast lane with it. Manfred arrives in Römersfeld with his nerves in shreds.

Silence has fallen in the mayor's office. Marion has outlined her suspicions, and now they are looking at each other in disbelief. Marion finds it simply incredible that there's no basis for all the speculation about the land near the animal sanctuary, and Joachim is puzzling over what benefit anybody could derive from starting such a rumour.

'Are you sure that it really is to do with that area? How could anyone think of developing an industrial zone on the west of the town when we've already got one on the eastern side?' Thoughtfully he rubs his forehead, and Marion watches the movement of his hand. His low hairline leaves little room for a forehead; he has a large Roman nose and his lips are too thin. He's certainly not handsome, but he's got something about him. Maybe the attraction lies in his clear grey eyes, which are now turned towards the door because someone's just knocked. 'Yes, what is it?'

Coffee is brought in and, while they drink, each in turn suggests possible explanations, until Marion starts to wonder what it might mean for her if this whole business isn't connected with the animal sanctuary. Is it possible that it never was? Did she draw false conclusions from the bits of information that she had? She tries to cast her mind back. It started with that weird cheque. Günther made a donation of 600 marks to the Animal Welfare League and explained away that magnanimous deed by saying he'd lost a bet with Klaus. And then the next day she met Regine at the animal sanctuary – and after all Regine *is* the wife of her husband's financial adviser. Marion can't get any further. As usual, no coherent picture emerges.

Joachim Wetterstein is brooding too. If Schmidt has withdrawn as much money as Marion says, then there's something afoot. Perhaps something that he, as mayor, ought to know about. In his mind he runs through the companies that are on the verge of bankruptcy right now. Is Günther planning to buy something up? Expand? Change direction? Merge? The whole thing makes no sense. But maybe it's got nothing to do with Römersfeld but his business interests in eastern Germany. Maybe he's having to push more money in that direction because not everything is going as swimmingly as he always claims.

'I really can't help you any further,' he says at last, leaning back in his armchair. 'I simply have no idea what could be behind it.'

'Well.' Marion takes the hint that she's being invited to leave. 'Thank you for giving me your time anyway.'

Joachim Wetterstein rises and accompanies her to the door. 'Not at all, I'm the one who should be grateful to you.'

Alone again, he goes over to the window, still puzzling over the matter. What could it all be about if not some huge profit-making deal? He remembers the strange phone call Günther made to him on the day after the birthday party, about Linda's makeup bag. It's not like him to trouble himself about such things. But this line of thought gets him nowhere either.

He remains standing for a while longer, lost in thought, then picks up the phone. 'I'm glad I've caught you,' he says when Monika answers. 'Marion's just told me a most peculiar story . . .' He gives her a brief outline of their conversation.

'Linda's makeup bag, you say?' With one hand Monika had been putting her shopping away while holding the phone in the other, but now she straightens up and stands motionless. 'Günther phoned you about Linda's makeup bag? Has he ever done anything of the kind before?'

Joachim shakes his head but makes no reply.

'Have you taken a good look at your son lately?' asks Monika slowly.

'What's he got to do with it?'

'Have you?'

Joachim thinks. 'I haven't seen him for days.'

'He seems as though he's in quite a bad way. Richi had to fetch him back from Stuttgart because he'd been in some seedy bar and couldn't pay and had to pawn his watch.'

Joachim is speechless. 'My wife never told me about that!'

'Even mothers don't get to hear about everything that goes on!'

Manfred has driven straight to the job centre. His instinct tells him that every minute counts. As he's backing into a parking space, his mobile rings. 'Not now,' he growls. He pulls forward a little to position himself better and finally lines the car up to his satisfaction, dead centre. The mobile's still ringing. He picks it up and looks at the display. It's a number he knows: Marion Schmidt's! Oh yes, that would just suit her! She can jolly well leave a message on his voicemail. As soon as the contract's in his pocket he'll call her back with a glass of champagne in his hand. 'Bottoms up, Marion – how does it feel to be a loser?' he'll say. That's a good line, he thinks as he gets out of the car – I must remember it.

· * ·

Marion has already left a message at Manfred's office that 'the animal sanctuary is dead', and now she repeats the same formula on to his voicemail. Fancy having a mobile and not keeping it with you! The wretched thing is called a mobile, not a stationary, she thinks crossly before she quickly leaves her message: 'Pity I couldn't get hold of you anywhere, Manfred. I just wanted to tell you that you can stop making your enquiries about the animal sanctuary. The whole thing was a misunderstanding. The land is just farmland without any special value and is going to stay that way. The town authorities aren't interested in developing an industrial estate over in the west – so it's back to square one. The mayor sends his compliments. Marion.'

So that's that done with. Now she just needs to locate her husband and make him explain himself.

Manfred couldn't get his signature on to the purchase contract fast enough. Once that was done the solicitor, Peter Lang, promptly departed. Now, with the smile of a man who knows victory is his, Manfred is counting out 180,000 marks in 1,000-mark notes on to the desk. Annemarie stacks them up in piles of ten so as to keep track. 'And the last 10,000, as agreed,' chuckles Manfred. 'Your little agency fee. We really ought to have a drink on it!'

She looks up briefly from counting the notes. 'It's not time for me to knock off yet.'

'Don't tell me you haven't got any champagne or glasses here? Don't you ever have anything to celebrate in a job centre?'

'The jobless don't usually have much money or much cause for celebrations.'

Manfred, positively fizzing with good humour, grins. 'Come on now,' he says, endeavouring to give his voice a sexy low reso-nance, 'are the two of us jobless? Do we look as if we are? You've just made a nice little profit, and I've bought a worthless patch of ground.' He almost splits his sides laughing at his own joke.

Annemarie puts the money into a large envelope, which she locks away in her desk drawer, then she stands up. 'Even so, people are waiting outside. I won't complain about you jumping the queue today, but other people have their rights too!'

'Don't be so strict,' he pipes, getting up too. 'We'll get round to having that drink together.' With this prophecy he shakes her hand and goes.

Scarcely has the door closed on him when Annemarie throws her arms in the air and spins round several times on the spot, laughing out loud. 'Wow!' she rejoices, rolling her eyes, 'I can't believe it! It's really happened!' She grabs the telephone and calls Regine's number. 'I've got the cash!' she laughs into the mouthpiece. '170,000 marks! I'm going to paint the town red tonight. Are you on? Can you come?'

Manfred gets into his car, kisses the contract and puts it down beside him. There – now he can go to the office with complete peace of mind, and this evening he'll really push the boat out. It would be the triumph of his life to take Günther out to the pub, polish off a bottle with him, and only then tell him what they've been celebrating. He grins to himself and reaches for the phone. Let's see if he can get hold of him. Günther's secretary says he's with his financial adviser. This almost makes Manfred laugh out loud. They're still messing about with the details of their grand coup while he's already got it in the bag. In exuberant mood he has himself put through to Günther at Raak's office.

Günther seems surprised to get the call, but Manfred explains that this is the only way to get hold of him and that he'd really like to go out for a few drinks with him. The way they used to. Old mates together, this evening if possible. The drinks will be on him, of course. That always goes down well with a Swabian.

But Günther isn't so keen. 'I'm up to my ears, and this evening I've got a major deal going down!'

Manfred smirks. This major deal is precisely the one he's just messed up for him. 'Oh well, another time, then,' he says and hangs up. In that case he'll contact Marion instead and spoil her good mood. He needs that satisfaction before he goes home. He remembers his voicemail, he'll just quickly listen to what she's got to say and then prepare to strike back. With a grin he keys in the number.

Manfred hears the message three times over. His smile has become frozen. But he refuses to believe what he's hearing. He dials the voicemail number again. And then again. It sounds so genuine. Did she really go and see Wetterstein? Or is she lying to him?

With trembling fingers he dials the switchboard number. He presses a wrong key and has to start again. A few moments later he's speaking to Günther again. 'Günther,' he blurts out, 'have you heard that the land next to the animal sanctuary is to be developed for an industrial estate?' He holds his breath. Now Günther must react.

'Industrial estate?' Günther's tone is impatient. 'You're not serious. That's nonsense! Who on earth would build there?'

Manfred swallows, his throat dry.

'Where did you get that idea from?' Günther wants to know.

'From somebody who ought to know,' he says, his voice shaking.

'That's utter rubbish. Nobody would invest money in that.'

Now it's clear to Manfred. He's gambled and lost – everything. He needs to think of something fast.

'What if it's some big project?' he asks, hoping to elicit something after all.

Günther hesitates. 'What sort of a big project – nobody's got the money for that sort of thing any more!'

'Well, I don't know.' Manfred thinks frantically: 'An airfield, maybe?'

'Don't be absurd!'

'A hospital, sheltered housing, an industrial park, how should I know!'

He hears Günther take a deep breath. 'How about a convent?' Günther sounds as if he's about to slam the phone down. 'What does our friend Wetterstein have to say?'

Manfred lowers his voice. 'He knows nothing about it yet!'

'He knows nothing about it?' Günther explodes with laughter. 'The grand panjandrum of the council knows nothing about it when his own lot are supposedly planning to build on a green-field site? Come on, forget it!'

Günther puts the phone down and looks doubtfully at Klaus.

'Do you think it's possible that the land by the animal sanctuary is going to be developed?'

Klaus wrinkles his forehead. 'Manfred reckons it might be an airfield . . .'

'An airfield?' Klaus raises his eyebrows. 'Have *you* got a pilot's licence?'

'No.'

'Well, there you are. Neither have I. So Römersfeld doesn't need an airfield!'

Günther grins. 'Seriously, though . . .'

'What put it into his head?'

'He says he was told it, but apparently Wetterstein doesn't know anything about it yet.'

Klaus gives a dismissive wave of the hand. 'Doesn't make sense. Unless,' he ponders, 'the reason why Wetterstein claims not to know is that it's too early to admit to knowing about it, then it could be a bit of a bargain . . .'

Günther stands up, goes over to the wall cabinet and folds Klaus's little bar down. 'Would you like one too?' he asks Klaus, reaching for the bottle of cognac.

In the mirror of the drinks cabinet he sees Klaus nod.

Returning to the desk with two well-filled glasses, he gives one to Klaus. 'And how could one find that out?' he asks.

'By buying the plot of land and then waiting to see what happens!' replies Klaus, pulling a face.

Manfred is still sitting in his car, at the same spot. He hasn't dared to start the car because he's so overwrought that he's afraid he'll drive straight into the nearest tree. He has a sense of being totally out of control; his whole body is in revolt and is alternating between violent sweating and bouts of shivering. His only hope is that Günther has taken the bait. Then he could sell him the land through some intermediary. If necessary at half the price he has paid himself.

He grasps the leather steering wheel with both hands and bangs his forehead against it several times. How could he be so stupid? How could it happen? What went wrong?

Then another thought enters his mind. He could go and retrieve the money. He knows where it is. In an envelope in the drawer of her desk. It would be easy to break into it. Or he could follow her when she leaves the job centre. It's too late for her to bank the money today. She'll have the envelope on her, and she'll be taking it home with her. Somehow he must get his hands on it. And then tomorrow the nightmare will be over. He'll pay the three outstanding accounts in cash, and everything will go back to the way it was.

In Römersfeld the evening rush-hour traffic is gradually starting to build up. Marion still hasn't managed to locate her husband, Linda has been pacing to and fro in her flat for hours, and Annemarie Roser is studying the view through her office window. Spread out below her is the job centre's big car park, which more and more cars are leaving, while opposite, looking across some low buildings, she can see the church tower.

Behind that rise the gentle contours of the vineyards, slightly indistinct in the haze. She gazes up at the sky. It's not brilliantly fine weather, certainly, but it's warm and at least there's no sign of rain on the way. Later on she'll meet Regine for an evening walk and then they'll drink to the 170,000 marks in some quaint old inn. The extra 10,000 will remain her secret, but the drinks will be on her tonight. She unlocks her desk drawer, takes out the envelope, presses it quickly to her lips and puts it in her handbag. Time to stop work – time to start living.

Manfred sees her approaching. He's still in his car, but he's driven it into one of the rows of cars at the far end of the car park. There are a few bushes and trees to give him some cover, and he watches Annemarie get into a smartly kept small car. She has a good figure, he thinks, but her short hairstyle suggests an excess of testosterone. And he can do without a woman with male hormones; he has his own. He starts the car. He has no plan yet – he's relying on his ability to think on his feet in crisis situations. Inspiration will come to him when it's needed. Annemarie Roser drives off without looking round. Manfred drops in behind her in the rush-hour traffic and pulls the visor down. You never know.

Linda has come to a decision. She's stopped her restless prowling round the flat and is sitting down at the table with a blank sheet of paper on which she has written columns of numbers. There is a quicker way of doing this, but she wants to have it all set out clearly before her:

1,000 DM
1,000 DM
1,000 DM
1,000 DM

1,000 DM
1,000 DM

When she's filled up a whole side of paper she stops. What she's written comes to exactly 100,000 marks. With that amount she could move to another town and start up a business of her own. A sunbed centre perhaps, or a copying and printing service, or anything that would make her independent. She lies back in her chair and props her feet up on the table. But that would mean having to put up with Günther's attentions at least a hundred times. One hundred times, that's an awful lot, even to get the start-up capital to launch her into independence. Who knows what new ideas he may come up with? He might even bring a mate with him or something, she wouldn't put it past him.

She crumples the paper into a ball and throws it into the waste-paper basket. How awkward that she has no one she can discuss it with. She thinks of Irena; she hasn't heard from her for some time and it would be nice to get together again for an evening and have a good gossip. But Irena is Richi's sister, and Richi is Dirk's best friend, so something would be sure to get back to him. And when all's said and done, it's nobody's business what she chooses to do in her own time.

'Choose' is hardly the right word; 'drift into' would be more like it, she thinks as she saunters over to the fridge. Maybe a slice of bread and cheese will take her mind off it all.

Annemarie is weaving her way through the traffic, humming to herself. She's happy. How suddenly her life's taken a turn for the better. She'll put the 10,000 marks into an interest-bearing account, and once she has enough holiday entitlement she'll splash out on a trip round the world. She doesn't need a new sofa, nor a bigger car, but she'd like to see foreign countries and experience foreign cultures, talk to people with quite different lives, find out what the world has to offer. She's already looking forward to it. She turns off into her own part of town. It consists of blocks of flats, all built parallel to each other and pretty dull architecturally, especially as you're always looking into the windows or on to the balconies of the block opposite, but the buildings are well maintained and set in gardens that won a 'towns in bloom' award five years ago. She parks in her parking space, no. 78 in the shared car park. That's the only thing that's strictly observed here – well, that and the sorting of household waste, another perennial topic. At first most people put their biological waste into the correct bin, but in plastic bags. And the tins were left in the yellow bags unrinsed and stinking – a disgrace to the neighbourhood.

Annemarie tucks her bag under her arm, carefully locks the car and follows the narrow path between the bushes to the refuse bins, which are close to the street and screened by a tall wooden fence. She has done this every evening since the occasion six months ago when, purely by chance, she discovered four newborn kittens in the bin for non-recyclable rubbish.

Manfred has parked between two other cars and sees his opportunity. He grabs the champagne bottle from the passenger seat and starts walking. Annemarie Roser is ahead of him, and if he's careful she won't hear him approaching. A discreet blow to the back of the head, a quick snatch for her bag, and off back to his car. It'll look like an ordinary mugging, and it's a fair bet that there are a few foreigners living not too far away, so every rightthinking German will know straightaway where to find the perpetrator of an attack on a helpless woman.

Manfred watches Annemarie closely, hastening his step. She seems lost in thought, and now he can hear her warbling away to herself. She's almost at the first bin. What's she doing there anyway? She's not carrying any rubbish. Is she planning to hide her money there? Surely she doesn't steal from other people's refuse?

Another three steps and then it'll be over and done with. He clutches the bottle by the neck like a club and is just raising it to get enough momentum to strike when suddenly he's knocked into from behind and pushed sideways so that he lands with a crash against the wooden fence. An animal of monstrous size has shot past him and is jumping up at Annemarie, who, strangely enough, shows no fear and makes no attempt to ward it off but instead turns round towards it with a laugh. The beast's muzzle is on a level with Annemarie's face. 'Bobby, old chap, are you here already? Where's your mistress?'

Then she notices Manfred, who is standing, disconcerted, by the fence, the bottle in his hand. 'Well I never, what are you doing here?' she asks, smiling at him. 'Do you live in this part of town too? What a coincidence!' She hugs the dog and, without paying any further attention to Manfred, immediately starts opening the bins one after another.

Manfred watches her, thinking. She's seen him. If he steals the money from her now, obviously she'll know who did it. He'd have to murder her. But is it worth it? And what would this loathsome dog do?

'Ah, there you are!' A woman's voice behind him. Now it's too late anyway. 'We were standing at your door waiting for you!' He turns his head. Regine Raak, that's all he needed. What on earth is she doing here?

'Oh, Manfred. What a surprise!' She offers him her hand, which he takes, thoroughly embarrassed. 'Did you come together?' She looks from Manfred to Annemarie and back again.

'Not as far as I know,' laughs Annemarie. 'He lives round here!'

The Raaks know where I live, thinks Manfred. You'd better

think of something! 'Round here?' Regine looks at him incredulously.

'No,' he slowly raises the champagne bottle, 'to tell you the
truth, this afternoon I thought Frau Roser and I might drink to
our bit of business, but unfortunately she didn't have time, so I
came here to see if we could do it after all . . .'

'Really?' Annemarie eyes him in astonishment.

'Yes . . .' Manfred gives an embarrassed shrug, which isn't difficult in the circumstances. 'If you really want to know, I find you
attractive.' He says it without a blush, and it's Annemarie Roser
who colours now. This has never happened to her before. An
admirer by the rubbish bins!

'I didn't hear you coming,' she says frankly.

'To be honest, I wasn't at all sure you wouldn't send me
packing. I sort of wanted to take you unawares and yet at the
same time I didn't . . . I'm not putting this very well' – he gives
her a look of abject apology – 'but do you understand what I
mean?'

'Were you going to try and grab the money back from her?'
Regine and Bobby are both scrutinising him with their heads on
one side.

'Are you off your head?' Manfred snaps at her. There's a
moment of silence. 'Why should I do anything like that? Added
to which,' he continues at last with a short laugh, 'in that case
surely I'd have come with a weapon, not a bottle of champagne!'

'Is it chilled, at least?' asks Regine, looking him in the eye.

'Well, not any more.'

Annemarie clears her throat. 'Well now . . .' she says indecisively.

Bobby has pressed himself up against Regine, but hasn't taken
his eyes off Manfred for one second. Regine scratches his massive head. 'Does this alter our plans for the evening?' she
questions Annemarie.

'We were going for a walk together, you see,' explains Annemarie, at which Manfred takes a step backwards.

'I wouldn't want to intrude in any way,' he says, and, thinking quickly, holds out the bottle decisively towards Annemarie. 'Perhaps another time. You could put it on ice in the meantime. Or else the two of you could drink it together, just as you like.'

Annemarie thanks him and nods to him. 'Well, in that case . . .' Manfred raises both hands in farewell and slowly retraces his steps to his car.

'Well, what do you make of *that*?' asks Regine, watching him as he gets in.

Annemarie reads the label on the bottle. 'A really expensive one. To be honest, I don't get it at all.'

Manfred starts his car, choking with rage. Did that bitch really have to get in his way, that adulterous slag who's never done anything worthwhile in her whole life? As though it was some kind of achievement to pinch other women's husbands! He drives away. He wishes he could have thumped her and her lousy cur over the head with another bottle, that would have done no harm. And what's happened instead? He's had to back off! He, Manfred Büschelmeyer, six feet tall and weighing fourteen stone, manager of a DIY store, successful, virile, has to admit defeat by a pair of totally insignificant women. The next person he meets will get a kick up the backside. There's an ear-splitting crash; he's thrown forward with an almighty jerk, his safety belt tightens and catapults him back into his seat, and the back of his head hits the head rest with a bang. Not knowing what's happened, he remains seated with his eyes shut for a few moments, then looks up. He's gone straight into the back of a car that was coming to a stop. He just didn't see the car, nor the red light. Why does there have to be a pedestrian crossing in this rotten bit of the town? Nobody here needs a pedestrian crossing. Fuming, he gets out and goes up to the car in front of him. Of course, he might have known it! A woman driver! Too stupid to drive on. He shouts at her through her open window, but she shows absolutely no reaction. She picks up her mobile and dials a number, says a few words and then gets out of her car. She looks about his age, short black hair, jeans and jacket.

'The police are on their way,' she remarks, looking coolly at the damage. There's glass on the road, the front end of his car is totally wrecked and the boot of hers is crushed. 'Not your day, is it?' she says at last with a mocking expression. That really is the last straw.

Marion has already been sitting idly at home for some time. She has no idea where Günther could be, and her mood is shifting between extremes of anger and anxiety. She can sense that there's something dark and menacing gathering above her head, but she can't identify it. And she doesn't know how to deal with it. Up to now her role has always been clearly defined, consisting of performing her social duties at Günther's side, giving him moral support, being there for him, relieving him of any burdensome tasks, seeing that his clothes were always impeccable, that he never missed an appointment at the barber's and always had good food, beautifully kept surroundings and a perfectly run household. For herself she'd taken on the role of the disciplined wife who lives according to set principles so that her husband has a strong partner. A woman finds her happiness through the success of a husband; that was drummed into her by her parents, and that's what she herself has always believed. And she's followed the parental decree to the letter. Her husband is successful; he's held in general esteem and is also a good-looking man, and that makes her happiness as a woman complete. What more is there to aspire to?

This was still what she felt – genuinely and deeply – on

Günther's sixtieth birthday. That was only a fortnight ago, but just recently all the strands of her life have seemed to be unravelling and going off in different directions, though she can't say why or where to.

Feeling tense and strained, she sits in the big armchair and lets her gaze roam round the big living room. Do I have a life at all? she suddenly asks herself, but before she can take this thought any further she abruptly gets to her feet. She had a strict Catholic upbringing, and finds it almost sinful to think about herself. It's wrong to put herself in the foreground, so the act of devoting thought to herself is as bad as looking at herself naked in a mirror. She remembers the *Penitent's Handbook* of her childhood, and how she used to say, 'I have been immodest by myself or with others.' She opens the big oak cabinet where she keeps the expensive glasses and the better quality spirits, and pours herself a cognac. That's another thing she's never done before at this time of day.

Günther has made sure that the basis for his new life is firmly in place, and now he can start building on it. Next week that fellow from Liechtenstein is coming for the meeting with the solicitor, and then after the divorce Marion can count herself lucky if he gives her anything of his own free will. He takes his leave of Klaus with a firm handshake, man to man, and once in his car immediately phones Linda. 'Tomorrow will see the start of a new life,' he declares, almost before she's had time to lift the receiver.

'How do you mean?' she asks.

'From tomorrow the world is ours – yours and mine.'

'I still don't follow!'

Amused, he laughs loudly down the phone. 'You'll see soon enough. This evening I'm going to go for it, no half measures! Put the champagne on ice!' He makes a loud kissing noise and hangs up.

Linda resumes her prowling round the flat. Since Günther entered her life she's seemed like a stranger to herself. Are there two sides to her? Or is she undergoing a personality change?

Eminently satisfied, like Günther, Klaus is leaving his office. That's it for today. Now he can indulge himself a little. Tomorrow he'll write Günther the first invoice, and as soon as the money's been received he'll spend it all, every penny of it, in the city of Regine's choice. This will be just the advance of all the sums he'll have coming in if he handles things with sufficient skill. His conversation with Günther has shown him very clearly that the opportunity is there for the taking. Günther, the uncrowned king of Römersfeld, always behaves as though he's totally au fait with every aspect of life, but in matters of finance he has a lot to learn. Soon enough he's pretty sure to lose track of all the dodges that Klaus is planning. And who can guess how Marion will react this evening when Günther, coldly smiling, tells her about the new plans he's made for his future. After all, she comes from a military family – perhaps she'll kill him on the spot. Then he'd have lost a friend – he'd be sorry about that – but he could make a fitting speech at the funeral and then see to it that Günther's wealth is immediately redirected to other purposes.

Marion is standing at the window when Günther comes through from the kitchen into the living room. He can't make out her face clearly because she has her back to the light. But her silhouette strikes him as somehow altered, and he suspects that she isn't exactly going to greet him with a smile. He decides to go on to the attack. 'Since when have you been spying on me? I won't have it!'

She doesn't move, except to fold her arms. 'Where is the million marks from our joint account?' she asks in a flat voice.

'Gone,' he replies coolly.

'I have a right to know. It's my money too!'

He grins. 'That's absurd! None of it's yours. I earned it all myself by my own hard work.'

She's silent for a moment, then she says with a firmness that surprises Günther, 'You know that isn't true. The capital that enabled you to start up in business came from me when I married you.'

He laughs disparagingly. 'That was your dowry, Marion. All over the world young men get money for taking a daughter off an ageing father's hands. When you married me that became mine. I don't know what you expect.'

Now she moves away from the window and comes slowly towards him. Günther notices that, rather unusually for her, she's wearing a plain black trouser suit and has combed her hair severely back.

She comes to a halt two steps away from him. 'What's going on?'

'I'm going to get a divorce from you, Marion. It's not because of anything to do with you, it's really purely about me. One phase of my life is over; I'm not old yet, I want to enjoy life, I'm starting again!'

She stares at him, and for the first time he notices that she has her father's eyes. Hard and cold, just like his. Blue steel.

'If you want a divorce,' she says slowly, emphasising each word, 'then that has a whole lot to do with me!'

'I can't see how.'

'Then tell me why. Why so suddenly?' Just don't break down now, Marion tells herself, tensing her stomach muscles. He's just waiting for you to start crying.

'I told you. I'm starting a new life!'

'And you'd like to cast me off like an old glove!'

'If that's the way you see it . . .'

So her feelings hadn't deceived her. Her gut feeling had told her what her head had no means of knowing yet. 'Don't you find this manner of demanding a divorce rather uncivilised?' she asks in the ensuing silence.

'I could have faxed you or got my lawyer to inform you, or not bothered to tell you at all, like other husbands,' he says with a slight shrug. 'But I'm standing here and talking to you and telling you that our time together has run out. That's fair, surely. Everything comes to an end sometime!'

If Marion had a pistol in her pocket, she would provide instant confirmation of his words. But she hasn't got one, and he isn't worth it. She turns away from him. 'What's her name?'

'That's irrelevant!'

'How old is she?'

'Young enough for it to be fun!'

'So what happens next?'

'You move out.'

'When?'

'As soon as possible. I'll let you keep your car.'

'Please don't go overboard with the generosity!'

'That's just my nature!'

Marion returns to the window, while Günther goes upstairs without another word. Up to now she'd always thought that in this sort of situation you'd feel the ground open up beneath your feet and you'd fall into a deep chasm, a bottomless pit. But there she is, still standing, and the flowers are waving gently in the breeze, and clouds are drifting across the sky. Actually, nothing shattering has happened. The world hasn't come off its axis. Marion stands there, staring and marvelling. She doesn't even shed a tear. She thinks what her father would have said. But she mustn't be guided by that, it's *her* life.

Only at this thought does her stomach suddenly tighten. Her life. What has she made of it? How is it to continue? It's the only one she has! She picks up her bunch of keys and marches into the garage. She'll go and seek legal advice, and if by any chance the lawyer's office is already closed she knows his private address. Then it occurs to her, as the garage door is just opening, that he's not her lawyer, but Günther's. She must get a different one.

Preferably a woman.

But where from? She doesn't know a single woman lawyer.

Günther has gone into the bathroom, and he grins to himself as he hears the sound of the automatic garage door. That went better than expected. Now she'll dash over to our lawyer's, and he'll give her the right advice. Then it'll be all up with her, and she'll be glad enough to come out of the whole affair without ending up in debt. Because she certainly won't want to take on the debts that he'll soon be able to show her. Günther, you're a sly old fox, he tells himself, turning on the shower.

Marion is sitting irresolutely in her car. It's too late in the day now to go hunting for a woman lawyer. It's stupid that they're not listed in the telephone book, like doctors. So she has to have a name before she can look up an address and phone number.

In her mind she runs through the people she knows. She remembers that Monika's been through a divorce. But is she prepared to bare her soul to that woman? They've never really liked each other. Though perhaps only because they've never got to know each other properly. Monika was always acting the high-powered businesswoman, and Marion disliked that. As far as she was concerned – in defiance of all movements for women's emancipation – a woman's place was at her husband's side.

And now look where it's got her!

She drives out of the garage and off towards the town. Where the speed camera had been sawn off there's now a new one. Just like my situation, she thinks: as soon as Günther has got rid of one, there's a new one in place. And to think that I nearly did the job for him! Her hacksaw comes to mind. So do a dozen gruesome film scenes. Or perhaps they aren't scenes from films, maybe it's her imagination putting together these scenarios of horror. At all events, the hacksaw's still in the garage. In good working order too.

The perfect implement for deceived wives.

Monika has just watched the television news and is searching through all the channels in the hope of finding a relaxing film when the doorbell rings. Oh? She looks at the clock. It'll just be one of her children. Forgotten to bring a key, typical! She presses the buzzer and opens the door a fraction and then goes into the kitchen. Better have a look straightaway to see what she can give her offspring to eat. Then she hears a hesitant knock and a long, drawn-out 'Hellooo?' In amazement she returns to the door. She does a double-take. It's Marion Schmidt standing in the doorway, looking somehow different, not as impeccably ladylike as usual, but unmistakably Marion Schmidt.

'Do excuse me for barging in on you like this, Frau Raak,' she says, standing motionless on the threshold. 'I would have phoned you on the way, but I'm afraid I couldn't find your number.'

'I'm ex-directory, Frau Schmidt.'

'Of yes, of course.'

Monika invites her unexpected guest into the living room, offers her a seat at the table and switches off the television. 'What would you like to drink?' she asks next. 'Wine, beer? Mineral water or juice?'

'To be honest' – it's obvious how hard Marion is finding all this – 'all I'd really like is some advice from you. And I couldn't wait till tomorrow, because I'm' – she's clearly having to search for the right words – 'too impatient, too restless. I needed to do something!'

'Ah,' says Monika, still poised indecisively between living room and kitchen. 'Why is that?' Without the drinks, she sits down on a chair facing Marion.

Marion swallows, then lifts her head and looks Marion straight in the eye. 'I need a good lawyer, a woman, and I don't know one. My husband has just informed me that he wants a divorce.'

There's a moment's silence.

'Just like that?' asks Monika at last.

'Yes, just like that!'

Alarm bells are going off in Monika's head. Surely he wouldn't do that on account of Linda? She gets to her feet. 'I need a brandy! How about you?'

Marion doesn't hesitate for a second. 'Yes!'

Günther has set out, freshly showered and dressed in youthfully casual style, with a chilled bottle of champagne from Marion's stock. He can celebrate today – why wait until tomorrow? Tonight is his night! On the way over to Linda's he keeps calling her number, but she doesn't pick up the phone. She'll be having a bath, preparing herself for him, because her feminine instinct is bound to tell her that he's coming tonight! He switches his radio on, right in the middle of a song with the refrain 'Men are pigs'. That's the limit, he thinks crossly, listening incredulously to a few more lines and then activating the seek-tuning control. 'These bastards who knock their own sex,' he grumbles aloud, but just then he recognises a few bars of 'Strangers in the Night', stops retuning and sings lustily along with it. He can identify with Ol' Blue Eyes, he was one for the ladies too.

Linda suspects that it's Günther who's responsible for the constantly ringing telephone. He said he would come tomorrow. She can face that, but she can't face him tonight. Tonight is her night, and even if he were to sit wailing on the doorstep that would make no difference. She needs her calm before the storm, because just in this past hour she's worked out how she's going to handle her new status as a kept woman. If he simply must have her, then she'll lose no time in telling him what *she* simply must have, namely a boutique in Stuttgart. And not in some downmarket part of town either, but right in the centre. Selling Joop, Gucci, Jil Sander, Thierry Mugler, either some lines from each of them or one label exclusively. He's supposed to have connections all over the place, so now he can use them in her favour for a change. On this basis she can put up with his old man's body with the floppy dangling bits.

Linda stands behind her curtain. She doesn't have to wait long before she sees his car turning into the estate. Let him believe he's the great hero, if he needs to. But not until tomorrow. She runs water into the bath and ignores his persistent ringing at the door.

Günther weighs up the situation. He can't give the game away to Marion by spending the night at home. She must believe that his new love life is all action. He'll drive home, quickly pack an overnight bag and take himself off to some hotel in Stuttgart for the night. Damn it, girl, where are you? he fumes as he restarts the car. Once she's his wife he'll soon teach her not to play games. In that respect she could afford to learn from Marion.

Marion has got everything off her chest. Hesitantly at first, but then with mounting fury, she gives vent to what she would have liked to hurl in Günther's face. Her constant self-restraint towards him, her dutifulness, the suppression of her own needs, the pressure of always having to keep up her role. 'And now he's just getting rid of me. As though there had been nothing between us, as though all those years had never happened! Thirty-five years of marriage, swept away just like that!' She fixes her gaze on Monika, and suddenly the dam breaks. The tears pour out and she sobs without restraint. 'How can anyone be like that?' she wails, and Monika hands her a packet of tissues.

'You just have a cry, it'll do you good. Let it wash out everything that's weighing on your soul. I'll make us a cup of tea.'

After some time Marion is just sobbing, dry-eyed. Eventually even that comes to an end. 'Why am I actually crying?' she asks herself after a while, as Monika pours her a cup of black tea and puts the brown sugar to hand. 'Am I crying about him? Or about myself? About an illusion that's been shattered? About the house? Or because I'm afraid of the future? Afraid of society, of people?'

'That would be the only justifiable reason for being afraid,' Monika interrupts, stirring her tea.

'People?' asks Marion, raising her puffy face questioningly.

'Do you remember Günther's sixtieth birthday?'

'How could I forget it?' Marion replies with a sigh.

'I haven't forgotten it either!' Monika rests her spoon next to her cup and gazes at her.

'You? Why? You weren't even there!'

'Exactly!' She lets the word hang in the air for a moment before adding, 'I wasn't invited.'

For a while neither speaks. Marion studies her hands, which are resting on the table near her cup. Then she nods. 'Yes, I understand.' She looks up. 'I understand what you're saying. It was wrong.'

'It's something that's wrong with society!'

'I was wrong. We *are* society!'

Again some minutes pass in silence. 'I'm very grateful to you,' says Marion at last. 'Our conversation has done me good, even if that sounds very selfish of me.'

'It was selfish, and that's a good thing,' smiles Monika. 'There are some women who need to learn that they have an existence of their own. We're not in this world to serve others. The provision of services belongs to the realm of business and commerce, and it gets paid for!'

'You're refreshingly different!' Marion stands up slowly. 'I really am most grateful to you! And for Frau Kell's address, too.'

'I'll ring her in the morning and tell her to expect a call from you.'

'Thank you.'

Monika also gets up, but shakes her head. 'You're surely not going home with a face that shows you've been crying?' she asks. 'Do you want to hand your husband a triumph like that?'

Marion feels her face with her fingers. 'Do I look such a fright?'

Monika frowns, and then has to laugh. 'If you ask me, you'd do better to stay here. On purely tactical grounds you shouldn't let your husband see you in this state. I have a guest room and a separate little shower room – you're welcome to make use of them. I'm sure that together we can find anything else you may need!'

Anna Kell has listened to what Monika Raak has to tell her. She knows the Schmidts, just as everyone else in Römersfeld knows them. Money-grubbing, ambitious, conventional. And influential with it. All just surface show, their snow-white villa typifies it, and beneath the surface lie intrigue, nepotism and corruption. You can take Günther Schmidt on and win, but equally you can take him on and lose everything. Who knows what else might be affected by this divorce case? Perhaps one's whole livelihood.

Swivelling round on her desk chair, Anna Kell looks out of

the window at the busy activity in the main street. Friday, the final sprint to the line. The whole of Römersfeld goes shopping as though the currency were about to be devalued. For Anna, who has spent much of her life in Berlin, it's a fascinating picture. In this town everything happens as regularly as clockwork. Each day has its rituals, and Saturday is the day of the collective worship of the golden calf. Anna has never seen queues as long as those for the two car washes in Römersfeld, not even when the Italian border officials went on strike – and she had to queue for a full two hours then. She finds it even more remarkable, though, that the freshly washed cars can only be parked when the bit of street outside the house, or the numbered parking space, has been swept as clean as a whistle, together with the porch, the hall and the balcony. Without the weekly clean, organised by rota, panic would be sure to break out in Römersfeld, decency and morality would collapse and the mayor would be deposed. Anna grins and lights a cigarette. She inhales deeply and leans back. But precisely because that's the way of Römersfeld people, she could be putting her own livelihood at risk by agreeing to represent this client. Just now, when she's bought this house, an old one, with a suggestion of art nouveau, and is planning to do it up in a rather unusual way. If her planning application is turned down she'll have poured her money down the drain, and if the banks start being difficult she may as well pack up and go. So she needs to think carefully whether or not to lock horns with Schmidt & Co. What was it she so blithely urged Monika Raak to do at the time of her divorce from that wanker, the financial adviser? Listen to the selfish part of you, she had told her; ultimately you're all that matters. Not the reasons, not the difficulties, not the ifs and buts, but you yourself. Have the courage to stand up for yourself and what's in *your* interests. Go all out for that! You'll be glad you did.

Great stuff, Anna, she thinks. And what is your own healthy egotism telling you right now?

Don't touch it!

Marion has come home and found that neither side of the bed has been slept in. So he really was capable of leaving her on the very first night. Instantly her heart sinks, but she quickly pulls herself together. She's just sorry that means he isn't aware that she didn't come home either. Perhaps the idea that she might have a lover in the background would have taken some of the wind out of his sails. Out of long-established habit, Marion makes herself her 'good morning' coffee, and immediately afterwards she fetches her bank statements. She finds out a case and puts everything into it, before going into Günther's study to find the corresponding documents of his. Various gaps in his filing cabinet tell her that he's beaten her to it and that things are really getting serious. He has no intention of playing fair. He wants to dump her: a BMW convertible and a toll pass for the bridge in exchange for thirty-five years of marriage. 'We'll see about that,' she hisses through her teeth, dialling the number that Monika Raak gave her yesterday. Monika is sure to have told the lawyer, Frau Kell, about her by now.

Günther has paid 280 marks for a night of frustration in a hotel, has got his own back by stuffing himself immoderately at the breakfast buffet, and is now cross about his round belly as he crawls along in the morning rush hour, stopping and starting all the time. It's all the women's fault, he grumbles to himself, Marion occupying his house like some Roman matron and Linda not at home when he needs her. Not even now. He's called her several times but nobody's answered. Has she gone to work? She can save herself the trouble in future, because once she's living with him she'll have enough to do looking after the house and garden. And any time that's left over she can devote to making herself look nice for him. At this thought his mood immediately improves. He's looking forward to this evening, because this time they have a definite date and her lovely body will be all his. Turning all this over in his mind, he thinks of a few little amusements that he'd like to try out with her. At the next traffic lights he does a U-turn and drives back the way he's come. He can still remember from earlier days where to find the Beate Uhse sex shop.

Since Monika said goodbye to Marion early this morning she's been considering what to do. She has coffee with Richi in the office while they discuss some business matters. As he goes back to his own office, she wonders why she hasn't asked him about Dirk. She has no concrete reason, just a vague anxiety that her suspicion might be correct. It's not that Linda has fallen for some Adonis who came in to buy some after-shave, but that Günther Schmidt has fallen for *her*. What a stupid business; does everything in life have to repeat itself? Or was Günther so impressed with what his friend Klaus did that he felt obliged to trump it? She wouldn't put it past him. Showing off is certainly part of Günther's makeup, and if what he needed for his image was a Zulu chieftain's daughter he would probably give that a try. Why on earth hasn't anybody ever told him how phoney his behaviour looks? And how awfully ridiculous? Or could it be that to other people he doesn't appear ridiculous or phoney, but manly? Strong? Enviable? She has no idea. Apparently no one sees through him. Or perhaps they don't want to see through him because they'd rather keep him as leader of the pack. But what about Linda? The thought makes Monika shudder, and she goes over to Richi, who looks up from his computer screen. 'Did we forget something?' he asks.

'I just remembered Dirk. How is he?'

'I wish I knew. I haven't been able to get hold of him any-where. He seems to have vanished into thin air.'

'A new love?'

Richi gives a short laugh. 'I think he's more likely still to be chewing over the old one!'

'And what's Linda doing?' asks Monika nervously.

'You'd have to ask Irena. She doesn't tell me her secrets.' He grins and after a pause adds a meaningful, 'More's the pity.'

'Men!' Monika shakes her head at her son and throws him a mocking look as she leaves his office.

When the call is put through, Anna Kell takes a deep breath. She doesn't find it easy to say no to a woman like Marion Schmidt. Not because of who she is, but because she senses that Marion's husband will pull out all the stops to inflict total defeat on her. If she didn't need to fear the consequences for herself, she would even enjoy the challenge. Taking on someone like Günther Schmidt requires not just professional expertise but also suffi-cient cunning to see through his tricks.

'Anna Kell speaking,' she says. 'Good morning, Frau Schmidt.'

Marion briefly outlines what she already knows, then waits eagerly for a reply.

'Documents missing and accounts emptied,' Anna reflects aloud. 'Hmm, the classic scenario. I dare say he has some plan worked out for his companies too?'

There's silence at the other end of the line.

'Frau Schmidt?'

'I don't know.' Her voice sounds despondent.

'You know what it means if . . .'

'So he's been carefully planning the divorce for some time!'

That wasn't what Anna was getting at – she meant the finan-cial disaster. But Marion has suddenly understood how Günther has been scheming, and this deception is more painful to her than anything else. She's close to losing her self-control and has to make an effort not to burst into tears.

Anna Kell considers. 'How exactly did he express his intention to seek a divorce?'

Every word is etched into Marion's memory, and she repeats the conversation almost word for word. '"Don't go overboard with the generosity," I said, when he offered me the car,' she concludes. 'I was being sarcastic, of course.'

'And what did he say to that?'

'I can still hear him saying it. He said, "That's just my nature!"'

It certainly is, you disgusting hypocrite, thinks Anna, but says instead, 'I can't make you any promises. He's very powerful in Römersfeld and has many influential connections.'

'I know,' Marion replies slowly. It's strange how everything that she's always taken pride in is now suddenly being turned against her. And to think of that noble promise he made about protecting her. He'd be her protector as long as she lived, he said to her on their wedding night. And now if anything he ought to protect her against himself. What crazy twists life can take. 'I'll risk it,' she adds. What choice have I got? she thinks.

Anna hesitates, then nods in a determined way into the telephone. 'Okay, so will I! I'll risk it too. If he should win, we'll both be on social security, I hope you realise that! The only way we have any chance is for you to put your best effort into the case too.'

'Oh, I will, don't worry!' Marion's voice is recovering its normal vigour. 'You can rely on that, Frau Kell. Thank you so very much . . .'

When Manfred woke up he immediately rolled over and went back to sleep. At some point later on he phoned the office, explained that he'd been involved in a car accident the day before and was in severe pain from a whiplash injury, and went back to bed. If he can go on making himself believe that for a while longer, perhaps he'll die of it, which is what he'd like best right now. Car smashed up, money gone, actual fraud and intent to commit murder. He tosses and turns. And the person he came so close to killing was the wrong person. That little Roser woman wasn't really at fault. It's Marion Schmidt who's to blame for everything. She's the one who's left him with these mountains of debt. And now she's sitting on her dosh, laughing at him fit to bust. While he has to rescue himself as best he can. He gets out of bed and fetches two sleeping pills. If people in Römersfeld get to hear that he paid 180,000 marks for a worthless bit of land he'll be the laughing stock of the town. And if anybody looks into it more closely . . . he daren't even think about that. He washes the pills down with a hefty swig of whisky straight from the bottle. He wants to forget the whole thing again for a while before he turns his mind to it seriously. And who knows, maybe the solution will come to him in a dream.

Annemarie Roser has not been in such a good mood for ages. This afternoon a reporter from the *Courier* is coming to see the animal sanctuary, and so is the editor of Römersfeld's local freesheet, because Regine has notified the press of Annemarie's achievements on behalf of the Animal Welfare League. Nobody on the papers could quite believe the story, but they immediately scented a sensation. And stories about animals always go down well with the readers, especially in the *Courier*'s weekend edition.

Joachim Wetterstein can't get Marion Schmidt's story out of his head. Günther's whole life revolves around business. He simply can't imagine him doing anything for purely private reasons, and linking his son with it seems to him quite misguided. Before he asks Dirk, he wants to look into it a bit himself. He phones the head of his building department and asks him for a plan of the area surrounding the animal sanctuary. If he knows who owns the plots of land there, maybe he'll be somewhat the wiser.

An hour later he asks his office to get Max Dreher on the phone, and hears that the plot adjoining the animal sanctuary has been sold.

'What's going on all of a sudden?' Max Dreher demands to know. 'Yesterday a woman called Schmidt was up here at the farm asking the same thing. What's so special about that bit of land?'

'Nothing, really,' replies the mayor, thinking: that's just it. Why are they all so interested in that plot? he wonders. He gets a subordinate to ask the planning office whether a change-of-use application has been received. The answer is negative, nothing of the kind as yet. Joachim thinks it over. So Annemarie Roser has bought a piece of land for the Animal Welfare League on spec. But has she actually bought it for the society? He studies the ownership of the adjacent areas of land. One field, between the plot in question and the farm, is still owned by the Drehers, but as for the rest . . . he stops short and grabs the telephone. This time instead of asking for a connection he dials the number himself.

He gets Monika at her desk in her office.

'Is your father's first name Berthold? Berthold Herzog?'

'Yes, why?'

'I thought so. I knew Herzog because of course that was your maiden name, but I couldn't remember for certain whether your father was called Berthold. Did you know that you own several hectares of land out by the animal sanctuary?'

'Yes, of course, it was my mother's when my parents married. Worth very little, unless I'm much mistaken.'

'How did your mother come by it?'

'Back then my grandfather was one of the bigger farmers around here. My uncle, one of my mother's two brothers, took over the farm and let it go downhill somewhat. He's very old now.'

'What was your mother's maiden name?'

'Why do you ask?'

'I'll tell you in a minute.'

'Dreher.'

'Max Dreher's sister?'

'That's right. But now . . .'

'We must get together! Straightaway!'

'As bad as that?' she asks smugly.

'Even worse!'

Linda is unpacking stock in the cosmetics shop and considering what to do with all her money. She doesn't want to pay it in at her bank, as she knows the clerks there and she's sure they'd start wondering about the constant deposits of cash. She'll open a savings account at another bank, possibly even one in Stuttgart, and whenever Günther slips her some money she'll deposit it there. She's already looking forward to that. She just hopes that Günther won't freak out and want anything too exotic sexually, but will be reasonable and stick to the sort of fare he's probably always had. Plain homely fare.

Monika set out immediately. It's less risky to meet at the municipal offices than in a restaurant or at the edge of the woods, let alone at her own house. In a place like Römersfeld people watch the mayor's every move. An affair could be fatal for him, and neither of them wants that. They've known each other since their schooldays; they were part of the same group of friends, liked each other a lot, did a bit of snogging on the quiet, took their exams together, and got married. Each of them to somebody else. Joachim had fallen in love with Ilse, who was then a beautiful young girl from the neighbouring town with a peaches-and-cream complexion, and Monika had found Klaus, the ambitious financial adviser, irresistible. As the years went by,

Joachim and Monika realised that they were still fond of each other, while their love for their partners had long since cooled off. And sometimes they discuss what might have been, if they had taken their youthful feelings for each other more seriously.

They meet in the council chamber, and Joachim locks the door behind them.

'I hope we don't get another surprise like yesterday's,' he says with a grin.

'I can tell you something about that,' Monika intimates. She informs Joachim of her unexpected visitor last night.

'Interesting,' says Joachim. 'So this business really is to do with Günther's private life. I'd never have thought it! Even so,' he lowers his voice, 'perhaps our friend Schmidt has inadvertently put us on to something!'

'How do you mean?' asks Monika. Joachim indicates that this is something just between the two of them, and they move two chairs so that they directly face each other. Monika smiles and sits down on one of them. 'Are we talking about an X-file?' she whispers conspiratorially.

'We may be talking big money,' replies Joachim quietly. A challenge lurks in the twitching at the corners of his mouth.

Two hours later Manfred wakes up. Buried deep beneath his quilt, he's slept as though in a coma, and now he's woken up with a splitting headache but no solution to his problems. I'll have to face up to things, he finally tells himself, and goes into the bathroom for a shave and a cold shower. He almost fails to hear the phone until he's alerted to it by his loud message on the answering-machine. He steps quickly through to the living room to take the call. He had reckoned with a call from his office, but to his surprise it's Monika Raak.

'They said in your office that you're not feeling well. I imagine that's because of the land by the animal sanctuary. You've spent a lot of money buying a worthless patch of grass and an old barn. I can understand why you have a headache.'

Manfred has subsided on to a chair. 'How do you know?' he asks weakly, placing the flat of his hand against his forehead.

'I expect everybody will know tomorrow, because the press are already out at the sanctuary. They think this rather sensational sale will make a great story!'

'Oh no, that'll be the end of me!'

'You're telling me.'

There are a few moments' silence. Then Manfred pulls himself together. 'What do you want?'

'To buy the land off you at a reasonable price.'

'Why?'

'Because my family owned it. Max shouldn't have sold it without discussing it with the family. Not to Frau Roser or anybody else!'

'I don't follow.'

'Max Dreher is my uncle – his farm was my mother's parents' home, where she grew up.'

'Oh!' Manfred suddenly sees the light. He can get himself off the hook. He's found a sucker! 'How much?' he asks.

'I'll offer you 90,000 marks.'

'That's only half of what it cost me!' he explodes indignantly.

'Half or nothing!' Monika's tone is determined.

'But I can't do that,' he protests, 'I paid 180,000 marks.'

'What can I say?' Monika laughs gently. 'It's your own fault, Herr Büschelmeyer. But it's even worse for me, because I'm having to pay 90,000 marks to buy back a piece of land that's worth only 10,000. And all because of your stupidity, if you'll forgive my saying so. So kindly show a bit more gratitude that I'm making you this offer at all! I could equally well leave you to stew and forget about my family feelings!'

Manfred slumps down in his chair.

'I have a problem,' he confesses after a few seconds of silence. 'I must have the other 90,000, or I'm done for!'

When Monika hangs up five minutes later, she's satisfied with herself and the world. She hadn't expected Manfred to concede defeat so easily. He really must have been going through agonies of dread. As arranged, Joachim phones her soon afterwards.

'I've got the land,' she tells him immediately, 'at the price we agreed. I've already let the solicitor know, and we can tie it all up today. So you can put it on the agenda for Tuesday.'

Günther has been browsing round the Beate Uhse shop for over an hour. Now that he's here, he'd like to have a good look at everything. When he leaves he's got two porn videos that he and Linda can watch and then imitate, and a battery-powered vibrator bigger than anything he could achieve even with three potency pills. She might well enjoy that, a bit of hand-operated fun, he thinks lasciviously as he trots towards his car with his plastic bag.

Marion has taken all the relevant papers that she can find to Anna Kell's office. Unfortunately the documents relating to his companies, properties and holdings of land are either in his office or with his financial adviser. Could Klaus be working hand in glove with him? She can't really believe that he would be. It's quite annoying that it's already Friday and nothing can be done over the weekend. Should she stay in the house over the weekend? Attempt another discussion with Günther? But who knows if he'll come home anyway? She has no choice but to wait and see.

To make good use of the time, she sits down at a table on the terrace and notes down everything that occurs to her about Günther's business affairs, but her thoughts stray to her approaching birthday, on Tuesday. How on earth has this happened? Only yesterday Günther was proposing a meal at the Palace Hotel to celebrate her reaching fifty-five, and today he wants to throw her out of the house. Fear starts to creep up on her, and she feels like hiding in a corner like a small child. Somehow things will turn out all right, get back to normal. And until they do she just wants to cover her face with her hands and pretend she's not there.

After a few minutes, though, she pulls herself together. She *will* celebrate her birthday, if not with Günther then with her bridge friends. She'll throw a party such as she's never thrown for herself before. A party worthy of the Schmidts. But this time just for *Marion* Schmidt! Marion fetches the phone at once and calls Ulrike Goedhart.

Her best friend is astonished – she hadn't expected an invitation to Marion's birthday party. 'But you never celebrate it!' she says.

'Well, I'm going to this time!' Marion declares. 'It's going to be a really glittering affair, with music and – if necessary – a male stripper!'

'A male stripper? You?'

'Yes, me. What's so unusual about that?'

'Well, I don't know . . .'

Ulrike Goedhart is an architect – and, given the male-dominated society of Römersfeld, a very successful one. She has to laugh. 'I must tell you something now, Marion, and if you fancy it you can come too. On your birthday I'm afraid our whole gang will be at another party.'

At first the news comes as a disappointment to Marion, but then she resolves, come what may, to take up the offer. 'And I could come along?'

'Absolutely. We'd be delighted – and it'll be great fun.'

'If you could just explain . . .'

To begin with Marion hears only merry laughter. 'Have you ever been to a lingerie party?' asks Ulrike at last.

'Never even heard of one. What is it?'

'It'll be a novelty for us too. It's at Greta Kremer's house, and apart from us there will be quite a few other women coming from Römersfeld and Kirchweiler, I don't know exactly who. But it's sure to be a real hoot.'

A lingerie party. Marion has no idea what that might involve. 'Do we dress in lingerie for the party, or how does it work?'

Ulrike roars with laughter. 'It's a party where you buy things. Like Tupperware, I suppose. But don't ask me, I've never been to one either. Bring some cash along, in case you want to buy something, and the evening is yours to enjoy!'

From her balcony Linda sees the big silver saloon turning in at the entrance to her estate. She stands up and goes into the bathroom for a minute to check her appearance. On the way back she stops near the phone and looks around her small living room. Flowers everywhere. During her lunch break she went to the most elegant china shop in Römersfeld and bought herself three really beautiful, huge vases. For someone in her circumstances they were much too expensive, but since right now her circumstances are changing from one day to the next, she bought them anyway. Now she contemplates the juxtapositions of colour with a certain pride, delighted to see how the gorgeous bouquets are shown off to even better effect by the vases, and waits for the phone to ring.

Just before driving into the garage, Günther calls her. 'What are you wearing?' he wants to know.

She looks down at herself. 'You'll like it,' she says in her sexiest voice.

'Describe it!'

'I'm wearing a low-cut top over my full breasts, no bra, and under my short skirt . . .' The concrete walls of the garage cut off communication. Relieved, Linda puts the receiver down. Let him see for himself what she's got on.

In a few moments her bell rings. Günther must have parked right by the lift. She opens the door, and he takes a deep breath. 'You look ravishing,' he declares with satisfaction, then kisses her and waves two tickets in the air as he goes into the flat. 'Return flight to Hamburg, just a taster. What do you think of that?'

A lot. She's never been to Hamburg.

Günther sets down his capacious executive case and lays the tickets on the table.

Linda throws her arms around his neck. 'That's brilliant! A really brilliant idea.'

'Bit of shopping, bit of sightseeing, bit of the Reeperbahn, get ourselves into the mood for Paris. The flight's tomorrow morning, returning on Sunday evening. Not long, but long enough . . .' He grins and tweaks her nipple gently through her top.

'Great! I'm absolutely bowled over!' Linda laughs. 'What should I bring?'

Günther puts a hand under her skirt and gives her buttock a firm squeeze. 'You've already got everything that matters! We can buy anything else we need. Have you got something in the fridge to drink, before I make a start on you?'

Marion probably wouldn't believe that this is her husband, Linda thinks as she goes to the fridge. 'I have some reserves in the car,' she hears him say, 'a case of champagne, one of red wine and one of white. Do you think that'll last another week?' He gives a resounding laugh, and as she returns with the bottle he puts two champagne glasses on to the table.

'Where do they come from?' she asks, surprised.

He points to his case and says mysteriously, 'This is the alchemist's poison cupboard.'

'What?'
'You'll see!'

Peace has gradually returned to the animal sanctuary. The news that Annemarie Roser had sold the piece of land soon got round. As well as journalists, a large number of animal lovers came – people who regularly supported the sanctuary, found homes for animals or were active in animal protection work. In no time at all more than twenty people had gathered, and Regine went off in her car to get drinks and sandwiches. Many of the people ended up simply sitting together in the yard, either on upturned boxes or on old chairs. The mood was exuberant and they all had their own ideas on how to use the large sum of money.

'First you must have back the money you pinched from your joint account, and your donation too,' Annemarie had said to Regine right at the start.

Regine protested, 'I won't take back the donation unless you take yours back too!'

This made Annemarie feel mean, so she came clean to Regine about having taken a commission.

'Well, what of it?' Regine retorted. 'You earned it! Manfred didn't pay the extra simply out of the kindness of his heart, you can be sure of that!'

Günther has taken the two filled glasses to the bedroom and now vanished into the bathroom. Linda stands irresolutely by the bedroom door. She's just showered, and it's obvious what's coming next. But the details are still something of a mystery. Whatever is he carting around in his executive case?

Günther comes out of the bathroom, beaming, with a towel round his middle and droplets of water on his skin. 'Where's your video-recorder?' he asks, looking round.

'I haven't got one.'

'Really? That's impossible!' He glances at the television in the corner. 'Why ever not?'

Linda reflects. 'I've never needed one,' she says lamely.

'If only I'd known! You need one of those combined systems for your bedroom. One of those little cube-shaped ones with a built-in video-recorder. Never mind, next time,' he deliberates aloud, and then mutters to himself, 'If there's any point!'

Linda has pricked up her ears. 'What do you mean?' she demands.

'Well,' he picks up the two glasses and hands her one, 'a lot of things could change very quickly. Perhaps you'll soon be moving out of here, and then you'll have a big widescreen TV and several videos all over the house.'

'Why should that happen?' Linda clinks glasses with him.

'Just wait and see!'

Manfred has just left Monika's office with conflicting feelings. On the one hand the 90,000 marks in his pocket are a great comfort, but on the other he can't rid himself of the idea that she may have pulled a fast one on him. He's not sure whether he can take her story at face value. Okay, so somebody might want to keep the family inheritance together, but at such a crazy price? How did she phrase it over the phone – 80,000 marks above its true value? For the other 90,000 he's going to get a loan from her bank, she's already given instructions for that too. On Monday he simply has to go along there and it'll all be settled. It seems too good to be true. Even so, he's not comfortable with his own role in all this. A woman arranging things for him; he doesn't like that, however much he benefits from it.

*

Linda, meanwhile, has gone along with Günther's little sex games. If he thinks he needs some extra reinforcement he can have it. She has no objections to a dildo, even though the idea would never have occurred to her with Dirk. As long as there isn't another man attached to that spare part, she doesn't mind. She can easily deal with a person like Günther. And quickly too, that's the main thing. Günther, all hot and flushed from his breathtaking bout of lovemaking, sits up and gazes at Linda, who turns on to her side and reaches out a hand for her glass. 'You have a heavenly body,' he says, running his fingertips down over her waist. 'When I look at you, I could start all over again.'

She laughs and takes a sip. 'I'm sure you could,' she says, sitting up. 'But we want to have our fun again tomorrow, don't we?'

'You bet!'

He stretches out on the bed and looks up at her. 'Would you have believed that we'd be so well matched sexually?'

'Well, you're an expert!'

'Yes, thanks, I know. But you're not bad either!'

It's the weekend in Römersfeld. Günther and Linda have set out for Stuttgart Airport, after Günther went back to his own house very early in the morning to pack a suitcase. Marion acted as though she couldn't care less, but as soon as Günther had gone she threw herself into gardening to work off her anger. Klaus has invited Regine to come to Stuttgart and have a stroll round the city, and Monika has taken a train to Munich to go to the opera with a friend that evening. Richi is doggedly trying to persuade Dirk to come to the beer garden with him, but Dirk is still using his exams as an excuse and burying himself in his books. And Irena is still away.

It was the first time Linda had ever flown. She enjoyed it, even if she felt a little odd sitting next to Günther. She could almost feel some of the people in the seats behind them wondering whether she was his daughter or his girlfriend. Not a very honourable position, she thinks at first, but after a while she really doesn't care. Nobody knows her here, so it makes no difference.

She's thrilled with Hamburg. Even the taxi ride to the hotel seems exciting. She likes the completely different way the houses are built here, the old villas with their high ornamental plaster ceilings, which can be glimpsed through the windows, the Inner Alster with the fountain in the middle, and the Jungfernstieg. 'I could really live here,' she says enthusiastically, impulsively squeezing Günther's hand.

'And we're lucky, the weather's being kind to us,' he says in a more matter-of-fact tone as he pays off the taxi. It's halted in front of the Four Seasons Hotel, and before Linda can say anything her door is swiftly opened. A commissionaire in hotel livery bids them welcome. She mounts the red-carpeted steps at Günther's side, as nonchalantly as she can manage, but the splendour of the foyer, with its superior kinds of wood, its precious tapestries and antiques, still takes her breath away. She would never have dared to dream of ever setting foot in such a luxurious hotel. Günther deals with the formalities and accompanies her to the lift, which is promptly held open by a lift attendant. Linda can scarcely believe it; it reminds her of the film of *Paradise for Three*, which she enjoyed as absolutely glorious kitsch because it contained this sort of thing. Now she sees that kitsch can be real.

'Well?' asks Günther as they walk along a corridor upstairs, 'Did I promise too much?'

'It's a dream,' Linda acknowledges, and she means it. He stops outside Room 516 and unlocks the door. Linda goes ahead of him into a bright double room with a huge bed and a view on to the Inner Alster. There's a knock behind them: the luggage has already been brought up. Günther fishes in his breast pocket for a tip. Then they're alone, and Günther turns towards her with a meaningful smile. 'Shall we unwind a little before we go and have a wander round the city?'

On Sunday evening, while Günther and Linda are flying home, Richi's telephone rings. To his surprise it's Dirk. 'Don't think I'm off my head, but I simply must get my own back on him, or else I'll never get back to my normal frame of mind!'

'Who? Who are you talking about?'

Dirk leaves the question unanswered. 'D'you fancy a beer?' he asks instead.

'Okay, I'll come and pick you up.'

Half an hour later they're sitting in Römersfeld's one and only beer garden, under Dirk's favourite chestnut tree. The table has only just become free, and Dirk had to sprint across to grab it before any other customers. 'Promise you'll keep this to yourself?' is his first question.

'You *are* making a mystery of it,' growls Richi, signalling to the waitress that they'd each like a Pils.

Dirk looks around. There are plenty of people in the garden, enticed by the fine weather, but he can't see anyone who knows them in the immediate area. That's good. He leans across the table to Richi and says softly but intensely, 'I'm absolutely livid, and if I don't give Günther Schmidt a hiding I'll end up murdering him!'

'Sorry if I seem a bit slow on the uptake, but why Günther Schmidt?' Richi puts down the menu that he had just picked up.

Dirk lowers his voice still further, so that it's barely more than a hiss. 'He's taken Linda away from me!' It takes a visible effort for him to say this, and Richi has to stop himself from laughing out loud.

'You're kidding,' he says disbelievingly.

'No, I'm not, damn it!'

Richi suddenly remembers his mother's strange comments. How could she have known already? Or do women really have an instinct for this sort of thing?

'I'm sorry, but I just can't believe it! What would a woman like

Linda want with a repulsive oaf like Günther?'

'If I knew that I'd feel better. Honestly, Richi, I thought I'd got over it, but I was just deluding myself. It's driving me mad!'

Their two freshly pulled lagers arrive, and they clink glasses and drink them down almost in one go.

'Phew, that's better!' They both bang their glasses down hard on the wooden table and wipe their mouths with the backs of their hands. Richi belches into his upper arm. '"Scuse me,' he says. 'Couldn't help it!'

'You're welcome,' nods Dirk, and waves a hand in the air to order two more.

Richi lowers his voice. 'Well? How did it happen?'

'Yeah, if only I knew! Looking back now, I get all mixed up, but it all started with a supper. She was insisting I should go round to her flat, and she did actually cook a meal and stuff. But, to be honest, Richi, I didn't want to go. I couldn't be bothered to move from my place, and I really didn't see why she couldn't just as well run something up at home!'

'Oh man,' groans Richi, 'you really screwed up there. She planned the evening, she cooked for you, maybe she had other things in mind too. She needed to do it and feel she'd made a real success of it! So what did you tell her?'

'That I couldn't find my car . . .' mutters Dirk sheepishly.

'You're hopeless! Then a young lover would jump on his bike, set a new marathon record, take a taxi – but not use a feeble excuse like that. What did she say?'

'The same.'

'The same?'

'The same as you've just said.'

'Well, can you wonder?'

'I wanted to marry her, really and truly, Richi, don't laugh. I'd imagined it all, the proposal down by the river, the champagne, the night of passion . . .'

'And that's as far as you got!'

'What do you mean?'

'The night of passion, man! You can't expect to get anything without making an effort!'

'But up to then everything *had* just happened of its own accord, honestly, and in my book about women it says that they need space but that they also like to have something familiar to hold on to, mainly out of a need for security. So what was there to worry about?'

Their beers arrive, and Richi orders a plate of salami and sausage to go with them. 'Well, now you've seen what there was to worry about. Linda knew all about wanting her own space, but unfortunately she doesn't seem to have read the bit about needing security!'

'Are you taking the piss?' Dirk bursts out, so loudly that some people at nearby tables turn round to look at them.

'I'm sorry, but really you've dug a hole for yourself. It's hard to accept that it should be Günther who is burying you in it, I grant you.' He thumps himself on the forehead. 'Günther and Linda, that makes even me feel sick!'

'I'd like to give him a real thrashing!'

'He's stronger than you are.'

'I thought you were my friend.'

Richi frowns. 'We can give it some thought. Maybe we'll have a brainwave. But first, I need to eat something.'

The new week begins with a glorious blue sky and frantic activity. Günther has spent the night at home because that is where his suits are, and his ironed shirts and cleaned shoes. And he needs all these things today because he plans to go to his bank to arrange for the sale of his building to the Liechtenstein Company. He's slept in the guest room to show Marion the boundaries, but when he looks in his wardrobe for his blue-and-white striped shirt with the button-down collar, the one that goes perfectly with the suit that he's already laid out, he gets cross.

'Marion! Where are my shirts?'

'Where do you think they are?' she says, appearing in her dressing-gown. That's something that's never happened before. Not at this time of the morning.

'Well, they're not here,' he snaps at her.

'Why should they be?' she asks in a bored tone of voice, running the fingers of both hands through her uncombed hair. 'Or do you think shirts can fly?'

'What's that supposed to mean?'

'Well, for instance, fly from the laundry basket to here. Via the washing-machine and the ironing-board. I'm going back to bed. You know where to find the coffee!' And she's gone.

Blazing with fury, Günther puts on a different shirt and swears she'll live to regret this. He's about to lay the first stone for his revenge.

No sooner has he gone downstairs than Marion too launches herself into feverish activity. She showers with lightning speed – doesn't spend time on blowing her perm into perfect shape with the dryer but instead quickly sprays her hair and pushes it back behind her ears – puts on a comfortable dress and shoes with low heels, and in minutes she's on her way to Anna Kell's with all the papers she's gathered and the notes she's made. She stops at a corner bakery and buys some croissants. She's assuming that her new lawyer will have a coffee machine, so this way at least she won't have to miss breakfast.

*

Meanwhile Monika is sitting in Richi's office, talking about the jobs, deadlines and plans for the week. 'And what's the matter with you?' she suddenly asks, for no obvious reason.

'Me? Why?' he asks, but his blue eyes can hardly manage to look her in the face.

'Come on,' is all she says.

'Leave it, Mum! It has nothing to do with you or the business. It really is purely a personal matter.'

'All right then. I've got something to tell you, too.' She snaps her organiser shut.

'What d'you mean, "too"?'

'Just what I say, "too".' She smiles at him.

'Fine! So, what is it?' Mothers can be quite impossible sometimes, he thinks.

'We're going to build!'

'Oh!' He looks at her as if he's genuinely afraid she's gone off her head.

'A car body plant. We're developing the West Römersfeld Industrial Estate. And we'll be the first firm to start up there, *and* the nearest to the access road. The best position! And a body plant will bring us profits that up to now we've had to leave for other people!' She stretches out contentedly in her chair.

Richi slowly taps his forehead. 'Are you mad? Why should that suddenly become an industrial estate? That land belongs to the animal sanctuary, doesn't it?'

Monika laughs. 'The area is on the agenda for tomorrow's council meeting as land to be scheduled for development. I've already expressed an interest and made concrete proposals. If we really can build there, the town will get the business rates. And we create jobs. So it's very much in the town's interest!'

Richi leans forward. 'In the interests of your friend the mayor, you mean!'

'What's that supposed to mean?' She gives him a disapproving look.

'Has he really got no personal interest in seeing the land turned into an industrial estate?' he asks innocently.

Yes, he has, thinks Monika, fifty per cent of the proceeds from the sale of the land will go to him. But that's only fair, since if it wasn't for him all the fields and meadows belonging to her family would remain agricultural land and thus more or less valueless. If she and Wetterstein together set something in motion, it's perfectly reasonable for both of them to profit from it.

'Of course he's got an interest in it, after all he represents the town. And anything that benefits the town benefits him, naturally,' she says evasively. 'He does want to win again at the next election!'

Richi leans back. 'So we build a car body plant. Okay, why not. But then we'd better get on with planning it a.s.a.p. The council meeting's tomorrow, and if I know you you'll start building the very next day!'

Monika laughs heartily. 'You really do take after me, you know.' She extracts some notes and small sketches from her organiser and spreads them on the table. 'Yes, I *have* given it some thought over the weekend . . .'

'I thought you went to the opera in Munich?'

'Where better to think about business, totally free from distractions, than the opera?'

Dirk is sitting at his desk, writing away. Yesterday, after the salami and country-style sausages, inspiration finally came to Richi. And since, unlike Richi, Dirk doesn't know much about real estate deals, he's looking things up in various reference books, writing, rejecting and rephrasing, until at last he phones Richi. 'I think I've got it now!'

Richi watches as his mother leaves his office, and tells Dirk to read it out.

'Okay, now how does this sound? "Good morning, Herr Schmidt, my name is Rainer Hoyer and I'm purchasing suitable plots of land in Berlin on behalf of the national government. I've established from the land registry that you are the owner of one of the plots that would very possibly be appropriate for our purposes. We've already looked into the market value and we'd like to make you an offer of 800,000 marks."' He clears his throat. 'What do you think?'

'Ye-es,' answers Richi slowly. 'And you're sure you're right about the land?'

'I told you yesterday, I was there when he was bragging about it to my father.'

'All right then. Well, go ahead and try your luck. Arrange where to meet, and don't forget to disguise your voice!'

'I know – I've been practising.'

A few minutes later Richi's phone rings again. Richi has just started working on an estimate and picks up the phone impatiently.

'He hardly let me finish, because he was in a hurry, but he said that it would suit him very well and that we should meet. He asked me for my phone number in Berlin, but I said I was on the move and that I'd get back to him.'

'Well done! And he didn't recognise your voice?'

'I'm sure if he had he would have reacted differently!'

'Well, that's great. That's the first step then.'

Linda is serving a customer. She's already shown her three ranges of products, describing them in great detail, and she's now on the fourth. She's feeling increasingly impatient and finds herself wondering whether the woman can actually afford these products or whether she just finds this a pleasant way of passing the time.

'Couldn't you suggest something to me?' the woman is saying. 'You can see for yourself what my skin type is.'

Linda studies her face. 'Your skin's the combination type,' she says.

'No, it *was* the combination type. But it's become more dry,' the customer contradicts her.

'I'm sorry, but here on your nose and forehead the skin does seem to be a little greasy. That points to the combination type . . .' Linda tries to convince her that her assessment is right.

'But I'm telling you that it's dry!'

'All right,' Linda says, turning to the displays. 'For dry skin, then, there's a cream here that is light but also rich, by . . .'

'But it says "for mature skin". My skin can hardly count as "mature" yet – I'm only thirty!'

Linda would have judged her to be nearer forty, but perhaps that's down to her stringy brown hair, which hangs down to her shoulders without any proper styling at all, and her badly done makeup, because her face is actually quite pretty.

'What are you using at the moment?'

'Well, it's all packaged in blue – with sort of white writing on it, you know, I can't quite remember . . .'

Behind Linda the shop is filling up, and she can't give the other assistants any help because she's stuck with a silly cow who can't make up her mind and doesn't even know what products she's using.

The outcome of it all is just what Linda has expected almost from the start. 'I'll think about it,' the woman says, looking at her meaningfully. 'Will you be here this afternoon?'

'Yes.' Linda nods in resignation.

'Fine, then I'll come in again this afternoon!'

I'm not going through all that again, thinks Linda, starting to put all the pots, jars and bottles back, though she doesn't actually think she'll ever see her again.

'A nice bit of business that was!' Renate says mockingly when the woman has gone.

'You can say that again.' says Linda angrily. 'All talk and no buy.'

'What we could do with is another customer like that man last week. Do you remember? The one who went off with a huge bagful of stuff!'

'That was two weeks ago,' says Linda absent-mindedly.

'Was it really? What a good memory you've got!'

Linda thinks about Günther. Yes, he certainly gets things moving, and life at his side is easy. But it also has its drawbacks. He obviously has it firmly fixed in his mind that he's going to start a new life with her. And yet he still hasn't asked her if that's what she wants. She wonders how he can be so sure of himself. Or has he always got his own way up to now, so that he simply can't imagine *not* getting it? No sooner conceived than achieved?

Günther encounters no obstacles at his banks. They all know his business acumen and so they assume that he's selling in order to speculate on some much bigger deal, and that he'll land a correspondingly bigger fish. Günther rings Klaus straightaway. 'It's all systems go!' he says. 'You can let your Dr Berger know.'

Manfred Büschelmeyer also gets his business affairs sorted out quickly this morning. After Monika Raak has put in a good word for him, the loan is no problem; only its conditions somewhat dampen Klaus's spirits. He'll have to tighten his belt for some while. But it's better to have lost 90,000 marks than 180,000, he tells himself in an attempt to cheer himself up at least slightly. He has paid the money into the firms' accounts in cash, so there should be no questions asked. He drives to work and sits down, relieved, at his desk. That adventure's over and done with. He's had enough excitement for the time being.

Marion has already been with Anna Kell for an hour, going through the facts of the case. 'How is it possible that you don't know how much money your husband has?' the lawyer finally asks her.

'He just didn't want me to have anything to do with business matters. He always said that he would look after it for both of us . . .'

'Yes, that's what he's doing probably right now,' says Anna Kell drily.

'How do you mean?'

'Well, I'm afraid he's probably one step ahead of you in sorting out his financial affairs. Up to the beginning of the divorce proceedings he can still manipulate all sorts of things to your disadvantage. But if he won't give you any information about his financial situation voluntarily, we'll have to apply for a disclosure order and then pursue your claim through what's called an action by stages.'

'Heavens!' Marion takes a deep breath. 'That sounds like a complicated process, and worst of all a lengthy one.'

'If you could get at the information some other way it would certainly be better, I agree.'

'And if not?'

'Then your husband will have to supply a list of all his property and swear an affidavit that it's correct.'

'And how is it decided what property comes to me after the divorce?'

'The state of your finances and the state of his finances at the beginning of your marriage will be recorded separately, and then compared with what you and he own at the end of the marriage. The difference represents the gain made by each of you during the course of the marriage. Whichever of you has gained more – and we can take it that that'll be Günther – has to pay over to the other partner half of the excess. So for instance, just as an example, if you brought 500,000 marks into the marriage and your husband the same, but now you've still got 500,000 marks while he's got three million, then he's made a gain of 2.5 million, and you're entitled to 1.25 million. Of course if you'd had unequal amounts of money to start with, then the calculation would be done differently, taking that into account.'

'Oh, it's so complicated. I wish I'd never got married!'

'You're not the only one to have wished that.'

Depressed, Marion closes her eyes for a moment, then she pulls herself together. 'I'll ask him how he proposes we should do this. Then we'll go on from there!'

'But please do it soon. Every second counts. With a man like Günther Schmidt, you never know! The sooner we foil his plans the better. And the safer.'

As Marion is just about to stand up, the phone rings. She signals to Anna to ask if she should leave, but the lawyer motions her to sit down again. When she puts the phone down she looks at Marion and makes a slight grimace.

'Has something happened?' asks Marion with foreboding.

'Yes. It's good for our case, but not good for you, unfortunately!'

Unconsciously Marion grips the arm rests of her chair. 'What do you mean?' she asks uncertainly.

'I now know who's at the centre of this merry dance that your husband is engaging in at the moment . . .'

'You mean . . . his girlfriend?' It's still so new and horrible to her that she has difficulty in pronouncing the word.

'Yes! Someone called Linda Hagen. Does that name mean anything to you?'

'Oh my God!' Marion claps her hand to her mouth. 'That's a young woman I invited to Günther's sixtieth birthday party. Together with her boyfriend, the mayor's son. And I even admired the two of them, the way their relationship was so happy and natural!' Marion shakes her head. 'I can't believe it! She's much too young!' And after a while she asks, 'How do you know?'

'A young man who works in the office at Monika Raak's firm happened to see the two of them at the Lufthansa counter at

Stuttgart Airport when he was seeing his brother off. And he mentioned it to Frau Raak because it seemed strange to him. That's how word gets round!'

'It comes as a real blow. And somehow I just can't believe it. What does he want with a young girl like that?' She stands up slowly, trying to regain her composure. 'Isn't it depressing to be replaced by a young thing like that?' she asks. 'After so many years! I was always there for him. And now suddenly all that no longer counts. All those years – just as if they had never been. It's simply unfair, and that's what hurts, Frau Kell. I didn't deserve to have this happen to me! Not like this.'

'I know how you feel.'

'Why – are you divorced too?'

'No. I'm a widow. My husband was killed in a car accident.'

Marion has stopped in the doorway. She looks back at her. 'It makes you wonder which is preferable!'

In the afternoon Marion rings Monika at her office, because she needs to hear it again directly from her. 'I can let you have a word with the young man who saw him,' Monika suggests.

'Oh no, I think it's too . . . private,' Marion objects, though she feels that's a stupid thing to say. 'Even so, Frau Raak, you ought to start a newspaper. Somehow you always get to hear about everything.'

Monika laughs, amused. 'I'll take that as a compliment.'

Marion is sitting in her spacious living room, in which she suddenly no longer feels comfortable. Everything is too big, too impersonal. She feels lost and alone. 'Did you have someone to help you to get over your divorce?' she asks, and then immediately apologises for such a personal question.

'You don't have to apologise. It's a perfectly fair question. Yes, I had my children. They helped me a lot.'

'Ah well, of course I don't have any.'

'But not all children support their mothers. When they're grown up they often have other interests.'

'You mean . . .'

'Going off to study abroad, that sort of thing. Cars, holidays, whatever. In most cases the wife isn't financially in a position to . . .'

'Does everything revolve around money?'

'You must know that better than anyone!'

There's a moment's silence. Marion looks out of the window and takes a deep breath. 'Yes, I suppose you're right. Money and power. Those seem to be the main things that motivate people.'

'And sex!'

'What?'

'You left out sex. Money, power and sex. Then I'm in agreement with you!'

'And what about love?' ponders Marion over the phone.

'You shouldn't be asking me about that. That's not my strong suit!' Monika is laughing again. 'But if you'd like to, you're more than welcome to come over and have supper with me this evening. Around eight o'clock?'

'Thank you very much, Frau Raak, I really appreciate your invitation, but it's my birthday tomorrow, and today I'd like to take stock and think about where my life is going. I think I need to.'

'I can understand that. All the same – the offer still stands.'

Linda has bought various salads from the delicatessen and is in her kitchen putting them out on to small coloured dishes for supper. She's made the table on the balcony more elegant with a new white tablecloth, and when Günther drives up punctually at eight o'clock she takes all the dishes outside and adds a fresh baguette. With a grin of pleasurable anticipation, Günther carries a television set past her into the flat and sets it down in the middle of the room. 'The latest model,' he says, '100 hertz, high-resolution picture and with a built-in video-recorder. I went straight ahead and got this, otherwise it would take too long.'

'What would take too long? I don't understand,' says Linda, greeting him with a kiss.

'Well,' he says, looking straight into her eyes, 'Marion will soon be packing her bags, and then we'll be living together at my house!'

'Why would she do that?'

'Because I'm getting a divorce, my love! What's for supper?'

This evening, unlike last night, there's lots of space in the beer garden, and when Richi and Dirk meet there at about half past eight dark clouds are gathering. 'Typical! The one time you manage to get a table here, there's sure to be a rainstorm.'

'Well, who cares?' They are sitting under the big chestnut tree again, and Richi studies his friend. 'At least you look much better today.'

'I feel much better, now that I know I shall get the chance to give that swine a kick in the balls.'

'Now then, is that the done thing among men?'

'Well, he wasn't bothered about mine!'

Richi laughs and orders two beers and some cheese noodles for himself. 'Aren't you hungry?' he asks Dirk. When he doesn't reply he goes ahead and orders some more. 'My treat! No arguments!'

Dirk gives a wry smile and looks around. A few tables behind him he thinks he can see Petra. He'd better tell Richi about her before she says something, it occurs to him, but then the girl moves and Dirk sees that he was mistaken. Involuntarily he heaves a sigh of relief, until it strikes him that Petra has never got in touch with him again. And that gives him food for thought. Has he really stopped making any impression on women? Was he so bad?

He sits there, mulling it over, until Richi jogs his elbow. 'Hey! Are you dreaming?'

'Yes, I was, actually!' Dirk starts to wonder about himself. 'It begins with daydreaming, then you start talking to yourself and eventually you don't know your own name any more!'

'That's your future mapped out, is it?'

Dirk laughs. 'No, of course not.' The lagers arrive, and they clink glasses. After drinking deeply he has another thought: 'By the way, Richi, what's going on with Karin? You two were always inseparable!'

'That's true, we were. But in the long run I found it too stressful with Karin. She always had a thousand schemes in her head, and as soon as we'd planned something she'd scrap it and start all over again. I may be a Capricorn, but I can't keep jumping around like that. At a certain point I just gave up.'

'I don't believe it. You?'

'Yes, me, why not?'

'Because men never give up!'

'Did you get that out of your famous psychology book?'

Dirk says no more and downs what's left in his glass.

'She's got a new bloke now, anyway. He's a Capricorn too and he's already looking rather pale!'

Dirk laughs out loud. 'You're kidding!'

'No, it's true, I assure you!'

The cheese noodles are brought to the table, and Richi orders two more beers. Dirk tries to get a forkful of food into his mouth, but the cheese forms stretchy strings right back down to the plate. 'That looks ridiculous,' Richi laughs uproariously.

'Well, see if *you* can do any better!' Challengingly, Dirk lays down his fork.

Richi tries to wind the noodles and the strands of cheese round his fork like spaghetti, but that doesn't work either. 'Okay,

I admit it, only Swabians born and bred can manage that!' he says, detaching the cheese with his fingers.

Dirk eats on, grinning. Halfway through he suddenly looks up. 'Shall we go through our plan one more time? If possible I'll do it this week and get it over with.'

'What do you mean, *you* will? How about thinking in terms of teamwork?'

'Well, maybe just this once.'

'You're a complete idiot.'

Marion had hoped that Günther would come home tonight, at least. But she soon discovers that his small suitcase has disappeared, and his toilet bag is missing too. So she can dismiss once and for all that faint glimmer of hope inside her that the whole thing has been some sort of game and that everything will return to normal. He won't come tonight, on the night before her birthday, and most probably not tomorrow either. In order to cope with this emotionally, she'll have to deal with it in a perfectly matter-of-fact way. 'You're an officer's daughter,' she reminds herself, as she goes out into the garden and sits down on the warm stone steps. Tomorrow morning she'll devise a strategy the army general staff would be proud of, she decides. For now, though, she tries to banish all thoughts from her mind. She looks up at the sky. It's slowly getting dark, menacing storm clouds are starting to block out the remaining light. A slight wind rises, presaging the storm, but it's still pleasantly warm. Marion takes off her shoes and places her feet side by side on the stones. Their warmth does her good. She looks at her feet, and the Catholic *Penitent's Handbook* comes into her mind again. All her life she has thought far too little about herself. She's failed to pay attention to herself, and hasn't noticed the changes wrought by time. Now she's fifty-five, and if it weren't for photographs she wouldn't be able to say how she looked or felt at thirty-five. She sits there looking at her toes in wonderment. Her feet have been carrying her through life for so long, and she's never even looked at them properly.

The first heavy raindrops fall. It's warm summer rain and Marion holds up her face towards it. At length she leans back against the stone steps and remains in that position, half sitting and half lying. Round about her the wind tears through the trees; there's a roaring and crashing and the heavens release their charge. Wild flashes of lightning rise above the horizon, and the thunder rolls ever closer. She knows she could be struck dead by the lightning, but that doesn't frighten her. On the contrary. The electricity in the atmosphere, the roaring and thundering around her, the lashing wind and rain – Marion has a sense of being reborn, of being truly alive for the first time in her life. She will enter her fifty-sixth year her own way. Perhaps there are more important things than acting the perfect wife. She laughs aloud and throws up her arms.

She has only one life. And it's hers alone.

At about nine o'clock the following morning Marion's doorbell rings. She opens the door and finds herself looking straight at an enormous bouquet. 'They're from Schmidt,' says the young woman behind it, pressing the flowers into her hand.

'Thank you, that's very nice,' says Marion, so surprised that she forgets to give her a tip. As she goes back into the house, she realises what she's carrying. Carnations! Günther has sent her fifty-five carnations! She tears open the little envelope and reads the card. It's true – he's actually sent her birthday greetings by Interflora, along with fifty-five cemetery flowers. This really is the limit! She feels like throwing them straight on to the compost heap, but after her experience the previous evening she hasn't the heart to do that. After all, they can't help being misused in this way. She arranges them in a vase and stands them in the living room. Perhaps she ought to dry them. Who knows, one day she might be able to lay that bunch of dried flowers on a mound of earth on top of him.

That evening two groups of people are getting ready to go out. One is going to the council meeting, the other to Kirchweiler. Ulrike Goedhart comes to pick Marion up. 'My goodness!' says Marion, after they have exchanged greetings and she's noticed Ulrike's new car. 'I would never have dreamt that you'd swap your sports car for an estate.'

'Only so that we have more room for the shopping . . .' Ulrike opens the passenger door for Marion.

'I feel really stupid, never having been to a thing like this before,' says Marion apologetically. 'I suppose I'm awfully out of touch.'

'Oh, it's a bit of a laugh, that's all. And just so that you know, the bridge ladies are going to buy you a set of lingerie for your birthday. So you can choose something really sophisticated!'

'Is there such a thing in my size?'

'Of course!' Ulrike gets in. 'You need a decent bust for lingerie to look good!'

Marion can't help laughing at this. 'Charming, charming. Well, we'll see!'

In cheerful mood, Manfred Büschelmeyer has been chatting to his party colleagues on the council and they've arranged where they'll be going afterwards for a beer. Eventually they all take their seats, and Manfred scans the agenda. Let's see which little hovel is getting a new bay window. He reads each item through carefully. First general information, then a report of the resolutions passed at the last closed meeting. Item no. 3 is the building of a clubhouse, and item no. 4 the purchase of a second-hand fire engine with a turntable ladder. Manfred yawns surreptitiously and looks across at the mayor. Joachim Wetterstein seems to be in the best of spirits, joking with his sharpest critic, Hanns Benz, which he never normally does.

Manfred reads on. Item no. 5 is the installation of a disabled toilet in the clubhouse at 147 Kirchweilerstrasse, item no. 6 adjustment of the kindergarten contributions. Then questions from the public. This is going to be a long meeting, he thinks, and again looks towards Wetterstein, who's already five minutes late in starting the proceedings. He's quickly skimming through the planning applications and enquiries when suddenly he catches his breath. He can't believe it! He reads it again: application for a change of use of land to create the West Römersfeld Industrial Estate. That simply isn't possible. Only yesterday it was said that the land next to the animal sanctuary would never be developed in any way – it was completely worthless, absolutely no plans, utter nonsense. Didn't Marion say that the mayor knew nothing at all about it? And he's now introducing the application himself? There must be some huge mistake! Manfred can't burst out with his questions straightaway, but he's almost dying of impatience. And what if there's *no* mistake? What if it goes through and the councillors approve the development of an industrial estate next to the animal sanctuary? Then he'll kill himself. No, he has a better idea: he'll murder that Raak witch, because it's now obvious to him that she's behind it all. And this time it won't be a champagne bottle that he'll use!

Linda has never set out for one of these events so unwillingly. Somehow she doesn't feel in the mood, though naturally the prospect of earning some extra money is enticing. Greta Kremer phoned her again this afternoon at work and enthused about the group of ladies that she'd invited. Women with money, all of them in good shape and keen to enjoy a fun night out. It could hardly be more promising. After finishing work Linda went to the lingerie boutique, tried on the latest items, and finally took a selection of them in all sizes. Together with what she still has at home, there'll be quite a good selection. As usual she puts her portable CD player into the car, chooses music that will nicely complement her modelling of the lingerie, and sets off. She's said something to Günther about a get-together with some women friends, and he's indicated that this suits him quite well, as he has a lot to catch up with at the office.

Linda arrives in Kirchweiler in good time, before the others. Greta has covered the big dining table, where the garments will be laid out, with a light-coloured cloth, and set out glasses and canapés on the coffee table. She's looking forward to this evening. She immediately presses a glass of champagne into Linda's hand. 'Thanks, but I won't have one before the demonstration,' Linda says, only to be overruled by Greta.

'Go on,' she laughs, quickly pouring herself one too. 'It'll make us all more relaxed. We're not going to be critical. We want it to be fun, that's the main thing!'

The main thing is that it should bring in a bit of cash for me, thinks Linda, clinking glasses with her.

'I also thought that we could give the evening a dramatic start!'

'How do you mean?' asks Linda, surreptitiously looking around. None of the furnishings here can be more than two years old: the dining table, a good ten feet long, and the narrow dining chairs in some superior wood, which Greta has moved to one side to create space; the slim sofa with the matching cocktail chairs, all upholstered in leather in different colours; the exclusive cabinet, which is undoubtedly the work of a top Italian furniture-maker; and the many large, brightly coloured pictures on the smooth painted walls. Above the dining table hangs a lamp of gigantic proportions, and the lighting scheme looks like

the work of a designer. Sometimes you could really believe that
the Germans are rolling in money, thinks Linda. And at other
times you have a sneaking feeling that Germany is full of people
living only just above the poverty line.

Then she starts listening again, but Greta has rushed on. 'I'm
sorry, what was that about the dramatic opening?' she interrupts
her hostess in mid-sentence.

Evidently this isn't Greta's first glass of the day, for she laughs
and gesticulates wildly, spilling a quantity of champagne without
even noticing.

'As soon as everyone's here and has sat down, I'm going to put
on the Rolling Stones number "I Can't Get No Satisfaction".'

'Aha,' Linda nods.

'And I'll also turn off the lights.'

'But it isn't dark yet.'

'Well, obviously I'll lower the blinds first!' Greta shakes her
head in irritation. 'So I'll turn the lights off, and when the song
reaches the first refrain the light will suddenly come on and
you'll appear!'

'I see.'

'Yes.' She points to a large doorway, temporarily draped with
some bright red material. 'You'll come out from behind this curtain, wearing your hottest lingerie!'

'Normally I only put on the lingerie if the ladies expressly
request it.'

'Well, I am expressly requesting it.'

'Hmm!'

'I thought you wanted to make some money this evening, or
am I wrong?'

Linda would like to throw the rest of her champagne into
Greta's face, but she controls herself. She remembers her father's
favourite saying. 'Money changes people for the worse,' he
always said when Linda complained that her schoolfriends had

so many things that she did not. At the time it seemed silly, but she's gradually beginning to see what he meant.

'Okay, so I come out from behind the curtain.'

'That's better.' Greta laughs again, quite openly appraising Linda's figure. '*You've* no need to worry!'

'It's not that. Some women find it embarrassing. They don't want to see a scantily clad woman, they want to see the lingerie!' After all, this isn't the Reeperbahn, she adds to herself. Of course she can compete with anything to be seen there. But that live show with couples was a bit too much for her, although Günther was immediately turned on by it and started putting his hand between her thighs.

Greta breathes out deeply, as though Linda were not just slow on the uptake but already at an advanced stage of dementia. 'My friends aren't like that, they have an excellent sense of humour,' she says, with a slightly supercilious curl of the lips.

'I just thought you might like to think about it . . . but that's fine, I'm game. And now I'd better unpack the garments or there won't be time!'

On the drive to Kirchweiler, Marion and Ulrike talk about everything under the sun except Günther. As long as Marion doesn't mention him, Ulrike also keeps off the subject. If, for the first time in all the years they've known each other, Marion isn't celebrating her birthday *à deux* with Günther but going out on her own instead, there must be a reason. And that this reason has something to do with Günther is fairly obvious to Ulrike. But Marion will open up when she feels ready. They have enough to talk about as it is. For instance that article about the animal sanctuary. Marion's copy of the weekend edition of the *Courier* is lying around at home, still unread. Her own problems seemed to her more urgent than anything in the paper, but now she's annoyed all the same. The one time she doesn't read the paper, something like this happens! Ulrike tells her that the whole town is agog to know who could have paid so much for that worthless bit of land.

'An animal lover, perhaps?' Marion suggests, recalling the way the mayor had answered her questions, assuring her that no one was interested in it, because how could anyone think of developing an industrial estate to the west of Römersfeld when there was already one to the east?

'An animal lover?' Ulrike repeats doubtfully, and firmly shakes her head. 'An animal lover would have donated the money, not bought the land from the Animal Welfare League. That would have made much more sense!'

'Yes, you're right,' Marion admits. It's annoying that she didn't know this before, or she'd have followed it up immediately. 'By the way, do you know a good hairdresser?' she asks out of the blue.

'A good hairdresser?' repeats Ulrike in astonishment. 'Why? You've already got one, surely?'

'I need a new style, something fresh and modern. I must change myself radically.'

'Why, have you got a boyfriend?' This quick-fire response makes Marion laugh.

'Not yet,' she says after a moment. 'But you can help me out, all the same. I'm also looking for a nearly new clothes shop.'

Ulrike looks at her, dumbfounded. 'Not to buy clothes from?'

'No!' Marion is laughing again. 'To *sell* clothes to. I want a different look. Simpler, more modern, different – I must cast off my old self!'

'Goodness, I've never known you like this before!'

'Precisely!'

Günther, meanwhile, is sitting in his office, making notes. He's glad of the opportunity to be able to work and think without interruption, because he wants to keep his eye on everything and not lose track of events for a moment. On Thursday he'll be seeing Rainer Hoyer, that fellow from Berlin who wants to buy the piece of land from him. Why the government wants a piece of land in that particular location he can't quite fathom, but that's not his problem.

On the very next day after that, Dr Berger will be arriving from Liechtenstein. They've had to bring forward the appointment by an hour so that the lawyer can fit it in. That'll make it all rather hectic, but at least it keeps things moving along. At the weekend he'll tidy out his office and destroy all important papers, and then on Monday he'll be able to go ahead and apply for his divorce. He'll show Linda that it's not just talk: a Schmidt's as good as his word. He gets up and puts his notes through the shredder. Once he's written something down it's firmly lodged in his memory. He knows he can rely on that.

By now all the women have arrived at Greta Kremer's. Marion is surprised, as she had not expected to see so many familiar faces, least of all Regine Raak. They shake hands, and from the unembarrassed way that Regine laughs and talks Marion assumes that she hasn't heard anything. Either Günther hasn't yet informed his financial adviser of his impending divorce, or else Klaus hasn't told his wife. Whichever. They interpret the electric whirr of the blinds being lowered as a sign that things are about to start, and sit down side by side on the sofa. Regine fills a side plate with salmon canapés and when Marion asks her casually how she is, Regine tells her, laughing, that she was involved in the animal sanctuary coup, so naturally she feels terrific. It takes Marion a moment to grasp the implication of Regine's words. Here, sitting next to her, is the person who has all the information she's after. But before she can put any questions to her the light suddenly goes out, everyone falls silent and the intro of a rock number rips through the room. The speakers vibrate, and a cone of light is directed on to the red curtain. 'I can't get no satisfaction,' yells Mick Jagger, the curtain rises, and out steps Linda. Marion shrieks and jumps up, accidentally knocking Regine's plate out of her hand. The salmon canapés fly through the air and the plate crashes into some glasses, which fall from the table and shatter on the parquet. Champagne splashes over the guests' shoes and there are splinters of glass everywhere. Appalled, Greta rushes for the light switch and gazes in horror at the scene before her, while Linda and Marion stare speechlessly at one another. Linda, in the merest wisp of lingerie, tanned, sexy and sensual, and Marion, with an expression and posture that suggest that she's about to summon the Inquisition. In the background the Rolling Stones number continues to blare out at full volume; everyone seems paralysed, sensing that something significant is taking place, but not knowing what. Instinctively Linda has stepped back a pace, as though to take refuge behind the curtain, and Marion stands there immobile, as though unsure whether to kill Linda or silently ignore her. In the end she walks the length of the coffee table and out to the hall without giving Linda another glance.

Greta rushes after her. 'Whatever is the matter?' she asks.

'Nothing!' Marion's facial muscles are tense, her eyes hard. 'Please call me a taxi and carry on with the party. I didn't mean to disrupt the evening.'

'But what is it? What is it about the girl?'

Ulrike comes running up. 'Marion, are you not feeling well? You look dreadful.'

'Thanks! That's nice to know!' Her hand is already on the doorknob.

'But where are you going?' asks Greta.

'Out. I'll wait outside.' She feels herself beginning to tremble all over. She's close to losing her self-possession.

'Please wait.' Ulrike is holding her by the arm. 'I'll drive you if you want to leave.'

'Just leave me alone, all of you! And don't ask why. Just get on with your party!' With that she's outside and standing at the edge of the road. For the first time since she's been trying to cope with her new situation and step out of her old skin, she has tears streaming down her face. She realises that she's left her handbag behind and has neither her keys nor money for the taxi, but even that isn't enough to make her go back into the house. If she has to give the taxi driver her diamond ring and break the glass of the verandah door to get in, she doesn't care. She hadn't expected to suffer such humiliation, such injury. Marion hurries down the road to meet the taxi.

At the very first junction a car stops behind her and a car door slams. 'I'll take you home!' Marion turns. Regine Raak is standing behind her. 'I've cancelled the taxi. I don't think you should be on your own!'

'You!' Of all people, it's the woman who stole another woman's husband, Linda's counterpart, as it were, who is saying this. 'Did you say the same thing to Monika at the time?' she asks, deliberately trying to hurt her, to make *someone* pay for the pain she is suffering.

'Come on.' Regine holds the car door open for her. 'At the time of the split Monika and Klaus had drifted totally apart. They were only staying together for the sake of social convenience and status. It wasn't the same as in your case.'

'Huh!' Marion snorts contemptuously. 'Did you ever discuss it with Monika? And what makes you think you know how things are in my case?'

'Quite honestly I don't know anything at all. I really just wanted to take you safely home.'

Marion slowly gets in. 'I've stupidly left my bag on the sofa, do you think you could possibly . . .?'

'Yes, of course.'

*

Behind the curtain Linda is shaking. What a nightmarish situation, she thinks. She has no idea how she should react. In the room beyond she can hear a hubbub of movement and voices, the music has been turned off, all the lights are on. Linda looks around for a coat or at least a blanket. She'd opposed the idea of making an appearance like that in the first place. And then to find she was doing it in front of Marion! She can't get her head round it. For a situation like this even Günther wouldn't have an instant remedy! She recalls how she fled into the toilet at the Lake Restaurant when Marion arrived, and feels that that was an omen. Linda in flight, Marion on the attack. But actually she, Linda, holds all the trumps. Günther wants *her*, not Marion. So why is she hiding? Why doesn't she just come out with a big grin on her face?

Because she can't. Because Marion is so much older and is still *the* Frau Schmidt, and because one shows respect to older people. That's the way she was brought up.

Greta Kremer comes to her behind the curtain. 'What *do* you think you're doing?' she barks at her. 'Frau Schmidt is a highly respected woman.'

'So? Was I trying to look at *her* underclothes?'

'Now, don't you start being rude to me! A woman like Marion Schmidt doesn't get upset about nothing.'

'You needn't speak to me in that tone, Frau Kremer. You may be older than I am, but in your case that isn't necessarily to your advantage.' Linda turns and walks in a deliberately sexy manner, in her lacy underwear, towards the bathroom. She knows that her body looks just as perfect from behind, and she can imagine Greta Kremer staring furiously after her.

Marion, sitting alongside Regine, has regained her composure. Regine drives out of Kirchweiler and on to the main road. 'It *is* kind of you to drive me home,' she says at last. 'I wouldn't have expected it.'

'Well, Ulrike Goedhart was going to drive you, but in all the confusion she couldn't find her car keys. But I'm more than happy to do so.'

Marion is silent for a while, looking straight at the road ahead. 'But I expect you have some questions . . .'

'I presume it's something to do with Linda?'

'And my husband, yes.'

Regine considers whether or not further questions might be too intrusive. And she's conscious of her own odd position as a sort of precursor of Linda. Marion is bound to see her in that light.

'I'm sorry,' she says finally.

Marion gives a quick, abrupt laugh. 'Last night I was actually congratulating myself. But I didn't know then that today I'd run into *her*!' And in a low voice she adds, 'And on my birthday, too!'

'That really is tough on you,' agrees Regine, and she means it. 'Perhaps you ought to talk to her,' she suggests just before they reach the sign at the entrance to Römersfeld.

'Have you ever talked to your predecessor?' counters Marion.

'Of course not.'

'Well, there you are! Why should I talk to Linda?'

They drive slowly through the centre of Römersfeld and halt at traffic lights.

'To be honest, I don't know either. In my case, I mean. In your case I just feel instinctively that it would be a good idea. But as to why, I can't tell you.'

The lights turn to green. Regine accelerates and pays attention to the traffic.

She's quite nice really, thinks Marion, yet it was only yesterday that she took quite a liking to Monika. Ought she to be emotionally on Monika's side, because she's spent the night at her house and sought her advice? But when it was a question of the invitations to Günther's birthday party she had no hesitation in choosing Regine and excluding Monika.

'I'll think about it. Perhaps we're all on the wrong track.'

Regine is surprised. 'How do you mean?' she says.

'Well, with all these ex-partners and current partners and status and form. When it comes down to it it's only the individual person that counts, don't you think?'

'You mean, really you think Linda's quite nice?'

'I didn't say that,' Marion demurs. She is glad that they're almost at her door, because she wouldn't be able to analyse exactly what she did mean. Only three weeks ago she thought Linda was nice, that's true. But you can think a cobra is nice, too, as long as it's safely behind glass.

Linda has turned from the bathroom, fully dressed, and is about to pack away the lingerie on the table, but the women are not prepared to let the incident spoil their evening. At first Ulrike wondered whether she should drive after Marion, but then she thought that after all she wasn't a child; one escort must be enough. And perhaps she'd prefer just to be alone.

Together the women urge Linda to start all over again: her opening appearance was splendid, and the evening will be a success despite everything. To get back into the mood again they all drink a glass of champagne with Linda, turn out the light, giggling, and wait for her show. Well, what the hell? thinks Linda, undressing again; if I left now I'd be admitting defeat. Of course she's aware that they are all dying to know the reason behind the scene, but she's damned if she's giving anything away. She's not going to give these sensation-starved ladies a juicy bit of scandal to chew on. However much she sells this evening, it won't be worth that.

Regine considers whether to drive back out to Kirchweiler or whether to go home. She doesn't know if Greta's show will go on or if the whole party has been broken up by their hasty departure. And anyway she's no longer in the mood for lingerie. She decides to give the two males in her life a nice surprise by returning home earlier than expected. Let's see what they can all make of the rest of the evening.

Monika hears about it before she's even had breakfast. Edith Jürgens managed to contain herself until exactly seven o'clock before picking up the phone.

'You won't believe it,' she begins, the moment Monika answers. 'There's a new scandal in the town! Soon nobody will be talking about you any more!'

'I'm delighted to hear it! Good morning, Edith. What is this exciting news?'

Edith tells her what happened yesterday at Kirchweiler.

Good heavens, thinks Monika. 'And did you buy anything?' she asks.

'Is that all you're interested in?' asks Edith, disappointed.

'No. Why did my replacement, of all people, drive Frau Schmidt home?'

Edith considers for a moment. 'Let me think, she came with Ulrike – I know. Ulrike couldn't find her car keys, so Regine stepped in. That's how it was.'

'Ah.'

'So, what do you think is going on there?'

Monika grins to herself and makes an effort to sound bored. 'Nothing much, I dare say. I expect Linda's figure was rather a provocation to her, if she showed herself in the way you just described to me.'

'What?'

'Has she got cellulite?'

'No, of course not.'

'Well, there you are, then.'

'What?'

'That's provocation for women of our age. It would have annoyed me as well!'

Edith hesitates, clearly unsure whether Monika is winding her up. 'Well, I thought you'd have more to say about it!'

'I'm really glad if that's all I've missed. Are you going to be playing a round of golf one of these days? Yes? Will you give me a ring?'

As soon as Monika has rung off she dials again, but then immediately disconnects again. That's no good, it's too early. Joachim can't possibly be in his office yet. She puts on some coffee and goes into the bathroom to do her makeup. In front of the mirror, as she applies her mascara, a grin suddenly spreads over her face. She looks into her own eyes and says to her reflection, 'Yes, go on, be happy! Why shouldn't you be happy for once!' Last night the councillors approved the application. The West Römersfeld Industrial Estate is going to be put in hand. How Joachim pulled it off, she doesn't know. But she holds all the trumps.

Manfred has phoned in sick again. This time he really does feel ill. He's lying in bed with raging stomach pains, plotting murder. He has a debt of 90,000 marks to pay off in instalments, which means he will have to miss out on all the pleasures of life, just because Monika Raak has pulled a fast one on him. He need only have waited, just four days, and then *he* could have cleaned up. 190,000 marks' profit, just thrown away. He pounds with his fists on the wooden bedhead. They've all cheated him, the whole lot of them!

A million ideas are buzzing around Marion's head. She's woken up early and is finding it hard to concentrate on anything. Everything seems so hopeless, and yesterday's feeling that she was making an exciting new start has gone. Seeing Linda gave her a visible demonstration of what really counts: youth, beauty, a sexy body. She has none of those things, and that hurts. So what is there left for her in this world? No one wants her, no one likes her, no one is interested in her. And no one needs her, either. She has not one real function, now that Günther has gone. Who would notice if she suddenly weren't here any more? Her gardener, perhaps, he sometimes greets her from afar.

She has no appetite at all, and doesn't feel like bothering with her usual ceremony of making frothy coffee. She doesn't even read the article about the Animal Welfare League in the weekend edition of the paper. It's still lying folded on the table, and she's not in the least interested in it. Suddenly she can feel what it's like when someone goes off the rails and sinks deeper and deeper. No energy, no motivation, no purpose – she too has lost the strength to fight. And the strength to live. It would be so easy, she thinks. Just to go to sleep and not to wake up. To leave everything behind. And no reincarnation, please! She couldn't bear it!

The ringing of the phone shakes her out of her brooding. She pulls herself together, and answers in a listless tone, 'Yes?'

'Frau Schmidt? This is Monika Raak here! Everybody's talking about it! Have you thought what action you intend to take in this matter?'

'This matter?'

'I'm in the office!'

'Oh, I see. No, I don't know . . . Nothing. What *can* I do?' She takes a deep breath, then it dawns on her what Monika has just said. 'What was that? How can everyone know about it?'

'I think quite a lot of people were there last night . . .'

'Oh my God! I shan't be able to show my face anywhere!'

'That's what I thought when it happened to me. And do you

know what? I'm really enjoying life now. I make my own decisions.'

'But you did that even before!'

'That's true!' Monika laughs heartily over the phone, and Marion can't help joining in.

'Do you know what?' says Monika. 'I'll come over and see you, and we'll figure out a plan of action. I know all about these things!'

'Would you really do that?'

'Yes, but only if you can make me a decent cup of coffee.'

'With frothed-up milk?'

'Is that a promise? I'll be with you in twenty minutes!'

Linda hasn't said a word about the incident to Günther. She managed to sell lots of lingerie, more than she'd expected, and now, in the absence of Renate, she's dealing with a sales rep when the glass door of the shop opens and one of her customers from last night comes in.

'Oh!' she says, trying to sound surprised. 'Is *this* where you work?' She stresses the word 'this' in such a contemptuous tone that Linda feels as if she's been found out.

'Please excuse me a moment,' she says to the rep. 'Can I help you, Frau . . . I'm sorry, I've forgotten your name.'

'Have you? It's Edith Jürgens. It doesn't matter, Linda. My husband is thrilled with the lingerie. But finding you here . . . what a surprise!'

'Why? Where do *you* work?'

'Me? You surely don't think . . .' She gives a short laugh and walks past Linda to look at the perfumes.

She didn't seem such a cow yesterday, Linda thinks as she follows her. Are they all going to show up here? Come and gawp at Schmidt's girlfriend?

*

Monika has just arrived at Marion's. They're sitting on the sofa drinking coffee and eating apple pastries. Between mouthfuls Marion describes briefly what happened at Greta Kremer's. 'And how did *you* hear about it?' she asks when she's finished.

'Römersfeld's walking newspaper goes by the name of Edith Jürgens. She has nothing else to do; her husband is the town's chief of works, their life is totally secure, and probably for that reason she's terribly bored. No matter what the occasion, she'll be there. She joins in whatever's going on.'

'Frau Jürgens?' Marion looks up. 'I know her. But she's never been to my house. I've never invited her.'

'Well, now you'll have to suffer for it. I'm sure she's already on the warpath!'

'I really seem to have handled everything wrongly!'

'One can only avoid making mistakes by never doing anything, so I expect you have made some. But it may have nothing to do with that at all.'

'More coffee?' asks Marion, getting up to go over to the espresso machine.

'Oh yes, please. It's excellent! And then I'd like to know how you get on with Regine Raak.'

Damn, so now we've reached that subject, thinks Marion as she goes into the kitchen. What is she to say? That she really rather likes her?

Monika is following her. 'What did she say yesterday when you were in the car?'

'That she really doesn't know why you and she have never talked things over together.' It just slips out. 'Because that was the advice she gave me about Linda!'

'Did she really?' Monika is clearly surprised.

It almost makes Marion laugh. Here they both are, about the same age – Monika Raak slim and of medium height, her short dark hair showing the first grey streaks, and she herself taller and heavier – at this significant stage in life, philosophising about their husbands' girlfriends. It's simply too absurd!

'You must tell me about it,' demands Monika. And while the freshly ground coffee trickles into the cups, Marion tries to repeat every word that Regine said.

'She could have thought about that before,' says Monika at length, as Marion hands back her cup. 'Then I could have given her a few home truths about my husband to take away with her. He snores, has sweaty feet and is losing his hair!'

'Mine has been for a long time!' They look at each other and burst out laughing.

'But seriously,' says Monika after a few moments, going over to the window, cup in hand, 'Regine is your key to success, you must see that. I suggest you ring her and ask her to come over.'

'Why?'

'Because she presumably knows what her husband's up to at the moment, so she may also know what your Günther's plans are! After all, I would assume that he's still working for him. Even if we only manage to draw some vague conclusions, that's still better than nothing!'

'And you?'

'I'll stay here and have a word with her too. We should have got together long ago, she's absolutely right about that.'

Manfred has forced himself into action. He is sitting at the dining table with a blank sheet of paper in front of him. If he stares at it for long enough, he tells himself, he'll think of something – it always happened that way at school. He looks in turn at the wall, the window, and then the piece of paper again. Nothing. Thinking that a bit of exercise will do him good, he walks over to the fridge and gets a beer. As he does so, his eye lights on the pile of newspapers for recycling in the corner, and sudden inspiration sends him back to the table. 'Wetterstein is corrupt' he writes as a heading, but immediately changes it to 'Wetterstein plays a crooked game'. He's still not satisfied with it, but when all's said and done he's not a journalist. He'll ring the newspaper and leave it to them. In any case, he'll unleash such a scandal that the mayor will have to resign and that wretched car-spraying firm will have to shut down at once.

Hastily Manfred searches in the phone book, dials the newspaper's number and asks to be put through to the news desk. He finds himself speaking to a member of the editorial staff whom he knows, Andrea Hertzig, a mousy little woman who dresses in rather outmoded fashions. Manfred asks for her boss. Not in this afternoon, he's told, won't be back before the evening. But if it's something for the paper, she can help him. Manfred is doubtful, for he knows the sort of articles this journalist, who used to cover rural affairs, tends to write. She rarely grasps the central issue of a subject – but actually, since she always manages to hide her lack of understanding behind virulent polemic, she could serve his purpose very well. He tells her in broad outline what's been going on over the last few days in connection with the land next to the animal sanctuary, and then he grins at her reaction. Just as he thought, she hasn't quite grasped all of it, but she can see that this has all the makings of a sensational story.

Regine has mixed feelings as she drives over to Marion Schmidt's. She's taken the precaution of not telling Klaus about meeting his ex-wife, as she doesn't know how he would react. Probably with complete incomprehension. And she's left Bobby at home, because she tacitly assumes that Marion would prefer it. To make up for it she's promised him a long walk this evening.

She sees Monika's car in the drive and parks right next to it. Her heart is in her mouth. Why on earth did you agree to this? she asks herself crossly, but her finger is already resolutely pressing the bell. Marion comes to the door herself. 'I do admire you for coming,' she says by way of a greeting, pressing her hand in her own.

'I admire you for inviting me,' Regine replies with a slight smile that she hopes conceals her nervousness. She follows Marion, who's briskly leading the way, and sees Monika in the living room. She's standing in the middle of the room with her arms hanging loosely at her sides, just as though she were waiting for a train and not for the woman who stole her husband.

Now she comes up to Regine and holds out her hand. 'I think it's very brave of you to have come. And I agree with what you said to Frau Schmidt in the car yesterday. You're right – we should have met and talked before now!'

There's not much left for Regine to say. She nods and returns the handshake.

'Where shall we sit, and what would you like to drink?' Marion, in her accustomed role as hostess, gestures towards the sofa, but Monika shakes her head. 'How about sitting at the table outside? The weather's so nice, and it's easier to discuss weighty topics at a table!'

'Quite the businesswoman,' Regine teases her.

Monika smiles. 'Possibly, yes. And you'll soon find out why!'

When Linda goes home at the end of the day her nerves are stretched to the limit. She feels as though she's in limbo between two worlds, and that she's just left one behind but not yet reached the other. She feels less and less at ease with herself and would love to take some time off. Two days by herself somewhere, perhaps staying at some inn in the surrounding countryside with some grass to lie on and bikes you can borrow, with supper in your room and no need to get up early in the morning. As she drives into the basement garage she sees Günther's Mercedes in the visitors' car park. So early? She wasn't expecting that, and she's not pleased. She shouldn't have been so ready to give him a key of his own when he asked for one.

Linda considers whether she should get on her bike and go for a quick ride straightaway, but she's not wearing the right clothes. But if she goes up to the flat to change she won't easily get away again. She thinks for a moment, and finally goes up in the lift and opens the door to her flat.

Günther comes towards her from the bathroom, wearing nothing but a towel round his middle. 'I'm glad you're back early too,' he greets her, beaming. 'I've been waiting for you!'

'Can you never get enough?' asks Linda, finding it difficult to hide her irritation.

'That's the effect you have! You should be proud of it! With you I'm like a young stallion!' He laughs and triumphantly points to the bulge under the towel. 'All for you! *And* I've been shopping!'

'Have you been to Stuttgart again?' she asks without enthusiasm.

'You bet!' He takes her in his damp arms and kisses her on the neck. 'You'll be amazed. Specially for you!'

'Why, what is it this time?'

'Handcuffs and a fantastic black rubber job with studs all over it! You'll like that, won't you?' He gently nibbles her earlobe. 'With that I can give you a really good seeing-to!'

When Regine drives home some hours later her feelings are in turmoil. She hit it off with Monika straightaway, and they discovered a host of things that they had in common, which they chatted and laughed about. It confirmed the widely held belief that a man always goes for the same type. Really, Klaus might just as well have stayed with Monika. Then they started to go into more detail, and Regine accused Monika of having left her with a man who was completely screwed up, who didn't want to allow her any space at all for fear that it would all go the same way as his first marriage. Monika listened, amused, and described how difficult it had been for her to find a path of her own after the divorce. Wherever she went she came up against barriers as a result of their previous life together. Klaus was simply able to carry on with that old life, with Regine, as though only he had a right to it. Marion listened closely, realising that she could learn from Monika's experience.

When they had had a good talk about all this, Marion produced some sandwiches and a bottle of wine and they turned to their main topic.

Now, as Regine is driving through Römersfeld virtually on automatic pilot, she's thinking about it all. If it's true that Günther is at this moment moving all his money out of Marion's reach, then that's a rotten trick, to put it mildly. With the speaker of the phone turned to loud, Marion had, in her presence, phoned first Günther and then Klaus. In an extremely friendly manner she asked Günther if he would draw up a list of all his assets as soon as possible, so that they could come to a fair settlement. But Günther just laughed and replied that he'd already said all that he was going to say on the matter. She could keep her car, but as far as anything else was concerned, surely she was still young enough to get a job? Other women of her age worked, after all.

As for Klaus, he was obviously doing his best to dissociate himself from everything. Both Regine and Monika could tell at once how Marion's questions about Günther's finances were making him uncomfortable. First he tried pleading confidentiality, but when Marion continued to press him he conceded that Günther had recently suffered some severe losses. When she told him bluntly that she didn't believe a word of it, he quickly rang off, claiming that a client who was late had just arrived.

It's certainly not fair, Regine says to herself and, a little later, to Bobby, whom she has come to collect for his evening walk. While Bobby exuberantly rushes around the house, Regine goes into Klaus's study and has a quick look for his laptop. It isn't there. It would be an amazing stroke of luck if he has transferred the data to his computer. Just to make sure, she switches it on and searches through the file names for any reference to Günther, and she also fetches his disks, not forgetting to keep an eye on the window in case he should just be driving up. No luck. It would have been too good to be true. In the correct order she opens the files he has used most recently, so that he won't notice any changes when he starts up the computer, and then she switches it off. She'll have to find another way. 'Come on, Bobby, let's go!' she calls to the dog, putting a formatted disk and the spare key to Klaus's office into her bag. She's determined to find out what's going on. After all, some day it could happen to her . . .

Monika has come to work because she wants to check up on what's been happening in her absence. The car park is empty, and all the outer doors are locked as they should be. She pops into her office and is looking through the notes that are lying on her desk, arranged in order of importance, when the phone rings. At this hour it must be someone who knows her direct line, she thinks, and looks at the display. It doesn't show a number. She lifts the receiver.

'You won't believe this! Just listen!' Joachim sounds absolutely stunned.

'No excitements, please, I've had more than enough excitement this afternoon!'

'Even so. Listen . . .'

'Where are you calling from?'

'A phone box at the car park in the woods. Next to the jogging track.'

'Have you taken up jogging?'

'Nearly . . .'

Monika can't help laughing. 'All right, let's hear it.'

Joachim tells her about the phone call he received this afternoon from the *Courier*, and the verbal assault the reporter had made on him.

'And what did you say?'

'I tried to explain all the facts, but I'm not sure she understood.'

'If she didn't understand she won't be able to write anything, so that's okay!'

'You can't be sure of that. With some people, that's exactly when they start to write!'

'Have you rung her boss?'

'I didn't want to create even more of a stir . . .'

'But you should. After all, he's the one you usually talk to, and he knows his way round politics.'

Joachim hesitates. 'You may well be right,' he admits.

Regine has parked her little car round the corner from Klaus's office and starts by strolling past, as though casually, with Bobby on his lead. The five parking spaces in front of the building are empty. That's what she'd expected at this time of the evening. She walks on another block and then turns back. Where could Klaus be? Still with a client? And what if he's carrying the laptop around with him? She quickly unlocks the outer door to the old building and dashes up the few stone stairs to the entrance of Klaus's office. Apart from this and a doctor's surgery there are three flats in the building, and she hopes to get in and out again without being seen.

A few minutes later she's in Klaus's personal office and is positioning Bobby by the door. 'Now keep guard, but no barking, Bobby, do you hear? No barking!' She looks around. She is terribly on edge and feels like a burglar. Then she finds it. There is the laptop, connected up to the printer, next to the computer. It looks as if he's just been working on it. But that might mean that he could come back at any moment. She swallows, but her throat is dry, then she opens the laptop and switches it on. 'Come on, come on,' she whispers impatiently to the machine as it hums into life and loads the program. At last it's ready, and with a ringing tone that to Regine sounds like an alarm bell it indicates that she can start. She opens the window to display the list of files; the very first one is HOFMEISTER.WPS. That's what he was working on last. Hofmeister? A client? Then she remembers that that was Marion's maiden name. She opens the file.

At that very moment there's a low growl from Bobby. With a start as though she'd received an electric shock, Regine switches off the laptop without any further procedure and softly runs over to Bobby. There comes the unmistakable sound of footsteps heading for the outer door of the office. There's a rattling at the door and Bobby jumps up indignantly from his lying position; Regine is only just able, at the last moment, to throw herself on him and hold his muzzle shut. She's on the verge of a heart attack. If Klaus comes in she'll have to keep her cool and put on an act about paying him a surprise visit. And if it's anyone else, she must angrily ask where Klaus is. 'Be quiet,' she whispers into Bobby's ear, then she hears a thud. More footsteps, then silence.

Regine remains kneeling down beside Bobby for a little while before creeping to the door. A large oblong envelope has been pushed through the letterbox, that's all.

She takes several deep breaths to calm herself down, and then runs back to the desk. Opening it up, she starts up the laptop again. She inserts her disk and copies the entire Hofmeister file. So she's got that, whatever happens. Only then does she look at what's in it. Over eighty pages of lists and tables, as well as dates and a kind of timetable. Liechtenstein is mentioned several times, as well as names she doesn't know, and on the last page is a draft contract in which Günther Schmidt is named. What on earth is this all about? She closes the program, the laptop signs off with its ringing sound, and with relief Regine pockets her disk. Now she must get out as fast as possible.

Minutes later she's in the nearest phone box, trying to get hold of Monika. She doesn't seem to be home yet, and at her office Regine only gets the answering-machine. After only a moment's thought she drives off. 'Sorry, Bobby, we'll have to postpone your walk. But a promise is a promise – we'll go later on!'

Meanwhile Dirk and Richi are sitting in Dirk's flat, finalising their plan of action. Dirk produces a truncheon wrapped in a plastic bag out of his wardrobe. 'Only the cops have these, normally,' he declares proudly, holding it aloft.

With a touch of repugnance, Richi asks, 'Can you buy those?'

'Of course not!' Dirk swings it through the air like a golf club. 'You need connections!'

'Ah! What sort of connections?'

'There are any number of radical activists at the university – it's easy!'

'That's encouraging!' says Richi mockingly. He stands up and walks past Dirk into the little kitchen. 'Have you got any beer in the fridge?'

'Sure. Help yourself. Bring me one too!'

By the time Richi has come back with the two bottles and a bottle opener, Dirk has put two pieces of stocking, each knotted at one end, on the table.

'Don't forget you only want to teach him a lesson,' Richi warns him. 'You're not supposed to be murdering him!'

Dirk takes one bottle from him and opens it. 'I just want to see the elegant Herr Schmidt flat on the ground. I want him scared shitless!'

'That's very nice, coming from a pacifist.'

Dirk takes a long swig and then looks at Richi with raised eyebrows. 'Even a priest can lift his cassock once in a while.'

'Absolutely,' Richi nods. 'That's a very persuasive analogy!'

Regine has arrived at Monika's work. Monika's car is there, as she expected. Now she must just attract her attention somehow. She stops her car in the middle of the forecourt, where she can be seen from all the office windows, and sounds her horn, which makes Bobby rush round the car like one possessed, barking as if to frighten it into silence. At last there's a reaction, a window is opened, and Regine recognises Monika and waves to her. Monika nods and motions for her to come over to the main entrance.

Only minutes later they're sitting in front of Monika's computer. 'I hope he uses Word rather than some outlandish kind of program,' says Monika as she inserts the disk.

'No, I can put you at ease there.' Regine has pulled up a chair. They sit beside one another and go through the notes page by page.

'You're brilliant!' When they reach the last page, Monika gives her a hearty clap on the thigh. 'The day before yesterday I couldn't stand you, and now I know what I was missing.'

Regine laughs. 'Thanks, that's just how I feel!'

Monika reaches for the phone. 'This disk is worth its weight in gold. Marion will never be able to repay you!'

'To think that Günther wants to rip her off like that,' exclaims Regine indignantly.

'And that our, or rather your, husband is prepared to help him do it.'

The two of them look at each other.

'It's really awful,' says Regine thoughtfully.

'The dirty little bastard. I always knew it!' Monika nods grimly and starts to dial.

'Oh, he's not quite as bad as all that,' Regine tries to mollify her, but she can't help laughing when she sees the look Monika gives her. 'But I still can't even tell him what I think of him. I'm afraid I'll burst when he comes home this evening.'

Monika has got through. 'Anna, just imagine, Regine Raak, yes, that's right, my replacement, has pinched some secret documents. Yes, I have the evidence here with me! An offence under Paragraph 314 of the criminal code? I thought as much! Can we have her arrested now?'

Regine's jaw drops.

Monika bursts out laughing. 'A little joke – sorry, I couldn't resist it. Now, Anna, could you come here to my office straightaway? We can really nail Schmidt now! Yes, I'm just about to ring Marion too!'

Dirk is writing out the details of the plan on a piece of paper.

'Right, I'll go over it again. Rainer Hoyer will arrive just as it's getting dark, because he's had other important appointments before that, and the next day, after the meeting with the lawyer, he has to leave straightaway. Time is money, Günther will accept that, it's the sort of language he understands. After all, the only thing he's interested in is money!'

'Well, almost the only thing . . .' says Richi meaningfully.

'Prat! Now then, the path from the car park to the Seven Stars Hotel passes between those tall hedges. At that time of the evening we'd have to be very unlucky for anyone to come along and get in our way.'

'But you can't rule it out.'

'Okay, well, then it won't work out this time. In that case it turns out that Rainer Hoyer couldn't come for some reason, and he'll ring again on Friday. No problem. We'll get him eventually.'

'But don't forget: pain and above all fear, but no permanent damage.'

'Do you see me as a killer?'

'No, of course not. So you'll phone him tomorrow and tell him the time and place to meet?'

'Right. Just as we said.'

'Be careful.'

'Don't worry.' Dirk stretches his back. 'He didn't recognise me last time. I'll tell him that when we've reached an agreement we can go to his lawyer in the morning.'

'And don't talk too much, or he *will* recognise your voice after all!'

Marion is almost beside herself. She's torn between delight and horror. She's absolutely stunned at what Günther was planning to do, and at the same time doesn't know how she can ever thank Regine enough for thwarting his plans and saving her from poverty. Monika has printed out four copies of the file, put them into separate spring binders and given one each to Anna Kell and Marion Schmidt on their arrival. They've been sitting for two hours in the room where Monika meets customers, drinking coffee and eating cakes, reading through the pages together and listening to Anna Kell's comments. 'It now depends on what you want to do, Frau Schmidt,' she says finally. 'Whether you want to take a hard or a soft line – naturally, there are various possibilities.' She taps the document with the flat of her hand and looks at each of the women in turn. Then, unexpectedly, she bursts out laughing. 'This case really is amazing! In all my years as a lawyer, I've never come across a conspiracy like this!' They all join in her laughter.

'You're right!' Monika stands up. 'We really ought to drink to it!

For not only will it restore all Marion Schmidt's rights, it's also brought us all together! Who knows what may yet come of that?'

Monika goes to the cupboard to fetch glasses, and Marion squeezes Regine's hand. 'I'll never forget what you've done for me! You must tell me what I can do in return!'

'The battle isn't over yet,' Regine points out. 'I'm afraid this may not be the last of it.'

Manfred has never waited for the local paper as impatiently as he does early this Thursday morning. Today he'll get the satisfaction he seeks. It can't compensate him for the 90,000 marks, of course, but at least it'll be balm for his wounded ego. He has just drunk his third cup of coffee, standing by the window and keeping his eye on the street, when at last he sees the paper boy approaching. Manfred rushes up to him, snatches the paper and disappears back into his flat. He hastily takes the local section out of the paper and opens it out on the dining table. Not the lead story, that's a pity. It would have been the obvious choice. And it's not on the front page at all – how annoying! He turns over the pages, and when he reaches the local sports and club reports he can't believe it and slowly turns the pages back, one by one. Perhaps in the main part? Page three? Under a heading such as 'Corruption rife in Germany'! He quickly picks up the main section, which he dropped on the floor in his hurry, and goes through it article by article. Trivial stuff about Indonesia, Kosovo and Afghanistan, but not a word about Römersfeld. Incredulously he sinks down into a chair. She's taken him for a ride. That stupid cow has written nothing at all!

It's as if the whole town has suddenly conspired against him. In olden times one would have known what to do. Just poison the well and that would be that. Somehow or other, he must pay them back for this.

*

Later that morning, Marion drives to Anna Kell's office. Anna has decorated her office in Mediterranean colours, with yellow, blue and muted tones of red predominating. When Marion arrives the sun is blazing in so strongly through the open window that Anna has to draw across some pale yellow curtains, which soften the harsh light and billow out with every breath of wind. 'This really is a good place to work,' Marion remarks, and Anna, going back behind her desk, answers, 'It's a good place to *live*, Frau Schmidt. I don't get home all that much, and I want to feel comfortable in the place where I spend most of my time.'

'You're quite right!' Marion sits down. 'I'm not comfortable in our house any more. When all this is over I'd like to have a little house with a smaller garden, instead of the great big park I've got now. A nice overgrown cottage garden, with lots of different flowers. I'll do everything quite differently!'

'As long as you have dreams, you have a future,' smiles Anna, opening the file.

'As long as you have a future, you're alive,' adds Marion, leaning forward expectantly.

The lawyer has already worked out a strategy and goes over every detail of it with Marion.

At last she leans back and winks at her. 'It's lucky that Herr Raak is such an efficient man. He has even given us the exact times of his appointments,' she says mockingly. 'So tomorrow afternoon this Dr Berger is coming. I think it'll be most effective if we arrive at the same time as him. Two o'clock, at your husband's firm, we should be able to manage that! And be sure to take a photo of the scene, with Dr Berger, the lawyer, your husband and the documents. A snap for the family album, of course!' She grins.

'I see,' Marion nods slowly. 'I'll treat myself to a suitable camera!'

'It needs to be a good one, small, automatic and with a zoom and a wide-angle lens. Let the shop advise you, and make sure you practise with it a bit.'

'And what will you do?'

'I'll see to everything else!'

Manfred has come to the conclusion that he needs a strong partner. He really doesn't seem able to handle this problem on his own. By the end of lunch he's come to a decision, and he rings Günther. He's in luck, Günther is in his office, though he acts as if he's too busy and pressed for time. Manfred tries to think of a way of getting Günther on his side without having to give too much away.

'I'm furious about a woman who's constantly treading on my toes,' he says, trying to rouse Günther's sense of male solidarity.

'Really? Who's that?' asks Günther, pricking up his ears.

'Monika Raak! She thinks she's the Almighty God of Römersfeld!'

'Oh, does she now?'

Manfred feels that his approach has been the right one. The status of God Almighty has hitherto always been reserved for Günther.

'Is she getting too big for her boots?' Günther wants to know.

'She interferes in everything and is about to make an absolute killing. Have you heard that some land is to be designated for development as West Römersfeld Industrial Estate . . .?'

'You've mentioned that nonsense before . . .'

'If you'd paid more attention you'd have been able to make a quick buck. Because the application's been approved. And that woman is reaping all the profit!'

He can actually feel Günther taking a deep breath. He's touched a raw nerve. A woman is threatening to usurp his position as the absolute ruler of Römersfeld and the most cunning fox in town.

'I never could stand that old battle-axe!' he says. His voice is quiet and dangerous.

'What can we do to stop her?' Manfred asks, rubbing his hands.

Günther lowers his voice. 'There are various cards I could play, Manfred. But we need to approach this cautiously. If I'm seen to be involved, it's too obvious. If *you* are able to tackle it and put her out of the game, that's another matter.'

'Will it be risky?'

'Rubbish. Not for you! I know one or two things about her and Herr Wetterstein. Also, various bits of council business have gone through faster because of the "understanding" between them. If the facts come out and there's a scandal, she can pack her bags!'

This far exceeds Manfred's hopes. Filled with hatred, he closes his eyes. He'll see her burned at the stake, the witch! Or he'll blackmail her. In return for 180,000 marks, cash down, he might be prepared to be reasonable. Or why not a nice round figure of 200,000 while he's about it – he certainly ought to get an extra 20,000 marks for all that pain and suffering.

'I don't know,' he says guardedly. 'And if Wetterstein has to resign because of the scandal . . . haven't you yourself . . .?'

'That's precisely why you have to be the one to set the ball rolling. I'll keep clear of things, and he's got nothing on you!'

'So you really think . . .?!'

'We men must stick together, or where will it all end?' He makes it sound like the battle cry of a secret alliance.

Manfred is still hesitant, and achieves what he's been aiming for.

'Come on, Manfred! Courage! Do it – you'll be doing us all a favour! Serve the realm, and finish her off!' Günther laughs maliciously. 'We don't need any women around us. Except in the sack!' He laughs again, and Manfred lets himself be persuaded.

'Quite right, show them where they belong!' he chimes in boorishly. Their unanimity on this point fills them with elation.

'How shall we go about it?' asks Manfred when they have calmed down.

'Come over to me in the morning – no, wait a minute, that's no good, I already have a meeting . . . no, we'll meet for supper at the Lake Restaurant. Around six, not too late, because I have something else planned after that. I'll bring all the necessary papers and we'll talk it all through again. I need to gather the stuff together first, and I shan't be able to do that before tomorrow afternoon. I hope I'll have enough time.' He thinks. 'Shall I be able to reach you later today?'

Manfred nods into the receiver. 'I'll be here until at least ten. I have a few things to catch up on – I've fallen a bit behind over the last few days.'

'Okay, just in case.' He lowers his voice. 'And Manfred, just between you and me, I'm really looking forward to seeing that slag brought down!'

Not half as much as I am, thinks Manfred, putting the phone down. He'll get his money back, but then he can still go on and ruin her completely. If Günther really possesses such damning evidence against her she won't be able to defend herself. This thought is so intensely pleasurable that he gives the front of his trousers a quick rub.

No sooner has Günther put the phone down than it rings again. He glances at his watch before picking it up. He ought really to have left by now; he seems to have one meeting after another. Now it's Rainer Hoyer, who wants to bring him the 800,000 marks for his plot in Berlin. He doesn't mind finding time for that.

'We'll have to discuss this again carefully,' Günther says, leaving himself room to manoeuvre.

'Fine!' says the man from Berlin, to Günther's surprise. 'I expected you to say that. But the government has sufficient funds, so that won't be an obstacle.'

This is what Günther likes to hear. Even so, he finds it hard to believe. 'Sufficient funds?' he says. 'The government? Since when?'

'Well, with taxpayers like yourself!'

Günther pulls a face at this painful thought. Not for much longer, he thinks. 'You're right there,' he agrees. 'Okay, it's rather late, but if that's the only possible time . . . I'll be at the Seven Stars Hotel at ten o'clock. I'll ask for you at reception.'

Dirk puts down the phone and gives Richi a triumphant dig in the ribs. 'Well? Brilliant, or what? It couldn't have been easier – he's going to walk right into a knuckle sandwich!'

To escape her anxieties, Regine has fled to the animal sanctuary, where she can give a hand to Annemarie and her helpers, calming herself down with physical work and finding some distraction from the thoughts that are plaguing her. Having to sit at the breakfast table with Klaus this morning, not being able to ask him about his questionable role, almost drove her mad. She couldn't go through that many more times, and she's glad that it'll all be over soon. Tomorrow morning, when Anna Kell and Marion Schmidt suddenly appear in the room where the contract is being agreed, he'll have to explain himself. One way or the other.

Regine is in one of the dog enclosures, hosing down the floor with a high pressure jet, and taking meticulous care. She's wondering if the meeting will mean the end of her marriage. After all, it'll be quite clear who supplied the information. She turns the water off, ready to go into the next cage. 'Can you take the dogs out, please?' she calls to Sonja. 'This one's done!' She'd be sorry if it led to their separating, because really she does still love Klaus. Even though he's obviously involved in some crooked dealings. She winds in the hose. And it's not like him, she thinks; he's not really a bad person!

*

Linda has put on the new dress and shoes that Günther bought her in Hamburg to get herself into the mood to do something special today. Without much deliberation she rings the hotline number for the musical *Beauty and the Beast* in Stuttgart and orders two tickets for this evening. After all, there must be more to life than screwing all the time.

Then she tries to get hold of Günther. At his office they say he's already left, so she tries his car phone. He's delighted to hear her, but he hesitates when she tells him what she's arranged.

'What's the matter, aren't you in the mood?'

'A Schmidt is always in the mood,' he says automatically, without thinking. He immediately realises that now he's trapped himself in a corner. How can he get out of it again?

'That's great! I've already changed, and if you come straight-away we'll have plenty of time to get to the theatre and even have an aperitif before the show.'

'An aperitif?' he repeats feebly, desperately trying to think of a way to get out of this unscathed.

'Yes, in the same building there's a hotel with a sort of indoor market, and . . .'

'I know, the Copthorne,' he interrupts.

'Right, fine, all the better. See you soon then – I'm really look-ing forward to it.' And she puts the phone down.

Günther stares at the receiver, then he too slowly hangs up. He can't go, damn it. Why didn't he just tell her that straight out? He's going to be collecting 800,000 marks later on, he can't just fail to turn up!

He reaches for the phone. He'll simply tell her he can't go, and that she should change back into her ordinary clothes and wait for him to come, though it may be quite late. Günther enters the first few numbers quickly, then hesitates. He can't do this. She won't wait for him, she might go with someone else. The image of Dirk appears before his mind's eye. He would be the biggest ass on God's earth if just for the sake of this bit of business he drove her into the arms of another man. Who knows what he might get up to with her! They're all randy bastards, the whole lot of them. He puts his phone away.

At the first opportunity he turns and drives back. As he drives on to the estate he thinks of a way to save the day: he'll get Manfred to run that errand for him! Günther hopes that he's still in his office as promised, and calls him.

Yes, he's in luck. Manfred answers.

'I need you to do me a favour, mate.'

'Always at your . . .'

'This evening, I'm supposed to be meeting a fellow at the Seven Stars Hotel, but now I can't. Of course, I could leave a message there, but I think it would look bad. If you could go instead . . .'

'I would, gladly, but my car's being repaired. Some stupid bitch drove into the back of me,' he interrupts.

Günther thinks quickly, it's 800,000 marks after all; it's worth tossing him a little sweetener. 'Use mine, it's no problem.'

'I could take a taxi . . .'

'Nonsense, I'll come by and bring it – just book me a cab so I can get off straightaway.'

'You really mean it?'

Günther can hear the delight in his voice, and turns round again just before he reaches Linda's basement garage. He has to drive back into town again!

'You know, I live just round the corner from the store, that's why I haven't bothered to hire a car, I don't really need . . .'

'No problem, Manfred, I'll be right with you. As long as you're at the Seven Stars on time, at ten o'clock, everything's sorted. You just tell the man, he's called Hoyer, remember that,

Rainer Hoyer, that we'll sort it out without any fuss tomorrow morning. I'll call him. And tell the hotel manager that the bill for his supper, no matter what he has to eat or drink, should be sent to me!'

The instant he's rung off, Günther dials again. 'Linda,' he says, 'we'll be going in your old rattletrap tonight, so get it ready for the off. I promise I'll sit quietly in the passenger seat and not say a word!'

Klaus is at home, but he has buried himself in his study, which suits Regine, as it means they won't cross each other's paths. He's probably brooding over his meeting tomorrow, she thinks. She considers whether, later on, when he's asleep, she should look at his laptop to see if any important changes or additions have been made. To pass the time she flicks through the TV channels and happens upon *Commissioner Rex*. As Bobby at once starts watching attentively, she decides to stick with that. She fetches some crisps for herself and some Doggy-Bone Treats for Bobby, and they settle down together for a cosy Thursday evening.

Günther, freshly showered and changed, is sitting beside Linda as they drive through Römersfeld, heading for the motorway.

Linda is really happy. She's looking forward to seeing the musical, but just as much she loves everything that goes with it: the feeling of expectancy, the aperitif to set the mood and the crowds of theatre-goers dressed up in their finery whom she loves to observe. Altogether she finds people-gazing enormously fascinating. She even enjoys looking at the occupants of approaching cars when she's stopped at traffic lights; sitting at a pavement café is better still.

'We ought to have a bite to eat at Cyril's,' she says cheerfully to Günther.

'Where?' he asks. He feels strange in this little car, and he's not used to being the passenger.

'Cyril – he has one of those little bistros on the marketplace, you know? Karin always goes there!'

'Who's Karin?'

'Richi's ex-girlfriend,' Linda laughs. 'Ever so pretty! The Jackie Kennedy type.'

'As pretty as that?' Günther casts her a quick glance, preferring to keep an eye on the road. 'Do I know her?'

'I don't think so,' Linda says. 'She's not in your age group.'

'Isn't she? How old *is* she?'

'Somewhere around thirty.'

They're just leaving the town, and Günther is about to make some reply when suddenly the car starts to jump and judder. The engine splutters and coughs as though it's about to die at any minute.

'What on earth's happening?' Linda asks, alarmed.

'Do you have enough petrol?'

Linda takes a quick look at the petrol gauge. 'Yes, it's half full.'

'Then there's something wrong. You'll have to turn back, or we'll break down on the motorway!'

Worrying that the engine is going to seize up somewhere along the way, she drives jerkily back home. Günther gets out. 'Take it straight on to a garage and leave it there. Put the car keys through their letterbox. I'll call you a taxi.'

Linda is close to tears. She was so looking forward to this evening!

On his way up to the flat, Günther thinks that now he could easily keep his appointment with Rainer Hoyer. All that rattling and jolting gave him just the excuse he needed to get out of the theatre. He tries to reach Manfred first in his office, then at home. No luck. He's probably out for a spin in the borrowed car, thinks Günther. Return trip for one, Römersfeld to Paris and back. He can't track him down on his own car phone – he took the precaution of turning it off – so he tries his last chance, Manfred's mobile, but he only gets voicemail. 'Please call me back on my mobile about our ten o'clock appointment – thanks, Günther.'

Damn! He could go along too of course, by taxi, but what impression will it make if they both turn up? They'll look like a pair of stupid provincials who can't get their act together. No. Günther sinks down on to the sofa. Better to make the most of the evening. After all, Linda would be sure to be disappointed if he just went off again now that it's this late. So would his little friend. Günther grins and calls a taxi for Linda.

Well before ten o'clock Richi and Dirk have got themselves into position. They've parked the car some distance away, and Dirk is carrying their gear in a small sports bag. The car park is almost empty – the hotel can't be very busy tonight, which suits them perfectly. They stride purposefully along the footpath to the hotel; it seems ideally designed for all manner of attacks. 'What a visionary architect,' murmurs Richi gratefully. From the hotel it's impossible to see very far down the path because of tall shrubs on either side, and even from the car park only a very short stretch is visible; after that it's obscured from view as it crosses the gardens before finally leading into the driveway in front of the hotel.

'I hope he won't drive right up to the door,' Dirk worries.

'He can't, the barrier's down. He can only do that if he's a hotel guest who has luggage to unload.'

'Good!' They decide on a spot for the ambush, a short section between two bends. Dirk will land him a blow from behind and, as he falls forward, another in the stomach, ideally in the solar plexus, so that he simply folds up. And then he'll say, 'That's for Linda, you swine! I could have your balls off you while I'm about it, but maybe Linda will do it herself sometime. I look forward to that day!' He'll spit on him and march off. Richi will keep watch in case anything goes wrong.

'And you're sure she's worth it?' asks Richi, before putting on his stocking mask.

Dirk just looks at him.

'Okay, okay! Make yourself ready – it's getting dark.'

Dirk looks at his watch before pulling on his mask. 'Ten to ten. You're right; it could be any time now.'

They hear a car approaching. Dirk creeps to the beginning of the path and comes straight back.

'His car! It's him!'

'Sure?'

'How many silver Mercedes with the registration GS 1 are there in Römersfeld?'

'Right then – here we go!'

Manfred has no idea what this meeting is about. But knowing Günther, it's sure to involve money. And if it's so important that this fellow Hoyer should be met in person at this time of night, it must be a lot of money.

He wouldn't be Manfred Büschelmeyer if he didn't try to get a bit of the action too. It'll be a golden opportunity to draw the guy out a bit. Supper together, a few lagers topped up by a couple of liqueurs to aid digestion – Manfred has managed to soften up plenty of others before now, and these big-city wankers can't usually hold their drink very well. He parks Günther's Mercedes and gets out. Nice motor! That's the first thing he'll do as soon as the Raak woman pays up: get himself one of these – but the next model up. And perhaps this meeting with Hoyer will help him run to a few extras! Manfred feels the barometer of his luck rising steeply.

Dirk hears rather than sees his enemy approaching. The twigs and branches of the hedge he is crouching behind cut off his view. The moment the shadowy figure has passed by, Dirk leaps out, brings the truncheon down hard on the back of his head and leaps into position for his next attack, because Günther will turn round to defend himself and he must counter that with a sideways blow to his stomach. Once Günther is lying in a heap on the ground, he'll say his piece. Günther will be retching and gasping, and every time he tries to have it off with Linda in future, he'll remember it.

But far from turning round, Günther collapses in the darkness without a sound. There's a peculiar splat as his face hits the ground. Dirk stands there, truncheon at the ready, prepared for Günther to make a grab at his feet, but nothing happens. Complete silence, nothing but the usual night-time noises.

Then Richi emerges from his hiding place. 'What's going on?' he whispers.

Dirk slowly lowers the weapon. 'You tell me!'

'He's not moving!' Richi cautiously moves closer to Günther. 'Hey!' he suddenly exclaims, 'this isn't Günther!' He crouches down. 'We've got the wrong bloke!'

'Don't be crazy!' Dirk steps quickly to look at the head. 'It's so bloody dark between the hedges. You can't see a thing!'

Richi gets a lighter out of his pocket and flicks it on. 'Christ Almighty! It's Manfred Büschelmeyer!'

Dirk kneels down next to him.

'His eyes are open.' Richi snaps the lighter shut again and looks at Dirk aghast. 'Dirk, he's dead!'

'Rubbish! He can't be!'

'How hard did you hit him?'

'You saw me . . . not really hard at all . . .' Dirk is silent for a while. 'Why him?' he asks helplessly. 'What's he doing driving Günther's car?'

'And what if Günther turns up now, too?'

They look at each other.

'Are you sure he's dead?' Dirk asks as they get to their feet.

'Just look at his eyes!'

'No! That's . . . ridiculous! I don't believe it!'

'Whether you believe it or not, we've got to get out of here! Right now! And let's make an anonymous call for an ambulance from the nearest phone box. That's the least we can do!'

Early in the morning there comes a ring at Marion's door. She's already in the bathroom, not having slept a wink for thinking about the meeting this afternoon with Günther and the fellow from Liechtenstein. She was far too worked up to sleep. She glances at her watch. Half past seven. A letter by special delivery? She can't think what it could be, so she slips into her dressing-gown and goes to the intercom.

'Yes?'

'Police. May we come in, please?'

The police? So they've found the sawn-off camera. Marion presses the button to unlock the door and goes into the hall, trying to work out what to say.

There are two men at the door, but the fact that they're not wearing uniform makes Marion uncertain. Are they about to attack her? she wonders, staying behind the door so that the men can't grab hold of her.

'We're from the criminal investigation department, Frau Schmidt. Could we speak to your husband, please?'

'My husband? Do you mind showing me some identification?'

The two men show their warrant cards, and Marion opens the door. 'Come in,' she says, and leads them into the living room. The criminal investigation department dealing with a sawn-off radar camera, she thinks – isn't that a bit over the top? Have the authorities got money to burn? Or too little to do? She stops in the middle of the room. 'My husband?' she says again. 'But why?'

'Is he here?'

'Could you please tell me what this is about?'

'Do you know a Herr Manfred Büschelmeyer?'

'Of course, he's a friend of my husband's, the manager of the DIY store. Why?'

'He was found last night with serious head injuries. He was the victim of an attack.'

'An attack?' A myriad thoughts race through Marion's head. 'But why? What was the reason for it?'

'That's precisely what we don't know yet. Herr Büschelmeyer still hasn't regained consciousness. That's why we're here.'

'Here? That's why you're here?' Her eyes open wide. 'What have we to do with it?'

The 'we' comes out so automatically that she only notices it after she's said it.

'Your husband's car was found at the scene of the crime. We'd like to know how it got there.'

'Where *is* the scene of the crime?' Marion asks in return.

'Outside the Seven Stars Hotel. Between the car park and the hotel entrance, to be precise, on the footpath. Would you please fetch your husband now?'

'My husband? He's not here.'

'Not here?' The two men exchange a glance as though that's all they need to know.

'Where is he . . .'

'. . . at this time of the morning?'

'Probably with his girlfriend.' She says it so calmly that the two men again exchange a look.

'You could have told us that before,' says one of them.

'Where does this girlfriend live, and what's her name?' the other one asks. He's already taken a notebook out of his jacket pocket.

'She's called Linda Hagen. I don't know where she lives. But she works in the cosmetics shop in the town centre – as a shop assistant!'

Günther has been sitting in his office with Klaus Raak, Jürgen Berger and his lawyer, Walter Kalthoff, for an hour. After much discussion three documents are now lying on the table before them. One relates to the sale of the firm of Schmidt Engineering to the Liechtenstein Co. Ltd, the second to the sale of Günther Schmidt's building to the same company, and finally there is a legal agreement by which Günther is entitled to purchase the shares of the Liechtenstein company. Günther has just signed the first two contracts when there is frantic knocking. The door is thrown open and his secretary, eyes popping, announces the criminal investigation department.

'Ah, has Manfred Büschelmeyer smashed up my car?' Günther asks by way of a greeting, for he can't think of any other reason. He hopes Manfred hasn't been the cause of a huge pile-up.

'Manfred Büschelmeyer is in hospital with serious injuries,' says one of the officers, looking around.

'How do you mean, he's injured? What are you saying? A road accident? That's awful!' Günther slowly rises to his feet. 'And what about my car?'

'It wasn't a road accident, he was hit over the head. We need you to answer a few questions, so we would like you to accompany us to the station,' says the second policeman, keeping his eyes fixed on Günther as though he might vanish into thin air at any moment.

'I think it's dreadful that Manfred is badly injured, but it's very inconvenient for me to go to the police station just now,' says Günther, indicating the other three men. 'Couldn't I come down this afternoon? These gentlemen have come a long way for this meeting.'

'*Herr Schmidt*. I'm very sorry, but we're talking about grievous bodily harm, not business matters! Added to which, there were certain items found in your car that we also need to ask you about.'

All eyes are turned towards Günther.

'I suppose luxury extras are against the law now?' he says aggressively.

'A roll of film that we found belongs inside a speed camera, not in a glove compartment. And the pills which were lying next to it are only available on prescription. At least in Germany. I expect you'll be able to provide evidence of how you obtained them. And perhaps of where you were last night, too.' He smiles at him with exaggerated friendliness. 'So you see, sir, we really must insist that you come with us!'

The colour has drained from Günther's face. 'Does this mean that I'm under arrest?' he asks, trying to make it sound like some absurd joke.

'That remains to be seen.'

They're hardly out of the door when it's thrown open yet again. This time it's Marion standing in the doorway.

'Marion!' says Klaus, flabbergasted. 'What on earth brings you here?'

'Günther's been driven away by the police! I've just seen him off. That's one of the duties of a good wife. And what are you doing here?'

Klaus immediately starts gathering up the papers in front of him, while Jürgen Berger and Walter Kalthoff stand up to greet her.

'May I also introduce these two ladies to you, Anna Kell and Regine Raak?'

The two women enter and are greeted politely by the two strangers. Klaus seems rooted to the spot. He stares at Regine as though he were seeing her for the first time.

'How nice to see you, Klaus.' Marion gives him a friendly nod. 'We've arrived a little later than intended, but no doubt there was a last-minute change in the time of the meeting.'

'Weren't you told of it?' asks the lawyer hastily.

'No, unfortunately not, but I'm sure you'll be able to explain to us how things stand.' Marion sits down in her husband's chair, Regine on a chair diagonally opposite Klaus, and Anna next to her.

Walter Kalthoff summarises the content of the meeting so far and takes pains to explain everything to the women in meticulous detail. Anna meanwhile reads through the contracts, and Klaus slumps further and further down into his seat. The only thing that still keeps him more or less upright is the fact that the women have come too late. Günther has signed, and the two contracts make him, Klaus, a rich man. But Regine? What's her part in all this? He avoids catching her eye; he can't think how best to behave towards her afterwards. How does she see him? Will she feel he's acted rightly or wrongly? And how does she see herself?

He wishes he and his two contracts could simply disappear.

Jürgen Berger adds a comment, which rouses Klaus from his thoughts. He starts paying attention again.

Walter Kalthoff is pushing his thick hair away from his forehead with one hand. Uncertainly, he looks at Berger. 'And now what do we do with the agreement for the purchase of the shares?'

Klaus answers hastily, 'We'll do that when this business with Günther and the police is sorted out.'

'Oh, that won't be necessary,' Marion says, smiling at him. 'We can deal with it.'

'I would prefer that, then the whole thing would be complete,' agrees Berger, looking at his watch.

'But wait a minute . . .' Klaus tries to save what is beyond saving. No one takes any notice of him. Marion taps the paper. 'Of course, it'll have to have *my* name on it.'

'No!' cries Klaus, outraged. 'You can't do that!'

'Of course she can,' Anna Kell interrupts him. 'You're the sole proprietor of the Liechtenstein Co. Ltd. The shares are in your name, and therefore – she holds up the two contracts – 'so is all the Schmidt property. Of course you can sell to Marion Schmidt. Alternatively, you can let Jürgen Berger do it, if you don't want to sign in person. As your authorised representative he is, after all, responsible for purchases and sales!'

Jürgen Berger nods. 'Undoubtedly.'

'Well then!' Marion gives Klaus a smile.

He shakes his head vehemently. 'No, I won't do it!' he says decisively. 'I won't even consider it! I won't sell!'

Regine gives him a sideways look.

Klaus sees it. And hesitates. 'Well, perhaps I will,' he says at last, in a quiet voice.

Marion looks at him with one eyebrow raised, and draws the purchase agreement towards her. 'How much for?' She skims the text. 'Oh really? For one Swiss franc? I can still just about rise to that!'

For a moment they are all silent, then Berger makes a slight bow in Marion's direction. 'Very well, in that case may I congratulate you on your acquisition of this successful company. And at such a good price!' He reaches out his hand. 'You are now the sole shareholder in our limited company. May I take this opportunity of inviting you to our next board meeting?'

Early this morning Linda was already at the garage seeing about her car when the police rang her doorbell. Only when she gets to work is she told that they have been asking for her there too. When Renate asks what the criminal investigation department want of her, she reacts quite calmly at first. 'No idea, but I may as well go down and find out. It's not all that far.' Renate agrees, so Linda heads off.

In front of Dirk's house she sees Richi's convertible parked in the no-parking zone. Not a good idea, she thinks, and goes to the nearest phone box.

Dirk answers at once. 'Tell your friend that the police round here won't stand any nonsense!' She starts to hang up.

'The police? Have they already been round to you?' Dirk's voice is almost cracking.

Linda hesitates. She's already taken the receiver away from her ear to hang up, but she changes her mind. 'Why? What on earth's going on?'

Suddenly it's Richi at the other end. 'Have the police been to see you? What did you tell them?'

'Richi! Is something the matter? Why all these questions?'

'Where are you ringing from?'

'Down here, in the street. I just wanted to warn you that your car's in the no-parking zone.'

'Hasn't it got a ticket yet?'

'No, not so far. You're in luck!'

'Damn!'

Linda doesn't understand, and says nothing.

'You'd better come up,' she hears Richi say.

'Me?'

'Yes. Why not?'

'I'm on my way to the police station and then I've got to go straight back to work.'

After a short silence at the other end, Richi clears his throat. 'Please come up, Linda,' he pleads. 'It's important.'

Minutes later Linda is sitting on Dirk's unmade bed, hardly able to believe her ears. What Richi and Dirk are telling her seems utterly weird.

'Why are you telling me this?' she asks at last. 'What if I go and report this to the police?'

'I don't really care. Things couldn't be much worse for me

anyway,' says Dirk, who sits drooping over a chair, unshaven and looking as if he hasn't slept a wink.

Linda looks at him and sighs. Then she draws a deep breath. 'To be honest, I'm stunned! I'd never have thought you two would be capable of such a thing. Are you really sure he's dead?'

Dirk covers his face with his hands. 'We both saw him. I can't live with something like that. It makes me quite ill! And besides, I'm terrified!'

Richi and Linda exchange a helpless glance.

'What are you planning to do?' asks Linda gently after a while.

'We must provide each other with an alibi.' Richi turns his chair round so that he can rest his arms on the chair back.

'Each other?' Linda shakes her head. 'Yes, it would even be true. You *were* together – at the scene of the crime!'

'That's not funny!' Richi draws his eyebrows together into a frown.

And Dirk mutters behind his hands, 'To think that a man had to die just because you went off with someone else!'

Linda lightly taps her forehead. 'Are you mad or something? Are you suggesting that I killed him? By telepathy or something?' She's shouting now. 'I could just leave and let you get on with it!'

'Shout even louder, why don't you, so the neighbours can hear all about it too,' Richi interrupts her.

'Okay,' Linda says to Dirk. 'So, what's the position? Have you got rid of the weapon? Thrown away your shoes? Worked out a good alibi?'

'I was hoping to get a parking ticket down there last night so I could prove I was here at the time of the attack. But that stupid warden seems to have lost interest in me!'

The doorbell rings. The three look at each other. 'It can't be anything special,' Dirk says slowly. 'Maybe it's the postman.'

He pushes himself up from his chair. 'They can't be here so soon.'

Dirk opens the door and finds himself facing two uniformed policemen. Terrified, he asks, 'Has something happened? To my father? My mother?'

'Something has happened, but not to your parents. Can we come in?'

Dirk leads the way, and grimaces as they walk into the room.

'Can we have your names?' asks one of them, looking first at Richi and then at Linda.

'Richard Raak,' says Richi simply.

The one officer looks at the other, who shakes his head.

'Herr Raak, if you don't mind, could you please leave us alone with Herr Wetterstein? You're not on our list.'

'On your list? Would you mind telling me what this is all about?' demands Dirk challengingly. 'You make this sound like an interrogation.'

'Just a few questions, Herr Wetterstein. And may I ask who you are?' he says, turning to Linda.

'Linda Hagen.'

The two look at each other, and one of them nods. 'That's very convenient. You can stay!'

Richi slowly gets up. 'Can't you tell me what it's about?'

'You're not involved, Herr Raak. This matter concerns only a small group of people. You are not one of them.'

'All right then.' Richi casts a helpless glance at Dirk and takes his leave.

'Herr Wetterstein, does the name Manfred Büschelmeyer mean anything to you?'

Dirk nods and slumps down in his chair.

'Yesterday evening Manfred Büschelmeyer was attacked, close to the Seven Stars Hotel, and seriously injured.'

Dirk looks up in surprise. 'Injured?' he asks.

'Yes, a blow to the back of the head.'

Whatever the policemen go on to say, Dirk is hardly listening any more. He's not a murderer – that's the best news of his whole life.

'And you've come here about that?' interposes Linda, sounding mystified.

'Yes,' says one of the policemen, looking at her. 'That's why it's quite a good thing that you're here too, Frau Hagen. Because Günther Schmidt says that it must have been a case of mistaken identity. He had an appointment at ten o'clock at the Seven Stars Hotel, and Manfred Büschelmeyer was to go in his place. This theory is supported by the fact that Herr Hoyer, whom Günther Schmidt was supposed to be meeting at the Seven Stars Hotel, at that time, isn't known there. We're currently trying to establish whether he exists at all. Herr Schmidt suspects that it may have been intended as an act of vengeance directed against himself, and that the assailant got the wrong man. According to him, you're the main suspect, Herr Wetterstein, because – and these are his own words – "he went off with your girlfriend". Before you comment, I must remind you that you are not obliged to say anything.'

'I'll have to say something sometime. And besides, it's all utter nonsense. I'm hardly going to knock somebody on the head just because he's got the hots for my girlfriend!'

'Where were you last night?'

'Here,' says Dirk, folding his arms.

'Are there any witnesses who can confirm that?'

Uncertainly, Dirk shrugs his shoulders. 'Well . . .' he begins, and Linda continues, 'Me!' She goes and stands next to Dirk.

'You?' One of the policemen pushes back his cap and looks at her in frank astonishment. 'That surprises me very much, because Günther Schmidt cited you as a witness to support *his* statement. That's why we were looking for you. Because if you had supported his story, then Günther Schmidt would be cleared of all suspicion!'

'Why is Günther Schmidt under suspicion anyway?' asks Dirk.

'Well, his car was at the scene of the crime and there was a call from Schmidt on Büschelmeyer's mobile saying that they were going to meet there at ten o'clock.' He looks incredulously at Linda. 'But that you . . .'

'What did he say?' Linda tosses back her hair.

'He claims that you spent the night together!'

'Not last night! I was here! We're back together again!'

The policeman pushes his cap forward again. 'Right, that puts a different spin on things!'

'You know that it's an offence to make a false statement?' asks his colleague.

'This isn't a false statement!'

'Then I would like both of you to come to the police station later today so that we can take written statements from you.'

Marion, Regine and Anna are standing in the car park in front of Schmidt Engineering, making valiant efforts not to break out into whoops of joy. 'Wait until Kalthoff and Berger have gone,' whispers Marion, grinning all over her face.

They wave to them both as they get into their cars. Then Klaus appears in the doorway to the building.

He stops in his tracks and looks at Regine.

'Well, I think the two of us have things we need to discuss,' says Regine to the other women.

'Will you come round later?' asks Marion.

'To Monika's?'

'Yes, that's what I had in mind. And for this evening I'm going to take you all out to the Lake Restaurant. For a victory celebration!'

Regine laughs. 'This really has been a victory, Frau Schmidt.'

'Well, if it hadn't been for you . . .'

Regine gives a modestly dismissive gesture and goes over to her husband. 'See you later,' she calls.

'Hmm. I'll be interested to see what happens there!' Anna shakes her head doubtfully.

'Are you on the lookout for a new case?' Marion teases her.

'Well . . .' Anna shrugs her shoulders.

'If it should come to that, I hope one thing is clear, Frau Kell . . .'

'Oh? What's that?'

'All Regine Raak's bills are to be sent to me!'

'Okay,' Anna chuckles, and she and Marion watch as Regine takes Klaus lightly by the sleeve and walks him over to the car.

'Let's wait and see.' Marion gets into her car. 'Shall you and I meet later at Monika's?'

'Absolutely!'

'Right, I'll just go and quickly buy a few things for then!' Marion slams the car door. Now she's alone with her feelings. But she still just can't believe it. Günther right out of the game – can it be possible? Big, powerful Günther? Stripped of all his property, and carted off by the police?

Beware of pity, she says to herself. You can forget that particular womanly virtue right away. Marion starts the engine and laughs out loud. I'll tell him that he can keep his car. Because I'm generous by nature.

Linda has seen the two policemen out. When she comes back Dirk is leaning on the door frame.

'Tell me . . .' he begins, but she places a finger on his lips.

'That's just how it is. When it comes down to it, I'd rather see Günther in jail than you. Even if you are a pig!'

Dick takes her in his arms and leans his head against hers.

Then he sinks down with her on to the floor. 'I'm absolutely
done in. I was sick with jealousy and now I'm blissfully happy
that that guy isn't dead and that you're standing by me –
although I can't imagine why.'

Linda rests her head against his shoulder. 'Günther will find a
way to get out of the mess he's in. But you – your whole life
would be ruined. That would do nobody any good, not even
Manfred Büschelmeyer.'

Dirk strokes her hair. 'Even so. I could kill myself, to think
that my idiotic emotions made me attack another human being
purely for revenge, when really I'm a committed pacifist. I can't
think what got into me! I ought to turn myself in – then I'd feel
better.'

Linda angrily pushes his hand away. 'Don't talk such rubbish.
It seems to me you're doing perfectly all right. After all, you've
got a new girlfriend, so what's all this stuff about seeking
revenge? You don't seem to know your own mind!'

Dirk stares at her. 'What on earth gives you that idea?'

'Don't try to deny it! It's not long since you had a girl staying
the night – a dark-haired girl, not even that pretty!'

Dirk sits up so that he can look into her eyes. 'And how come
you know all about it, if I may ask?'

'I was sitting on the stairs.'

'So I was right!' He claps his thigh.

'What do you mean, you were right?'

'I smelled you! I swear it, all at once I could smell you and I
thought it was extra-sensory perception!'

'This figment of your extra-sensory perception would have
liked to hit you over the head!'

Appalled, they both fall silent. Then Dirk sighs and runs his
fingers over his stubble. 'So, what's to become of us now?'

Linda turns towards him. As she does so her foot collides
with the overflowing waste-paper basket, which falls over,

scattering some of its contents on to the floor. Linda quickly collects up the crumpled pieces of paper that are nearest to her, but then stops and unfolds one of them. She sits up with a start. 'You two must be absolute idiots,' she says, shaking her head, flattening out a clumsily screwed-up sheet of paper. 'Plan,' she reads aloud. 'Rainer Hoyer arrives 10PM . . .' She looks at Dirk. 'How can you just throw it into the waste-paper basket like that? I bet you still have the murder weapon in your wardrobe, too!'

Dirk pulls himself together and sits down beside her. He pulls a face.

Linda shakes her head. 'Honestly, if you carry on in such a stupid way I won't be able to help you! For goodness' sake get rid of everything before they come back with a search warrant. And the shoes as well, yours *and* Richi's!' She stands up, smoothing her skirt. 'Dirk, you really have got to get your act together if you don't want to get yourself convicted. And me too, for perjury. See to your stuff, and come and join me at the shop when you've got it all sorted out.'

She looks down at him. 'And as for the two of us, it's a matter of *wanting*. Take me, for instance, I really *want* to live. In the manner that I would have lived in if I'd become Frau Schmidt. And you should *want* to be able to offer me that. So you need somehow to get yourself established in your career as quickly as possible. It won't just fall into your lap!' She laughs at his astonished expression and raises both her hands. 'Of course you may need to think whether that's what you really want.' Slowly she retreats towards the door, keeping her eyes fixed on Dirk. 'This evening, at eight o'clock, I'll give three short rings at your door. If you *want* to, open it. I mean, if you really want to. If not, then don't. I'm not going to force you into anything . . .' Linda blows him a kiss, slips through the door and runs lightly down the stairs. We'll see what happens, she thinks; he is sweet, really. On the pavement she looks at her watch. Damn, it's later than she'd intended. Let's hope the shop hasn't been too busy and that Renate won't moan at me.

She dashes across the road and hears a squealing of brakes. Startled, she turns round. It's a dark-blue BMW convertible with a woman at the wheel. She's about to indicate that she's sorry for not looking properly before crossing when she recognises Marion. On an impulse she opens the passenger door. 'Could I have a quick word with you, Frau Schmidt?'

Marion, who is wearing a simple grey trouser suit, seems to take it in her stride. 'Yes, of course,' she says, gesturing towards the seat. As Linda quickly gets in, Marion says with a slight smile, 'Günther's been arrested. Did you know? How will you manage without him?'

'You're asking me that?!' Linda is utterly astounded.

Marion moves in to the kerb, turns off the engine and looks at Linda in a friendly way. 'Well, who else? You're the one who's with him now . . .'

'But truly, Frau Schmidt, I'm so sorry . . . and about that business in Kirchweiler. I felt awful about it. I'm really pleased to have met you like this, else I would have phoned you. You can have your husband back!'

'What?' Marion looks at her as though she were completely out of her mind.

'It's true! I haven't behaved well, I admit it. I let myself be dazzled by everything – the presents, the travel, the lifestyle, the champagne, all of it. And you were the one who suffered. I really am terribly sorry!'

'But I don't want him back!'

'You don't . . . what?'

'No, thanks, Linda. You've opened my eyes. If it hadn't been you it would have been someone else. He never loved me, he used me. Now he's used you; that's the way life goes!'

'Is that really how you see it?'

'Yes, it really is! Believe me. In all those years I never probed beneath the surface, I never made any demands, never understood anything! For years I was locked in a prison of roles and duties and couldn't break out. Now it's his turn!'

'To be in prison?'

Marion gives a short, dry laugh. 'Why not? Don't worry, he'll soon be back on his feet again.'

Monika is on the phone to Römersfeld Hospital when Anna Kell is announced. 'Ask her to come in,' she says, without interrupting her call. She nods to Anna and turns up the volume on the telephone speaker.

'. . . all in all, he's been lucky. He's got a cerebral oedema, which means that the brain is swollen. He regained consciousness briefly and said some things that can't be taken seriously, and then we put him into an artificial coma . . .'

'Artificial coma?' Monika interrupts, signalling to Anna to sit down.

'Yes, the swelling has got to subside, and that's most easily achieved if the brain is completely at rest. That's why we do it.'

'I see. So his condition isn't life-threatening?'

'As things stand at present, I'd say not.'

Anna is making signs to her. Monika understands. 'What was it that Manfred said?'

They hear a laugh at the other end of the line. 'He wants to give you money, Moni. You of all people! Completely unintelligible nonsense. Wait a minute, his actual words were something like "And give Frau Raak the 90,000 marks that I still owe her"! No sense to it at all. Or can you make head or tail of it? Does he owe you 90,000 marks?'

Monika suppresses a laugh. 'Perhaps he means the other Frau Raak?'

'Do you think so?'

'Or perhaps he's gone off his head and wants to give money away all the time. That would be quite a change for Manfred Büschelmeyer . . .'

'If he's got such a lot, why not? But Moni, I must go, I'm behind as it is.'

'Moni?' asks Anna, smiling slightly after Monika has hung up.

'My brother . . .' She shrugs her shoulders apologetically.

Anna Kell laughs. 'You can't beat a close family!'

There is another knock, and in come first Regine and then Marion. Marion is carefully balancing a silver tray with kitchen foil over it, and Regine is carrying a cool-box.

'What's all this?' asks Monika.

'The victory celebration! Or rather the pre-victory celebration, because the real celebration is this evening at the Lake Restaurant. Has Anna already told you?'

'We hadn't got that far yet,' says Anna apologetically, and as they set out the food, open a bottle and fetch plates and glasses, she tells them of the conversation with Monika's brother.

'That's right,' Marion nods, as she fills the glasses, 'he's the senior consultant surgeon at the hospital. I know him. A good man. Why has he never married?'

'He can't make up his mind.' Monika makes a dismissive gesture. 'Besides, he's always involved in research and conferences, and he travels a lot, and he's seen from my example that one can get along quite nicely without being married!'

'Aha!' says Marion.

'Perhaps he's just gay?' asks Regine, and they all laugh.

'Or else he's the right man for Linda,' it occurs to Marion; she tells them briefly of her meeting with Linda earlier on.

'Poor Günther,' says Regine with pity, theatrically wiping a pretend tear from her eye. 'Forsaken by everyone!'

'And what about Klaus?' asks Monika curiously.

'He's afraid that I'll want a divorce . . .'

'And will you?' demand all three instantly.

Regine can't help laughing. 'The outlook is: serious talk, yes; divorce, no.' Seeing the others' faces, she says, grinning and with a sideways glance at Anna, 'After all, it costs money!'

'Which brings us to what we need to talk about,' says Marion, raising her hand. 'But only after we've drunk to our triumph and everyone has had a bite to eat!' They all do as she says, toasting each other loudly and taking a sandwich from the tray, then start to look at her expectantly. Marion folds her hands. 'I'm just going to suggest this idea,' she starts. 'We can decide whether to take it further, or not.'

'Fire away,' says Monika eagerly, munching at her prawn sandwich.

'I think we should aim to become *the* businesswomen in Römersfeld,' says Marion, emphasising every word, to Monika. 'Together we could start up a factory that would complement this workshop here.'

'I already have a plan along those lines,' Monika nods. 'On the future West Römersfeld Industrial Estate I'm going to build a factory that produces car bodies. Didn't you know that?'

'No, I'm not quite in the swing of things yet, but that would do admirably well. If you'll let me, I'll invest money of mine in your projects – perhaps there will be more than just the one – and we'll bring a bit of life into the new industrial area. Your know-how and my capital, and vice-versa!'

'It sounds great,' says Regine enthusiastically.

'My immediate reaction too.' Monika puts her head on one side, then gives a slight nod and raises her glass. The others do likewise.

'Just a moment.' Marion looks at Regine. 'If it hadn't been for you I'd have nothing left at all. Everything we'd have done would have been too late, and we probably would never have caught on to what Günther was doing. So I'd like to use 500,000 marks to set up a bank account for you – and I suggest you keep it a secret from any man. And if you'd like to work too, I'm sure we'd have a good job for you.'

'What?!' Regine chokes on her sandwich. As she coughs and splutters, Anna taps her gently on the back. 'But . . .' she begins, as soon as she has got her breath back.

But Marion cuts her short. 'It's my dearest wish that you should accept it. And it's little enough considering what you've done for me!'

Stunned, Regine flops down into the nearest armchair and then immediately leaps up again. 'I'll work for the animal sanctuary! I'd enjoy working with Annemarie Roser – I'm sure we'd really be able to get something done!' She pirouettes across the room to Marion, kisses her on the cheek and twirls excitedly on.

'And Anna will look after all our legal affairs,' suggests Monika, unperturbed.

Laughing, and touching her cheek, Marion nods. 'That should keep the wolf from the door for the rest of your days!'

'A magnificent offer! Thank you!' Anna Kell picks up her glass and raises it to each of them. 'Then let's drink a toast to the new Römersfeld! Its name harks back to the men of ancient Rome . . .'

'But the future,' interrupts Monika, 'belongs to the *women*!'